Nobel Quotes

詞窮到詞王，就是這麼簡單！

詹森 著

用諾貝爾金句
拯救你的破英文！

思路變清晰、語感變靈動、作文變好玩，打開腦袋讓靈感發光！

一句話勝千言，教你怎麼說才動人

話要寫得漂亮，讓語錄成為你的作文祕笈

每天一句，跟諾貝爾得主一起醒腦又醒心！

目 錄

■ 1991-2000 多元聲音與思想碰撞　　　　　　005

■ 2001-2010 跨界融合與人文關懷　　　　　　115

■ 2011-2020 科技反思與人性的回望　　　　　247

■ 2021-2024 危機年代的希望之聲　　　　　　391

■ 編譯者後記　　　　　　　　　　　　　　　453

目錄

1991–2000
多元聲音與思想碰撞

1991 年

Your Majesties, Your Royal Highnesses, Ladies and Gentlemen,

This is the first, and probably the last, time in my life where I have dinner with queens and princesses. I am worried. I suspect that with the chimes of midnight I will be turned into a pumpkin.

I have come often to this beautiful city of Stockholm. As a matter of fact, once in 1974 I attended a banquet in this very same room. This was during a conference on liquid crystals. And I was asked to give a 3 minutes talk. But in those days I still had some common sense, I said： No, this is too hard. My friend Tony Arrott took over and did very well.

But now I finally understand why I have been given this fabulous prize, not because of some scientific achievement but because the Swedes are stubborn. They wanted me to give a 3 minute talk in this hall.

Now this is done, but what remains to be said is my admiration for this country.

1991-2000 多元聲音與思想碰撞

I was in Lund and in Stockholm 2 months ago. I was in Göteborg last Friday. I can testify that our young science of soft matter has found some of its best men or women here in Sweden.

But my words go far beyond science: I am especially proud of being distinguished in this country, the home land of Carl von Linné and Alfred Nobel —— but also the land of Ingmar Bergman and Ingrid Thulin —— the land which, through them, became the dream land of the world. (Pierre-Gilles de Gennes)

尊敬的陛下，各位殿下，女士們，先生們，

這是我此生第一次，很可能也是最後一次，與王后和公主們共進晚餐。我很擔心。我懷疑隨著午夜鐘聲，自己會變成一顆南瓜。

我經常到斯德哥爾摩這個美麗的城市。事實上，1974 年，就在這同一個房間裡，我參加了一個宴會。那是在一次液晶會議期間。我被要求做一個 3 分鐘的演講。不過在那些日子，我還是有些拘於常理的，我就說：「不行，這太難了。」我的朋友安東尼‧亞洛特接替了我，講得也非常好。

而現在我終於明白了，我之所以被授予這一個神奇獎項，不是由於若干科學成就，而是由於瑞典人太固執。他們就是想讓我在這個大廳裡做 3 分鐘演講。

現在演講做了，然而我還要說的是對這個國家的讚美。

兩個月前我在隆德和斯德哥爾摩。上星期五我在哥特堡。我可以證明，我們年輕的軟物質科學已經在瑞典此地發現了一些最優秀的男女學者。

不過我的讚美遠遠超出科學：我為自己在這個國家獲得成就而分外驕傲。它是卡爾‧林奈和阿佛烈‧諾貝爾的故鄉 —— 又是英格瑪‧伯格

曼和英葛黎‧蘇琳的國度 [01]——這個國度經由他們揚名天下，成為世界的夢想之國。（皮埃爾－吉勒‧德熱納）

All along there was a very close cooperation between experimentalists and theorists —— in each group the optimal ratio being 1 theorist to 5 experimentalists. (Pierre-Gilles de Gennes)

長久以來，實驗專家和理論專家之間都有著非常密切的合作——每組的最佳比例為一個理論專家對五個實驗專家。（皮埃爾－吉勒‧德熱納）

It is indeed a great moment for me to stand where I am standing to express my deep gratitude to the Nobel Foundation for this extraordinary honor. Obviously, most of the glory should fall on those standing behind me, my teachers, my colleagues, my coworkers, my school, my 700 years old country, those whom I represent here as their scientific spokesman. The presence of all the former Nobel Laureates gives me a feeling of being carried by a swarm of wild geese, some real high fliers, like in Nils Holgersson, and I am afraid of falling down. (Richard R. Ernst)

對我來說，站在這個位置，為此盛譽向諾貝爾基金會表達深切謝意，確實是個非凡的時刻。很明顯，絕大部分榮耀都應當屬於我身後那些人和事物，我的老師，我的同事，我的合作者，我的學校，我的700年悠久歷史的國家，我作為科學發言人在此充當其代表。到場的所有前諾貝爾獎得主，令我感覺像是被一群飛得很高的野鵝背著帶上了天空，宛如在《騎鵝歷險記》[02]中，而我深怕掉下去。（理察‧恩斯特）

---

[01] 卡爾‧林奈是瑞典植物學家，英格瑪‧伯格曼和英葛黎‧蘇琳分別為瑞典導演和女演員。
[02]《騎鵝歷險記》，瑞典作家塞爾瑪‧拉格洛夫的童話名著。

1991–2000 多元聲音與思想碰撞

Science prizes have a tendency to distort science history. Individuals are singled out and glorified that should rather be seen embedded in the context of the historic development. Much luck and coincidence is needed to be successful and be selected. Prizes can hardly do justice to those brave men and women who devote, in an unselfish way, all their efforts and energy towards a goal that is finally reached by others. (Richard R. Ernst)

科學獎有扭曲科學史的傾向。個人被挑選出來予以讚譽,而其人其事本應置於歷史發展的背景下看待。想要成功並被選中,需要很大的運氣和巧合。科學獎很難公允地表彰那些勇敢的男男女女,他們無私地勞力盡心,都是為了一個最終由別人實現的目標。(理察·恩斯特)

I am one of the very fortunate scientists who have achieved what many claim to be the ultimate form of recognition or even the ultimate form of happiness in this exuberant, splendid, almost unearthly setting. However, I think more important is the responsibility that is being loaded on the shoulders of the laureates who are supposed to suddenly behave like unfailing sages although they might have been just work addicts in the past. (Richard R. Ernst)

我屬於非常幸運的科學家,在這個熱烈、輝煌,幾乎超凡出世的場合,獲得了許多人所說的終極形式的認可,乃至終極形式的快樂。不過,我認為更重要的是責任,它被置於獲獎者肩頭,這些人忽然被認為如聖人一般,儘管他們先前大概只是個工作狂。(理察·恩斯特)

You do what you like because you just follow your curiosity, and you are happy when you find new things about nature, about how things work around us and inside us. (Erwin Neher)

> 1991 年

你做你喜歡做的事是因為追隨自己的好奇心；而當你發現關於自然的新事物，關於事物在我們周圍和我們體內如何作用時，你會很快樂。（厄溫・內爾）

Of course I have other interests, but on the other hand, science is a lifestyle in the sense that it's a combination of profession and hobby. (Erwin Neher)

當然了，我有別的興趣；但另一方面，科學是一種結合職業與愛好的生活方式。（厄溫・內爾）

So once it's published you should do everything to make the result and all the techniques involved available to other people but as long as you're in the process of following an idea, first of all you have to have an idea, then you follow it. You find out whether you can falsify it or whether it is true and then publish it. (Bert Sakmann)

所以一旦發表成果，你就應該盡力讓結果和全部有關技術都可供他人使用，只要你處於跟進它的過程。首先你得有個想法，然後你跟進它。你要確認自己是否能夠證其為偽，或它是否為真，然後發表出來。（伯特・薩克曼）

We had limited funding and this can be a benefit even because you think of how you can solve a problem without spending too much money. (Bert Sakmann)

我們的資金有限，但這也可能是一種好處，因為你會想著怎樣才能不花太多的錢而解決難題。（伯特・薩克曼）

1991–2000 多元聲音與思想碰撞

Responsibility is what awaits outside the Eden of Creativity. (Nadine Gordimer)

創造的伊甸園之外等待的是責任。（納丁・戈迪默）

The truth isn't always beauty, but the hunger for it is. (Nadine Gordimer)

真理並不總是美麗的，但對它的渴望是。（納丁・戈迪默）

I always repeat: read, read, read. (Nadine Gordimer)

我一再地說：「閱讀，閱讀，閱讀。」（納丁・戈迪默）

When the Nobel Committee chose to honor me, the road I had chosen of my own free will became a less lonely path to follow. (Aung San Suu Kyi)

當諾貝爾委員會選擇授予我這一項榮譽時，我自願選擇的自由之路將變得不再那麼孤獨。（翁山蘇姬）

I've been wrong so often, I don't find it extraordinary at all. (Ronald H. Coase)

我經常犯錯，完全不覺得它有何特別。（羅納德・寇斯）

I am very much aware that many economists whom I respect and admire will not agree with the opinions I have expressed and some may even be offended by them. But a scholar must be content with the knowledge that what is false in what he says will soon be exposed and, as for what is true, he can count on ultimately seeing it accepted, if only he lives long enough. (Ronald H. Coase)

我非常清楚，許多我敬重和欽佩的經濟學家不會贊同我的意見，有些人甚至可能被它們冒犯。然而身為學者，必須為理解這一點而滿足：自己說法中的錯誤將很快被揭露，而只要他活得足夠長，就能看到正確的言論終將被接受。（羅納德・寇斯）

1992 年

The official photographer informed me that I was the 137th Nobel Laureate of whom he has had to make a portrait. Certainly all of you know that 137 is a magic, quasi-mystical number in physics. It is equal to the velocity of light times the reduced Planck constant divided by the square of the electron charge! This number governs the size of all objects in the Universe. Some people claim that if this value were to be slightly different life would not be possible. (Georges Charpak)

官方攝影師告訴我，我是他拍攝肖像的第 137 位諾貝爾獎得主。大家當然都知道，137 是物理學中一個神奇的、近乎神祕的數字。它等於光速乘以約化普朗克常數除以電子電荷的平方！這個數字影響著宇宙中所有物體的大小。有些人說，假如這個數值稍有不同，生命就不可能存在了。（喬治·夏帕克）

My very modest contribution to physics has been in the art of weaving in space thin wires detecting the whisper of nearby flying charged particles produced in high-energy nuclear collisions. It is easy for computers to transform these whispers into a symphony understandable to physicists. (Georges Charpak)

我對物理學的小小貢獻，展現於在太空中結網的技藝。這張網疏而不漏，探測著附近飛舞的帶電粒子的低語，這些粒子是由高能核碰撞產生的。電腦並不難將這些低語轉換成物理學家能夠理解的交響樂。（喬治·夏帕克）

My mother used to wheel me about the campus when we lived in that neighborhood and, as she recounted years later, she would tell me that I would go to McGill. (Rudolph A. Marcus)

我們住在那一帶時,母親常常開車帶我圍著校園轉,而且,像她多年後所描述的那樣,當時她告訴我,我會進麥基爾大學。(魯道夫・馬庫斯)

During my McGill years, I took a number of math courses, more than other students in chemistry. (Rudolph A. Marcus)

就讀於麥基爾大學期間,我選修了若干數學課程,超過化學專業的其他學生。(魯道夫・馬庫斯)

Being exposed to theory, stimulated by a basic love of concepts and mathematics, was a marvelous experience. (Rudolph A. Marcus)

在對概念和數學的基本熱愛刺激下,得到理論薰陶是種奇妙的體驗。(魯道夫・馬庫斯)

It is commonly said that a teacher fails if he has not been surpassed by his students. There has been no failure on our part in this regard considering how far they have gone. (Edmond H. Fischer)

人們普遍認為,如果沒有被學生超越,老師就失敗了。考量到他們已邁出的進展,我們在這方面沒有失敗。(埃德蒙・費希爾)

It was in Hopkins's laboratory where I saw for the first time at close quarters some of the characteristics of what is sometimes referred to as "the British way of life." The Cambridge laboratory included people of many different dispositions, convictions, and abilities. I saw them argue without quarrelling, quarrel without suspecting, suspect without abusing, criticize without vilifying or ridiculing, and praise without flattering. (Edwin G. Krebs)

正是在霍普金斯大學的實驗室裡，我第一次近距離地看到有時稱為「英國生活方式」的一些特徵。劍橋實驗室的成員有著各式各樣的性格、信仰與能力。我看到他們辯論而不爭吵，爭吵而不懷疑，懷疑而不辱罵，批評而不詆毀或嘲笑，讚揚而不奉承。（埃德溫‧克雷布斯）

I used to think that if you won the Nobel Prize, you should turn to the hardest problem of all: how people think. But I've decided that's a bit arrogant. Instead, our research has continued to guide itself. (Edwin G. Krebs)

我一度認為，你要是得了諾貝爾獎，就應當轉向最困難的問題：人們是如何思考的。但我意識到這有點狂妄了。實際上，我們的研究還是繼續走自己的路。（埃德溫‧克雷布斯）

The future happens. No matter how much we scream. (Derek Walcott)

未來總會到來。無論我們如何尖叫。（德里克‧沃爾科特）

Peace cannot exist without justice, justice cannot exist without fairness, fairness cannot exist without development, development cannot exist without democracy, democracy cannot exist without respect for the identity and worth of cultures and peoples. (Rigoberta Menchú Tum)

和平離不開正義，正義離不開公平，公平離不開發展，發展離不開民主，民主離不開對各種文化與族群的特性與價值的尊重。（里戈韋塔‧曼朱）

What I treasure most in life is being able to dream. During my most difficult moments and complex situations I have been able to dream of a more beautiful future. (Rigoberta Menchú Tum)

生活中我最珍惜的是能夠夢想。在最困難的時刻和最複雜的情況下，我都能夢想更美好的未來。（里戈韋塔・曼朱）

I am like a drop of water on a rock. After drip, drip, dripping in the same place, I begin to leave a mark, and I leave my mark in many people's hearts. (Rigoberta Menchú Tum)

我就像落在岩石上的水滴。一滴，一滴，總是落在同一個位置之後，我開始留下印記，我在許多人的心中留下我的印記。（里戈韋塔・曼朱）

This world's not going to change unless we're willing to change ourselves. (Rigoberta Menchú Tum)

這個世界不會改變，除非我們願意改變自己。（里戈韋塔・曼朱）

This Prize gives recognition in the most influential way possible to all economists who endured many obstacles, criticisms, and even ridicule to study and analyze broader aspects of behavior than is traditional in economics. (Gary S. Becker)

這個獎項以最具影響力的可能方式，表揚所有不顧各種障礙、批評甚至嘲笑，研究和分析比傳統經濟學更廣泛的行為方面的科學家。（蓋瑞・貝克）

Economics is a very young science in comparison with the physical and biological sciences. Still, much is now known about economic and social life, although perhaps even more remains to be learned. For the economic and social world is mysterious, and it sometimes changes quickly and in surprising fashion. Every time we peel away some of the mystery, deeper challenges rise to the surface. (Gary S. Becker)

與物理學和生物科學相比，經濟學是一門非常年輕的科學。然而，現在對經濟和社會生活的了解已很可觀，儘管也許還有更多的東西有待學習。由於經濟和社會世界神祕費解，有時會以令人驚訝的方式迅速改變。每當我們揭開一些謎團，又浮現更深的挑戰。（蓋瑞‧貝克）

Economics surely does not provide a romantic vision of life. But the widespread poverty, misery, and crises in many parts of the world, much of it unnecessary, are strong reminders that understanding economic and social laws can make an enormous contribution to the welfare of people. (Gary S. Becker)

經濟學的確不提供浪漫的生活願景。不過，遍及世界許多地方的貧困、痛苦和危機，許多並非必要，都強烈地提醒著，理解經濟和社會規律可以為人民的福祉做出巨大的貢獻。（蓋瑞‧貝克）

1993 年

I do not pretend to be anything like an accomplished expert in all of the many things that I have ever been or am presently involved in doing. My most fundamental urge has always been just to spend time on what I found the most interesting, trying of course to match this up somehow with the more practical demands of life and a career. (Russell A. Hulse)

在所有自己曾經或正在參與的眾多事務中，我完全沒有假裝自己是

1991–2000 多元聲音與思想碰撞

專家之類的人物。我最根本的迫切願望,一直是只把時間用於自己覺得最有趣的事情上,當然也嘗試使之與生活和職業更實際的需求相互協調。(拉塞爾‧赫爾斯)

By now, it is surely clear that my interest in science has never been so much a matter of pursuing a career per se, but rather an expression of my personal fascination with knowing "How the World Works", especially as it could be understood directly with hands-on experience. This central motivation has been expressed over the years not only in my career but also in a wide range of hobbies. Notable amongst these "hobbies" have always been interests in various areas of science beyond whatever I was professionally employed in at any given time. (Russell A. Hulse)

直到現在,我很清楚自己對科學的興趣從來就不是追求職業本身,而是我個人一心了解「世界如何運轉」的展現,尤其是在它能夠由實務經驗直接理解的情況下。多年來,這種核心動機不僅展現在我的職業生涯中,也展現在廣泛的愛好上。這些「愛好」中最顯著的總是各種科學領域中的興趣,且超出了我當時的專業工作範圍。(拉塞爾‧赫爾斯)

Science was a defining part of my approach to life for as far back as I can remember. My parents fostered and supported this interest, and I thank them very much for being my first and, by far, most uncritically supportive funding agency. I ran through a seemingly endless series of interests involving chemistry sets, mechanical engineering construction sets, biology dissection kits, butterfly collecting, photography, telescopes, electronics and many other things over the years. (Russell A. Hulse)

從能想得起來的時候起,科學就屬於我生活方式中決定性的一部

1993 年

分。父母培養並支持這種興趣,我極其感謝他們作為我的第一個、也是迄今最不問青紅皂白的贊助人。多年來,我曾有過沒完沒了的一長串興趣愛好,包括化學裝置、機械工程建設設備、生物解剖用具、蝴蝶收藏、攝影、望遠鏡、電子產品以及許多別的事物。(拉塞爾·赫爾斯)

I remember spending weekends and summers helping my father put in place walls, rafters, siding and everything else that goes into a house. Among other things, it produced an early familiarity with tools and a do-it-yourself approach which has stood me in good stead over the years. My parents' friends and relatives were apparently not too sure that I should have been given such freedom to work with power tools at an early age, but fortunately I came through the experience with all of my fingers intact. (Russell A. Hulse)

我記得在週末和夏天時幫助父親用牆體、椽架、壁板和其他各種材料搭建房子。別的姑且不論,這使我早早就熟悉了各種工具和自己動手的方式,使我多年來受益匪淺。父母的親友顯然不確定是否應該准許年紀還小的我使用電動工具;幸好我度過了這段經歷,十指完好無缺。(拉塞爾·赫爾斯)

We have heard earlier today that scientific discoveries come at unpredictable times. Just as a person cannot say "I shall write poetry," another cannot say "I shall make a scientific discovery."

Russell Hulse and I did not set out in 1973 to detect gravitational waves, or even to conduct experiments into the fundamental nature of gravity. Instead, we set out to chart the celestial globe with a new type of star —— aware only that we were sailing a route none had explored before, and that wondrous new lands might be revealed beyond the next horizon.

We were young, well-prepared, and receptive, but not yet wise. We were playing a detective game, gathering clues and solving logical puzzles as they presented themselves.

One special new island, at first only faintly visible in our telescope, later showed its bounty in full relativistic glory. When its treasures were gathered and brought home, some after many years of labor, they provided keys to long-locked gates and added new notes to the symphony of natural law.

In discovering this new island and gathering its exotic fruits, Russell Hulse and I, and other colleagues in later years, were enjoying the privilege of doing what we like best: satisfying our own curiosities, by asking and answering questions. We sought no other reward than the pleasure of an exciting journey. To be honored by being here tonight is beyond our wildest youthful dreams of nineteen years ago, and brings us joy that mere words cannot express. (Joseph H. Taylor Jr.)

我們今天早些時候聽人說，科學發現在無法預知的時候到來。正像一個人不能說「我要寫詩」一樣，另一個人也不能說「我要做出一項科學發現」。

1973 年，拉塞爾・赫爾斯[03]和我並沒有著手探測引力波，或進行了解重力基本性質的實驗。實際上，我們開始藉助一種新星來觀測天體——只知自己駛上一條無人先行的航線，而那些令人驚奇的新陸地也許出現在前方的地平線上。

我們年輕，準備充分，樂於接受，但還不明智。我們在玩偵探遊戲，收集線索，於邏輯謎題出現時解開它們。

---

[03] 拉塞爾・赫爾斯，與泰勒同獲 1993 年諾貝爾物理學獎。

1993 年

一座非同尋常的新島，起初只是在望遠鏡中隱約可見，後來在充足的相對論之光下大放異彩。島上的寶藏被收集起來運回家後，經過多年探究，其中一些為長期閉鎖的大門提供了鑰匙，為自然法則的交響樂增添了新的音符。

在發現這座新島並收集其奇珍異寶時，拉塞爾·赫爾斯和我，以及後來歲月裡的其他同事，都享受著做我們最喜歡之事的特權：以提出和解答問題滿足自己的好奇心。我們不求其他回報，只是享受一次令人激動之旅的快樂。今晚能來到這裡的殊榮，超出我們 19 年前最瘋狂的青春夢想，帶給我們的歡樂單憑言語無法表達。（約瑟夫·泰勒）

Almost instantly the phone rang again. He had heard me just as he'd hung up. "Congratulations, Dr. Mullis. I am pleased to be able to announce to you that you have been awarded the Nobel Prize." "I'll take it!" I said. (Kary B. Mullis)

電話幾乎馬上又響了。他剛要結束通話時聽到了我說話。「祝賀你，穆利斯博士。我很高興能夠通知你，你獲得了諾貝爾獎。」「我接受！」我說。（凱利·穆利斯）

We have this inaccurate perception that everything that is real is perceptible by at least one of our senses, and invisible things are kind of freaky. (Kary B. Mullis)

我們都有這樣的錯覺，即所有真實的事物皆可由我們至少一種感官所感知，而無形的事物則有點怪異。（凱利·穆利斯）

This was typical of a chemist; chemists always believe they're smarter than biochemists. Of course, physicists think they're smarter than chemists, mathematicians think they're smarter than physicists, and, for a while, philosophers thought they were smarter than mathematicians, until they found out in this century that they really didn't have anything much to talk about. (Kary B. Mullis)

這是化學家的典型特徵,化學家總是相信自己比生物化學家聰明。當然了,物理學家認為自己比化學家聰明,數學家認為自己比物理學家聰明,而一度,哲學家認為自己比數學家聰明,直到進入 20 世紀發現自己真的沒有多少值得一提。(凱利·穆利斯)

For any human interaction to work both parties must believe they are getting the better deal. (Kary B. Mullis)

任何人與人交往要發揮作用,雙方都必須相信自己占了便宜。(凱利·穆利斯)

I look forward to shedding all my administrative responsibilities in another couple of years and returning to my first scientific love, working at the bench and having more time for sailing and for skiing. (Michael Smith)

我期待著在接下來的幾年裡卸下所有的行政職責,重歸自己最初的科學愛好,在實驗臺邊工作,有更多的時間去航海和滑雪。(麥可·史密斯)

Much of my work in biology has been driven by my early training in chemistry. When studying a new chemical compound, the first and most important thing is to determine its detailed molecular structure. (Richard J. Roberts)

我的許多生物學工作都是由早期的化學訓練推動的。在研究一種新的化合物時,首先並且最重要的是確定其詳細的分子結構。(理察·羅伯茨)

1993 年

The beauty of research is that you never know where it's going to lead. (Richard J. Roberts)

研究之美妙在於，你永遠不清楚它將引向何處。（理察・羅伯茨）

I am a passionate reader, having been tutored very early by my mother. I avidly devoured all books on chemistry that I could find. Formal chemistry at school seemed boring by comparison, and my performance was routine. In contrast, I did spectacularly well in mathematics and sailed through classes and exams with ease. (Richard J. Roberts)

我是一個熱愛閱讀的人，很早就一直受到母親的薰陶。我貪婪地吞下了找得到的所有化學書籍。相形之下，學校裡正規的化學課就顯得很無聊，我的表現也普通。我的數學反而尤其出色，輕鬆地通過了課程和考試。（理察・羅伯茨）

There is need for more science in politics and less politics in science. (Richard J. Roberts)

政治中需要更多的科學，而科學中需要更少的政治。（理察・羅伯茨）

This experience taught me many things, including the power of novel methodology and how a simple experiment can transform the understanding of an important problem. (Phillip A. Sharp)

這一次經歷教我許多事情，包括新的方法論的力量，以及簡單的實驗如何能夠改變對重要問題的理解。（菲利普・夏普）

If there's a book that you want to read, but it hasn't been written yet, then you must write it. (Toni Morrison)

1991-2000 多元聲音與思想碰撞

要是有一本書你想讀,可是還沒人寫,你就必須寫出來。(托妮‧莫里森)

Freedom is choosing your responsibility. It's not having no responsibilities; it's choosing the ones you want. (Toni Morrison)

自由是選擇你的責任。不是沒有責任,是選擇你所要的。(托妮‧莫里森)

At some point in life the world's beauty becomes enough. You don't need to photograph, paint or even remember it. It is enough. No record of it needs to be kept and you don't need someone to share it with or tell it to. When that happens —— that letting go —— you let go because you can. (Toni Morrison)

在人生的某個時刻,世界的美麗變得足夠了。你無須拍照、繪畫,甚至無須記住它。這就足夠了。無須保存任何紀錄,也不需要與什麼人分享或知會。當這種情況發生時 —— 順其自然 —— 你順其自然,因為你做得到。(托妮‧莫里森)

Nowadays silence is looked on as odd and most of my race has forgotten the beauty of meaning much by saying little. (Toni Morrison)

如今沉默被視為怪異,我們大多數人都忘卻了言簡義賅之美。(托妮‧莫里森)

The greatest glory in living lies not in never falling, but in rising every time we fall. (Nelson Mandela)

生活中最大的榮耀不在於從不跌倒,而在於每次跌倒都爬起來。(納爾遜‧曼德拉)

I learned that courage was not the absence of fear but the triumph over it. I felt fear myself more times than I can remember, but I hid it behind a mask of boldness. The brave man is not he who does not feel afraid but he who conquers that fear. (Nelson Mandela)

我體認到勇氣並不是沒有恐懼，而是戰勝它。我自己也記不清有多少次感到害怕，但我把它藏在勇敢的面具後面。勇敢的人不是不知害怕的人，而是能夠戰勝恐懼的人。（納爾遜·曼德拉）

After climbing a great hill, one only finds that there are many more hills to climb. I have taken a moment here to rest, to steal a view of the glorious vista that surrounds me, to look back on the distance I have come. But I can rest only for a moment, for with freedom comes responsibilities, and I dare not linger, for my long walk is not yet ended. (Nelson Mandela)

爬上一座大山後，你只會發現還有更多的山要爬。我在這裡稍事休息，掃一眼四周的壯麗景色，回顧自己走過的路程。但我只能休息片刻，因為責任隨著自由而來，我不敢逗留，因為自己的長途跋涉尚未結束。（納爾遜·曼德拉）

Peace does not simply mean the absence of conflict. (Frederik Willem de Klerk)

和平並不僅僅意味著沒有衝突。（弗雷德里克·威廉·戴克拉克）

People want more and more leisure time, which means the freedom to do what they want to do, not what they have to do, and as we get richer and richer, more and more people will be able to afford that. (Robert W. Fogel)

人們想要越來越多的休閒時間，這意味著自由地做自己想做的事，而非做不得不做的事。而且隨著我們變得越來越富裕，越來越多的人將負擔得起。（羅伯特·福格爾）

As we get rich, the basics of life – food, clothing and shelter – become a very small part of total expenditure. And people have enough money to purchase things that enhance them spiritually, and I mean the word 「spiritual」 not necessarily in a religious sense but in the sense that it adds to your feeling of well-being. (Robert W. Fogel)

隨著我們富裕起來,生活的基本要素——食物、衣服和住所——在總支出中成為很小的部分。人們有足夠的錢購買精神上提高自己的東西,而我所說的「精神上」一詞,指的未必是宗教上,而是其在增加幸福感方面。(羅伯特‧福格爾)

Remember, what does "retirement" mean? It doesn't mean that you're a couch potato. Leisure is not the same thing as rest. If you're bicycling five miles a day, that's leisure, but it certainly takes a lot of effort. (Robert W. Fogel)

記住,「退休」的意思是什麼?它並不意味著你是個「沙發馬鈴薯」。休閒跟休息不同。你要是每天騎 5 英哩腳踏車,這就是休閒,但它確實需要很多努力。(羅伯特‧福格爾)

To predict the future we would have to know today what we will learn tomorrow which will shape our future actions. (Douglass C. North)

為了預測未來,我們今天必須清楚明天自己將學習什麼,這將構成我們的未來行動。(道格拉斯‧諾斯)

1994 年

On the pragmatic view the only thing that matters is that the theory is efficacious, that it "works" and that the necessary preliminaries and side issues do not cost too much in time and effort. (Bertram N. Brockhouse)

依照實用主義的觀點，唯一重要的是理論是有效的，它「發揮作用」，所需鋪陳和枝節問題不需耗費太多時間和力氣。（伯特倫·布羅克豪斯）

The wonderful reward we have received today seems to indicate that some of nature's secrets are indeed vulnerable to this tool of the physicist. We are indeed appreciative of the honor. (Clifford G. Shull)

我們今天接受的絕妙獎項似乎表明，自然界的一些祕密的確容易受到物理學家的破解。我們衷心感激這個榮譽。（克利福德·沙爾）

There are many facets of chemistry. Mankind's drive to uncover the secrets of life's processes and use this knowledge led to spectacular advances in the biological and health sciences. Chemistry richly contributes to this by helping our understanding at the molecular level. Chemistry is, however, and always will be a central science of its own. (George A. Olah)

化學有很多方面。人類不斷探索生命過程的奧祕並運用這種知識，推動了生物及健康科學領域的驚人進步。對此，化學在分子層面上幫助我們的理解而貢獻良多。然而，化學本身是，而且永遠都是一門核心科學。（喬治·安德魯·歐拉）

1991–2000 多元聲音與思想碰撞

The Prize is also wonderful for the individual. I've jokingly said it's like being given a lifetime depot injection of Prozac. (Alfred G. Gilman)

諾貝爾獎對於個人來說也棒極了。我曾開玩笑地說，這就像打了一針終生有效的百憂解[04]。（艾爾佛列·古曼·吉爾曼）

You need to find an area of importance and something where there are big questions, hopefully more than one and to begin to hone in on an area first. I don't think that the questions need to get too specific too soon. (Alfred G. Gilman)

你需要找出一個具有重要意義且存在重大問題的領域，但願不止一個，然後開始磨鍊其中一個領域。我不認為問題需要過快地提出得太具體。（艾爾佛列·古曼·吉爾曼）

Life, like the first blooming, emerges tantalizing to the curious:

Why, How, When, Where;

Interlocked questions arising from the mysterious

encompassing matters quite serious. (Martin Rodbell)

生命，猶如初次開花，引得好奇者遐想：

為什麼，怎麼樣，什麼時候，什麼地方，

其不可思議引起連串問題

裡面有一些富於嚴肅意義。（馬丁·羅德貝爾）

In many respects, my career and my experiences with people and events have been seamless in that I cannot separate one from another. Without doubt, the thread of one's life should be within the matrix of the total human experience. (Martin Rodbell)

---

[04] 百憂解，一種抗憂鬱藥。

1994 年

　　在很多方面，我的職業生涯跟待人處事的經歷一直密切相關，兩者無法截然分開。毫無疑問，一個人的生命線索應該處於整個人類經驗的矩陣中。（馬丁・羅德貝爾）

　　As a child, I wanted to be a physicist. I begged my mother to let me go to Tokyo to study physics. I promised I would win the Nobel Prize for Physics. So, 50 years later, I returned to my village and said to my mother, "See, I have kept my promise. I won the Nobel Prize." "No," said my mother, who has a very fine sense of humor, "You promised it would be in physics!" (Kenzaburo Oe)

　　小時候，我想成為物理學家。我懇求母親讓我去東京學物理。我承諾我會得到諾貝爾物理學獎。於是，50 年後，我回到村裡，對母親說，「看，我信守了諾言。我得了諾貝爾獎。」「沒有，」母親說，她的幽默感非常微妙，「你承諾要得物理學獎的！」[05]（大江健三郎）

　　I am one of the writers who wish to create serious works of literature which dissociate themselves from those novels which are mere reflections of the vast consumer cultures of Tokyo and the subcultures of the world at large. (Kenzaburo Oe)

　　我屬於一心創作嚴肅文學作品的作家，這種作品有別於那些只是反映東京廣大的消費者文化乃至整個世界次文化的小說。（大江健三郎）

　　The fundamental style of my writing has been to start from my personal matters and then to link it up with society, the state and the world. (Kenzaburo Oe)

　　我寫作的基本風格，始終是從個人生活出發，然後將其與社會、國家和世界連繫起來。（大江健三郎）

---

[05]　大江健三郎是 1994 年諾貝爾文學獎得主。

1991-2000 多元聲音與思想碰撞

The writer's job is the job of a clown… the clown who also talks about sorrow. (Kenzaburo Oe)

作家的行業即小丑的行業……那種也會談論悲傷的小丑。（大江健三郎）

I have survived by representing these sufferings of mine in the form of the novel. (Kenzaburo Oe)

我以小說的形式表現自己的這些艱難困苦，從而存活。（大江健三郎）

Fundamentally a good author has his or her own sense of style. There is a natural, deep voice, and that voice is present from the first draft of a manuscript. When he or she elaborates on the initial manuscript, it continues to strengthen and simplify that natural, deep voice. (Kenzaburo Oe)

從根本上來說，好的作者有自己的風格。有一種自然的、深沉的聲音，這個聲音出現於作品最初的草稿。當他或她對初稿進行詳細闡述時，作品繼續強化並簡化這種自然的、深沉的聲音。（大江健三郎）

I don't have faith nor do I think I will have it in the future, but I'm not an atheist. My faith is that of a secular person. You might call it "morality." Throughout my life I have acquired some wisdom but always through rationality, thought, and experience. I am a rational person and I work only through my own experience. My lifestyle is that of a secular person, and I have learned about human beings that way. (Kenzaburo Oe)

我沒有宗教信仰，也不認為將來會有，但我不是無神論者。我的信仰是世俗之人的信仰。你可能稱其為「道德」。經由此生我獲得了若干智

> 1994 年

慧，但總是經由理性、思考，以及經驗。我是個理性的人，只根據自己的經驗行事。我的生活方式是世俗之人的生活方式，我以這種方式了解人類。（大江健三郎）

I kept trying to run away. And I almost did. But it seems that reality compels you to live properly when you live in the real world. (Kenzaburo Oe)

我一直試圖逃跑。而我差點就這麼做了。不過當你生活在現實世界中時，看來是現實迫使你好好地生活。（大江健三郎）

To be upright and to have an imagination: that is enough to be a very good young man. (Kenzaburo Oe)

正直，有想像力：如此即足以成為非常好的年輕人。（大江健三郎）

In Japan itself there have all along been attempts by some to obliterate the article about renunciation of war from the Constitution and for this purpose they have taken every opportunity to make use of pressures from abroad. (Kenzaburo Oe)

在日本國內，一直有些人力圖從憲法中廢除關於放棄戰爭的條款，為了這個目的，他們抓住一切機會利用來自國外的壓力。（大江健三郎）

Today I come bearing an olive branch in one hand, and the freedom fighter's gun in the other. Do not let the olive branch fall from my hand. (Yasser Arafat)

我今天來，一隻手拿著橄欖枝，另一隻手拿著自由鬥士的槍。不要讓橄欖枝從我手中落下。（亞西爾·阿拉法特）

In Israel, a land lacking in natural resources, we learned to appreciate our greatest national advantage: our minds. Through creativity and innovation, we transformed barren deserts into flourishing fields and pioneered new frontiers in science and technology. (Shimon Peres)

在以色列，一塊缺乏自然資源的土地上，我們學會了重視我們最大的國家優勢：自己的頭腦。透過創造和創新，我們把貧瘠的沙漠變成繁榮的田野，開闢了科學技術的新領域。（希蒙·佩雷斯）

When you have two alternatives, the first thing you have to do is to look for the third that you didn't think about, that doesn't exist. (Shimon Peres)

當你擁有兩個選擇時，你必須做的第一件事是尋找你沒想到也不存在的第三個。（希蒙·佩雷斯）

The Jews' greatest contribution to history is dissatisfaction! We're a nation born to be discontented. Whatever exists we believe can be changed for the better. (Shimon Peres)

猶太人對歷史的最大貢獻就是不滿！我們是個天生不知滿足的民族。任何事物出現，我們都相信可以加以改進。（希蒙·佩雷斯）

The older generation had greater respect for land than science. But we live in an age when science, more than soil, has become the provider of growth and abundance. Living just on the land creates loneliness in an age of globality. (Shimon Peres)

老一輩的世代尊敬土地勝過科學。然而我們生活在這樣一個時代，科學超越土壤成為成長和富足的來源。在全球化的時代，僅以土地為生會造成孤獨。（希蒙·佩雷斯）

They thought that I was a man with reasonable judgment, so I was never under pressure from my parents; I could do whatever I wanted. I never had a

1994 年

negative word from them, nothing whatsoever. (Shimon Peres)

父母認為我是個有合理判斷力的人,所以我從未受到他們的壓力,我可以做任何想做的事。我從未聽到他們否定的話,一句都沒有。(希蒙·佩雷斯)

Count the dreams of your mind; if the numbers of the dreams exceeds the number of achievements, you are young. (Shimon Peres)

數一下心中的夢想。如果夢想的數量超過成就的數量,你就是年輕的。(希蒙·佩雷斯)

My greatest mistake is that my dreams were too small. (Shimon Peres)

我最大的錯誤是我的夢想太小了。(希蒙·佩雷斯)

I never was after money. It never attracted me. (Shimon Peres)

我從未追求過金錢。它永遠吸引不了我。(希蒙·佩雷斯)

I thought all my life that optimists and pessimists pass away the same way, so why be a pessimist? (Shimon Peres)

我一生都認為,樂觀主義者和悲觀主義者的死法是一樣的。那麼,為什麼要當悲觀主義者?(希蒙·佩雷斯)

I'm trying to learn the lessons of the past, but not to make speeches about the past. (Yitzhak Rabin)

我在盡力汲取過去的教訓,而非針對過去發表演講。(伊扎克·拉賓)

There's nothing harder than defining oneself. (Yitzhak Rabin)

沒有什麼比定義自己更困難了。(伊扎克·拉賓)

1991–2000 多元聲音與思想碰撞

Of course, we all feel greatly honored by the decision of the Royal Swedish Academy of Sciences to award the Nobel memorial Prize to us. But from a more general point of view, we also feel great satisfaction by the fact that, by this award, game theory has now received international recognition as an important branch of economic analysis. (John C. Harsanyi)

不言而喻，對瑞典皇家科學院將諾貝爾獎授予我們的決定，我們都感到非常榮幸。不過，出於更普遍的觀點，我們還對如下事實感到非常滿足：由於這個獎項，賽局理論現已得到國際認可，成為經濟分析的一個重要分支。（夏仙義・亞諾什・卡羅伊）

I did have an appreciation of maths and science as a child, and even at elementary school I would like to do more in mathematics than the other students were doing in one way or another. So I did have that at an early stage. Like maybe almost comparable to Mozart in music. Of course he had a father who was a musician. (John F. Nash Jr.)

當我還是個孩子時，我就特別欣賞數學和科學，即便在小學，跟同學相比，我也會更樂於盡可能學習數學。所以這方面我確實早慧。也許幾乎可以與學音樂的莫札特相比。當然，他有一位音樂家父親。（約翰・富比士・納許）

I was affected in this way for a very long period of time, like 25 years, so it was quite a portion of a life's history. (John F. Nash Jr.)

我如此承受折磨很長的時期，大約 25 年，所以這佔據了我個人生命史相當大的一部分。[06]（約翰・富比士・納許）

I have other areas of research I'm about to publish and my work really

---

[06] 納許久患精神分裂症，飽受其擾。

1994 年

relates to game theory, a project… and I have other areas of study. I don't know how long I will live and how much I will be able to do, but at least I am active. (John F. Nash Jr.)

我還有另一些研究領域行將發表成果，我的工作的確關係到賽局理論，一個項目……我還有另一些探討領域。我不知道自己會活多久，自己能做多少事，但至少我是活躍的。（約翰·富比士·納許）

Statistically, it would seem improbable that any mathematician or scientist, at the age of 66, would be able through continued research efforts, to add much to his or her previous achievements. (John F. Nash Jr.)

從統計學角度來看，任何數學家或科學家，到了 66 歲，還能透過後續的研究努力，使自己已有的成就更上一層樓，這似乎不大可能。（約翰·富比士·納許）

It's very productive scientifically; I often get some very good ideas for my research while hiking. (Reinhard Selten)

從科學角度來說，這非常有成果；在徒步旅行中，我經常產生一些關於研究工作的出色想法。（賴因哈德·澤爾滕）

If you take an oppositional point of view, people look at it with interest even if they don't accept it completely. They may say Oh, that's original. Of course you have to present it in the right way, but the scientific world is not the enemy of young imaginative people. (Reinhard Selten)

如果你持相反的觀點，人們會懷著興趣看待它，即使並不完全接受。他們可能說，哦，這挺有獨創性的啊。當然你得以正確的方式呈現它，不過科學世界並不是富於想像力的年輕人的敵人。（賴因哈德·澤爾滕）

Nobody should enter a field if he is not attracted to it, he has to have a real feel, a real attraction to it so that he can be kept captivated by the questions there. Because you have to get emotionally involved in these questions, you have to become a drug addict for this kind of scientific activity, because if you just want to do it in order to get a career it's already wrong. I mean, people ask me what do you have to do in order to get the Bank of Sweden Prize? Then I say if you ask this you already on the wrong track. (Reinhard Selten)

誰都不應該進入一個不感興趣的領域。他得有真正的感覺，真正受到吸引，才能被其中的問題迷住。因為你得對這些問題投入情感，你得成為這種科學活動的癮君子；因為如果你若只是為了得到一份職業而想做此事，就已經錯了。我的意思是，人們問我，為了獲得瑞典銀行獎，你得做什麼？我就說，你要是問這個，你已經走錯路了。（賴因哈德‧澤爾滕）

1995 年

The popular image of a scientist and how one does science is very distorted and that is what drives many young people away from careers in science. And so I want to tell you what I have learned in the course of fifty years of doing experiments in physics. I will summarize in 13 maxims what I have learned and it is these maxims that make doing experimental science enjoyable and exciting. I will use examples from my own life.

You must take account of your personality and temperament in choosing your science and your interests in that field.

I have a mechanical view of the universe, I am competent in mathematics but I don't excel in mathematics and so I have been an experimenter. I speculate about experiments that might be interesting but I don't work in physics theory. I like to work on equipment because I am mechanically handy. But don't try to fit yourself into any particular image of what a scientist should be. You don't have to be a mathematical genius, you don't have to be mechanically handy. You just have to want to find out new things about nature and you just have to have the strength to keep working on an experiment when no one knows the answer. The great joy will then occur when you are the first one to know the answer.

It is best to use your own ideas for experiments.

You can't always use your own ideas because you may be part of a larger science group with defined goals, but it is always more fun to work on your own ideas.

You don't have to be a fast thinker or a fast talker. In fact, it is best to avoid such people.

When you begin to get a new idea it may be badly formulated or even wrong. Beware of fast thinkers and fast talkers who delight in showing that your idea is wrong. This is because by working on a somewhat wrong idea you often can get a good idea. But this takes time and you need sympathetic and helpful colleagues, not fast-talking critics.

You don't have to know everything. You can learn a subject or a technology when you need it.

Science moves very fast these days and if you try to get into a new area you may think you will have to first spend all your time studying the subject before you get into it. It is best to jump fairly fast and then learn what you need from colleagues or books or courses or from experience.

For every good idea, expect to have ten or twenty bad ideas.

But expect that most of your own ideas will not work out, but when you get a good idea that works it is marvelous.

It is often impossible to predict the future of a technology used in engineering or science.

I was a chemical engineer before I was a physicist and in late 1940's I worked for the General Electric Company. I worked on an R&D project to make very small electron vacuum tubes so that radios could be made smaller and use less power. Meanwhile the transistor was invented at Bell Laboratories.

You must be interested in, even enchanted by, some of the technology or mathematics you use. Then the bad days are not so bad.

There will always be bad days when you do experimental science when nothing works or you discover that designs have to be changed. It is crucial that you be enchanted with some parts of the experiment so that you can get through these bad times.

Another advantage of being enchanted by the technology or the mathematics is that you will be more likely to think of improvements and variations.

This is obvious.

You may dislike, even dread, some of the technology or mathematics used in a large experimental or engineering projects, and you may be happy to leave these areas to colleagues. But don't be surprised if you have to get into one of these areas yourself.

Although I started my career as a chemical engineer these are many areas of chemistry that I don't like. But our present searches for fractional electric charge particles in meteoritic material uses much colloidal chemistry. I have had to learn it.

You should be fond of the technology or mathematics that you use, but not too much in love with the technology or mathematics. There may be a better way.

This is obvious.

You must learn the art of obsession in science and technology.

When working on an experiment it is important to be obsessed with it. When you wake up in the middle of the night you should be thinking about the experiment. But with all experiments there will come a time when you cannot improve it substantially or when someone else has devised a more fruitful experiment in the same area. Then you should end the present experiment and move on. This is the art of obsession in science.

In many areas of science it is getting harder and harder to have the time to do both experimental work and original theory. In some areas, such as particle physics and astrophysics it is usually impossible.

I believe that in many parts of science the design and building of modern experimental apparatus has become a full time job, as has doing original theoretical work. It is sad, but there is usually not enough time in the day and the night to do both.

Theory should be a good companion to the experimenter, inventor and engineer, sometimes leading, sometimes following. The experimenter or engineer should not let theory set the fashion or dictate what is important.

Theory, even very speculative theory has come to dominate the thinking and presentation of science inside and outside the science community. These days, experimenters do experiments because a theory, often a very speculative theory, suggests the experiment. If you are doing the experiment anyway you will not waste much time in also testing the speculation, but you will be happier and find out more about nature if you do the experiments in which you believe. In the end the validity of science depends upon experimental results and measurements. (Martin L. Perl)

大眾心目中的科學家形象以及科學研究過程大為失真，這是許多年輕人對科學職業敬而遠之的原因。所以，我想跟諸位談談自己 50 年物理學實驗事業的心得。我把它們總結成 13 條常識，而正是這些常識使從事實驗科學愉快而令人興奮。我將以自己為例。

在選擇所從事學科和該領域中感興趣的事時，必須考慮個性和稟賦。

我對宇宙持機械性看法，具備數學能力但並不出眾，所以一直是個實驗者。我思考很有趣的實驗，但不研究物理學理論。我喜歡在設備上工作，因為我在機械方面很拿手。不要試著賦予自己科學家應該是什麼樣子的特定形象。你無須身為數學天才，無須擅長機械。只要你想找出關於自然的新鮮事，只要你在沒人知道答案時有毅力堅持工作。一旦最

1995 年

先得知答案，巨大的喜悅會隨之而來。

做實驗最好運用自己的想法。

你無法總是運用自己的想法，因為你可能屬於一個目標明確的更大的科學團體，不過運用自己的想法工作總是更有趣的。

你無須身為反應快或談鋒健的人。實際上，最好避開這樣的人。

你剛得出新想法時，它可能難以說清楚，甚至可能是錯的。小心熱衷於指出你的想法錯誤、反應快或談鋒健的人。這是因為，經由研究一個有些錯誤的想法，常常可以得出好想法。但這需要時間，而你需要富有同理心、樂於助人的同事，而不是刀子嘴的批評者。

不必無所不知。可以在需要的時候學習一門學科或一項技術。

如今科學發展非常迅速。如果試圖進入一個新領域，你可能認為必須先把所有時間都用於學習這門學科上。最好還是迅速地大致了解一下，然後經由同事、書籍、課程或經驗學習所需知識。

對於每一個好主意，免不了出現一、二十個壞主意。

但是要知道自己的大部分想法都行不通，而一旦得出一個好想法，便是一件了不起的事情。

我們通常無法預言工程或科學所使用技術的前景。

在成為物理學家之前，我是個化學工程師。1940 年代末，我為奇異公司工作。我從事一個研發項目，製造非常小的電子真空管，以便把收音機做得更小、更省電。不料與此同時，貝爾實驗室發明了電晶體。

必須對所使用的一些技術或數學感興趣，甚至痴迷。這樣，糟糕的日子就不那麼糟糕了。

從事實驗科學時，在處處碰壁或發現必須改變設計時，總會有糟糕的日子。痴迷於實驗的某些部分很重要，這樣你才能渡過這些糟糕的時候。

痴迷於技術或數學的另一個好處是，你更有可能想到改進和改變。

這個顯而易見。

你可能不喜歡，甚至畏懼，一些在大型實驗或工程項目中使用的技術或數學，可能很高興把這些領域留給同事。但如果得親自進入這些領域，也不要吃驚。

儘管是化學工程師出身，我不喜歡化學的很多領域。但我們目前對隕石物質中分級電荷粒子的研究用到許多膠體化學。我就得學會它。

應當喜歡所使用的技術或數學，但不要過分鍾愛技術或數學。也許有更好的辦法。

這個顯而易見。

必須學會執著於科學與技術的藝術。

做實驗時，執著是很重要的。半夜醒來，你應該滿腦子還是實驗。然而所有的實驗總有你對它做不出實質性改進的時候，或者同一領域有別人設計出更有成效的實驗。這時你就應當結束當前的實驗而往前走。這是執著於科學的藝術。

在科學的許多領域，人們越來越難有時間既做實驗工作又從事原創理論。在一些領域，如粒子物理學和天體物理學，這通常是不可能的。

我相信，在科學的許多領域，現代實驗裝置的設計和建造已經成為全職工作，跟從事原創理論工作一樣。這很令人悲傷，但通常即便日以繼夜也沒有足夠時間同時做兩件事。

1995 年

　　理論應當是實驗者、發明家和工程師的好夥伴，有時引領，有時跟隨。實驗者或工程師不應任由理論開風氣之先或決定何者重要。

　　理論，甚至非常具推測性的理論，已經逐漸主導了科學界內外的科學思考和表達方式。如今，實驗者做實驗是基於一種理論，往往非常具推測性的理論，而提出了實驗。你如果在做自己相信的實驗，不管怎樣都不會花費太多時間去驗證理論假設，而會更樂於多了解一些自然。說到底，科學的有效性取決於實驗結果和測量值。（馬丁・佩爾）

　　Experimental science is a craft and an art, and part of the art is knowing when to end a fruitless experiment. (Martin L. Perl)

　　實驗科學是手藝也是藝術，而藝術的一部分在於知道何時結束無果的實驗。（馬丁・佩爾）

　　The physics world may not show much gratitude in the future for our work. Our discoveries may have brought up more problems than we solved. (Martin L. Perl)

　　將來，對於我們的工作，物理學界可能不會表示太多感謝。與所解決的問題相比，我們的發現所帶來的問題可能更多。（馬丁・佩爾）

　　Life is much harder for the young women and men who are in science in present times. But they are smarter and better trained than I was at their ages; they know more and have better equipment. I wish them good fortune. (Martin L. Perl)

　　對於現在身處科學領域的年輕男女，日子辛苦得多。不過他們比年輕時的我更聰明，受過更好的訓練；他們所知更多，擁有更好的設備。我祝他們好運。（馬丁・佩爾）

My activities over the past 40 years could not possibly have been accomplished by myself alone. They have required the dedicated and tireless support of many talented coworkers. One in particular I must mention —— my very good friend and colleague Clyde Cowan, who was an equal partner in the experiments to discover the neutrino. I regret that he did not live long enough to share in this honor with me. (Frederick Reines)

我過去40年的作為不可能單憑一己之力。它們需要許多才華洋溢的合作者熱誠的不懈支持。必須特別提到的一位是 —— 我的摯友、同事克萊德·科溫，他在發現中微子的實驗中是與我平等的夥伴。遺憾的是，他沒有活到分享這一項榮譽的時候。（弗雷德里克·萊因斯）

But natural sciences I became interested in, I don't know how, it's just by reading books and the first books maybe were about explorations you know, the people, the Jules Verne books, the stories about the march to the North and to the South Pole and so on. (Paul J. Crutzen)

不過，無意之間，我對自然科學產生了興趣，也就是由於閱讀。起初讀的書可能是談論探險的，你們知道，儒勒·凡爾納作品，探險家們進軍北極和南極的故事等等。（保羅·克魯岑）

Because I could not afford doing the more experimental courses which take time, you have to spend a considerable amount of hours in the lab and I couldn't afford that. One of the reasons why I became a theoretician is because of practical reasons. (Paul J. Crutzen)

因為我無法負擔耗時的實驗課，你必須把大量的時間用在實驗室裡，而這個我做不到。我成為理論家的原因之一是實際原因。（保羅·克魯岑）

1995 年

On July 1, 1959, we moved to Stockholm and I started with my second profession, that of a computer programmer. The great advantage of being at a university department was that I got the opportunity to follow some of the courses that were offered. By 1963 I could thus fulfil the requirement for the "filosofiekandidat" (corresponding to a Master of Science) degree, combining the subjects mathematics, mathematical statistics, and meteorology. (Paul J. Crutzen)

1959年7月1日,我們搬到斯德哥爾摩,我開始從事第二個職業——電腦程式設計師。在大學的系所工作有一大好處,即有機會旁聽學校提供的一些課程。因此,到1963年,我已能滿足對理學碩士學位的要求,包括了數學、數理統計學和氣象學等科目。(保羅·克魯岑)

The planet is just too small for these developing countries to repeat the economic growth in the same way that the rich countries have done it in the past. We don't have enough natural resources, we don't have enough atmosphere. Clearly, something has to change. (Mario J. Molina)

就開發中國家而言地球實在是太小了,這些國家無法以富裕國家昔日的方式複製經濟成長。我們沒有足夠的自然資源,我們沒有足夠的大氣層。顯然,模式不得不改變。(馬里奧·莫利納)

Clearly the Nobel Prize is widely recognised and honoured and it's sort of as though your name has just been changed. It's not Sherwood Rowland, it's Sherwood Rowland Nobel Prize winner. And that certainly is a difference. (F. Sherwood Rowland)

顯而易見,諾貝爾獎得到廣泛的認可和尊敬,我的名字也多少彷彿就此更改了一般。不是舍伍德·羅蘭,而是諾貝爾獎得主舍伍德·羅蘭。這當然是不同的。(弗蘭克·舍伍德·羅蘭)

The question of if you have a problem that you would like to work on where the answer is not known, all of us go through undergraduate school, high school, undergraduate school being asked to solve problems where the answers are known, and where as often as not they're in the back of the book. That's different from being, from posing a problem and knowing that no one knows the answer to it. And so if you think you have the right answer then you're the only person that can judge it and you have to decide that you know enough now, have you thought of everything that's involved. And that's just an entirely different kind of intellectual challenge. And if you like that challenge then it's a very favourable kind of employment for a career. (F. Sherwood Rowland)

如果有個未解的問題，你想要解答，該怎麼做？我們都上過大學，從高中到大學，被要求做許多已解的題目，未解的也往往是答案印在書末。這跟提出一個你知道無人知道答案的問題不同。於是，如果你認為自己有正確的答案，你就是唯一能夠判斷它的人，你就得判定自己是否已經考慮周全，是否已充分了解。這是一種截然不同的智力挑戰。而如果你喜歡這種挑戰，那麼，這就是一種非常值得作為事業而投入的工作。（弗蘭克・舍伍德・羅蘭）

It isn't necessary to seek out adventure. Opening to what is around you will produce the most extraordinary experiences. (Edward B. Lewis)

沒必要尋求冒險。向周圍的事物敞開自己，就會獲得極不尋常的體驗。（愛德華・巴茨・路易斯）

We define ourselves by the best that is in us, not the worst that has been done to us. (Edward B. Lewis)

> 1995 年

我們採用自己內在最好的東西定義自己,而非自己曾遭受到最壞的部分。(愛德華・巴茨・路易斯)

Creativity is combining facts no one else has connected before. (Christiane Nüsslein-Volhard)

創造就是將他人不曾加以連繫的事實結合起來。(克里斯汀・紐斯林—沃爾哈德)

I remember that already as a child I was often intensely interested in things, obsessed by ideas and projects in many areas, and in these topics I learned much on my own, reading books. (Christiane Nüsslein-Volhard)

我記得當我還是個孩子的時候,就對各種事物興趣十足,為許多方面的觀念和項目著迷。並且透過閱讀,我在這些主題中也自己學到了很多東西。(克里斯汀・紐斯林—沃爾哈德)

Although the work we did was often tedious and sometimes frustrating, it was generally great fun and a deep pleasure and joy to get an understanding to what seemed initially to be a great mystery. (Christiane Nüsslein-Volhard)

儘管我們所從事的工作經常冗長乏味,有時還令人沮喪,整體而言,破解一個最初看來巨大的謎,仍是極大的樂趣和深深的喜悅。(克里斯汀・紐斯林—沃爾哈德)

Follow your interesting, your ambition, your passion. (Christiane Nüsslein-Volhard)

追隨你的興趣、你的抱負、你的熱情。(克里斯汀・紐斯林—沃爾哈德)

1991–2000 多元聲音與思想碰撞

In mathematics and science, there is no difference in the intelligence of men and women. The difference in genes between men and women is simply the Y chromosome, which has nothing to do with intelligence. (Christiane Nüsslein-Volhard)

在數學和科學中,男女智力沒有差別。兩性之間的基因差異僅為Y染色體,它與智力毫無關係。(克里斯汀·紐斯林—沃爾哈德)

Theory without practice —— that's ignorance! (Eric F. Wieschaus)

空有理論而不實踐 —— 那是無知!(艾瑞克·威斯喬斯)

Nothing you do in the lab absolutely matters. All you are doing is desperately trying to fight against ignorance. (Eric F. Wieschaus)

在實驗室裡做什麼完全無關緊要。你所做的一切都是在極力對抗無知。(艾瑞克·威斯喬斯)

When I first encountered the name of the city of Stockholm, I little thought that I would ever visit it, never mind end up being welcomed to it as a guest of the Swedish Academy and the Nobel Foundation. (Seamus Heaney)

初見斯德哥爾摩這座城市的名稱時,我幾乎沒想到自己會到訪,更不用說居然獲得它的歡迎,作為瑞典皇家科學院和諾貝爾基金會的客人。(西默斯·希尼)

There is risk and truth to yourselves and the world before you. (Seamus Heaney)

對於你們自己和你們面前的世界,風險和真理並存。(西默斯·希尼)

I can't think of a case where poems changed the world, but what they do is they change people's understanding of what's going on in the world. (Seamus Heaney)

我想不出詩歌改變了世界的例子；不過它們所做的，是改變人們對世界上正在發生的事情的理解。（西默斯・希尼）

From my earliest days I had a passion for science. (Joseph Rotblat)

我從非常小的時候就對科學滿懷熱情。（約瑟夫・羅特布拉特）

At a time when science plays such a powerful role in the life of society, when the destiny of the whole of mankind may hinge on the results of scientific research, it is incumbent on all scientists to be fully conscious of that role, and conduct themselves accordingly. (Joseph Rotblat)

當科學在社會生活中發揮如此重要的作用，當整個人類的命運可能取決於科學研究的結果時，所有的科學家都應義不容辭，充分意識到這種作用，並據之自覺行動。（約瑟夫・羅特布拉特）

If I developed a reliable, systematic way for approaching economic problems I would end up at the right place. (Robert E. Lucas Jr.)

我若能發展出一種可靠的、系統的方法來解決經濟問題，我最終會找到正確的方向。（小羅伯特・盧卡斯）

A deal is a deal. It's hard to be unpleasant after winning a prize like that. (Robert E. Lucas Jr.)

說話要算數。得到這樣的獎很難不滿意了。[07]（小羅伯特・盧卡斯）

---

[07] 盧卡斯夫婦的離婚協議規定：自 1988 年 10 月 31 日離婚後 7 年內，男方若獲諾貝爾獎，「女方應得獎金的百分之五十」。不料盧卡斯獲獎，並於 1995 年 10 月 10 日公布，所以他得拿出 60 萬美元。

1991–2000 多元聲音與思想碰撞

1996 年

I look back upon graduate school as being a very happy period in my life. The chance to be thoroughly immersed in physics and to be surrounded by friends pursuing similar goals was a marvelous experience. (David M. Lee)

回過頭看，我感到研究所是此生非常快樂的一段時光。有機會完全沉浸於物理學之中，身邊都是追求相似目標的朋友，是一種妙不可言的體驗。（戴維・李）

Basic science provides long-term benefits for ourselves and our fragile planet and should be supported by all the world's societies. (David M. Lee)

基礎科學為我們自身和這個脆弱的星球提供了長期的益處，應當得到世界上所有社會的支持。（戴維・李）

The general wisdom was that the superfluidity of helium-3 was a pipe dream of the theorists. But in fact, it did occur. (Douglas D. Osheroff)

學界普遍認為，氦-3 的超流體只是理論家的白日夢。然而事實上，它的確出現了。（道格拉斯・奧謝羅夫）

I suppose my fascination with "physics" began at age six, when I tore apart my electric train in order to play with the electric motor inside. The non-event that was then crucial to my continued movement toward a career in science was that my parents did not scold me for this, but rather my father took the time to show me how the motor worked. He seemed fascinated with my fascination. As time went on, he would bring me other objects that he felt might interest me, such as a box of magnets from the electric power company, and boxes of parts from the telephone company. At age eight, he gave me the camera he had used as a child. Within an hour, it too, had succumbed to my curiosity. After this, my father brought home a mechanical watch with a set of jeweler's screwdrivers, suggesting that I see if I could take it apart and put it back together. Such was the sort of gentle nurturing that sustained my interest in science.

In grade school I learned almost no science, save what was provided in our Weekly Reader magazine. I do recall learning about phonons there. However, middle school was different. Here we took two years of health and science, followed by one full year of science. My teacher for health and science, Mr. Miller was rumored to beat children who disturbed his classes, and I was quite frightened of him. He gave weekly quizzes in class based on filmstrips he had shown that week. During the first test, I was so scared I could barely write my name on the exam sheet. However, when Mr. Miller turned back our exam he said he was certain I could do much better than this, and asked if there was anything he could do to help. He had done enough, though this simple act of kindness and concern. For the next two years no one in any of Mr. Miller's five classes ever scored higher than I did on a single one of these tests.

In high school it was my chemistry teacher who had the most impact on how I thought about science. Mr. Hock had spent time as a graduate student in chemistry, and explained to his classes how one could learn about nature by asking the right questions and then finding the answers through experimentation. It was very different from my tinkering with high voltage electricity and gunpowder, but just as exciting. I should add, however, that few of my classmates appreciated Mr. Hock's efforts in this regard.

    I attended Caltech for college, and was fortunate to be there when Professor Richard Feynman was teaching entry-level physics. Imagine, a brilliant man spending his time on freshman and sophomores! Many years later, when Caltech was offering me a faculty position, I thanked him for his educational gift. (Douglas D. Osheroff)

    我想我對於「物理」的痴迷始於六歲，當時我拆開了我的玩具火車，以便玩裡面的電動馬達。看似尋常、然而對我繼續追求科學事業十分重要的事情是，父母並未因此責備我；父親倒是花時間為我展示了馬達是如何運作的。他似乎被我的痴迷所吸引。我逐漸長大，他會為我找來其他可能引起我興趣的東西，比如電力公司的一盒磁鐵、電話公司的幾盒零件。我八歲時，他把自己小時候用過的照相機送給了我。不到一小時，它也被我的好奇心大卸八塊了。在這之後，父親帶回家一支機械錶和一套鐘錶匠用的螺絲刀，建議我試試看，能不能把它拆解並復原。正是這種和風細雨的栽培，維持了我對科學的興趣。

    在小學時我幾乎沒學到科學，除了我們的《每週讀者》雜誌所提供的知識。我確實記得從中了解到聲子。然而，初中時就不同了。在那裡，我們上了兩年的健康與科學，接著是整整一年的科學課程。我的健康與科學老師，米勒先生，傳言說他會揍擾亂課堂的孩子，我很怕他。他每週都進行隨堂小測驗，內容出自該週放映的幻燈片。第一次考試時，我嚇得幾乎不敢在考卷上寫下自己的名字。然而，發還答案卷時，米勒先生說他肯定我能考得更好，還問有沒有什麼事他幫得上忙。雖然只是善意和關心之舉，但他做得已經足夠了。在接下來的兩年裡，米勒先生教的五個班級之中，任何一次考試，都沒有一個人的分數高過我的。

1996 年

　　在高中階段，對於我如何看待科學，影響最大的是我的化學老師。霍克先生曾經是化學研究生。他向學生講解如何提出正確的問題，然後經由實驗找到答案，進而得以了解自然。這跟我把玩高壓電和火藥大為不同，但同樣令人激動。只是，我應該補充一句，同學之中很少有人欣賞霍克先生這方面的努力。

　　我大學就讀於加州理工學院，而且幸運的是正當理查·費曼教授教初級物理的時候。且想像一下，一位才華洋溢的人，把時間花在大一、大二學生身上！許多年後，當加州理工學院提供我教職時，我深為感激他的教育禮物。（道格拉斯·奧謝羅夫）

To me, physics is not a body of knowledge, nor just a way of thinking about things. It is a lifelong pursuit of knowledge of how the universe behaves and how it evolves. It is the exploration of our universe. As long as I can ask questions to which there are no answers, and then find the answers through experimentation, I will always be an explorer. (Douglas D. Osheroff)

　　對於我，物理學不是一門知識，也不僅是思考事物的方式。它是攸關於宇宙如何執行和如何演化的知識的畢生追求。它是對我們的宇宙的探索。只要能夠提出沒有解答的問題，然後透過實驗找到答案，我就會永遠是個探索者。（道格拉斯·奧謝羅夫）

It doesn't matter what is it that you study as a graduate student —— the important thing is learning how to study. (Douglas D. Osheroff)

　　作為研究生，學習的是什麼無關緊要 —— 重要的是學會如何學習。（道格拉斯·奧謝羅夫）

I do not remember having any special scientific interests during childhood but I did love school. (Robert C. Richardson)

我不記得兒童時期有任何特別的科學興趣，但我確實喜歡學校。（羅伯特‧科爾曼‧理查森）

When I was nine years old, my parents gave me a chemistry set. Within a week, I had decided to become a chemist and never wavered from that choice. As I grew my interest in chemistry grew more intense, if not more sophisticated. (Robert F. Curl Jr.)

我9歲的時候，父母送給我一套化學實驗設備。不到一個星期，我就決定要成為一名化學家，而且從未動搖過這個選擇。隨著長大，我對化學的興趣越來越濃厚，甚至更加深入。（羅伯特‧柯爾）

Science is a very social occupation. The image of the scientist is the mad fantasist who lives on top of a mountain top and only has his faithful servant Igor to help him is a complete myth. Has nothing to do with the way science is actually done. In fact, I claim that the people who really work in solitary are the humanists, they go to the library and closes themselves with the books and sit there and try to write their books and their papers and have far less human contact than the daily activities of their profession than scientists do. (Robert F. Curl Jr.)

科學是非常社會化的職業。科學家的形象是個瘋癲的幻想者，住在山頂上，只有忠實的僕人伊高爾助一臂之力，這是徹頭徹尾的神話，跟科學的實際做法毫無關聯。實際上，我認為真正獨自工作的人是人文學者，他們一頭栽進圖書館，坐擁書城，奮筆書寫專著與論文，比起職業上的日常活動，他們與人接觸的程度比科學家更少。（羅伯特‧柯爾）

We haven't become brilliant overnight. Getting the Nobel Prize did not increase our intelligence. (Robert F. Curl Jr.)

1996 年

我們並不曾一夜之間光芒四射。獲得諾貝爾獎並沒有增加我們的智力。（羅伯特·柯爾）

Saying that we should stop nanoscience is tantamount to saying we should stop science. (Harold W. Kroto)

說我們應該停止奈米科學研究，無異於說我們應該停止科學研究。（哈羅德·克羅托）

Imagine if we had stopped science in 1904. Yes, there would have been no nerve gas and no Bhopal, but there would also have been no penicillin. All science is a trade-off. (Harold W. Kroto)

假設我們在 1904 年停止了科學研究。是的，那就不會有神經毒氣，不會有博帕爾[08]；但也不會有青黴素。全部科學研究都是權衡。（哈羅德·克羅托）

Scientific discoveries matter much more when they're communicated simply and well —— if you can't explain your work to the man in the pub, what's the point? (Harold W. Kroto)

當科學發現能夠被簡單清楚地的說明時，它們的價值就更加重大 —— 要是不能對酒吧裡的人解釋你的工作，那還有什麼意義呢？（哈羅德·克羅托）

We live in a world economically, socially, and culturally dependent on science not only functioning well, but being wisely applied. (Harold W. Kroto)

我們生活在一個在經濟、社會和文化上都離不開科學的世界，科學不僅充分發揮作用，還得到明智的應用。（哈羅德·克羅托）

---

[08] 指 1984 年發生在印度博帕爾的氰化物洩漏事件，是典型的工業災難。

Attitude is the most important thing. Give it your best effort. (Harold W. Kroto)

最重要的是態度。務必盡力而為。（哈羅德·克羅托）

My strength lies solely in my tenacity. (Harold W. Kroto)

我的力量完全在於韌性。（哈羅德·克羅托）

Never, ever, compromise on science. (Harold W. Kroto)

永遠、永遠不要在科學上妥協。（哈羅德·克羅托）

If doing something with second-rate effort satisfies you, find something else to do —— where only your best effort will satisfy you personally. (Harold W. Kroto)

如果做某事無需十分力氣即可讓你滿意，就換一件事吧 —— 做只有竭盡全力才能使你自己滿意的事。（哈羅德·克羅托）

Having chosen something worth doing, never give up, and try not to let anyone down. (Harold W. Kroto)

選定了值得做的事情，就決不放棄，也盡量別讓人失望。（哈羅德·克羅托）

Some people think that science is just all this technology around, but NO it's something much deeper than that. Science, scientific thinking, scientific method is for me the only philosophical construct that the human race has developed to determine what is reliably true. (Harold W. Kroto)

有些人以為科學不過是隨處可見的這些技術；然而絕非如此，科學是更深刻的事物。科學、科學的思考、科學的方法，在我看來，是人類為確認可靠真理而發展出來的唯一哲學概念。（哈羅德·克羅托）

Many think of the sciences as merely a fund of knowledge. Journalists never ask scientists anything other than what the applications are of scientific breakthroughs. Interestingly, I doubt they ever ask a musician, writer, or actor the same question. I wonder why. (Harold W. Kroto)

許多人以為，科學不過是大量的知識。採訪科學家的記者只對科學突破的應用感興趣，而完全不問其餘。有意思的是，我不信他們問過音樂家、作家或演員同樣的問題。我想知道何以如此。（哈羅德·克羅托）

Science is based solely on doubt-based, disinterested examination of the natural and physical world. It is entirely independent of personal belief. There is a very important, fundamental concomitant —— that is to accept absolutely nothing whatsoever, for which there is no evidence, as having any fundamental validity. (Harold W. Kroto)

科學完全建立於對自然和物理世界的懷疑和不計利害的檢驗之上。它完全獨立於個人信念。科學伴隨著非常重要、根本的要求，即絕對不接受任何不具基本有效證明的東西。（哈羅德·克羅托）

Without evidence, anything goes. Think about it. Common sense says the sun goes round the Earth. Who agrees with me? (Harold W. Kroto)

不問證據，什麼事都講得通。想一想。假如常識告訴我們太陽繞著地球轉。誰同意呢？（哈羅德·克羅托）

You've accepted a lot of things without evidence. Find out what the evidence is for that. Find out what the evidence is for everything that you accept. (Harold W. Kroto)

你不問證據地接受了許多事物。找出它們的證據何在。找出你所接受的所有事物的證據何在。（哈羅德·克羅托）

I've always felt that the Nobel Prize gives me nothing as far as science is concerned. (Harold W. Kroto)

我一直覺得，就科學而言，諾貝爾獎沒有為我帶來任何幫助。（哈羅德・克羅托）

Rather than proceeding directly to graduate school, I decided to take a job in the chemical industry in order to buy a bit of time to see what I really wanted to do in science, and to live a little in the "real" world. It turned out to be a terrific decision. (Richard E. Smalley)

我並未直接進入研究所，而是決定在化工產業界找一份工作，以便有些時間去了解自己在科學領域真正想做什麼，並在「現實」的世界裡生活一段時間。結果證明，這是個非常棒的決定。（理察・斯莫利）

I know that, except for carbon, there would be no life in the universe. Except for this one atom, there would be no life. Well, why? When you think about it, it does get spooky. Encountering these molecules are spiritual experiences similar to what I remember in church as a child, only these are more serious. (Richard E. Smalley)

我知道，若非由於碳，宇宙中就不會有生命。若非由於這一個原子，就不會有生命。那麼，何以如此？想到這一點，確實令人驚異莫名。邂逅這些分子屬於精神體驗，近乎兒時的教堂記憶，只是這些更加嚴肅。（理察・斯莫利）

The thing I love about science is finding out something new and different. (Peter C. Doherty)

對於科學，我所鍾愛的是發現新的、不同的東西。（彼得・杜赫提）

1996 年

My characteristics as a scientist stem from a non-conformist upbringing, a sense of being something of an outsider, and looking for different perceptions in everything from novels, to art to experimental results. I like complexity and am delighted by the unexpected. Ideas interest me. (Peter C. Doherty)

我作為科學家的特質來自於非同常規的養育，一種類似身為局外人之感，以及經由小說、藝術、實驗結果之中尋求各種不同的觀點。我喜歡複雜性，意外令我欣喜。創意引發我的興趣。（彼得·杜赫提）

Good scientists are perpetual adolescents. They never grow up. (Peter Doherty)

優秀的科學家是永恆的青少年。他們永遠不會長大。（彼得·杜赫提）

To ask questions, to search for answers, to do research —— I mean research in nature, what is already there, but has not been revealed so far is the most fascinating and the most exciting thing we can dream of doing and what we would like to continue doing. We researchers are a bit like musicians —— and the Nobel Foundation and this assembly tell us we are reasonably good musicians —— who are re-creating as best as possible what true creators, as a Mozart or Rossini once have conceived. Peter, let us face it: We have been very lucky! Had we not found the rules of restricted immune T cell recognition, somebody else would have later. Without Isaak Stern or Luciano Pavarotti, we would still have Mozart's violin concerto or Don Giovanni, but we all recognise that without Mozart The Enchanted Flute would not exist. (Rolf M. Zinkernagel)

提出問題、尋找答案、著手研究（research）—— 我的意思是再度探究（re-search）—— 已經存在，但尚未被人揭示的事物，是我們夢想做且樂於繼續做的最令人著迷和興奮之事。我們研究人員有幾分像音樂家 —— 諾貝爾基金會及這一場大會告訴我們，我們是相當不錯的音樂家 —— 正在盡可能地再度創造真正的創造者，一如莫札特或羅西尼曾經設想的那般。彼得[09]，讓我們面對現實吧：我們原來是非常幸運的！我們要是沒發現限制性免疫 T 細胞辨識的規則，別人早晚會發現。沒有艾薩克·斯特恩或盧奇亞諾·帕華洛帝，我們仍會有莫札特的小提琴協奏曲或《唐·喬凡尼》；但大家都承認，沒有莫札特，《魔笛》就不會存在了。[10]（羅夫·辛克納吉）

Inspiration is not the exclusive privilege of poets or artists generally. There is, has been, and will always be a certain group of people whom inspiration visits. It's made up of all those who've consciously chosen their calling and do their job with love and imagination. It may include doctors, teachers, gardeners —— and I could list a hundred more professions. Their work becomes one continuous adventure as long as they manage to keep discovering new challenges in it. Difficulties and setbacks never quell their curiosity. A swarm of new questions emerges from every problem they solve. Whatever inspiration is, it's born from a continuous "I don't know." (Wislawa Szymborska)

靈感通常並非詩人或藝術家專有的特權。無論現在、過去和將來，靈感總是造訪特定的人群。他們是由有意選擇自身職業並滿懷愛心與想像力從事的人所組成，可能包括醫生、教師、園丁 —— 我還可以列出上百種行業。只要不斷在工作中發現新的挑戰，他們的工作就變成了一場持續的探險。困難與挫折永遠無法平息其好奇心。每一個被解決的問題

---

[09] 彼得，即彼得·杜赫提，與辛克納吉同獲 1996 年諾貝爾生理學或醫學獎。
[10] 斯特恩，美國小提琴家；帕華洛帝，義大利歌唱家；《唐·喬凡尼》，著名歌劇；《魔笛》，莫札特所作歌劇。

> 1996 年

中又浮出大量的新問題。不管靈感是什麼，它都源自於持續的「我不知道」。（維斯瓦娃・辛波絲卡）

In daily speech, where we don't stop to consider every word, we all use phrases like "the ordinary world," "ordinary life," "the ordinary course of events"… But in the language of poetry, where every word is weighed, nothing is usual or normal. Not a single stone and not a single cloud above it. Not a single day and not a single night after it. And above all, not a single existence, not anyone's existence in this world. (Wislawa Szymborska)

日常說話時，我們不會停下來斟酌每一個字，我們都會使用「平常的地方」、「平常的日子」、「平常的情況」之類的話……但在詩歌語言中，每一個字都要經過衡量，沒有什麼是通常或正常的。沒有哪塊石頭也沒有上空的哪朵雲彩，沒有哪個白天也沒有隨後的哪個黑夜，尤其是，這個世界上沒有哪種存在，沒有任何人的存在是尋常的。（維斯瓦娃・辛波絲卡）

I cannot speak for more than an hour exclusively about poetry. At that point, life itself takes over again. (Wislawa Szymborska)

只談論詩歌，我無法超過一小時。講得差不多時，生命本身就將再次佔據話題。（維斯瓦娃・辛波絲卡）

This terrifying world is not devoid of charms, of the mornings that make waking up worthwhile. (Wislawa Szymborska)

這個可怕的世界並不缺乏讓醒來的早晨變得值得的魅力。（維斯瓦娃・辛波絲卡）

So poets keep on trying, and sooner or later the consecutive results of their self-dissatisfaction are clipped together with a giant paperclip by literary historians and called their "oeuvres." (Wislawa Szymborska)

於是詩人不斷地嘗試，而早晚有一天，他們自我不滿的連續結果會被文學史專家用一枚特大迴紋針夾在一起，稱為其「畢生之作」。（維斯瓦娃‧辛波絲卡）

Any knowledge that doesn't lead to new questions quickly dies out: it fails to maintain the temperature required for sustaining life. (Wislawa Szymborska)

任何不能引發新問題的知識很快就會消亡：它保持不住維持生命所需的溫度。（維斯瓦娃‧辛波絲卡）

Get to know other worlds, if only for comparison. (Wislawa Szymborska)

去了解其他的世界，僅僅為了比較也罷。（維斯瓦娃‧辛波絲卡）

When I pronounce the word Future,

the first syllable already belongs to the past.

When I pronounce the word Silence,

I destroy it.

When I pronounce the word Nothing,

I make something no non-being can hold. (Wislawa Szymborska)

當我說出未來這個詞，

第一個音節已經屬於過去。

當我說出寂靜這個詞，

我破壞了它。

當我說出無這個詞，

1996 年

我造成了虛無所不能具有的東西。（維斯瓦娃·辛波絲卡）

Every beginning is only a sequel, after all, and the book of events is always open halfway through. (Wislawa Szymborska)

畢竟，每一個開端均僅屬續集，記事之書總是到了半途方才打開。（維斯瓦娃·辛波絲卡）

Nothing can ever happen twice. In consequence, the sorry fact is that we arrive here improvised and leave without the chance to practice. (Wislawa Szymborska)

任何事都不可能發生兩次。結果，令人遺憾的事實為，我們即興式地來到這裡，沒機會練習就離去了。（維斯瓦娃·辛波絲卡）

Life lasts but a few scratches of the claw in the sand. (Wislawa Szymborska)

生命只是在沙地上留下幾道爪痕。[11]（維斯瓦娃·辛波絲卡）

Nothing's a gift, it's all on loan. (Wislawa Szymborska)

從無贈予之物，一切均屬借出。（維斯瓦娃·辛波絲卡）

Let the people who never find true love keep saying that there's no such thing. Their faith will make it easier for them to live and die. (Wislawa Szymborska)

就讓從未找到真愛的人不斷說沒有這種東西吧。他們的信念會使其生死輕鬆一些。（維斯瓦娃·辛波絲卡）

I'm old-fashioned and think that reading books is the most glorious pastime that humankind has yet devised. (Wislawa Szymborska)

---

[11]　對照：人生到處知何似，應似飛鴻踏雪泥。泥上偶然留指爪，鴻飛那復計東西。（蘇軾）

1991–2000 多元聲音與思想碰撞

我很老派,認為讀書是人類迄今發明的最了不起的消遣。(維斯瓦娃·辛波絲卡)

I prefer the cinema.

I prefer cats.

I prefer oak-trees by the Warta.

I prefer Dickens to Dostoyevsky.

I prefer myself liking humans

to myself loving humanity.

I prefer having a thread with a needle close at hand.

I prefer green.

I prefer not claiming that

the intellect should be blamed for everything.

I pefer exceptions.

I prefer leaving before.

I prefer talking to doctors about something else.

I prefer old marked illustrations.

I prefer being laughable because of writing poems

to being laughable because of not writing them.

I prefer odd anniversaries in love life,

to be celebrated every day.

I prefer moralists

who do not promise me anything.

1996 年

I prefer calculated goodness to goodness that is too gullible.

I prefer the earth in civvy street.

I prefer conquered countries to the conquering ones.

I prefer having my objections.

I prefer the hell of chaos to the hell of order.

I prefer Grimm tales to the first pages of newspapers.

I prefer leaves without flowers to flowers without leaves.

I prefer dogs with their tails unclipped.

I prefer fair eyes since mine are dark.

I prefer drawers.

I prefer many things I have not listed above

to many others unlisted here.

I prefer noughts that are loose

to those queueing for a digit.

I prefer insect time to stellar time.

I prefer touching wood.

I prefer not asking how much longer and when.

I prefer considering even such a possibility

that existence has its reasons. (Wislawa Szymborska)

我偏愛電影。

我偏愛貓。

我偏愛瓦爾塔河兩岸的橡樹。

1991-2000 多元聲音與思想碰撞

我偏愛狄更斯而非杜斯妥也夫斯基。

我偏愛自己喜歡人們

而非自己熱愛人類。

我偏愛手邊備有針線。

我偏愛綠色。

我偏愛不聲稱

理智應對任何事情負責。

我偏愛例外。

我偏愛提前離去。

我偏愛跟醫生聊別的話題。

我偏愛老式的插圖。

我偏愛寫詩之可笑

而非不寫詩之可笑。

我偏愛愛情生活中不定的紀念日，

可以天天慶祝。

我偏愛

不向我做任何承諾的道德家。

我偏愛精明的善良而非輕信的善良。

我偏愛家常日子的地球。

我偏愛被征服的國家而非征服者。

我偏愛保留異議。

我偏愛混亂的地獄而非有秩序的地獄。

1996 年

我偏愛格林童話而非報紙頭版。

我偏愛無花的葉勝過無葉的花。

我偏愛尾巴沒被截短的狗。

我偏愛淺色的眼睛因為我的是黑的。

我偏愛抽屜。

我偏愛上面未曾提及的許多事物

而非這裡沒提的其他許多東西。

我偏愛無拘無束的零

而非列於數字後的零。

我偏愛昆蟲時間而非天體時間。

我偏愛輕擊木頭。

我偏愛不問還有多長時間和什麼時候。

我偏愛思考甚至這樣的可能：

存在自有其理由。（維斯瓦娃·辛波絲卡）

Dear youth, I quote from memory the great Indian poet Rabindranath Tagore: "Youth, as a Lotus flower, flourish just once in life." Do not let it wither on the way. (Carlos Filipe Ximenes Belo)

年輕人們，我記得印度大詩人羅賓德拉納特·泰戈爾說：「青春，猶如蓮花，一生只盛開一次。」不要讓它中途凋謝。（嘉祿·斐理伯·西門內斯·貝洛）

Innovation is important because it brings in new creative approaches on tackling issues around development and extreme poverty. (José Ramos-Horta)

1991–2000 多元聲音與思想碰撞

創新是重要的，因為它為了處理發展和極端貧困問題帶來了新的創造性方法。（若澤‧拉莫斯‧奧爾塔）

It became clear I wanted to be a development economist. I mean, I said I wanted to work on the economics of poor countries. And I'd actually say that I don't think that was so much about narrowing the gap as about increasing their incomes, which means economic growth, which is really my prime interest. (James A. Mirrlees)

顯然，我想成為一名發展經濟學家。我的意思是，我想研究貧窮國家的經濟問題。實際上我想說，我認為問題與其說是縮小差距，不如說是增加他們的收入，也就是經濟成長，這是我最關心的問題。（詹姆士‧莫理斯）

As you may know, according to economic theory, a prize once awarded should actually induce recipients to work less hard; and is therefore supposed to be not entirely good. But now I am of the opinion that, in the words of a Cambridge colleague, it is not entirely bad either. (James A. Mirrlees)

你們可能知道，根據經濟學理論，一個獎項一旦頒發，實際上可能會引起獲獎者不那麼努力工作了，所以它本來並不完全是好的。不過現在我認為，用劍橋一位同事的話說，這也不完全是壞事。（詹姆士‧莫理斯）

I define genuine full employment as a situation where there are at least as many job openings as there are persons seeking employment, probably calling for a rate of unemployment, as currently measured, of between 1 and 2 percent. (William Vickrey)

我對於真正的充分就業的定義為，就業的機會至少跟找工作的人一樣多，按目前衡量，失業率大約為百分之一至二。（威廉‧維克里）

1997 年

Education in my family was not merely emphasized, it was our raison d'etre. (Steven Chu)

教育在我們家不只是得到重視,它就是我們的存在理由。(朱棣文)

I approached the bulk of my schoolwork as a chore rather than an intellectual adventure. The tedium was relieved by a few courses that seem to be qualitatively different. Geometry was the first exciting course I remember. Instead of memorizing facts, we were asked to think in clear, logical steps. Beginning from a few intuitive postulates, far reaching consequences could be derived, and I took immediately to the sport of proving theorems. (Steven Chu)

我把大部分作業都當成了苦差事而非智力冒險。乏味的學習由於幾門看來截然不同的課程而改觀。幾何學是我記憶中第一門令人興奮的課程。它所要求我們的並非記憶事實,而是以清晰的、合乎邏輯的步驟思考。從幾個直覺的假設開始,就可以推演出深遠的結論,我立即接受了這種證明定理的遊戲。(朱棣文)

I joined Bell Laboratories in the fall of 1978. I was one of roughly two dozen brash, young scientists that were hired within a two year period. We felt like the "Chosen Ones", with no obligation to do anything except the research we loved best. The joy and excitement of doing science permeated the halls. The cramped labs and office cubicles forced us to interact with each other and follow each others' progress. The animated discussions were common during and after seminars and at lunch and continued on the tennis courts and at parties. The atmosphere was too electric to abandon. (Steven Chu)

我於1978年秋天加入貝爾實驗室，是僱用期兩年的大約24名急切的年輕科學家之一。我們感覺彷彿「被神選中之人」，除了自己鍾情的研究，沒有義務做任何事情。樓房間瀰漫著從事科學研究的歡欣和興奮。擁擠的實驗室和辦公室隔間迫使大家互相交流，隨時了解各自的進展。研討會上及會後、午餐時活躍的討論是稀鬆平常，並且持續到網球場上和聚會中。那種氣氛電力十足，根本無法捨棄。（朱棣文）

In the scientific world, people are judged by the content of their ideas. Advances are made with new insights, but the final arbitrator of any point of view are experiments that seek the unbiased truth, not information cherry picked to support a particular point of view. (Steven Chu)

在科學的世界裡，人們以其思想的內容受到評判。新的見解帶來進步，然而任何觀點的最終裁判都是尋求公正真理的實驗，而非為支持特定觀點而有意選出的資訊。（朱棣文）

The obvious compromise between mathematics and physics was to become a theoretical physicist. My heroes were Newton, Maxwell, Einstein, up to the contemporary giants such as Feynman, Gell-Mann, Yang and Lee. (Steven Chu)

數學和物理學之間顯然的折中是成為理論物理學家。我心目中的英雄是牛頓、馬克士威、愛因斯坦，以至同時代的巨人，如理查·費曼、默里·蓋爾曼、楊振寧和李政道。（朱棣文）

We professors are free to choose the topics of our lectures. The only rule is that these lectures must change and deal with different topics every year, which is very difficult and demanding. It is, however, very stimulating be-

1997 年

cause this urges one to broaden one's knowledge, to explore new fields and to challenge oneself. No doubt that without such an effort I would not have started many of the research lines that have been explored by my research group. (Claude Cohen-Tannoudji)

我們這些教授可以自由選擇自己講課的主題。唯一的規則是，這些講座必須逐年變換，談論不同的主題。這很困難，要求很高，可是非常令人興奮，因為這促使人拓展知識，探索新領域並挑戰自我。毫無疑問，如果沒有這樣的努力，我就不可能開創我的研究小組所探索的許多研究路線。（克洛德‧科恩－塔諾季）

I was initially more attracted by mathematics but met at Ecole Normale Supérieure a physics professor, Alfred Kastler, whose lectures were so stimulating and whose personality was so attractive that I decided to change to Physics. I deeply believe in the influence that an outstanding personality can have for arousing a scientific vocation. (Claude Cohen-Tannoudji)

我起初對數學更感興趣，但在巴黎高等師範學院遇到了物理學教授阿爾弗雷德‧卡斯特勒。他講的課是那麼充滿啟迪，他的個性是那麼富於魅力，以致於我決定轉而學習物理專業。對於科學行業的選擇，我深信傑出的人所能產生的影響。（克洛德‧科恩－塔諾季）

A researcher remains a student forever. He has always something new to learn, some new tools to master. (Claude Cohen-Tannoudji)

研究人員永遠是學生。他總是有新東西要學，有新工具要掌握。（克洛德‧科恩－塔諾季）

After my thesis, I got a position at the University of Paris. I very much enjoyed teaching. I think that research and teaching are complementary activities which cannot be dissociated. If one gives lectures without doing research one becomes rapidly obsolete because the lectures that one gives do not follow the progress of science. On the other hand, giving lectures is very important for improving one's research because when one tries to explain scientific concepts in the clearest possible way, one gets in general new interesting ideas and physical insights which can stimulate new directions of research. (Claude Cohen-Tannoudji)

畢業後，我在巴黎大學得到了一個職位。我非常喜歡教學。我認為研究和教學是相輔相成的活動，二者不可分離。如果一個人不做研究就講課，他很快就會過時，因為所講的課跟不上科學的發展。另一方面，講課對於改進研究非常重要，因為當一個人力圖以盡量清晰的方式來解釋科學概念時，他通常得到新的有趣的想法和具體的深入見解，能夠激發新的研究方向。（克洛德·科恩－塔諾季）

Science is a fantastic adventure. Every new discovery changes our vision of the world where we live. It is an integral part of the human culture, like painting, music or poetry. Understanding the basic laws which govern the huge variety of phenomena that we observe is the greatest achievement of mankind. In addition, the applications which result from the progress of basic science can bring a solution to the various problems that we have to face; finding new clean sources of energy, protecting our environment, providing enough food to everybody, improving human health… (Claude Cohen-Tannoudji)

科學是奇妙的冒險。對於我們棲身的世界，每一項新發現都改變了它的面貌。科學是人類文化不可或缺的部分，猶如繪畫、音樂或詩歌。

1997 年

理解支配我們所觀察到的各種現象的基本規律，是人類最大的成就。此外，基礎科學的進步所產生的應用，能夠解決我們必須面對的各種難題，發現新的清潔能源，保護我們的環境，為所有人提供足夠的食物，改善人類健康……（克洛德·科恩－塔諾季）

In high school, I enjoyed and profited from well-taught science and math classes, but in retrospect, I can see that the classes that emphasized language and writing skills were just as important for the development of my scientific career as were science and math. I certainly feel that my high school involvement in debating competitions helped me later to give better scientific talks, that the classes in writing style helped me to write better papers, and the study of French greatly enhanced the tremendously fruitful collaboration I was to have with Claude Cohen-Tannoudji's research group. (William D. Phillips)

上高中時，我喜歡也得益於精采的科學和數學課；不過回想起來，可以看出強調語言和寫作技能的課程對於我科學事業的發展跟科學和數學一樣重要。我確實覺得，高中時參加辯論比賽有助於後來發表更好的科學演講，寫作風格課程有助於寫更好的論文，而法語學習大為促進了我後來跟克洛德·科恩－塔諾季研究團隊卓有成效的合作。（威廉·丹尼爾·菲利普斯）

Surely the Nobel Prize is the highest award a scientist could hope to receive, and I have received it with a sense of awe that I am in the company of those who have received it before. But no prize can compare in importance to the family and friends I count as my greatest treasures. (William D. Phillips)

諾貝爾獎無疑是科學家所能期望得到的最高獎項，我也懷著一種敬畏之心接受了它，因為忝居迄今的獲獎者之列。然而，什麼獎都比不上

我的家人和朋友重要,我將他們視為自己最大的財富。(威廉‧丹尼爾‧菲利普斯)

More by example than by word, my father taught me logical reasoning, compassion, love of others, honesty, and discipline applied with understanding. (Paul D. Boyer)

我的父親更多地透過身教而非言傳,他教我邏輯推理、同情心、對他人的愛、誠實正直和寬嚴並濟。(保羅‧博耶)

Mountain hikes instilled in me a life-long urge to get to the top of any inviting summit or peak. (Paul D. Boyer)

登山運動向我灌輸了一種畢生的渴望,我想要登上任何吸引自己的頂點或高峰。(保羅‧博耶)

A painstaking course in qualitative and quantitative analysis by John Wing gave me an appreciation of the need for, and beauty of, accurate measurement. (Paul D. Boyer)

約翰‧溫的定性和定量分析的艱深課程,使我深刻體會到準確測量之必要與美妙之處。(保羅‧博耶)

I have a tendency to be lucky and make the right choices based on limited information. (Paul D. Boyer)

我很幸運,往往能基於有限的資訊做出正確的選擇。(保羅‧博耶)

The experience reminds me of a favorite saying: Most of the yield from research efforts comes from the coal that is mined while looking for diamonds. (Paul D. Boyer)

这个经验让我想起一个非常喜欢的说法：研究的努力成果，大都来自于寻找钻石时所挖掘的煤炭。（保罗·博耶）

The high resolution structure of the catalytic domain of the ATP synthesizing enzyme has provided new insights into our understanding of how ATP is made in biology. Nevertheless, challenging structural experiments lie ahead in the quest to understand the generation of rotation by transmembrane proton transport through its membrane sector. A short poem written by Robert Frost provides an appropriate summary of the current state of affairs.

We dance round in a ring and suppose

The secret sits in the middle and knows

I am glad to have played a role in arriving at our present level of understanding of ATP synthesis, and in the future I hope to contribute to the revelation of the secret sitting in the middle. (John E. Walker)

三磷酸腺苷合酶催化范围的高解析结构，为了解三磷酸腺苷合成的生物学机制提供了新的洞察。然而，为了探究凭藉跨膜质子传输的循环之生成，还需要进行富于挑战性的结构实验。罗伯特·佛洛斯特[12]的一首短诗，可谓对研究现状的生动刻划：

我们跳著环舞百般猜测

祕密端坐中央怡然自得

我很高兴为达到目前对三磷酸腺苷合成的理解程度发挥作用，今后也希望对揭示端坐中央的祕密有所贡献。（约翰·E·沃克）

The Nobel Prizes and the ceremony around the awards put focus not only

---

[12] 罗伯特·佛洛斯特（1874—1963），美国著名诗人。

on the work done by the Prize-Winners, but arouse in the public a more general interest in science, and give us scientists a very important opportunity to tell what science is and the importance of science. (Jens C. Skou)

諾貝爾獎及頒獎典禮不僅把人們的注意力吸引到獲獎者的成就上，也激發了大眾對科學更廣泛的興趣，並給予我們科學家一個非常重要的機會，講述科學是什麼，以及科學的重要性。（延斯・克里斯蒂安・斯科）

In 1988, I retired, kept my office, gave up systematic experimental work and started to work on kinetic models for the overall reaction of the pump on computer. For this I had to learn how to programme, quite interesting, and amazing what you can do with a computer from the point of view of handling even complicated models. And even if my working hours are fewer, being free of all obligations, the time I spent on scientific problems are about the same as before my retirement. (Jens C. Skou)

1988年，我退休了。保留辦公室，放棄系統的實驗工作，開始在電腦上研究泵浦的整體反應動力學模型。為此我得學會程式設計，這非常有趣，從處理甚至複雜模型的觀點來看，用電腦可以做的事情令人驚嘆。即便工作時間更少，我也全無義務，但我花在科學問題上的時間，跟退休前大致相當。（延斯・克里斯蒂安・斯科）

The Nobel Prizes are much more than awards to scholars; they are a celebration of civilization, of mankind, and of what makes humans unique —— that is their intellect from which springs creativity. (Stanley B. Prusiner)

諾貝爾獎遠非僅為對學者的褒獎，更是對文明、對人類、對人類獨特性來源的頌揚——這個來源就是激發創造力的人類智慧。（史坦利・布魯希納）

1997 年

Concepts are vindicated by the constant accrual of data and independent verification of data. No prize, not even a Nobel Prize, can make something true that is not true. (Stanley B. Prusiner)

經由資料的持續累積和對資料的獨立驗證，概念獲得了證實。任何獎項，甚至諾貝爾獎，都無法使並非真實之事成為真實。（史坦利‧布魯希納）

A theatre, a literature, an artistic expression that does not speak for its own time has no relevance. (Dario Fo)

戲劇、文學、藝術表現若不能代表其所屬的時代就毫無意義。（達里奧‧霍）

What am I supposed to be, a pompous fool because I got a medal? (Jody Williams)

我應該成為什麼，一個由於得了一塊獎牌而洋洋自得的傻瓜嗎？（喬迪‧威廉斯）

For me, the difference between an "ordinary" and an "extraordinary" person is not the title that person might have, but what they do to make the world a better place for us all. (Jody Williams)

在我看來，「平凡」與「非凡」之人的區別，不在於可能擁有的頭銜，而在於他們為了讓世界變得更美好所做的努力。（喬迪‧威廉斯）

I think there's a mythology that if you want to change the world, you have to be sainted, like Mother Teresa or Nelson Mandela or Archbishop Desmond Tutu. Ordinary people with lives that go up and down and around in circles can still contribute to change. (Jody Williams)

有一種說法為，你要是想改變世界，就得是聖人，類似德蕾莎修女、納爾遜·曼德拉或戴斯蒙·屠圖大主教，我認為這是神話。普通的人，人生起落反覆，仍然可以促成改變。（喬迪·威廉斯）

I think in the case of my father, in terms of the things that influenced me, he never pressed me to go into academics or pressed me to go to a field, and indeed, my behavior was largely to move as far the other direction. I don't think that's uncommon with people with very successful parents. And so for a long time I think what I really absorbed from him was a sense of a work ethic; a sense that if you are going to do something it should be of top quality. (Robert C. Merton)

我認為，就我父親而言，在影響我的事情上，他從不強制我從事學術研究或強迫我進入某個領域。事實上，我的舉動大都反其道而行。對於父母事業有成的人們，我不認為這是罕見的。所以，我長時間認為，自己真正從他那裡學到的是一種職業道德感，一種觀念，即果打算做某件事，它就應當是最高品質的。（勞勃·科克斯·莫頓）

My first reaction on being awarded the Nobel Prize was, actually, I thought of Fischer Black, my colleague. He unfortunately had passed away. And there was no doubt in my mind that if he were still alive, he would have been a co-recipient of the Nobel Prize. (Myron S. Scholes)

實際上，我被授予諾貝爾獎的第一個反應是想到了我的同事，費雪·布雷克。他不幸過世了。我真心相信，他如果還活著，就會成為諾貝爾獎的共同得主。（麥倫·舒爾茲）

The easier, simpler to understand and more comfortable you make it for your customer, the more complex you make it for yourself. (Myron S. Scholes)

為使用者把產品做得越簡單易懂、使用舒適,你就使事情對自己越複雜。(麥倫·舒爾茲)

1998 年

I realized that nature is filled with a limitless number of wonderful things which have causes and reasons like anything else but nonetheless cannot be foreseen but must be discovered, for their subtlety and complexity transcends the present state of science. The questions worth asking, in other words, come not from other people but from nature, and are for the most part delicate things easily drowned out by the noise of everyday life. (Robert B. Laughlin)

我意識到大自然充滿了無限的美好事物,它們與其他任何事物一樣有各種原因與理由,但是都無法預見而必須被探索,因為它們的精妙與複雜超越了科學的現狀。換句話說,值得探究的問題並非來自其他人,而是來自大自然,而且大部分是微妙的事物,很容易被日常生活的喧囂所淹沒。(羅伯特·勞夫林)

The important laws we know about are, without exception, serendipitous discoveries rather than deductions. (Robert B. Laughlin)

我們所知的重要法則,無一例外,皆為偶然發現而非演繹得之。(羅伯特·勞夫林)

Real understanding of a thing comes from taking it apart oneself, not reading about it in a book or hearing about it in a classroom. To this day I always insist on working out problems from the beginning without reading up on it first, a habit that sometimes gets me into trouble but just as often helps me see things my predecessors have missed. (Robert B. Laughlin)

對事物的真正了解來自於親手剖析它,而非在書本中讀到它,或在課堂上聽到它。直到今天,我總是堅持從頭開始解決問題,而不是先閱讀相關資料。這種習慣有時致使我陷入麻煩,但的確經常幫助我看到前人錯過的東西。(羅伯特・勞夫林)

We believe in universal physical law not because it ought to be true but because highly accurate experiments have given us no choice. (Robert B. Laughlin)

我們相信普遍的物理定律,不是因為它應該是正確的,而是因為高度精確的實驗使我們別無選擇。(羅伯特・勞夫林)

If I knew what leads one to the Nobel Prize, I wouldn't tell you, but go get another one. (Robert B. Laughlin)

我要是知道什麼能讓人得諾貝爾獎,我不會告訴你,而是去獲得另一個諾貝爾獎。(羅伯特・勞夫林)

Science throws off old skins as it grows. (Arthur Lewis)

科學在成長時會蛻去舊皮。(威廉・阿瑟・路易斯)

I always wanted to become a physicist. Supposedly, at age six, I had told just that to a technician, who was repairing a TV set in our home. Obviously, I had little clue as to what a physicist did. (Horst L. Störmer)

> 1998 年

我一直想成為一名物理學家。據說，我在 6 歲的時候，曾把這件事告訴了一名技工，他正在我們家修電視機。顯然，我對物理學家的工作一無所知。（霍斯特·施特默）

One of my teachers stood out, Mr. Nick. He taught math and physics. A new teacher, basically straight out of college, young, open, articulate, fun, he represented what teachers could be like. His love and curiosity for the subjects he was teaching was contagious. (Horst L. Störmer)

我的一位老師很出色，尼克先生。他教數學和物理。新教師，基本上剛從大學畢業，年輕、開放、善於表達、性情詼諧，代表了好老師的樣子。他對所教科目的熱愛和好奇心富於感染力。（霍斯特·施特默）

I have no fascinating story about childhood science experiments, or moments of grand insight. But curiosity has been my bent, and it led me to the edges of scientific knowledge where it was my fortune to determine, by experiment, phenomena that continue to generate new findings and understandings. (Daniel C. Tsui)

我沒有關於童年科學實驗的動人故事，也沒有偉大的頓悟時刻。但好奇心一直是我的傾向，它把我帶到了科學知識的邊緣。在那裡，我有幸經由實驗來確定不斷產生新發現和新理解的各種現象。（崔琦）

For me, at least, "discoveries" came from doing (and redoing) varying experiments, talking with other scientists at the then provocative Bell Labs, thinking over related theoretical ideas, taking advantage of various technical advances, and working together with others. It was only in time, as experiments the confirmed some of my hunches, and yielded more information, that what might be found became clearer. (Daniel C. Tsui)

1991–2000 多元聲音與思想碰撞

　　至少就我而言,「發現」來自做(和重做)各式各樣的實驗,在當時令人興奮的貝爾實驗室與其他科學家們交流,思考相關的理論主張,利用各種技術進步,以及與人合作。只有隨著時間的推移,經由實驗證實我的一些預感並產生更多的資訊,所期待的結果才清晰起來。（崔琦）

I realized quite early that I wanted to do experimental physics and that I lacked the aptitude for colossal experimental setups and also the taste for grandeur. I wanted to do tabletop experiments and be allowed to tinker. Royal Stark trusted me and let me try my hands on everything in his laboratory. I was given the best opportunity to learn from the bottom up: from engineer drawing, soldering, machining, and design, to construction and building of our laboratory apparatus. (Daniel C. Tsui)

　　我很早就意識到自己想研究實驗物理學,然而我缺乏運用龐大實驗裝置的天賦,對大型項目也沒什麼興趣。我想從事桌面實驗,並被允許做零碎工作。羅亞爾・斯塔克信任我,讓我在他的實驗室裡一試身手。我得到了從頭學起的極佳機會:從工程製圖、焊接、機械加工和設計,到我們實驗室設備的製作建造。（崔琦）

Many of my friends and esteemed colleagues had asked me: "Why did you choose to leave Bell Laboratories and go to Princeton University?" Even today, I do not know the answer. Was it to do with the schooling I missed in my childhood? Maybe. Perhaps it was the Confucius in me, the faint voice I often heard when I was alone, that the only meaningful life is a life of learning. What better way is there to learn than through teaching! (Daniel C. Tsui)

　　許多朋友和我所敬重的同事問過我:「你為什麼選擇離開貝爾實驗室到普林斯頓大學?」即使在今天,我也不知道答案。與童年錯過學校教

1998 年

育有關？也許吧。也許來自內心的古代聖賢，我獨處時經常聽到的微弱聲音，說唯一有意義的生活就是學習的生活。還有比教學相長更好的學習方式嗎？（崔琦）

Looking back I feel very fortunate to have had a small part in the great drama of scientific progress, and most thankful to all those, including family, kindly "acting parents", teachers, colleagues, students, and collaborators of all ages, who made it all possible. It has been an interesting journey. (Walter Kohn)

回顧此生，我感到非常幸運，能夠在科學進步的偉大舞臺上扮演一個小角色；我極其感謝包括家人、善良的「代理父母」、老師、同事、學生和年齡各異的合作者在內的所有人，他們使這一切成為可能。這是一次有趣的旅程。（華特·科恩）

At a certain theoretic level chemistry and physics are very close to each other, but also at the lowest level they're very close to each other. (Walter Kohn)

在一定的理論層面上，化學和物理學彼此非常接近；不過在最低層面上，它們依然彼此非常接近。（華特·科恩）

I am delighted to have had students, friends and colleagues in so many nations and to have learned so much of what I know from them. This Nobel Award honours them all. (John Pople)

我很高興在這麼多國家都有學生、朋友和同事，並從他們身上學到了這麼多。這一項諾貝爾獎的榮譽歸於他們所有人。（約翰·波普）

Life with a scientist who is often changing jobs and is frequently away at meetings and on lecture tours is not easy. Without a secure home base, I could not have made much progress. (John Pople)

1991–2000 多元聲音與思想碰撞

　　與一位經常改變工作、頻繁外出參加會議和巡迴演講的科學家一起生活並不容易。沒有一個穩定的家庭基地，我不可能獲得多大的進步。（約翰·波普）

　　Within the first couple of years of high school, I knew that I would like to be a scientist. My parents were encouraging: they gave me chemistry sets and a small microscope as presents. I liked to read popular books about scientists, although there were not many available at that time. My father subscribed to the Sunday New York Times, in which there was often a column on science that I found very exciting. (Robert F. Furchgott)

　　上高中的前幾年，我就知道自己想成為一名科學家。父母很支持：他們送給我一些化學儀器和一臺小顯微鏡作為禮物。我喜歡閱讀關於科學家的通俗讀物，雖然當時這樣的書不多。父親訂閱了《週日紐約時報》，上面經常有令我感到興奮的科學專欄。（羅伯·佛契哥特）

　　In thinking back about what aspects of my research have given me the greatest pleasure, I would not place the honors and awards first. I think that my greatest pleasure has come from each first demonstration in my laboratory that experiments designed to test a new hypothesis developed to explain some earlier, often puzzling or paradoxical finding, have given results consistent with the hypothesis. It is not just the immediate pleasure of obtaining such results but also the anticipated pleasure of discussing the results with others doing research in the same area —— obviously an ego supportive aspect. (Robert F. Furchgott)

　　當我回想研究的哪些方面給了我最大的快樂，我不會把榮譽和獎項放在第一位。我認為最大的快樂來自於我的實驗室中，每一次首度證實

1998 年

為了檢驗一個新假設（提出以解釋某個早期的、經常令人費解或矛盾的發現）而設計的實驗，得到了與該假設相符的結果。這不僅是獲得如此結果的直接樂趣，也是與同一領域其他研究者討論這些結果的預期快樂——這顯然是一種自我支持的方面。（羅伯・佛契哥特）

I still enjoy doing bench work in the laboratory with my co-workers. The research still is rather "old fashion" pharmacological research. (Robert F. Furchgott)

我仍然喜歡跟同事一起在實驗室裡進行實驗臺工作。這一項研究仍然是相當「老派」的藥理學研究。（羅伯・佛契哥特）

I had been invited to Nice, France, to give a talk and also to Naples, Italy, to give another talk, so I was in Nice on October 12th in the morning and I was waiting to board the aeroplane when the airport attendant came over to me with a cellular phone and she said, "Are you Dr Ignarro", I said "Yes", she said "There's an important phone call from the United States". So she gave me the cellular phone and I said "Hello" and it was one of my colleagues, who's a physician at UCLA and he usually jokes around with me and so on and he calls me all the time. He asked me how I was doing, how was the weather, how was the trip, and I said "Fine, fine but I'm very busy, I have to get on the plane, let me call you when I get to Naples in about an hour". He said "Okay, but before you go I have to tell you something" and I said "Well, please make it in a hurry because I have to board the plane" and he said "You won the Nobel Prize" and then we got disconnected, the cellular phone, you know the power was lost, we got disconnected and I gave back the phone and I boarded the plane but I never really knew if I had won the Nobel Prize or not.

1991-2000 多元聲音與思想碰撞

So I boarded the plane and I remember I was looking at the people on the plane, I thought maybe if it was true, maybe this was in the newspaper and people would recognise my face and so I kept looking at everybody to see if anybody would recognise me. But nobody recognised me so I sat down and again I wasn't sure, so about an hour later, when the plane landed in Naples, the Professor who invited me to give a talk at the University of Naples was waiting for me, not in the terminal building where you wait for most people who are coming in by plane, but he was actually standing on the runway with the airport police waving a piece of paper and so I looked at him from the window of the aeroplane and I'm wondering, what is he doing there?

And then I suspected, you know, maybe he's trying to tell me some important news, maybe it is true, so I exited the plane and I get to the ground and he says "Lou, Lou, have you heard the news" and I said "No, no", I didn't want to tell him what I heard, I said "No, I haven't heard any news". He said "Quickly, come over here and read this". So he holds up this piece of paper, but later I found it, it was written in Swedish, it was the press release I guess, but I recognised the first five letters of this very long word and it started off Nobel and then my eyes drifted downward and I saw my name and I actually dropped to the ground, I was so surprised and so jubilant and that's how I first heard about the Nobel Prize, far away from home. (Louis J. Ignarro)

我受邀到法國尼斯進行演講，還要到義大利拿坡里做另一場，所以10月12日早晨我在尼斯，等候登機。這時機場服務人員走過來，拿著手機。她問：「您是伊格納羅博士嗎？」我說：「是的。」她說：「您有一通美國來的重要電話。」於是她把手機交給我。我接電話：「你好。」原來

1998 年

是我的一個同事，加州大學洛杉磯分校的醫生，經常跟我說一些玩笑話之類的，總是打電話給我。他問我過得怎麼樣，天氣如何，旅行如何，我說：「很好，很好，不過我很忙，我得上飛機了，等我大約一小時後到拿坡里時再打給你。」他說：「好吧，但是在你走之前我得告訴你一件事。」我說：「哦，請快講吧，因為我得登機了。」他說：「你得了諾貝爾獎！」隨即我們就斷線了。你們知道，手機沒電了。我們斷線了，我交還電話並上飛機，可是我根本不知道自己是否真的得了諾貝爾獎。

於是我上了飛機，我記得自己看著飛機上的人們，我想假如消息是真的，也許它登在報紙上，人們就會認出我的臉，所以我一直看著每個人，看有沒有任何人會認出我。但是沒有人認出我。於是我坐下來，又游移不定起來。大約過了一小時後，當飛機降落在拿坡里時，邀請我到拿坡里大學演講的教授正在接機。但他不是待在迎候大多數乘客的航廈大樓裡，事實上是由機場警察陪同站在跑道上，揮舞著一張報紙。我隔著舷窗看著他，一邊納悶，他在那裡做什麼？

然後我猜測，你們知道，也許他是在急於告訴我什麼要聞，也許消息是真的，我走出機艙，來到地面，他說：「路，路，你聽到消息了嗎？」我說：「沒有，沒有啊。」我不想告訴他我所聽到的，我說：「沒有，我沒聽到任何消息。」他說：「快，來看看這個。」於是他舉起那張報紙。然而我隨之發現，它是用瑞典文寫的，應該是新聞稿。不過我認出這篇長文的起首五個字母，它以 Nobel 一詞開頭。接著我往下瀏覽，看到自己的名字，這才落實了消息。我是如此震驚，如此歡欣。這是我第一次遠在異國他鄉聽說諾貝爾獎。（路易斯‧伊格納羅）

My greatest joy each morning was building gigantic sand castles using dripping sand wetted by the incoming tide. All my friends believed and predicted that I would grow up to become an architect or engineer. This view was reinforced by my eagerness even as a young child to disassemble anything I could find and put it back together again. The joy of discovering that I could actually get the object to function again was quite rewarding and satisfying. But my greatest joy came when I was 8 years old. To my surprise and delight, mother and father finally responded favorably to my relentless request to have a chemistry set, and bought me one. I can recall vividly following every step of every experiment and becoming overjoyed at the success of each one. This was much more fun than building sand castles on the beach. My inquisitiveness drove me to the library to study more applied aspects of chemistry. (Louis J. Ignarro)

每天早晨，我最大的快樂就是用被漲潮浸溼的沙子堆起龐大的城堡。所有的朋友都相信並預言，我長大後會成為建築師或工程師。我很小就熱衷於把能到手的任何東西拆開再裝上，從而強化了這個看法。當我發現自己真的能讓物品恢復功能，其中的喜悅令人感到非常值得而滿足。不過，最大的快樂來自於我8歲的時候，母親和父親終於善意地回應了我的反覆要求，為我買了一套化學儀器裝置，令我又驚又喜。我清楚地記得自己遵循每一項實驗的每一個步驟，並為每一次實驗的成功而欣喜若狂。這比在沙灘上堆城堡有趣多了。我的好奇心驅使我到圖書館學習更多的化學應用知識。（路易斯·伊格納羅）

We want the clinical people to work more closely with the basic research people so that each person will understand the other person's problems and questions and I think in that way, we can approach the solution of these problems, that is developing new methods of diagnosis and prevention

1998 年

and treatment of these cardiovascular diseases in a much faster way. (Louis J. Ignarro)

我們希望從事臨床工作的人與從事基礎研究的人更緊密地合作,從而人人都能了解對方的困難與疑問。我認為以這種方式,我們就可以解決這些難題,以更快的方式開發診斷、預防和治療這些心血管疾病的新方法。(路易斯・伊格納羅)

The restaurant business had a profound effect on my future and that of my two brothers. When we were able to stand on a stool to reach the sink, we washed dishes, and later, when we could see over the counter, we waited tables and managed the cash register. (Ferid Murad)

家裡的餐廳生意對我和兩個兄弟的未來具有深遠的影響。當我們能夠站在凳子上、碰得到水槽的時候,我們洗盤子;後來,當我們長高到視線高於櫃檯的時候,我們便服務顧客並管理收銀機。(費瑞・慕拉德)

My parents always encouraged us to get an education and establish a profession. However, my brothers and I grew up with considerable freedom, whether it was saving or spending our tips from the restaurant or our career choices. (Ferid Murad)

父母總是鼓勵我們上學和建立專業。不過,我和兄弟們的成長都享有相當大的自由,無論在餐廳所得小費的處置還是職業的選擇。(費瑞・慕拉德)

I knew I wanted considerable education so that I wouldn't have to work as hard as my parents. (Ferid Murad)

我知道我想受到良好的教育,這樣就不用像父母那樣辛苦工作了。(費瑞・慕拉德)

1991-2000 多元聲音與思想碰撞

I am the same person I was before receiving the Nobel Prize. I work with the same regularity, I have not modified my habits, I have the same friends. (José Saramago)

我跟接受諾貝爾獎之前的我是同一個人。我以同一種規律工作，我不曾改變習慣，我有同樣的一些朋友。（喬賽·薩拉馬戈）

With no help or guidance except curiosity and the will to learn, my taste for reading developed and was refined. (José Saramago)

除了好奇心和學習意願，在沒有幫助或指導的情況下，我的閱讀品味也發展起來並得到提升。（喬賽·薩拉馬戈）

Words were not given to man in order to conceal his thoughts. (José Saramago)

人類被賦予語言，不是為了隱藏自己的思想。（喬賽·薩拉馬戈）

Without people any country is only a jungle. But if people are not educated then they will not be creative. (John Hume)

沒有人民，任何國家都不過只是叢林。但如果沒受到教育，人民就不會有創造力。（約翰·休姆）

Politics can be likened to driving at night over unfamiliar hills and mountains. Close attention must be paid to what the beam can reach and the next bend. (David Trimble)

政治就像是夜間在陌生的山中開車。必須密切注意車燈光線能及之處和下一個彎道。（大衛·特林布爾）

When the Nobel award came my way, it also gave me an opportunity to do something immediate and practical about my old obsessions, including literacy, basic health care and gender equity, aimed specifically at India and Bangladesh. (Amartya Sen)

诺贝尔奖颁发给我之际,它也给了我一个机会,得以立即实行我的夙愿,包括识字教育、基本医疗保健和性别平等,尤其是针对印度和孟加拉。(阿马蒂亚·森)

A defeated argument that refuses to be obliterated can remain very alive. (Amartya Sen)

一个拒绝被抹去的失败论点可以仍然富有活力。(阿马蒂亚·森)

1999 年

"A man who knows everything." This, reportedly, was my reply to a school teacher asking me what I'd like to become when I grow up. I was eight years old, or thereabouts, and what I wanted to say was "professor", but, still not knowing everything, I had forgotten that word. And what I really meant was "scientist, someone who unravels the secrets of the fundamental Laws of Nature". (Gerardus 't Hooft)

「一个无所不知的人。」据说,一位老师问我长大了想成为什么样的人,我是这么回答的。当时我大约 8 岁,我想说的是「教授」,可是当时还懵懂,忘记了这个词彙。我真正想说的是「科学家,揭开自然基本法则祕密的人」。(杰拉德·特·胡夫特)

Taming the Laws of Physics, this is what caught my imagination, when I was a child. Automobiles, bicycles, radios had been invented by people who had understood how the forces of Nature work. How did they do that? I figured that these inventions must have been preceded by an insight that, perhaps, I could understand: the wheel. Wheels are marvelous; they allow us to move heavy weights over smooth surfaces with very little resistance. The world of animals and plants does not know about wheels. Wheels must have been discovered by someone. I envied this person. How has this discovery come about? Would I have been smart enough to invent the wheel if it had not yet existed? Probably not.

Questions like these were keeping my mind busy. Maybe not everything has been discovered yet. Certainly not all diseases could be cured, the gravitational force could not be cancelled out, nobody had yet flown to the Moon. Immense forces were thought to exist inside atoms, but it was said that these "smallest particles" were not yet well understood. Huge monsters called dinosaurs lived on Earth millions of years ago. Surely, many more things had to be out there that still had to be discovered, and, if so, I decided to discover all of them.

The nice thing about Nature's Laws is that they are fair. They are the same for everybody, and nobody has the power to change them, unlike the Laws that humans have invented themselves： you should speak politely, use your knife and fork when you eat, go to school and brush your teeth. Those rules could be changed by someone overnight without advance warning, but they can't do that with Nature's Laws. Also, these Laws do not contain contradictions. They can't.

I was extremely fortunate to have good teachers. They told me about mathematics. Mathematics is a superior language if you want to describe Nature's Laws, better than the languages normally used by humans. Mathematics describes things that are true: 1/2+1/3=5/6 Nothing, nobody can change that. There are many properties of numbers and geometrical figures that you can figure out using mathematics. If you make a triangle whose sides have the ratio 3:4:5 in length, then one of its angles is perfectly straight. This is something that one can understand. I figured that, since I planned to make discoveries about Nature, I had to master mathematics.

My friends at school did not care much about these things. That did not bother me. I became very good at mathematics. When I went to the University I already knew a lot about physics, or so I thought. Actually, there still was a lot more to be learned. Simple mechanical laws of motion could be handled much more elegantly by mathematics than I had realized before. There were many more things known about the atom. There existed a fantastic scheme that controls the tiny particles called "Quantum Mechanics", and it is based on even more extravagant mathematics. Superb laws of logic underlie all of this. Nature turned out to be even more beautiful than I had ever imagined.

And indeed, there was a lot that still had to be discovered. There is so much that still has to be discovered today that every scientist, not only the smartest ones, is making discoveries. Making a discovery gives you a kick, it is wonderful. So, indeed, I made discoveries. Small ones and big ones. Sometimes, you don't believe your own eyes: an equation that I had worked on for months turned out to describe exactly some basic forces of Nature, but I hadn't dared to believe it; I hadn't fathomed all logical consequences of this equation, and I had always thought that this simple identity would be too perfect to apply to the real world. Now, we know that it indeed does.

Paul Dirac had the same experience. He had derived a new equation for the electron, using pure logic. But then he noticed that his equation implies the existence of anti-particles, electrons whose electric charge is positive instead of negative. Dirac did not have the courage to predict new particles from a simple equation, so he suggested that these must be the protons. Several properties of the proton do not agree with this, but, Dirac thought, maybe I haven't understood it all yet. Well, the anti-particle of the electron was soon discovered experimentally, exactly in agreement with Dirac's own equation. "This equation is smarter than its inventor!" Dirac was quoted as saying.

Of course, I realized how lucky I have been. I was lucky to have been born with a curious mind, wanting to investigate the world that we live in, but I was also very lucky with the teachers around me, and the opportunities given to me.

In the mean time, the world has changed. Most of these changes are due to scientific discoveries. People have been on the Moon now. We now understand the particles out of which atoms are made, and the forces by which they are controlled. But many more discoveries are still waiting ahead of us. We haven't traveled to Mars yet, and the other planets and moons. The particles in the atom in turn must be controlled by even tinier objects that we do not understand, strings, or sheets, or something else. We do not understand how the gravitational force squares with what we know about these particles. Biologists are unraveling the DNA codes of life, but they cannot yet cure all

1999 年

diseases, and they do not know how to improve DNA codes by hand, or how to write entirely new DNA codes for organisms that do not yet exist. The memory chips in our computers are still stone-age compared to what should be possible theoretically.

Future generations of smart kids should be able to figure these things out. Perhaps we are all dinosaurs compared to the generations of the distant future, if today's children decide to exploit the tremendous opportunities science is likely to offer, by making their own new discoveries. It is like playing chess with Nature, but then better: the rules haven't been made by man. The rules are fair. The ones with the smartest ideas get there first. Only a few decades ago, people from poor countries, or, countries separated from the West by an Iron Curtain, were in a severely disadvantaged position to make any discovery at all. Today, the situation is much better: all you need is an Internet connection, and you will have access to the most up-to-date knowledge of the most reputable centers of science in the world. (Gerardus 't Hooft)

小時候，我就一心想馴服物理定律。汽車、腳踏車、收音機，都是由懂得自然力如何作用的人發明的。他們是怎麼做到的？我認為在這些發明之前一定有一種深刻的洞察，那是我或許能夠理解的：輪子。輪子很神奇，使我們得以在光滑的表面上以很小的阻力移動重物。動物與植物界不了解輪子。輪子一定是某個人發現的。我羨慕這個人。這個發現是怎麼來的？假如輪子尚未存在，我會聰明到發明它嗎？很可能不會。

我滿腦袋都是諸如此類的問題。可能並非所有的東西都已經被發現了。當然不是所有的疾病都能被治癒，引力也不能被抵消，還沒有人飛往月球。人們認為原子內部存在巨大的力量，但據說這些「最小的粒子」

尚未被充分了解。數百萬年前,地球上生活著稱為恐龍的巨大怪獸。肯定還有更多的東西有待發現,這樣的話,我決定把它們全部探索出來。

自然法則的好處在於它們是公平的。它們對每個人都一樣,沒有人有能力改變它們,不像人類自己發明的規矩:你應該說話有禮貌,吃飯時使用刀叉,你必須上學,還要刷牙。這些規矩可能由某人於一夜之間毫無預警地改變,但人們無法對自然法則這麼做。而且,自然法則不包含矛盾。

我極其幸運遇到好老師。他們向我講解數學。如果你想描述自然法則,數學就是一種優勢的語言,勝過人們通常使用的語言。數學描述真實的事情:$\frac{1}{2}+\frac{1}{3}=\frac{5}{6}$。任何力量、任何人都改變不了。有許多數字和幾何圖形的屬性可以用數學計算出來。如果一個三角形其邊長比是3:4:5,則有一角為直角。這個不難理解。我想,既然我打算探索大自然,就必須掌握數學。

學校裡的朋友們不太關心這些事情。這並沒有對我造成困擾。我變得非常擅長數學。上大學的時候,我已經了解許多物理學知識,或者自認如此。實際上,還有大量的知識有待學習。運動的簡單力學法則可以用數學處理,比我先前理解的更加優雅。還有許多關於原子的知識。有一種控制微小粒子的奇妙系統,叫做「量子力學」,它基於更加複雜的數學。這一切的基礎是高超的邏輯法則。大自然原來比我先前想像的還要美麗。

確實,還有許多東西有待探索。今天仍有這麼多的東西有待探索,以至於每一位、不僅是最聰明的科學家,都在持續探索。創造發現令人極度興奮,妙不可言。於是,我確實有所發現,有小的也有大的。有時候,你不相信自己的眼睛:我研究了數個月的方程式,結果準確地描述了自然界的一些基本力量,但我不敢相信,我還未曾透澈了解這個方程式的全部邏輯結果,我一直以為這個簡單的恆等式會完美到不適用於真實世界。現在,我們知道它的確適用。

保羅・狄拉克也有同樣的經歷。他運用純邏輯推演出電子的新方程式。然而此時他注意到,方程式意味著存在反粒子,電荷為正而非負的電子。狄拉克沒有勇氣由一個簡單的方程式預言新粒子,所以他提出這些一定是質子。質子的一些性質與此不符;然而,狄拉克想,自己也許尚未完全理解。結果,電子的反粒子很快就經由實驗被發現了,與狄拉克自己的方程式完全吻合。「這個方程式比它的發明者更聰明!」有人曾援引狄拉克如是說。

當然,我意識到自己是多麼幸運。我慶幸天生有一顆好奇的心,想要探索我們置身其中的世界,而我也非常慶幸身邊有許多老師,以及給予我的各種機會。

如今,世界已經改變了。這些變化大部分歸功於科學發現。現在人們已經登上月球。我們現在了解構成原子的粒子,以及控制它們的力。然而更多的發現還等在前面。我們還沒有前往火星,以及其他行星和衛星。原子中的粒子必定由我們所不了解的更小的物體,弦、片或別的什麼控制。我們不了解引力如何與我們關於這些粒子的知識相符。生物學家正在破解生命的 DNA 密碼,但他們還不能治癒所有的疾病,他們不知道如何人工改寫 DNA 密碼,或如何為尚不存在的有機體編寫全新的 DNA 密碼。與理論上可能實現的記憶體晶片相比,我們電腦中的記憶體晶片仍處於石器時代。

後代的聰明孩子應該能夠釐清這些問題。如果今天的孩子決心透過自己的全新發現,開發科學可能提供的巨大機遇,那麼與遙遠未來的後

1991–2000 多元聲音與思想碰撞

代相比，我們恐怕都是恐龍。這就像跟大自然下棋，但條件更好：規則不是由人制定的。規則是公平的。擁有最聰明想法的人會先到達目的地。僅僅幾十年前，貧窮國家或被鐵幕與西方國家相隔的人們，從事任何發現都處於極為不利的處境。如今，情況就好多了：只需要網際網路連線，就可以獲得世界最著名科學中心的最新知識。（傑拉德·特·胡夫特）

On your way towards becoming a bad theoretician, take your own immature theory, stop checking it for mistakes, don't listen to colleagues who do spot weaknesses, and start admiring your own infallible intelligence. (Gerardus 't Hooft)

若你一心成為糟糕的理論家，便採取自己不成熟的理論，停止檢查其中的錯誤，不要聽取洞察其弱點的同事之言，並開始讚賞自己絕對正確的智慧。（傑拉德·特·胡夫特）

Research brings you into situations you didn't know. (Martinus J.G. Veltman)

研究帶你進入未知的情境。（馬丁紐斯·韋爾特曼）

We go into the domain of particle physics and you start with an experiment and you see results coming, and you find it very exciting discovering new particles and interactions and stuff, and my whole life which started out by looking at a neutrino experiment, and that experiment was a total failure otherwise, but standing there and seeing these events coming and seeing these reaction coming, and try to guess what's going on, it's a very exciting something. It's like entering a domain that no other person has been before. That's the very wonderful stuff about this. And in physics, you are in another domain, unknown, you are truly an explorer. I liked that very much. (Martinus J.G. Veltman)

我們進入粒子物理學領域,你以一個實驗開始,看到結果產生,發現新的粒子、相互作用等非常令人激動。而我的整個人生始於觀察一個中微子實驗,雖然實驗就其他方面而言是徹底的失敗,但站在現場,眼見這些事件出現,眼見這些反應發生,並試著猜測其進展,是非常令人激動的事情。就像進入一個此前從無他人涉足的領域。這就是整件事最棒的部分。在物理學中,你身處另一個未知的領域,你是真正的探索者。我非常喜歡這樣。(馬丁紐斯・韋爾特曼)

I have found out that many physicists owe their career to a good high school teacher. (Martinus J.G. Veltman)

我發現,許多物理學家都把自己的事業歸功於一位優秀的高中老師。(馬丁紐斯・韋爾特曼)

And then a main factor in my life has been the high school teacher of my high school. When I did my final exam he jumped on his bicycle and he drove to the other end of town where I lived and he told to my parents that I should go study physics at University of Utrecht. Had he not done that I would not be sitting here, and it is an example of what a teacher can do. I liked the man very much at the time, and I guess he liked me and he saw something in me. So he did that, he did the extra piece that sometimes somebody does and which has big consequences for your life. (Martinus J.G. Veltman)

當時在我的生活中,有一位高中老師發揮了重大的作用。當我參加期末考試時,他跳上腳踏車,騎到我家所在的城鎮另一端,告訴我父母,我應該去烏特勒支大學攻讀物理學。假如他沒這麼做,我就不會坐

1991–2000 多元聲音與思想碰撞

在這裡。這就是一位教師所能做到的榜樣。當時我非常喜歡他，我猜他也喜歡我，看出了我內在的某種東西。於是他這麼做了，有時候有些人會像他一般做一些額外的事，並且對你的一生產生重大影響。（馬丁紐斯·韋爾特曼）

As a boy it was clear that my inclinations were toward the physical sciences. Mathematics, mechanics, and chemistry were among the fields that gave me a special satisfaction. Social sciences were not as attractive because in those days much emphasis was placed on memorization of subjects, names and the like, and for reasons unknown (to me), my mind kept asking "how" and "why". This characteristic has persisted from the beginning of my life. In my teens, I recall feeling a thrill when I solved a difficult problem in mechanics, for instance, considering all of the tricky operational forces of a car going uphill or downhill. Even though chemistry required some memorization, I was intrigued by the "mathematics of chemistry". It provides laboratory phenomena which, as a boy, I wanted to reproduce and understand. (Ahmed H. Zewail)

少年時，我的興趣明顯傾向於自然科學。其中數學、力學和化學是尤其帶給我滿足的領域。社會科學就不那麼有吸引力了，因為那時更強調對事件、名稱之類的記憶，然而出於我所不知道的原因，我的頭腦總是在問「怎麼樣」和「為什麼」。這個特性與生俱來。記得十幾歲時，解開力學難題使我非常激動，例如，思考汽車上下坡時發揮作用的各種難以捉摸的力。即便化學需要一些記憶，「化學數學」仍使我著迷。作為一個孩子，我想要重現並理解其中的實驗室現象。（亞米德·齊威爾）

Arriving in the States, I had the feeling of being thrown into an ocean. The ocean was full of knowledge, culture, and opportunities, and the choice

1999 年

was clear: I could either learn to swim or sink. The culture was foreign, the language was difficult, but my hopes were high. I did not speak or write English fluently, and I did not know much about western culture in general, or American culture in particular. My presence —— as the Egyptian at Penn —— was starting to be felt by the professors and students as my scores were high, and I also began a successful course of research. My publication list was increasing, but just as importantly, I was learning new things literally every day —— in chemistry, in physics and in other fields. I was working almost "day and night," and doing several projects at the same time. Now, thinking about it, I cannot imagine doing all of this again, but of course then I was "young and innocent". (Ahmed H. Zewail)

到了美國，我有種被扔進大海的感覺。大海充滿了知識、文化和機遇，而我的選擇很明確：若不學會游泳，就會沉下去。儘管文化很陌生，語言很困難，但我仍充滿希望。我的英語口說和書寫都不流利，對普遍的西方文化，尤其是美國文化所知不多。由於成績很高，我的存在——作為賓夕法尼亞大學的埃及人——開始被教授與學生們注意到，我也走上了成功的研究之路。發表的論文數量漸多，而同樣重要的是，學到的新東西與日俱增——在化學、物理學和其他領域。我幾乎沒日沒夜地工作，同時做好幾個項目。現在回想起來，我無法想像再度做到這一切；不過當然了，那時的我還是初生之犢。（亞米德·齊威爾）

There is no "master plan" on the road to the Nobel Prize. It represents a lot of hard work, a passion for that work and… being in the right place at the right time. For me, that place was Caltech. (Ahmed H. Zewail)

通往諾貝爾獎之路沒有「整體規劃」。它代表了大量的艱苦工作、對

這份工作的熱情以及……在適當的時間處於適當的地點。對我來說，這個地點就是加州理工學院。（亞米德·齊威爾）

I've always had fun, I mean I was, my entire research sort of was hypothesis driven therefore I always imagined how things would be and then some of my fantasies of course turned out to be wrong and one must not be wet to one's fantasies, one must when data come which aren't compatible with one's fantasies, one must abandon them. There are beautiful hypothesis killed by ugly facts and so one has to, but one has to also pursue and see whether one can get evidence for or against it and it's wonderful to take a phenomena and then think about them and then imagine how it could possibly work and then see whether one can provide some evidence for or against it. (Günter Blobel)

我總是自得其樂。我的意思是，我的全部研究有幾分是由假說驅動的，所以我總是想像事情會如何。當然，隨後我的一些幻想被證明是錯的。人不可沉迷於幻想。當得出的資料與幻想不一致時，必須放棄幻想。有些美麗的假說被醜陋的事實扼殺，於是人就得再努力看看是否能夠得到支持或反對它的證據。找出一個現象，然後思考，然後想像它如何有可能成立，然後看看是否能夠提供什麼支持或反對它的證據，這是很美妙的。（古特·布洛貝）

A good mentor is a person who is not overpowering but is gently stimulating you and is opening up, helping you to open up a new world of ideas and that is what a good mentor is and who is passionate about what he or she is doing. That's the most important thing, to be passionate, to be really involved in what you want to do. (Günter Blobel)

好的導師是這樣的人，他並不強勢，而是一直溫和地激勵你、打開心扉，幫助你開啟思想的新天地，這才是好導師的特性。他對正在做的事情充滿熱情。這是最重要的，滿懷熱情，全心投入你想做的事情。（古特・布洛貝）

A writer must face up to the test of reality, including political reality, and that can't be done if he keeps his distance. A literary style cultivated like a hothouse plant may show a certain artificial purity, but it won't really be pure. (Günter Grass)

作家必須面對現實的考驗，包括政治現實。他如果保持距離，考驗就無法完成。像溫室植物一樣培養的文學風格可能會表現出某種人為的純粹性，但它不會是真正純粹的。（鈞特・葛拉軾）

Art is uncompromising and life is full of compromises. (Günter Grass)

藝術是不妥協的，而生活充滿妥協。（鈞特・葛拉軾）

There was never a doubt in my parents' mind that their sons would receive the best possible education. Although none of my forefathers graduated from high school, my parents regarded highly the merits of a good education as a tool for social advancement. In their value system knowledge always ranked above wealth —— although not rejecting a possible fortuitous marriage of both. (Robert A. Mundell)

在我父母心中，兒子們毫無疑問要得到盡可能最好的教育。儘管長輩沒有人讀完高中，但是，我的父母高度重視良好教育作為出人頭地的工具的益處。在他們的價值體系中，知識總是高於財富——雖然也不排斥二者偶然結合的可能性。（勞勃・孟岱爾）

1991-2000 多元聲音與思想碰撞

2000 年

The Nobel Prize in Physics 2000, at the change of centuries, has a special meaning. The twentieth century was not only the century of wars and social explosions, it was the century of Physics and first of all quantum Physics. Positive progress of human kind (unfortunately not only positive) was linked with discoveries and development in this field of sciences. (Zhores I. Alferov)

正當世紀之交，2000 年諾貝爾物理學獎有著特殊的意義。20 世紀不僅是戰爭和社會震盪的世紀，它是物理學的世紀，也是量子物理學的第一個世紀。人類的正面進步（不幸的是，不僅是正面的），與此科學領域的發現和發展息息相關。（若列斯・艾費洛夫）

I did have one major problem in school, though: Discipline! I was often bored, and entertained myself in various disruptive ways. A frequent punishment was an entry into the "Klassenbuch," the daily class ledger. These entries were considered a very serious matter, and if I had not been excellent academically, I would have risked being expelled. Once, after I had again been entered as having disturbed the class, the teacher who had overall responsibility for the class —— Dr. Edith Richter, whom I adored —— asked me in great exasperation: "Why again?" I told her that I had been bored, whereupon she exploded: "Mr. Kroemer, one of the purposes of a higher education is that you learn to be bored gracefully." I will never forget that outburst —— nor have I ever really learned to be bored gracefully. (Herbert Kroemer)

不過，我在學校裡確實有一個大問題：紀律！我常常百無聊賴，於是以五花八門的破壞性方式自娛，因而頻繁受到被記入班級分類日誌的懲罰。這些記載被視為非常嚴重的問題，要不是學業成績出眾，我早就有除名之虞了。有一次，我又被記入擾亂課堂，班導──伊迪絲‧里克特博士，我所崇拜的老師──勃然大怒，問我：「為什麼又這樣？」我告訴她我覺得無聊，於是她發火了：「克勒默先生，高等教育的目的之一，就是讓你學會優雅地無聊。」我永遠不會忘記那次發火──我也從未真正學會優雅地無聊。（赫伯特‧克勒默）

I ceased to be a "real" theoretical physicist ── if I ever was one. Call me an Applied Theorist if you want. However, the awareness of doing something truly useful helped overcome the uneasy feelings over ending a theorist career as soon as it had begun. By hindsight, maybe it wasn't such a bad career move after all! (Herbert Kroemer)

我不再是個「真正的」理論物理學家──如果我曾經是的話。願意的話，你不妨稱我為應用理論家。不管怎樣，做確實有用之事的意識，幫助我克服了才剛開始理論家生涯之際就結束的不安感。回過頭看，也許這不是一次糟糕的職業轉換！（赫伯特‧克勒默）

I've reached the age where young people frequently ask for my advice. All I can really say is that electronics is a fascinating field that I continue to find fulfilling. The field is still growing rapidly, and the opportunities that are ahead are at least as great as they were when I graduated from college. My advice is to get involved and get started. (Jack S. Kilby)

我已經到了年輕人經常向我尋求建議的年齡。我真正能夠說的是，電子學是個迷人的領域，我依然覺得它令人有成就感。這個領域仍在快速發展，未來的機會至少跟我大學畢業時的同樣不凡。我的建議是投身其中並開始行動。（傑克‧基爾比）

I'm sure there will continue to be exciting new products and major changes, but it looks as if the existing technology has a great deal of room to grow and prosper. (Jack S. Kilby)

我確信會繼續出現令人興奮的新產品和重大改變,不過看來現有技術似乎擁有非常大的成長與繁榮空間。(傑克・基爾比)

It's gratifying to see the committee recognize applied physics, since the award is typically given for basic research. I do think there's a symbiosis as the application of basic research often provides tools that then enhance the process of basic research. Certainly, the integrated circuit is a good example of that. Whether the research is applied or basic, we all "stand upon the shoulders of giants," as Isaac Newton said. I'm grateful to the innovative thinkers who came before me, and I admire the innovators who have followed. (Jack S. Kilby)

很高興看到委員會認可應用物理學,因為諾貝爾獎通常頒發給基礎研究。我認為二者存在共生關係,因為基礎研究的應用通常提供了工具,從而有助於基礎研究的過程。不言而喻,積體電路就是個很好的例子。無論這項研究是應用的還是基礎的,如艾薩克・牛頓所說,我們都「站在巨人的肩膀上」。我感激在我之前出現的創新思想家們,也欽佩在我之後的創新者。(傑克・基爾比)

Four decades of hindsight is perhaps a unique experience among those who have been awarded the Nobel Prize in Physics. As I noted in my lecture, there were various efforts to solve the electronic miniaturization problem at the time I invented the integrated circuit. Humankind eventually would have solved the matter, but I had the fortunate experience of being the first person with the right idea and the right resources available at the right time in history. (Jack S. Kilby)

40年後的回首往事,也許是諾貝爾物理學獎得主們的特有經驗。如我在演講中所指出,在我發明積體電路的時候,為解決電子裝置微型化問題,人們做出了各式各樣的努力。人類終將解決這個難題,只是我有幸成為歷史上第一個在適當時間擁有適當想法和適當資源的人。(傑克·基爾比)

It's true that the original idea was mine, but what you see today is the work of probably tens of thousands of the world's best engineers, all concentrating on improving the product, reducing the cost, things of that sort. (Jack S. Kilby)

的確,最初的概念是我提出的,但你們今天所見到的,是大概數以萬計世界上最優秀的工程師的工作成果,他們都專注於改進產品、降低成本等諸如此類的事情。(傑克·基爾比)

In science, creativity and discovery are related, but they are not the same. Scientific breakthroughs typically result from a combination of creativity and discovery. (Alan J. Heeger)

在科學領域,創造力和發現是相互關聯的,但它們並不相同。科學上的突破通常來自創造力和發現的結合。(艾倫·黑格)

Perhaps the greatest pleasure of being a scientist is to have an abstract idea, then to do an experiment (more often a series of experiments is required) that demonstrates the idea was correct; that is, Nature actually behaves as conceived in the mind of the scientist. This process is the essence of creativity in science. I have been fortunate to have experienced this intense pleasure many times in my life. (Alan J. Heeger)

也許作為一名科學家最大的樂趣就是有一個抽象的想法,然後做一個實驗(更多的是需要一系列的實驗)來證明這個想法是正確的;也就是說,大自然實際上是依照科學家腦海中設想的那樣運作的。這個過程是科學創造力的本質。我很幸運,一生中曾多次體驗過這種強烈的快樂。(艾倫·黑格)

There is a statement on the wall of my study at home in suburban Philadelphia which reads, "I am a very lucky person and the harder I work the luckier I seem to be"! (Alan G. MacDiarmid)

在費城郊區我的家裡,書房牆上掛了一幅字,上面寫道:「我是個非常幸運的人,我工作越努力,看起來就越幸運!」(艾倫·麥克德爾米德)

As my parents always said, "… an 'A's grade in a class is not a sign of success." Success is knowing that you have done your best and have exploited your God-given or gene-given abilities to the next maximum extent. (Alan G. MacDiarmid)

就像我父母常說的,「上課得個 A 並不代表成功」。成功是知道自己已經盡力,並最大限度地運用了上天賦予或與生俱來的能力。(艾倫·麥克德爾米德)

We all owe so much to those who have gone before us —— "we stand on the shoulders of giants." (Alan G. MacDiarmid)

我們都受惠於前人如此之多 ——「我們站在巨人的肩膀上。」(艾倫·麥克德爾米德)

Long after I became a polymer scientist, I occasionally remembered a short composition I had written during my last year in junior high school. At that time students compiled a commemorative collection of compositions describing our future dreams. As I recalled, I wrote something about my wish to be a scientist in the future and to conduct research on plastics useful for ordinary people. I cannot be sure what I wrote exactly because I lost the book of essays during repeated moves afterwards. I had long regretted this loss because I wanted to know more about why and how a junior high school boy decided on a future research career in plastics. Much to my surprise, I found that the full composition I had lost was printed in every Japanese newspaper the day after the Royal Swedish Academy of Sciences announced its award of the Nobel Prize in Chemistry for 2000 to two friends and myself. After 45 years, I could finally read the complete composition again. I was deeply impressed with the great power of the Nobel Prize. (Hideki Shirakawa)

在成為聚合物科學家很久之後，我偶然想起自己在國中最後一年寫的一篇短文。當時，學生們編了一本講述大家未來夢想的紀念集。我記得自己寫到了個人願望，希望將來當個科學家，研究對一般人有用的塑膠。我不太確定確切內容，因為在後來的一再搬家之中遺失了這本文集。對此損失我惋惜不已，因為我想更多地了解一個國中生為什麼和如何認定了未來從事塑膠研究事業。令我大為驚奇的是，在瑞典皇家科學院宣布將 2000 年諾貝爾化學獎授予我的兩位朋友和我本人的隔天，我發現我所遺失的文章，被全文刊載在日本所有的報紙上。45 年之後，我終於可以再度讀到完整的文章了。諾貝爾獎的巨大威力給了我深刻的印象。（白川英樹）

My childhood and youth were characterized by a happy life in a stable environment with loving and supportive parents. I was probably just about average in terms of disobedience and escapades. At school, which I found fairly endurable, I had very good marks without too much effort. (Arvid Carlsson)

我的童年和青少年時期過得很幸福，生活在穩定的環境中，有父母的慈愛支持。在叛逆和冒險方面，我大概只處於平均程度。對於學校生活，我發現很容易接受，我不需要付出太多努力就能獲得好成績。（阿爾維德·卡爾森）

You should only go into science if you really have a yearning to make scientific discoveries. (Paul Greengard)

只有當你真正渴望創造科學發現時，你才應該投身於科學領域。（保羅·葛林加德）

My philosophy is that we should ask the most important question that's capable of being solved. (Paul Greengard)

我的理念是，我們應該問最重要的、能夠被解決的問題。（保羅·葛林加德）

I'm sure our brains are working unconsciously. When you have a creative thought, it's parts of the brain talking to each other without your awareness. (Paul Greengard)

我確信我們的大腦正在無意識地運作。當你有一個創造性的想法時，大腦的不同部分在你不知情的狀況下互相交流。（保羅·葛林加德）

Science is not the glamour that's portrayed in films. It's a lot of drudgery work, along with the wonderfully exciting periods when you discover something. (Paul Greengard)

科學並不是電影裡描繪的那種迷人的美。它是大量單調沉悶的工作，伴隨著有所發現之際令人非常激動的時刻。（保羅·葛林加德）

The fact is all of the most highly successful scientists I know work practically all the time. (Paul Greengard)

事實上，我認識的所有極其成功的科學家都是全部時間在工作。（保羅·葛林加德）

It's a tragedy for society to spend decades training people and then depriving them of work at some arbitrary age. (Paul Greengard)

花幾十年時間培訓人才，然後在某個年齡剝奪他們的工作，這對社會是一場悲劇。（保羅·葛林加德）

I have a philosophy that has guided me throughout all of my scientific career, and that is, I think of myself as a fairly thoughtful person. I don't go into projects impetuously, and I try to select important problems. (Eric R. Kandel)

在整個科學生涯中，我有一種始終指引我的哲學，那就是我自認是個深思熟慮的人。我不會由於一時衝動而投入研究，而會盡量選擇重要的問題。（埃里克·坎德爾）

In college and medical school I was never a good note-taker. I always preferred sitting back, enjoying the lecture, and just scribbling down a few words here and there. (Erik R. Kandel)

在大學和醫學院，我從來都不是認真做筆記的學生。我總是喜歡靠在椅背上，享受聽課之樂，只是潦草地亂寫幾筆。（埃里克·坎德爾）

There was little in my early life to indicate that an interest in biology would become the passion of my academic career. In fact, there was little to suggest I would have an academic career. (Eric R. Kandel)

在我的早年生活中，幾乎沒有什麼跡象表明，對生物學的興趣會發展成為我學術生涯的熱情。事實上，幾乎沒有什麼跡象暗示我會有個學術生涯。（埃里克·坎德爾）

I like problems at the borders of disciplines. One of the reasons that neurobiology of learning and memory appeal to me so much was that I liked the idea of bringing biology and psychology together. (Eric R. Kandel)

我喜歡處於學科交界地帶的問題。學習與記憶的神經生物學如此吸引我的原因之一,是我喜歡將生物學與心理學結合起來的概念。(埃里克·坎德爾)

I would not necessarily say that scientists and artists need to collaborate with one another, but it would be helpful for them to talk to one another to, perhaps, give rise to specific ideas that may or may not be carried out together. (Eric R. Kandel)

我不會非要說科學家和藝術家需要彼此合作,但互相交流也許會有助於他們產生一些具體想法,無論是否真的共同付諸實現。(埃里克·坎德爾)

I found working in the lab is so completely different than reading a textbook about it. You know, you're planning strategies; you're working with your own hands. There's essential satisfaction in running experiments. (Eric R. Kandel)

我發現,在實驗室工作與閱讀教科書實在是截然不同。你知道,你在運籌謀劃,你在用自己的雙手工作。從事實驗能帶來本質上的滿足感。(埃里克·坎德爾)

I had many moments of disappointment, despondency, and exhaustion, but I always found that by reading the literature and showing up at my lab looking at the data as they emerged day by day and discussing them with my students and postdoctoral fellows, I would gain a notion of what to do next. (Eric R. Kandel)

我有過許多失望、洩氣和精疲力竭的時刻；然而我總是發現，透過閱讀文獻和親臨實驗室觀察逐日資料，並跟學生和博士後研究人員討論，我會知道接下來該做什麼。（埃里克・坎德爾）

Accepting the Nobel Peace Prize, the honoree is committed to an endless duty. (Kim Dae-jung)

接受諾貝爾和平獎，獲獎者就承擔了無窮的責任。（金大中）

In 1980, I was sentenced to death by the military regime. For six months in prison, I awaited the execution day. Often, I shuddered with fear of death. But I would find calm in the fact of history that justice ultimately prevails. (Kim Dae-jung)

1980 年，我被軍人政權判處死刑。我入獄 6 個月，等待行刑日到來。我常常由於對死亡的恐懼而戰慄。然而，我會在正義終將獲勝的史實中找到平靜。（金大中）

There is a responsibility that goes with winning the Nobel Prize, and the responsibility is that if you have a forum, you should use it wisely. (James J. Heckman)

獲得諾貝爾獎伴隨著責任。這份責任是，你如果有個論壇，就應當明智地運用。（詹姆士・赫克曼）

An innovative design can advance the science. Whether it is a well-written novel, a well-made wine, a fine dish, a clever computer chip, or a well-crafted microeconometric analysis, good design instructs, brings pleasure, and lifts the human spirit. (Daniel L. McFadden)

創新的設計能夠促進科學發展。無論是精心撰寫的小說、精心釀造的葡萄酒、精美的菜餚、精巧的電腦晶片，還是精心設計的個體計量經濟學分析，優秀的設計提供指導、帶來快樂並且提振人心。（丹尼爾‧麥克法登）

If you're not careful, the Nobel Prize is a career-ender. If I allowed myself to slip into it, I'd spend all my time going around cutting ribbons. (Daniel L. McFadden)

要是不小心，諾貝爾獎會終結獲獎者的事業。我要是允許自己沉醉其間，就會把時間全都花在到處剪綵上。（丹尼爾‧麥克法登）

The term "economics", in its original Greek, means "of the hearth", the ancient and practical science of household management. Over the millennia, the discipline has transformed itself into a grander enterprise, speaking sagely of the organization of economies, and admonishing capitalists and kings on incentives, constraints, and unintended consequences. This is important business, but economists have felt the loss of their practical side. In the words of John Maynard Keynes, "If economists could manage to get themselves thought of as humble, competent people, on a level with dentists, that would be splendid!" I think of the public edifice of economics as being like the inflatable buildings that cover tennis courts in cold climates, entirely supported by air. Yet, the air has a direction and purpose, and is the result of carefully designed and systematically maintained mechanical equipment that provides stability and form. It is at this practical, mechanical level, closer to the hearth than to the throne, that the science is put into economic science. Measurements are taken, designs are tested, and new machines are constructed. (Daniel L. McFadden)

「經濟學」一詞源自希臘語,意為「壁爐邊的」,是古代實用的治家之道。幾千年來,這門學問已經轉型為更宏大的事業,睿智地談論經濟組織,還諄諄告誡資本家和國王們要注意激勵、約束和意外後果。這是一項重要的工作,不過經濟學家已經感到自身實用精神的喪失。用約翰·梅納德·凱因斯的話來說,「經濟學家要是能夠設法讓自己被認為是謙恭、能幹的人,就像牙醫一般,那就太好了!」我認為,經濟學這座公共大廈,就像寒冷氣候下覆蓋網球場的充氣建築,完全由空氣支撐。然而,這一股空氣有方向和目的,是精心設計和系統維護的機械設備造成的結果,提供穩定性和外形。正是在這種實用的、機械的層面上,更接近壁爐邊而非寶座旁,科學性融入了經濟學。實施測量、檢驗設計,新的機制得以建構。(丹尼爾·麥克法登)

1991–2000 多元聲音與思想碰撞

2001–2010
跨界融合與人文關懷

2001 年

Most of my teachers probably found I made less trouble if they let me read. (Eric A. Cornell)

我的大多數老師很可能發現，如果他們讓我看書，我就不太淘氣。（艾瑞克·康乃爾）

I was partly old-fashioned and partly modern. (Eric A. Cornell)

我的一部分是老派的，一部分是現代的。（艾瑞克·康乃爾）

Bose and Einstein had triggered low-temperature experiments that have led to the discovery of new matter. I owe my work and my Nobel to them. (Wolfgang Ketterle)

玻色和愛因斯坦曾發起低溫實驗，從而發現了新物質。我將自己的工作及諾貝爾獎歸功於他們。（沃夫岡·克特勒）

Maybe if you win a Nobel Prize in economics, you make a lot of money by giving talks... but not in my area. (Wolfgang Ketterle)

要是得了諾貝爾經濟學獎，你也許憑演講就能賺很多錢……但在我

這個領域卻不然。[13]（沃夫岡·克特勒）

The true nature and strength of science is that it is a grand staircase formed by the steps built by many individuals over many years, and often important steps come from very unexpected places. (Carl E. Wieman)

科學的本質和力量在於，它是一座宏偉的階梯，由許多年來、許多人所建造的臺階構成，而重要的臺階經常出自意想不到之處。（卡爾·威曼）

I don't like the word serendipity. I prefer luck. Because I think serendipity, in my mind, doesn't seem to imply much intelligence. It seems there were these guys wandering around and lucky things happened to them. To me it doesn't, I like to think I had luck, but I like there was a little intelligence behind this. (William S. Knowles)

我不喜歡意外發現這個詞。我寧願說運氣。因為我認為意外發現，在我心目中，似乎並不意味著很多智慧。似乎是有這麼一些人在閒晃之中，幸運的事情就發生在他們身上了。就我而言並非如此。我喜歡認為自己有運氣，但我喜歡它的背後有幾分智慧。（威廉·斯坦迪什·諾爾斯）

At least certainly the breakthroughs in science, you almost have to be active and your lucky break comes along. Never where or when you expect it, and the ones that succeed take advantage of that lucky break. And most people don't bother to take advantage. (William S. Knowles)

至少科學上的突破肯定如此，你幾乎只有積極進取，好運方才隨之而來。它永遠不會出現在你所期望的位置或時間，而成功者會藉助這種好運。但是大多數人不會利用這一點。（威廉·斯坦迪什·諾爾斯）

---

[13] 克特勒為 2001 年諾貝爾物理學獎得主。

Doubt is really a wonderful friend to life. The comfort with doubt is what enables one to be more curious than others. You can't be really a curious person unless you're comfortable with doubt. (William S. Knowles)

懷疑確實是人生中的好朋友。慣於懷疑使人比其他人更好奇。若非慣於懷疑，你無法成為真正好奇的人。（威廉・斯坦迪什・諾爾斯）

I was one who liked to work with my hands as well as my brain. (William S. Knowles)

我是個喜歡手腦並用的人。（威廉・斯坦迪什・諾爾斯）

Our individual knowledge is tightly bound to the combined knowledge of all humanity. Science is destined to make progress. In every age, it's the young who venture to explore new frontiers that are based on the intellectual assets passed on their predecessors. (Ryoji Noyori)

我們個人的知識與全人類的整體知識密不可分。科學注定造成進步。每一個時代，都是年輕人在前人相傳的知識資產的基礎上，勇於探索新的領域。（野依良治）

Research should be driven by curiosity. (Ryoji Noyori)

研究應該由好奇心驅動。（野依良治）

Discoveries are made accidentally, but that's not real accident. (Ryoji Noyori)

發現是偶然中獲得的，但那並非真正的偶然。（野依良治）

There are many important and useful compounds in nature. But that's not enough. We need many other, more important artificial compounds, which can be synthesised by chemists. (Ryoji Noyori)

自然界中有許多重要而有用的化合物。但這還不夠。我們需要許多其他的、更重要的人造化合物，它們可以由化學家合成。（野依良治）

The scientific research has been analytical. However that should be more scientific. So the integration of many simple elements generating anew our functions. (Ryoji Noyori)

科學研究一直是分析性的。然而這應該更科學。因此，許多單一元素的整合重新產生了我們所需的功能。（野依良治）

The chemists are being interested in the structure of molecules. And now we can fully understand the structure, but that's not enough. So important is the creation of functions from organic molecules, that's integrated matter and very difficult to understand. I think that we should know more about biology and also physics. (Ryoji Noyori)

化學家們對分子的結構興趣不斷。現在我們可以充分了解這個結構了，但這還不夠。從有機分子中創造功能非常重要，這是整合而成的物質，很難了解。我認為，對生物學以及物理學我們應該所知更多。（野依良治）

A clear-cut solution to a long-persistent problem, when accomplished, often results in an enormous scientific or technological impact. (Ryoji Noyori)

一旦完成某個長期難題的明確解決方案，通常會造成巨大的科學或技術衝擊。（野依良治）

The life issue, the complexity, is a fascinating area. (K. Barry Sharpless)

錯綜複雜的生命問題是個令人著迷的領域。（卡爾·巴里·沙普利斯）

2001 年

The serendipity one is a bit too much like really luck. Sometimes people are calling intuitive as well, which is related to this idea of they're going to be able to take advantage of serendipity more because they're actually open to it. And I think intuitive is a way that people who aren't creative will describe creative people because they don't see the method by which the information leads these people to the answer they get. I mean people that are intuitive often take in as much, if not more information, facts and feelings and connections than the people who are linear. So I think intuitive people actually are just using their information in a different way. (K. Barry Sharpless)

意外發現有點太像運氣了。有時人們也稱之為直覺，這跟他們的這種想法有關：自己將能更多地藉助意外發現，因為他們實際上對此持開放態度。我認為，直覺是缺乏創造性的人描述有創造性的人的說法，因為前者看不到資訊引導後者獲得答案的方法。我的意思是，直覺型的人所接收到的資訊、事實、感覺和連結往往與線性型的人一樣多，或者更多。所以我認為，直覺敏銳的人實際上只是在以不同的方式運用資訊。（卡爾・巴里・沙普利斯）

It almost seems like life systems want to be near the edge of chaos because his image is riding a wave, you know, surfer riding a wave. If you're up high on the wave and the wave goes forever and you can stay in the zone and you have movement, you have power, potential energy. If you get over the top of the wave, you could die. But if you're down back on the wave in a trough, you can't move. And move means evolve. You have to be having movement and life is attracted to instability and creative discoveries come from points of instability in chaos. You have chaos in catalysis. And catalysis is life really.

You need to be near this slippery area, partly because you need speed. Speed is really crucial. (K. Barry Sharpless)

這幾乎看起來就像生命系統想要接近混亂的邊緣，因為它的形象是乘著波浪，你知道，就像是衝浪者乘著波浪。如果你立於浪峰，海浪奔湧不停，你就可以待在這個區域，你在運動，你有能量，你有位能。如果你越過波浪頂部，你可能就退出了。但如果你從波峰落回波谷，你就無法運動。而運動意味著發展。你得不斷地運動，生命被不穩定吸引，創造性的發現來自於混亂中的不穩定點。催化過程中存在混亂。而催化實為生命。你需要接近這個難以站穩的區域，部分是因為你需要速度。速度十分重要。（卡爾‧巴里‧沙普利斯）

The chemist has a set of intuitions that enables him to control reaction and understand reactivity. The biologist has the same kind of creativity, it's a different set of blocks and principles. And we shouldn't be doing both jobs because the human mind is really needed to encompass those areas, they can overlap a little, but we need to collaborate. I don't like this idea that we have to know, we're not going to be able to know molecular biology, cell physiology, chemistry, physics, no, it's not going to be possible. I don't even think Goethe or Leonardo da Vinci could do it. So I think you need to have collaboration. More communication between the biology people and work with them hand in hand. But you do what you do best and they do what they do. (K. Barry Sharpless)

化學家有一套直覺，使他能夠控制反應和理解反應性。生物學家有同樣性質的創造力，另一套思路和原理。而我們不應該同時進行這兩種工作，人的心智確實需要涵蓋這些領域，它們可以稍有重疊，但我們需要合作。我不喜歡我們什麼都得懂的想法，我們不可能懂得分子生物學、細胞生理學、化學、物理學，不，這是不可能的。我甚至不認為歌德或李奧納多·達文西做得到。所以我認為你們需要合作。與生物學界加強交流，攜手工作。不過你們做你們最擅長的，他們做他們的。（卡爾·巴里·沙普利斯）

We get attracted to things we can understand and we go in deep on solving puzzles, but we don't notice, and we like to see things sitting still. If something is moving it's blurry usually and that's what our area is, the three of us, we work on catalysts. (K. Barry Sharpless)

我們被自己能夠理解的事物吸引，我們深入探究解謎，然而我們卻沒有注意到，我們喜歡看到事物靜止不動。如果什麼東西在移動，它通常是模糊的，而這就是我們的領域所在，我們三人[14]，我們研究催化劑。（卡爾·巴里·沙普利斯）

I often come up with ideas in the shower! (K. Barry Sharpless)

我常常在淋浴時冒出想法！（卡爾·巴里·沙普利斯）

The goal of science, as we all know, is to discover simplicity in the midst of complexity. Yet when Paul Nurse, Tim Hunt and I and our students and colleagues began studying how cells divide, any sensible scientist should have expected to find only hopeless complexity. If you think of cell division as a symphony, we knew that the symphony had to be performed by thousands of musicians each playing a different instrument. So —— our research can only be described as motivated by a kind of foolish optimist. Sometimes nature rewards foolish optimism. Continuing with the metaphor of cell division as a

---

[14] 即諾爾斯、野依良治和沙普利斯。三人同獲 2001 年諾貝爾化學獎。

symphony, our research paths led each of us, independently and by great luck, smack into the conductor of the symphony. And, it turned out that the same conductor performed this symphony in all types of cells —— yeast, fruit flies, sea urchins, frogs and humans. I really have no idea how often nature rewards such foolish optimism, but I am pleased to report that the Nobel committee is rather fond of foolish optimism. (Leland H. Hartwell)

眾所周知，科學的目標是在複雜中發現簡單。然而，當保羅·納斯、蒂姆·亨特和我以及我們的學生和同事們開始研究細胞分裂過程時，任何明智的科學家都應當預料到，只會發現令人絕望的複雜。如果將細胞分裂設想為交響樂，我們知道這首交響樂得由成千上萬的音樂家演奏，每一個人演奏不同的樂器。所以——我們的研究只能說是被一種愚蠢的樂觀主義所驅使。大自然有時候鼓勵愚蠢的樂觀主義。繼續以細胞分裂作為交響樂的比喻，我們的研究路徑引導我們極其幸運地各自遇到了交響樂的指揮。結果，真相竟是，同一位指揮在所有類型的細胞中，上演的都是這首交響樂——不論酵母、果蠅、海膽、青蛙還是人類。大自然如何地經常鼓勵這種愚蠢的樂觀主義實在無從得知；不過我很高興地告訴大家，諾貝爾委員會相當欣賞愚蠢的樂觀主義。（利蘭·哈特韋爾）

Through my experience, I learned that you only make discoveries when you are sort of stumbling and bumbling about, turning over stones at random. Making small mistakes in experiments is fine, because you stand a chance of making startling discoveries. If you stick to a very narrow path, then you'll probably simply conform to what other people already know, whereas the purpose of research is to try and discover something new that nobody knows. (Tim Hunt)

依據個人經驗,我了解到只有在跌跌撞撞、跟跟蹌蹌、亂翻石頭的時候,你才能有所發現。在實驗中犯小錯是好的,因為你有機會獲得驚人的發現。如果你堅持一條非常狹窄的道路,那麼你很可能只是遵循別人已經知道的東西,然而研究的目的,是盡力發現不為人知的新事物。(蒂姆・亨特)

I agree that choosing a research question may be difficult and a researcher can't always rely on luck. Over the years, I have come to realize that the most difficult aspect of research is to find a good problem to work on. It's really hard to find (a) an interesting problem, (b) an important problem, (c) a problem that people will be interested in knowing the answer to, and (d) a problem that can actually be solved. A researcher also has to be mindful of timelines. We are not talking about a trivial problem you could solve overnight nor are we talking about something that would go on forever, beyond your lifetime. In principle, you want to have larger problems that you can break down into smaller problems and solve those smaller issues during the period of a grant application of about 3 to 5 years. (Tim Hunt)

我同意選擇研究問題可能很困難,研究者不能總是依靠運氣。多年來,我逐漸了解到,研究工作最難的方面是找個好的問題來做。的確難於找到:一、一個有趣的問題,二、一個重要的問題,三、一個人們會有興趣知道答案的問題,四、一個實際上可以解決的問題。研究者還得充分考量時間因素。我們不是在談論一個可以一夜解決的小問題,也不是在談論什麼沒完沒了的事情,超出一輩子的。一般而言,你想要一些較大的問題,可以拆成稍小的問題,然後在三至五年的撥款申請期間解決它們。(蒂姆・亨特)

Winning a Nobel Prize isn't about being clever at all. It's about making... at least in physiology or medicine, it's about making discoveries, and you don't have to be clever to make a discovery, I don't think; it just comes up and punches you on the nose. (Tim Hunt)

獲得諾貝爾獎跟聰明全無關係。它關係到創造⋯⋯至少在生理學或醫學方面，它關係到創造發現。我不認為你一定要很聰明才能創造發現；它就是冒了出來，一拳打在你的鼻子上。（蒂姆・亨特）

I confess that until I actually received the medal itself, held it in my hand, I half expected the Nobel Committee to realize that they had made an unfortunate mistake, and feared the King would say, "Sorry, the award is not for you; it's actually for the other Tim Hunt!" (Tim Hunt)

我承認，直到真正拿到沉甸甸的獎牌之前，我有一半心思等著諾貝爾委員會意識到他們犯了一個不幸的錯，我生怕國王會說：「對不起，這個獎不是你的，實際上是另一個蒂姆・亨特[15]的！」（蒂姆・亨特）

I also remember that when we started out, we had to do a lot of background work to understand exactly how we would proceed and I guess that is common. Another thing that happened is that we kept being sidetracked from the main problem. Studying controls gave us a lot of fresh insight into other related mechanisms. Along the way, I also discovered that when your results challenge already established or accepted studies, you face a harder time from many people, including journal reviewers. This is the reason why you have to be completely sure of your results even if this means that you have to be your own harshest critic. That is better than having someone else question you or

---

[15] 蒂姆・亨特屬於常見姓名。

shoot your work down. (Tim Hunt)

　　我還記得，剛起步時，我們不得不做大量的背景工作，以確切了解我們將如何進行，我想這是很常見的。發生的另一個情況是，我們不斷地偏離主要問題。研究控制使我們對其他相關機制得到大量新的洞察。在這個過程中，我還發現，當你的研究成果挑戰已經建立或被接受的研究時，你就面臨來自許多人的困難，包括期刊審稿人。所以你得完全確信自己的成果，即便這意味著你得成為自己最苛刻的批評者。這勝過於讓別人質疑你或否定你的工作。（蒂姆・亨特）

　　Growing up in Cambridge, I knew a lot of Nobel Laureates and I think the one thing that was most striking was their heterogeneity —— some of them were very clever, some not so clever; some were modest, some were arrogant. They worked on a wide variety of things in a wide variety of ways. The only common thing was that there was a certain simplicity about them when you took a deeper look at their personalities. It's fine to work on really complicated brainy problems, but you should be able to understand it thoroughly and boil it down to something really simple. When I started out, I rather think we were trying to be far too clever and sophisticated, whereas all we needed to do was to keep things simple. I see this tendency in many young researchers: they learn too much and make things very grandiose. They don't concentrate on the essentials. They don't get back to basics. I think it is crucial to go back to the basics and keep things simple. On the whole, it is important to remember that although there are many ways to succeed, there are even more ways to fail. (Tim Hunt)

　　我成長於劍橋，認識很多諾貝爾獎得主。我認為最引人注目的一件事，是他們的各自不同 —— 有的非常機智，有的不那麼機智；有的謙虛，有的傲氣。他們以各式各樣的方式從事各式各樣的工作。更深入地觀察其性格，他們唯一的共同之處是展現出一種簡單性。鑽研極其複雜的腦力問題很好，但你應當能夠徹底理解它，並把它歸納為極其簡單的事情。剛開始的時候，我認為人們過於力求聰明世故，但我們需要做的只是保持事情簡單。我在許多年輕研究人員身上看到這種傾向：他們無所不知，把事情弄得很浮誇。他們沒有把注意力集中在基本的事情上。他們沒有回歸本源。我認為回歸本源、保持事情簡單十分重要。總而言之，重要的是記住，儘管成功的途徑很多，失敗的途徑甚至更多。（蒂姆·亨特）

Well, I think you certainly have to be lucky, and in my experience, intelligent scientists who also work hard seem to get luckier. My piece of advice to researchers aspiring to make it big: Keep your feet on the ground, your eyes on the horizon, and your nose to the grindstone. It is a matter of not getting lazy and being on the lookout for clues. I think the one thing I have been quite good at is realizing the significance of little clues when they come along. If there's something, an idea or a hunch, at the back of your mind but you haven't been able to figure out how to solve the problem, keep at it – follow your instinct instead of waiting for the problem to solve itself. I don't think I have ever known a problem yield to direct attack actually. So find other ways to get answers. While pursuing a research question, you will realize that there are problems you can attack directly and there are those you can't because you don't know enough about them. So you have to try different ways to find a solution; and this is where luck plays a part. I do think that success also depends on being in the right place at the right time. (Tim Hunt)

2001 年

　　嗯，我認為你肯定需要運氣。依我的經驗，既聰明又勤奮的科學家似乎更幸運。對於胸懷大志的研究人員，我的建議是：腳踏實地，放眼未來，埋頭苦幹。這關係到絕不偷懶而緊盯線索。我認為自己一直相當擅長的一件事，是在細微線索出現時意識到其重要性。如果你的頭腦深處有什麼東西，某種想法或預感，可是你還思索不出怎麼解決問題，那就堅持下去 —— 遵循你的直覺，而不是等待問題自行解決。我想不起來自己聽說過哪一個難題是被直接攻克的。所以要尋求另外的辦法獲得答案。著手於一個研究問題時，你會發現有些問題可以直接突破瓶頸，也有一些無法這麼做，因為你對它們不夠了解。所以你得嘗試不同的方法來尋找答案，而這就是運氣發揮作用之處。我確實認為，成功也有賴於在適當的時間處於適當的地點。（蒂姆・亨特）

　　Mere luck and hard work are not enough. Ambition is important, too. During a recent interview with Miranda Robertson, I said that, quite often, Nobel Prizes are given for things that people thought were impossible to achieve. For example, when I was still in college, people said that DNA sequencing was impossible. But Fred Sanger proved everybody wrong. Another example is that of the ribosome. We were taught that the structure of the ribosome could never be fully revealed because it was too complex and ribosomes would never crystalize. Even if they did crystalize, there would be too much data to decipher. It was a formidable problem, but people did tackle it. Now we know what the ribosome looks like and you can pretty much see how they work! So a certain degree of ambition is necessary. (Tim Hunt)

　　單憑運氣和努力是不夠的。雄心也很重要。在最近接受米蘭達・羅伯遜的採訪時我就說，諾貝爾獎經常頒發給人們認為不可能實現的成就。例如，當我還在上大學的時候，人們說 DNA 定序是不可能的。但弗雷德里克·桑格證明所有人都錯了。另一個例子是核糖體。我們被告知，核糖體的結構永遠不可能完全揭示，因為它太複雜，核糖體也永遠不會結晶。即便它們真的結晶，也會有太多的資料需要解碼。這是個令人卻步的難題，但人們終歸解決了它。現在我們知道核糖體是什麼樣子了，而你可以清楚看到它們如何工作！因此，一定程度的雄心是必要的。（蒂姆·亨特）

The research scene today is highly competitive. There are probably more scientists working in my own field than ever before. I often joke to younger researchers about how glad I am that I am not 20-something years old anymore, because I sense that it's tough out there. The tools are very advanced and problems that you thought would never ever be attacked have been attacked. I never thought we would know as much in my lifetime as we know today, particularly about areas like developmental biology. It's fantastic, but it's also really hard. (Tim Hunt)

如今的研究領域競爭非常激烈。在我本人所處領域工作的科學家很可能比以往任何時候都多。我常跟年輕的研究人員開玩笑，說我有多高興不再是 20 幾歲的人了，因為感到外面的日子不好過。各種工具非常先進，你以為將永遠無人問津的一些問題已經獲得解決。我從未想到，在我的有生之年，我們會像今天這樣知識豐富，尤其在發育生物學之類的領域。這非常美妙，但也非常困難。（蒂姆·亨特）

I don't think it made any difference. If anything, journal editors and reviewers possibly became stricter. Incidentally, my last paper, of which I am rather proud actually, was published in Science, but was rejected without a

2001 年

review by Nature. I am not too surprised about this, because things are so specialized these days. So it doesn't matter who you are. If your work is good, your paper will be accepted, but if it is rejected, you should try again. There are genuine matters of taste as well in this business. (Tim Hunt)

我不認為獲諾貝爾獎造成了任何不同。如果有所不同,也就是期刊編輯和審稿人可能變得更嚴格了。順便說,我最近的論文,事實上頗為得意的一篇,發表在《科學》上,但被《自然》未經審查就拒絕了。對此我並不感到太驚訝,因為如今的一切都非常專業化。所以你是誰並不重要。如果你的工作很出色,論文會被採用;但如果被拒絕,你應該再試一試。這個行業也有純粹的品味問題。(蒂姆·亨特)

My parents were neither wealthy nor academic, but we lived comfortably and they were always extremely supportive of my academic efforts and aspirations, both at school and university. (Paul M. Nurse)

我的父母既不富裕也無關學術,不過我們生活舒適,而且他們對我的學業和抱負總是全力支持,無論是在高中還是大學。(保羅·納斯)

I was never very good at exams, having a poor memory and finding the examination process rather artificial, and there never seemed to be enough time to follow up things that really interested me. (Paul M. Nurse)

我從來都不擅長考試,記憶力差,覺得考試方法實在僵化,而且好像總是沒有時間做好我真正感興趣的事。(保羅·納斯)

I think it was this curiosity about the natural world which awoke my early interest in science. (Paul M. Nurse)

我認為正是對自然界的這種好奇心,喚醒了我對科學的早期興趣。(保羅·納斯)

I am still asking questions in science although they are more complex now, or at least the language I use to ask the questions is more complex. Which raises the question of what I think is key for keeping an interest in science. For me, two points are important. The first is keeping a real curiosity about the world and the second is a determination to find explanations for what we see. Without that curiosity and a wish to know answers, the passion for science is soon lost. (Paul M. Nurse)

我仍然持續在問科學上的問題,儘管它們現在更複雜了,或者至少我用於提問的語言更複雜了。這就引出一個問題,即我認為保持科學興趣的關鍵何在。對我來說,有兩點很重要。第一是對世界保持真正的好奇心,第二是決心為所見現象找出解釋。沒有好奇心和求知欲,對科學的熱情很快就會消失。(保羅‧納斯)

Scientific understanding is often beautiful, a profoundly aesthetic experience which gives pleasure not unlike the reading of a great poem. (Paul M. Nurse)

合乎科學的理解往往很美,是一種深刻的美學體驗,帶給人的愉悅感與閱讀一首偉大的詩無異。(保羅‧納斯)

Most people are not really free. They are confined by the niche in the world that they carve out for themselves. They limit themselves to fewer possibilities by the narrowness. (Vidiadhar Surajprasad Naipaul)

大多數人並不是真正的自由。他們被局限在他們為自己打造的小天地裡。他們把自己限制在狹窄的可能性之中。(V‧S‧奈波爾)

Life doesn't have a neat beginning and a tidy end, life is always going on. You should begin in the middle and end in the middle, and it should be all there. (Vidiadhar Surajprasad Naipaul)

生活沒有清晰的開端和整齊的終點,生活總是在繼續。你應該從中間開始,在中間結束,一切都應該在那裡。(V·S·奈波爾)

Knowledge is power. Information is liberating. Education is the premise of progress, in every society, in every family. (Kofi Annan)

知識就是力量。資訊使人解放。教育是進步的前提,在每一個社會、每一個家庭都是如此。(科菲·安南)

Education is a human right with immense power to transform. On its foundation rest the cornerstones of freedom, democracy and sustainable human development. (Kofi Annan)

教育是具有巨大變革力量的人權。自由、民主和永續人類發展的基石就建立在它的基礎上。(科菲·安南)

It has been said that arguing against globalization is like arguing against the laws of gravity. (Kofi Annan)

有句話說得好,反對全球化就像反對萬有引力定律。(科菲·安南)

Little by little, step by step, women and men of ideas across the centuries and across the continents have wrested from nature a greater understanding of ourselves and also of God's creation. Let that endeavor continue. (George Akerlof)

幾個世紀以來,各個大陸的男女智者一點一點、一步一步地從自然界獲得了對我們本身和上帝創造的更深的理解。願這種努力持續下去。(喬治·阿克洛夫)

The one thing that you could do to make people better off and able to lead self-fulfilling lives was if people have more money then they'll have fewer constraints on their lives, and so they can make more of themselves and lead happier lives. So that was actually another reason for studying economics. (George A. Akerlof)

為了使人們過得更好,能夠擁有自我實現的生活,你所能做的一件事就是,人們如果有更多的錢,人生就會少受一些限制,於是可以更充分地發揮自己,擁有更美好的生活。這其實是學習經濟學的另一個原因。(喬治‧阿克洛夫)

You have to really understand the details and when you understand the details the markets are actually much more interesting than you would otherwise think. (George A. Akerlof)

你必須真正了解細節。一旦了解細節,市場實際上比你以為的有趣得多。(喬治‧阿克洛夫)

I was not thinking about infinite multipliers when I was 10. But I did have a father who was a Ph.D. in commerce and finance and an intellectual man. And so I had a feeling, probably about the time I went to college, that I would try to be a scholar and teacher, but I didn't know which field. (A. Michael Spence)

我並非在 10 歲時就思考著無限倍數。但我確實有個身為商業與金融學博士的學者父親。因此很可能是在上大學的時候,我有種感覺,自己想嘗試成為學者和老師,只是不知道該選擇哪個領域。(麥可‧史彭斯)

The overall effect of my parents upbringing was to provide a great sense of security, being surrounded by love and affection, a great (perhaps too great) sense of self-confidence (there really weren't any challenges that were deemed beyond reach for any reason), and an equally great sense of intellectual adventure, a world populated by opportunities and challenges rather than obstacles and roadblocks. (A. Michael Spence)

　　父母的養育，整體效果是給了我非凡的安全感（被愛和溫情環繞）、非凡的（也許過大的）自信感（實在沒有任何挑戰因為任何原因而被認為遙不可及），和同樣非凡的智力冒險感（一個充滿機遇和挑戰而非艱難險阻的世界）。（麥可‧史彭斯）

　　I picked economics at the end of my undergraduate time because it seemed to be a really nice combination of theory, including mathematical theory on one hand, and things that are quite practical that you can touch and see and feel. So I picked it, and I consciously thought of it as an experiment to see if I liked it. And it worked. (A. Michael Spence)

　　我在大學畢業時選擇了經濟學，因為它看來實在是個很好的理論組合，既包括數學理論，又有一些你可以觸摸、看到和感受到的實用事物。所以我選擇了它，並有意將其作為一次嘗試，看看自己是否喜歡它。而我確實喜歡。（麥可‧史彭斯）

　　I can't imagine people making decisions about what to study on the basis of how much something would contribute to their winning a Nobel Prize or a John Bates Clark Medal. A large amount of winning such prizes is randomness. To win a Nobel you have to be a certified genius, which I am not, or lucky, which I have been. But you can't bet on it, so it doesn't enter into the decision-making. You spend so much time doing this, that if you don't enjoy what you are doing, it just wouldn't work. (A. Michael Spence)

我無法想像人們決定研究課題時，會基於某項研究對其獲得諾貝爾獎或約翰·貝茲·克拉克獎[16]可能發揮多大作用。這些獎項的獲得，大都是隨機的。要獲得諾貝爾獎，你得是個真正的天才，而我不是，或者很幸運，我曾經是。但你不能把賭注押在這個上面，所以它與決策無關。你花這麼多時間研究這項課題，那麼如果你不喜愛所做的事，它就不會成功。（麥可·史彭斯）

The research side of academic life is often viewed from the outside as a solo and at times lonely activity. In fact it is quite the opposite, a communal activity in significant part where interaction and interchange generate ideas and critiques of them. (A. Michael Spence)

學術生活的研究這一方面，常被外界視為單獨行為，有時甚至是孤獨的活動。事實上全然相反，它是群體活動，很大部分為互動和交流產生想法以及對它們的評判。（麥可·史彭斯）

The combination of a workable basic formula and the capacity to improve over time is what one hopes for in any aspect of society: business, government, the non-profit sector. (A. Michael Spence)

可行的基本準則和隨時改進的能力兩者的結合，是商業、政府、非營利部門等社會各方面的人都希望的。（麥可·史彭斯）

One way to measure the size of a company, industry, or economy is to determine its output. But a better way is to determine its added value——namely, the difference between the value of its outputs, that is, the goods and services it produces, and the costs of its inputs, such as the raw materials and energy it consumes. (A. Michael Spence)

---

[16] 約翰·貝茲·克拉克獎是著名的經濟學獎項。史彭斯於1981年獲得該獎。

衡量公司、產業或經濟規模的一種方式是確定其產出。但更好的方式是確定其附加價值——也就是產出價值（即所提供的商品和服務）與投入成本（如原物料和所消耗能源）兩者之間的差額。（麥可・史彭斯）

The facts shouldn't get in the way of a pleasant fantasy. (Joseph E. Stiglitz)

事實不應該妨礙愉快的幻想。（約瑟夫・史迪格里茲）

The notion that every well educated person would have a mastery of at least the basic elements of the humanities, sciences, and social sciences is a far cry from the specialized education that most students today receive, particularly in the research universities. (Joseph E. Stiglitz)

以為每一個受過良好教育的人都至少掌握了人文、科學和社會科學的基本要素，這與當今大多數學生所接受的專業教育，尤其是在研究型大學所接受的教育相去甚遠。（約瑟夫・史迪格里茲）

The best teachers still taught in a Socratic style, asking questions, responding to the answers with still another question. And in all of our courses, we were taught that what mattered most was asking the right question——having posed the question well, answering the question was often a relatively easy matter. (Joseph E. Stiglitz)

最好的老師仍然採用一種蘇格拉底式的教學風格，提出問題，接著以另一個問題作答。而在所有課程中，我們都被教導，最重要的是提出正確的問題——提出好的問題之後，回答問題經常是相對容易的事情。（約瑟夫・史迪格里茲）

I love mathematics, but I decided I really wanted to work on problems of society. (Joseph E. Stiglitz)

我喜歡數學，但我決定真正致力於研究社會問題。（約瑟夫・史迪格里茲）

While I spent most of my time teaching and doing research, I learned a great deal from the limited amount of consulting I did, and I thought it important to engage in issues of public policy. (Joseph E. Stiglitz)

雖然我將大部分時間用於教學與研究，我從有限的諮詢業務中也獲益良多，我認為參與公共政策議題是很重要的。（約瑟夫・史迪格里茲）

Once I undertook the analysis of a problem, I often looked at it from a variety of perspectives. I approached the problem as a series of thought experiments —— unlike many other sciences, we typically cannot do actual experiments. (Joseph E. Stiglitz)

當我著手分析問題時，我常常從各種角度看待它。我將問題視為一系列的思想實驗 —— 與其他許多科學領域不同，我們通常無法做實際上的實驗。（約瑟夫・史迪格里茲）[17]

GDP tells you nothing about sustainability. (Joseph E. Stiglitz)

關於永續性，GDP 什麼都說明不了。（約瑟夫・史迪格里茲）

Growth is not an objective in itself; we should be concerned with standards of living. (Joseph E. Stiglitz)

成長本身不是目標，我們應該關心生活水準。（約瑟夫・史迪格里茲）

Development is about transforming the lives of people, not just transforming economies. (Joseph E. Stiglitz)

---

[17] 史迪格里茲是 2001 年諾貝爾經濟學獎得主。

2001 年

發展不僅是改變經濟,更是改變人們的生活。(約瑟夫·史迪格里茲)

Macroeconomic policy can never be devoid of politics: it involves fundamental trade-offs and affects different groups differently. (Joseph E. Stiglitz)

總體經濟政策永遠不可能缺乏政治:它牽涉基本的權衡,並以不同的方式影響不同的群體。(約瑟夫·史迪格里茲)

Society can't function without shared prosperity. (Joseph E. Stiglitz)

沒有共同繁榮,社會就無法正常運作。(約瑟夫·史迪格里茲)

Some people say we have this inequality because some people have been contributing much more to our society, and so it's fair that they get more. But then you look at the people who are at the top, and you realize they're not the people who have transformed our economy, our society. (Joseph E. Stiglitz)

有些人說,我們之所以有這種不平等,是由於有些人對我們的社會做出了更大的貢獻,因而他們所得更多是公平的。然而看看處於頂端的人,你就會意識到他們並不是改變了我們的經濟、社會的人。(約瑟夫·史迪格里茲)

There have always been two theories about inequality. One is that it reflects just deserts. The other is that there are large elements of exploitation and inequality of opportunities. The evidence is overwhelmingly that the increase in inequality is associated with those negative factors. If it were all social contribution, then when the top did better, they would be contributing to everybody's well-being. That trickle-down hasn't happened. We've seen median income, people in the middle, actually worse off than they were 25 years ago. (Joseph E. Stiglitz)

2001–2010 跨界融合與人文關懷

關於不平等，歷來有兩種理論。一種是，它反映了應得的懲罰。另一種是，存在大量剝削和機會不平等的因素。壓倒性的證據表明，不平等的加劇與這些負面因素有關。如果這一切都攸關社會貢獻，那麼，當頂層的人做得較好時，他們會為每個人的福祉做出貢獻。這種涓滴效應並未發生。我們看到中等收入者，處於中間的人們，實際上過得比 25 年前更差。（約瑟夫‧史迪格里茲）

American inequality didn't just happen. It was created. (Joseph E. Stiglitz)

美國的不平等現象並非偶然發生。它是人為的。（約瑟夫‧史迪格里茲）

2002 年

My first act, on arriving at Brookhaven, was to report to the chairman of the Chemistry Department, Richard Dodson, and ask him what I was expected to do. To my surprise and delight, I was advised to go to the library, do some reading and choose a project of my own, whatever appealed to me. Thus began a long career of doing just what I wanted to do and getting paid for it. In the library, I read a 1948 review paper by H.R. Crane in Reviews of Modern Physics which led me to decide on an experiment in neutrino physics, a field in which little was known at the time, and which seemed well-suited to my background in physical chemistry. (Raymond Davis Jr.)

到了布魯克黑文，我做的第一件事是向化學系主任理查·多德森報到，並問他我需要做什麼。讓我又驚又喜的是，他建議我去圖書館，看看資料，選擇一個自己的項目，不管吸引我的是什麼。一段漫長的職業生涯於是開始了，只做自己想做的事並獲得報酬。在圖書館裡，我讀到了 H.R. 克蘭 1948 年發表於《現代物理評論》上的一篇綜述文章，它讓我決定做一項中微子物理實驗，這個領域當時還鮮為人知，並且看來很適合我的物理化學背景。（小雷蒙德·戴維斯）

I have made some mistakes. No, a lot of mistakes. If you want to develop a new thing, a lot of mistakes will be inevitable. We should be allowed to make mistakes. (Masatoshi Koshiba)

我曾經犯了一些錯。不，很多錯誤。如果你想開發新東西，很多錯誤將是不可避免的。我們應當被允許犯錯。（小柴昌俊）

Science is to do research because of the target's fascinating and interesting characteristics. (Masatoshi Koshiba)

科學就是由於目標迷人有趣的特點而進行的研究。（小柴昌俊）

Science in textbooks is not fun. But if you start doing science yourself, you will find delight. (Masatoshi Koshiba)

教科書中的科學並無趣味。然而自己研究科學的話，你會發現樂趣。（小柴昌俊）

There are cases when it takes 50 or 100 years for fundamental science to achieve results. (Masatoshi Koshiba)

有些情況下，基礎科學需要 50 或 100 年才能獲得成果。（小柴昌俊）

At first, upon learning that we have become Nobel Laureates there is a feeling of personal pride which we share with family and friends. Then the realization hits us that the work for which we are honoured is the result of the cooperative effort of many many people over the years. Finally we feel a sense of continuity with the quest, initiated thousands of years ago for an understanding of the cosmos in which we live. While enormous strides have been made in the last decades, one of the most fundamental questions still have no answers, and so the quest goes on. (Riccardo Giacconi)

起初，得知自己成為諾貝爾獎得主，我們感到自豪，並與家人和朋友分享。隨即我們意識到，自己獲獎的工作是許許多多人歷年共同努力的成果。最後我們體會到，始於數千年前對所處宇宙的探索的延續感。雖然過去幾十年獲得了巨大進步，但最基本的問題之一仍無答案，所以探索還在繼續。（里卡爾多·賈科尼）

Now I, along with others contributing to this project, have been asked to explain how and why we have achieved some success in science. The easy and most truthful, but least satisfying, response to that question is simply: "I don't really know!" In fact, Werner Heisenberg's uncertainty principle, in which most modern scientists believe, asserts the impossibility of predicting in detail the future physical behavior of any particular atom or molecule. The reason is that the very act of interrogating such an individual particle about its behavior inevitably affects that behavior by an uncertain amount. Indeed, one can perceive an analogy to Heisenberg's "uncertainty principle" in Sigmund Freud's concept of the "unconscious mind" by which the behavior of an individual human can be governed by mental processes of which that individual is completely unaware! (John B. Fenn)

> 2002 年

　　現在，我和為這個項目做出貢獻的其他人，被要求解釋我們是如何以及為何在科學上獲得一些成功。對這個問題最簡單也最真實、但最不令人滿意的回答就是：「我真的不知道！」事實上，大多數現代科學家相信維爾納‧海森堡的不確定性原理，斷言不可能詳細預測任何特定的原子或分子未來的物理行為。原因在於，正是詢問個別粒子行為的動作本身，便不可避免地對該行為產生不確定的影響。的確，我們可以在西格蒙德‧弗洛伊德的「潛意識」觀念中，意會出海森堡「不確定性原理」的類比，即個人的行為，可以取決於本人全然不知的心理過程！（約翰‧貝內特‧芬恩）

　　I too became a book-lover like my mother, and from the 5 grade on, was a frequent "customer" of the public library and read an average of three or four books a week till I finished college. One of the earliest books I remember was called Stories of Everyday Wonders out of which my parents would read to me at bedtime. It described and explained the intricate and marvellous systems that supplied the vital components of our lives which we so often take for granted like hot and cold running water, electricity, gas, coal and the blocks of ice that kept food and drink cool before the days of mechanical refrigerators. When I was a about seven or eight, Dad and Mother invested what was for them a considerable sum in a 20 volume encyclopedia for young people entitled The Book of Knowledge. I became so entranced with those books that I often say, without undue exageration, that "I got through college on The Book of Knowledge!" (John B. Fenn)

　　我也跟母親一樣，成為了愛書人。從五年級開始，我就是公共圖書館的常客，平均每週閱讀三到四本書，直到大學畢業。我記憶中最早的書有一本叫《每日奇觀故事》，父母會在我睡前為我讀一些內容。它描述和解釋一些複雜而奇妙的系統，它們為生活提供了十分重要的組成部分，而大家常常認為它們理所當然，比如冷熱水、電、燃氣、煤，以及機械冰箱出現之前讓食物和飲料降溫的冰塊。我七、八歲時，父母拿出對他們來說數量可觀的一筆錢，買了一套 20 卷本的青少年百科全書，名為《知識之書》。我完全被這些書迷住了，經常毫不誇張地說：「我憑《知識之書》讀完了大學！」（約翰・貝內特・芬恩）

When I entered college (with the class of 1938) I had decided to major in Chemistry, probably because of my affection and respect for Julian Capps, Professor of Chemistry. He and his charming wife Hilda, along with our next door neighbors, George and Eleanor Bent, were my parents' closest friends so I got to know Julian very well. He was a great raconteur who could recite Milton and Shakespeare at length. He had a rare sense of humor and an amazing storehouse of knowledge of all kinds, from natural history to soap-making. Any doubts I might have had were swept away in his freshman chemistry course. He was a magnificent teacher who made his subject live, in part because he had worked in industry and could relate the classroom to the real world of both commerce and everyday life, much more convincingly than did any textbook. I really looked forward to going to class, a rare sentiment among today's first year students in chemistry. As now taught in too many universities, introductory chemistry courses have become crucibles in which interest in the subject is cremated rather than ignited. (John B. Fenn)

我上大學（1938 年）時，決定主修化學，多半出於對化學教授朱利安・卡普斯的喜愛和尊敬。他和他迷人的妻子希爾達，還有我們的鄰居本特夫婦喬治和埃莉諾，是我父母最親密的朋友，所以我對朱利安非常了解。他是個極其健談的人，可以詳細地背誦米爾頓和莎士比亞的作品。他具備一種難得的幽默感，擁有豐富得驚人的百科知識，從自然史到肥皂製造。在他的大一化學課上，我可能懷有的任何疑惑都被一掃而空。他是一位傑出的教師，講起課來活潑生動，部分原因是在產業部門工作過，能夠把課堂與現實世界連繫起來，無論商業和日常生活，這比任何教科書都更具有說服力。我真的很期待去上課，這種心情在今天的化學一年級學生中是罕見的。就像如今在許多大學裡所教的那樣，基礎化學課程已經成為熔爐，學生對這門學科的興趣被焚燒殆盡而非點燃。（約翰‧貝內特‧芬恩）

In sum, for me —— and probably for most other people who have been fortunate enough to taste some of the fruit of what passes for success —— it has been my parents and my teachers, from kindergarten on, whom I must salute. They molded the raw material. (John B. Fenn)

總而言之，對我來說 —— 很可能對大多數有幸品嘗過所謂成功果實的人來說也是如此 —— 從幼稚園開始，我就必須向父母和老師致敬。他們打造了毛坯。（約翰‧貝內特‧芬恩）

Forget about your text books, science is fun! The text books are terrible. (John B. Fenn)

忘掉你的課本吧，科學很有趣！課本很糟糕。（約翰‧貝內特‧芬恩）

You ask the average student, why are you going to college? So I get a better job. And ask their parents. Why are you sending your child to college? So he can get a better job. That is entirely the wrong emphasis. They ought to go to college to get educated. To learn how to think. To know what other people have thought. (John B. Fenn)

你問一般學生：為什麼上大學？為了得到較好的工作。再問學生家長：為什麼送孩子上大學？他能得到較好的工作。這是完全錯誤的初衷。他們上大學理應為了受到教育。學會如何思考。了解他人思想。（約翰‧貝內特‧芬恩）

From my father, I learned the importance of working sincerely at things to which I had committed myself, and to persevere untiringly even in the face of little progress. (Koichi Tanaka)

從父親那裡，我領會到盡心做好自己承諾之事的重要性，即便沒什麼進展也堅持不懈。（田中耕一）

I have always thought that I was doing what I desired to do, doing what was interesting to me. However, upon reflecting on my life in this way, it seems that my life is a product of my relationship with such factors as my birth, my family, teachers, friends, companions at work, and even the business world, geographical regions, the natural environment as well as my cultural environment. (Koichi Tanaka)

我一直認為我在做自己想做的事，做自己感興趣的事。然而，這樣反思我的一生，看來我的一生，是自己與種種因素，諸如我的出身，我的家庭、老師、朋友、同事，甚至行業、地域、自然環境乃至文化環境等等之關係的產物。（田中耕一）

Most of the work performed by a development engineer results in failure. However, the occasional visit of success provides just the excitement an engineer needs to face work the following day. (Koichi Tanaka)

開發工程師所做的工作大部分以失敗告終。然而，成功的偶然光顧帶來興奮，那正是工程師第二天面對工作時所需的。（田中耕一）

2002 年

I feel very fortunate that my field of specialization thus leads me to an education in biology from people who have high standards, and who sometimes even tend to consider me as one of their own. (Kurt Wüthrich)

我感到非常幸運，因為我的專業領域使我能夠接受高標準的生物學教育，他們有時甚至傾向於將我視為其中一員。（庫爾特‧維特里希）

From 1970 through 2002, 229 students, postdoctoral research associates, and technical and administrative staff worked with me at the ETH Zürich. I am deeply indebted to all of them for their enthusiasm and dedication. (Kurt Wüthrich)

從 1970 年直到 2002 年，229 名學生、博士後研究同事，以及技術和管理人員，與我在蘇黎世聯邦理工學院合作。我深深感激他們所有人的熱情和奉獻。（庫爾特‧維特里希）

During this time (at high school) I discovered the Public Library... It was here that I found a source of knowledge and the means to acquire it by reading, a habit of learning which I still follow to this day. I also became interested in chemistry and gradually accumulated enough test tubes and other glassware to do chemical experiments, using small quantities of chemicals purchased from a pharmacy supply house. I soon graduated to biochemistry and tried to discover what gave flowers their distinctive colours. I made the (to me) astounding discovery that the pigments I extracted changed their colours when I changed the pH of the solution. (Sydney Brenner)

在這段時間裡（在高中）我發現了公共圖書館。……就是在其中，我找到了知識的來源和以閱讀求知的方法，這種求學習慣我沿用至今。我也對化學產生了興趣，逐漸累積了足夠的試管等玻璃器皿，用從藥局買來的少量化學製劑做化學實驗。我的興趣很快升級到生物化學，試圖揭示是什麼賦予花朵各自的顏色。我得出（對我而言）驚人的發現：當我改變溶液的 pH 值時，我所提取的色素改變了顏色。（西德尼·布瑞納）

Basic research can lead in unexpected ways to insights of substantial practical importance. Time and time again, truly basic studies of simple experimental organisms have proved directly relevant to human biology and human disease. (H. Robert Horvitz)

基礎研究能夠以意想不到的方式，引發具有重大實際意義的深刻見解。一次又一次，針對簡單實驗有機體的純粹基礎研究，已被證明與人類生物學和人類疾病直接相關。（H·羅伯特·霍維茨）

For me, it's been like climbing up from a valley and reaching a col: suddenly you can see new territories, stretching away into the distance, and you wonder. (John E. Sulston)

對我來說，這就像自谷地中攀登，抵達山口：豁然開朗，你看到新的領域，延伸向遠方，令你驚奇。（約翰·蘇爾斯頓）

The important purpose of science is to explore, discover and understand. I'm glad if I've been able to contribute a little to that process, and hugely grateful to all my colleagues, both here and elsewhere, for their achievements and for the fun. And I hope that we can apply our ever increasing knowledge wisely, for the good of all. (John E. Sulston)

科學的重要目的是探索、發現和理解。如果在此過程中有所貢獻，我很高興。我非常感謝所有的同事，無論在場或不在場，感謝大家的成就和樂趣。我希望我們能夠明智地運用不斷累積的知識，造福所有人。（約翰·蘇爾斯頓）

2002 年

From them both I gained a sense that there is not, or need not be, any clear distinction between work and play, and that one has a duty both to serve others and to do the best one can in everything. (John E. Sulston)

從他們身上我理解到,工作和娛樂之間沒有、也無須有明顯區別,而且,每個人都有責任為他人服務,並事事盡力而為。(約翰‧蘇爾斯頓)

A man turns into a writer by editing his own texts. (Imre Kertész)

人以編輯自己的文本而成為作家。(因惹‧卡爾特斯)

A good autobiography is like a document: a mirror of the age on which people can "depend." In a novel, by contrast, it's not the facts that matter, but precisely what you add to the facts. (Imre Kertész)

好的自傳就像一份文獻:一面時代的鏡子,人們可以「以之為鑑」。反之,在小說中,重要的就不是事實,而是你對事實所做的新增。(因惹‧卡爾特斯)

I believe that anyone can be successful in life regardless of natural talent or the environment within which we live. (Jimmy Carter)

我相信,無論自然稟賦或所處環境如何,在生活中人人都可以成功。(吉米‧卡特)

I have one life and one chance to make it count for something… My faith demands that I do whatever I can, wherever I am, whenever I can, for as long as I can with whatever I have to try to make a difference. (Jimmy Carter)

我只有一次生命和一次讓它具有價值的機會。……我的信念要求我盡我所能,無論身在何處,無論何時能夠,但求能以任何自己所具有

的,盡力做出改變。(吉米‧卡特)

We must adjust to changing times and still hold to unchanging principles. (Jimmy Carter)

我們必須適應變化的時代,而仍舊堅持不變的原則。(吉米‧卡特)

Faced with the choice between changing one's mind and proving that there is no need to do so, almost everyone gets busy on the proof. (Daniel Kahneman)

面對改變自己的想法和證明沒有必要這樣做之間的選擇,幾乎每個人都忙於證明。(丹尼爾‧康納曼)

The gorilla study illustrates two important facts about our minds: we can be blind to the obvious, and we are also blind to our blindness. (Daniel Kahneman)

關於我們的心智,大猩猩研究說明了兩個重要的事實:我們可以對顯而易見的事物視而不見,也對自己的盲目視而不見。(丹尼爾‧康納曼)

Don't follow the path of least resistance. (Vernon L. Smith)

不要走阻礙最少的道路。(弗農‧史密斯)

Young people in economics are well advised to read widely outside of economics. (Vernon L. Smith)

建議經濟學領域內的年輕人廣泛閱讀經濟學以外的書籍。(弗農‧史密斯)

2003 年

For me the inspiration was always experiment. Some experimental facts which were strange, could not get an immediate explanation, and so on. These were always my source of inspiration, and I think that only that. Yes, I am very closely connected to experiment. Not mathematics, not models, nothing but experimental data. And so of course after that, what Tony said, the thinking and so on, even sleepless nights, that is of course how it comes. (Alexei A. Abrikosov)

就我而言，靈感始終來自於實驗。一些奇怪的實驗事實，無法得出立即的解釋等等。這些一向是我的靈感來源，我認為唯有如此。是的，我與實驗密切相關。不是數學，不是模型，而是實驗資料。隨後當然同樣還有東尼[18]說的話、反覆思考等等，乃至無眠之夜，這當然是靈感之由來。（阿列克謝‧阿布里科索夫）

Of course, there must be luck, of course, definitely, but there must be also something else. And this else is the knowledge. A person must keep in his brain a lot of, I would say, different knowledge about different materials and so on. He must have that all in his brain, and if he has that so then at the proper moment it will click. (Alexei A. Abrikosov)

當然了，肯定存在運氣，不過肯定還有其他因素。這個其他因素就是知識。我想說，一個人必須在頭腦中保存很多關於不同材料的不同知識等等。他必然把這一切記在腦海中，而如果他的確如此，那麼在適當的時刻就會靈光一閃。（阿列克謝‧阿布里科索夫）

---

[18] 東尼，即安東尼‧萊格特，他與阿布里科索夫同獲 2003 年諾貝爾物理學獎。

Usually one should not divide the problems into small and large problems, because every small problem can become a large problem, or eventually, you know, develop into something. So therefore one must just, if one has a problem, one has to solve it. And that's all. That is the main important thing. (Alexei A. Abrikosov)

通常，人們不應該把問題分成小的和大的問題，因為每個小問題都可能成為大問題，或者最終，你知道的，發展成非同尋常之事。因此，如果遇到問題，就務必得解決它。就是這樣。而這是最重要的事情。（阿列克謝·阿布里科索夫）

All my life, I have felt regret that I do not know languages, that I could know more about this and about that. However, when your work is in progress and there are so many interesting things in it, will you learn verbs or the names of constellations? I for one have never been capable of doing that. (Vitaly L. Ginzburg)

我一生都感到遺憾，自己不懂得多種語言，無法更多地了解紛繁的事物。然而，當你的工作正在展開，其中又有那麼多有趣的事，你還會學習動詞或星座名稱嗎？拿我來說就根本做不到。（維塔利·拉扎列維奇·金茲堡）

No educational institution would make one into a very good writer, physicist, or mathematician, unless he exhibits the corresponding aptitude. However, first, inclinations alone would not suffice. How many talented people never "realized" their potentialities and what role was played by the shortcomings in education? Second, a good background, training, etc. are supposedly able to make a worthy professional out of a person of average abilities, who would otherwise be a drudge, become a failure, find no satisfaction in work, etc. (Vitaly L. Ginzburg)

沒有哪一個教育機構會把一個人培養成優秀的作家、物理學家或數學家,除非他展現相應的天資。然而,首先,僅有傾向是不夠的。有多少不乏才氣的人從未「實現」自己的潛力,教育的缺陷又發揮了什麼作用?其次,良好的背景、訓練等,可能使能力普通的人成為出色的專業人員,而他本來會是個苦力,成為失敗者,在工作中得不到滿足……等等。(維塔利·拉扎列維奇·金茲堡)

A sportsman who covered, say, a 100-m distance in 9.9 seconds to become an Olympic champion and a sprinter who did it in 10.2 seconds proved to be the fourth to miss even the bronze medal (the figures are, of course, arbitrary). Here, random circumstances might have played their part: how he had slept, what he had eaten, how he had pushed off the shoe, etc. Fortunately, in science this is not the case: the lot of the fourth is much better, he makes his contribution, writes good papers (with the understanding that the first writes very good ones). But the role of chance and of good luck may still be critical. This is not so for titans like Einstein, for too large is the "safety margin" and the outstripping of others. The talents of Maxwell, Bohr, Planck, Pauli, Fermi, Heisenberg, and Dirac were scarcely dependent as well on the fluctuations of good luck, accidental idea, etc. De Broglie, and even Schrödinger, were, it seems to me, a different matter, to say nothing of numerous Nobel Laureates. Max von Laue was a well-qualified physicist, but they state that the idea of X-ray diffraction in crystals was a "beer idea" (Bieridee). Braggs, Roentgen, Zeeman, Stark, Lenard, Josephson, Penzias and Wilson, Hewish and Ryle,

Cherenkov, Basov and Prokhorov, as well as 3/4 of the entire list were largely strokes of luck rather than "divine" revelations. I only want to emphasize that chances of success depend both on a lucky strike and a variety of factors, which include health, a timely read article or book, activity, ambition (as a stimulus), and perhaps many other things. An interesting topic. (Vitaly L. Ginzburg)

　　比如，一名運動員以 9.9 秒跑完 100 公尺，成為奧運冠軍；又有一名短跑選手以 10.2 秒跑完同樣距離，結果是第四名，連銅牌都沒拿到（秒數當然是隨口說的）。在這裡，隨機的情況可能發揮了作用：他睡得怎樣、吃了什麼、起跑如何等等。幸運的是，在科學領域並非如此：第四名的命運就好得多，他做出了自己的貢獻，寫出了相當好的論文（如果第一名寫得非常好）。但機會和好運的作用可能仍然是關鍵性的。對於愛因斯坦這樣的巨人不是這樣，因為「安全邊際」太大，遙遙領先。馬克士威、波耳、普朗克、包立、費米、海森堡和狄拉克的才能也幾乎不依賴好運、靈光一閃等因素。德布羅意，甚至薛丁格，在我看來，就是另一回事了，更不用說眾多的諾貝爾獎得主。馬克斯·馮·勞厄是位了不起的物理學家，卻認為晶體中的 X 光線繞射是「荒唐的想法」。布拉格父子、倫琴、塞曼、史塔克、萊納德、約瑟夫森、彭齊亞斯和威爾森、休伊什和賴爾、契忍可夫、巴索夫和普羅霍羅夫，以及整個名單上四分之三的人，相當程度上都受到幸運的眷顧，而非「神」的啟示。我只想強調，成功的機會既取決於一次幸運的眷顧，也取決於各式各樣的因素，包括健康、正好讀到的文章或書籍、活動、抱負（作為一種激勵），或許還有許多其他因素。一個有趣的話題。（維塔利·拉扎列維奇·金茲堡）

A tremendous progress of science has led to its deep internationalization. There is no such thing as American, Russian, Jewish or whatever else national physics. There is only one physics in the world, and when we are speaking, for instance, about British or Russian physics, we only mean the organization or the state of physics in Britain or in Russia… Whereas in the field of the social sciences and the sciences related to them, like sociology, psychology, economics and so on, the true depth and internationalization are still far from being achieved. But, I hope, here also the time of great success is near. Such is one of the factors which enable us, as it seems to me, to look into the future with hope. (Vitaly L. Ginzburg)

科學的巨大進步造成了它的深度國際化。不存在美國、俄羅斯、猶太或諸如此類國家的物理學這種東西。世界上只有一種物理學。當我們說到，例如，英國或俄羅斯物理學的時候，所指只是英國或俄羅斯的物理學組織或狀況。……然而在社會科學及其相關科學的領域，如社會學、心理學、經濟學等，真正的深度和國際化程度還遠未實現。不過，我希望，這方面，大功也即將告成。在我看來，這是使我們能夠滿懷希望、展望未來的因素之一。（維塔利·拉扎列維奇·金茲堡）

I suppose the people who do make big discoveries are ones who somehow manage to free themselves from conventional ways of thinking and to see the subject from a new perspective. (Anthony J. Leggett)

我想，真正做出重大發現的是這樣的人，他們想方設法擺脫傳統的思考方式，從新的角度觀察問題。（安東尼·萊格特）

In the scientific discovery, luck plays an enormous role, but I think one thing one can be fairly sure about is that if you've not been thinking about the problem continuously and perhaps even when you're lying awake at night for some time, perhaps some weeks or even some months, then it's unlikely that you'll get the sudden flash of discovery that makes it work. (Anthony J. Leggett)

在科學發現中，運氣發揮了巨大的作用。然而我認為，可以相當肯定的一件事是，如果你未曾持續不斷思考有關問題，也許以致失眠一時，也許數週乃至數月，那就未必能突然靈光一現而使運氣大行其道。（安東尼・萊格特）

I always find that the main stimulus to theory is some curious experimental result that seems totally outrageous and unnatural. And one tries to understand it⋯ Then if one's lucky, one may be able to make predictions about some experiment which has not been done, one would like it to be done and come out the way you say. (Anthony J. Leggett)

我一再發現，對理論的主要刺激是某些怪異的實驗結果，它顯得完全離譜而反常。於是當事人試圖理解它。⋯⋯而如果夠幸運的話，他也許能夠就某個尚未完成的實驗做出預測，希望這些實驗能被完成並呈現預期的結果。（安東尼・萊格特）

Some of the most stimulating experiments, to a theorist, are those which don't come out as you confidently expected them to. (Anthony J. Leggett)

對於理論家來說，最令人激動的實驗，其結果往往不是像你滿懷信心地預期的那般。（安東尼・萊格特）

As a Nobel Laureate one gets asked many questions, some of them very peculiar indeed, but one frequent question that is quite reasonable is: What advice would you give to a student hoping to embark on a career in theoretical physics?... here it is:

First, if there's something in the conventional wisdom that you don't understand, worry away at it for as long as it takes and don't be deterred by the assurances of your fellow physicists that these questions are well understood.

Secondly, if you find a problem interesting, don't worry too much about whether it has been solved in the existing literature. You will have a lot more fun with it if you don't know, and you will learn a lot, even if what you come up with turns out not to be publishable.

Thirdly, remember that no piece of honestly conducted research is ever wasted, even if it seems so at the time. Put it away in a drawer, and ten, twenty or thirty years down the road, it will come back and help you in ways you never anticipated. (Anthony J. Leggett)

作為諾貝爾獎得主，我接到很多提問。有些確實很特別，而一個經常提出又非常合理的問題是：你會給希望從事理論物理工作的學生提供什麼建議？……如下即是：

第一，如果傳統智慧中有什麼東西你不理解，不安下去好了，隨它持續多久。不要被物理學家同事們的自信嚇住，他們咬定對這些問題理解透澈。

第二，如果發現一個問題有趣，不要過於操心它是否已在現有文獻中得到解決。如果不知道，你會有更多的樂趣，你會學到許多，即便所想出的東西最後發表不了。

第三，切記任何用心從事的研究都非屬徒勞，即便當時看來如此。把它收到抽屜裡去，10年、20年或30年後它會回來，以完全料想不到的方式幫助你。（安東尼·萊格特）

My entry into my eventual career in physics was extremely unorthodox. In fact, at my high school in Britain, I specialized in classical (Greek and Latin) languages and literature, and took no science courses at all. However, after I had obtained a scholarship (in classics) to Oxford University, I had two trimesters to kill at school. At some point in that period I was buttonholed in the corridor by a retired priest who was living on the premises, who had at one time been a university professor of mathematics; noticing that he and I both had time on our hands, he volunteered to give me a couple of hours' informal tuition a week in modern mathematics. Although at that time I had no inkling that I would ever need any such thing, I found to my initial surprise that not only could I do the problems he set me but that I rather enjoyed doing them. That early experience was, in retrospect, probably the turning point in my career.

The course I followed at Oxford was a four-year one; for the first five trimesters one studies classical languages and literature, then for the last seven an equal mix of "ancient" (Greek and Roman) history and philosophy. The philosophy component of the course is mainly modern, and I enjoyed it very much and did well on it (as well as on the ancient history); and one obvious choice of career was to go on to do a doctorate in philosophy and eventually try to become a faculty member in that subject. However, as I started, towards the end of my third year, to contemplate this prospect, I began to realize that somehow it was not what I really wanted to do in life. On the other hand, the prospect of an academic career was in the abstract very attractive. I therefore started to try to analyse exactly what it was about a career in philosophy that I found unattractive. And the answer I eventually came up with was that it was because, at least as the subject was practiced in Oxford in those days, what counted as good or bad work in philosophy seemed to be so much a matter of fashion, and of the exact nuances of one's phrasing; there seemed to be no objective, external criterion of whether what one did had any validity, and I felt in my bones that it was just such a criterion that I wanted. I did briefly contemplate going into pure mathematics, but rejected it on the grounds that in that subject, by its very nature, to be wrong means to be stupid; I wanted the possibility of being wrong without being stupid, and physics seemed to offer just that opportunity. So I applied to do a second undergraduate degree in physics, and after some vicissitudes was accepted and launched my new career.

I don't think I have been disappointed; over the last 40 years I have been able to make a string of nontrivial conjectures about various parts of the physical world, and some of them have turned out to be wrong but hopefully not stupid (they are the ones you don't hear about), while others have apparently been shown by experiment to be along the right lines (and in one case have been recognized by the award of the Nobel Prize). Right or wrong, it is just this confrontation of my theoretical ideas with real-world experiments which I find infinitely exciting, and which has kept me going in physics; I have never regretted the choice I made. (Anthony J. Leggett)

我最終進入物理學職業生涯的過程極不正統。事實上，我在英國上高中時，專門學習古典（希臘語和拉丁語）語言與文學，完全沒讀過科學課程。不過，在獲得牛津大學古典文學獎學金後，我有兩個學期要在學校逗留。那段時間中有一天，在走廊裡，我被一位退休牧師拉住了。他住在這裡，曾任大學數學教授。注意到我和他都有大把的時間，他主動提出，每週非正式地為我講幾個小時現代數學。雖然當時沒有任何跡象表明自己會需要任何這種東西，我起初驚訝地發現，自己不僅能夠做他為我設定的問題，而且相當享受。早年的那段經歷，回想起來，很可能是我事業的轉捩點。在牛津，我學的是一門四年的課程。前五個學期學習古典語言和文學，後七個學期一併學習「古代」（希臘和羅馬）歷史和學分相當的哲學。這門課的哲學部分主要是現代的，我非常喜歡它，並且學得很好（古代史學得也不錯）；一個明顯的職業選擇是繼續攻讀哲學博士，並最終爭取這一科的教職。然而，接近第三年年底，考慮起這個前景時，我開始意識到，不知何故，這不是我一生中真正想做的事。另一方面，學術生涯的前景，抽象說來倒是非常吸引人。因而，我開始試著釐清，自己覺得哲學職業缺乏吸引力是怎麼回事。

我最終找出的原由為，至少作為當時牛津的研究課題，對哲學工作成果的考量，似乎更多地關乎時尚風氣，關乎咬文嚼字；對研究效果似乎沒有客觀的、外在的衡量標準，而我本能地覺得這正是我想要的標準。我確實短暫地考慮投身於純數學研究，不過仍舊否定了，理由為在這門學科中，其性質決定，出錯就意味著愚蠢；我想要出錯而不算愚蠢的可能性，而物理學看來正好提供了這種機會。於是我申請攻讀物理學的第二個學士學位。幾經周折，我被錄取並開始了新事業。

我想自己並沒有失望。過去40年裡，我已經能夠就物理世界各個領域提出一系列不平常的推論，其中一些結果是出了錯但希望不算愚蠢（都是諸位所不曾聞知的），而另一些顯然被實驗證明思路正確（且有一例已由諾貝爾獎認可）。無論對錯，正是自己的理論設想與現實世界的實驗這種印證，讓我感到無比振奮，促使我在物理學之路上不斷前行。我

2003 年

從未後悔自己做出的選擇。（安東尼・萊格特）

Written in 1895, Alfred Nobel's will endowed prizes for scientific research in chemistry, physics, and medicine. At that time, these fields were narrowly defined, and researchers were often classically trained in only one discipline. In the late 19th century, knowledge of science was not a requisite for success in other walks of life. (Peter Agre)

阿佛烈・諾貝爾立於西元 1895 年的遺囑，為化學、物理學和醫學方面的科學研究提供獎金。在那個時代，這些領域界定狹窄，研究人員往往古板地受到僅屬單科的訓練。在 19 世紀晚期，科學知識並非在各行各業獲得成功的必要條件。（彼得・阿格雷）

It is a remarkable honor to receive a Nobel Prize, because it not only recognizes discoveries, but also their usefulness to the advancement of fundamental science. (Peter Agre)

獲得諾貝爾獎是一種非凡的榮譽，因為它所認可的不僅是各種發現，還有它們對基礎科學的促進作用。（彼得・阿格雷）

In my whole life since my kids became teen-agers, this is the first time they've come home and said, "Dad, my friends think this is so cool." (Peter Agre)

此生自從我的孩子成為青少年，這還是他們第一次回家說：「爸爸，我的朋友們認為這太酷了。」（彼得・阿格雷）

I didn't do this work; the young people in the lab did it. I just made the coffee and sharpened the pencils. (Peter Agre)

我沒做這項工作，是實驗室裡的年輕人做的。我只是煮了咖啡，削了鉛筆。（彼得・阿格雷）

Chemistry was my worst subject in high school! I imagined my chemistry teacher aspirating his cornflakes when he found out his worst student had won the Nobel Prize! (Peter Agre)

化學是我在高中學得最差的科目！我想，當我的化學老師發現他最差的學生得了諾貝爾獎時，他會驚奇得被口中的玉米片嗆到！（彼得‧阿格雷）

I always say to my students that being a scientist is like being an explorer, and I really mean that because, in a sense, I think in science we explore the world, the universe around us. (Roderick MacKinnon)

我總是對學生說，當科學家就像當探險家。我的意思是，在一定意義上，我認為在科學中我們探索的是世界，我們周圍的宇宙。（羅德里克‧麥金農）

Just take a risk. Go for it. I think if you crash and burn trying, it's still going to be better than if you never tried at all. (Roderick MacKinnon)

就冒一下險。去吧。我認為就算你的嘗試徹底失敗，也勝過試都沒試。（羅德里克‧麥金農）

I always say, "Let your experiment speak to you." What I mean by that is I —— actually, we, or, at least, I'm not smart enough, actually, to guess how nature is working, but by looking and doing the right experiments and paying close attention to the subtleties of it, you start to catch on. (Roderick MacKinnon)

我總是說：「讓實驗告訴你。」這句話的意思為，我 —— 實際上是我們，或者至少是我，實際上並未聰明到足以推測大自然的運作方式，不過藉助觀察和進行適當的實驗，並密切注意其細微之處，你就會開始明白。（羅德里克‧麥金農）

2003 年

Working with membrane proteins was very difficult as expected. We had our periods of despair, but every time we felt left without options something good happened and despair gave way to excitement. Persistence and dedication eventually paid off. (Roderick MacKinnon)

與膜蛋白打交道，不出所料地極其困難。絕望的時期一再出現。不過每逢山窮水盡，總會峰迴路轉，絕望也讓位於興奮。堅持不懈和奉獻精神終於得到回報。（羅德里克·麥金農）

My parents provided a happy environment and made their expectations clear to us. Television is bad for you, reading is good for you, and you better get an A for effort in school. What you end up doing in life is up to you. Just make sure you enjoy what you do because then you will do it well. We all pursued completely different walks of life. I became the scientist. (Roderick MacKinnon)

我們的父母提供了快樂的環境，並使我們清楚了他們的期望。電視對你有害，閱讀對你有益，但願你在學校裡盡力做到最好。生活中的作為取決於你自己。確保喜歡自己所做的事，因為這樣就會做得好。我們選擇了完全不同的行業。我成了科學家。（羅德里克·麥金農）

I suppose there were some early indications of my tendency to a life of curiosity. Apparently from a very young age I had a habit of asking lots of questions: "what would happen if …?" was a favorite. (Roderick MacKinnon)

我想，有些早期跡象表明，自己傾向於充滿好奇心的生活。顯然，從很小的時候起，我就養成了問許多問題的習慣，「要是……會怎麼樣」是最喜歡的一個。（羅德里克·麥金農）

I was a daydreamer. Teachers kept telling me to pay attention. (Roderick MacKinnon)

我是一個愛做白日夢的人。老師們總是提醒我注意聽講。（羅德里克·麥金農）

What you end up doing in life is up to you. Just make sure you enjoy what you do because then you will do it well. (Roderick MacKinnon)

你一生最終做什麼取決於自己。只須確保喜愛自己所做之事，因為這樣你就會把它做好。（羅德里克·麥金農）

Some people look at big things, and other people look at very small things, but in a sense, we're all trying to understand the world around us. (Roderick MacKinnon)

有些人著眼於大的事物，另一些人則著眼於非常小的事物，然而在一定意義上，我們都在力圖了解周圍的世界。（羅德里克·麥金農）

You hear a lot of scientists say the same thing. It doesn't have to be a big thing because the thing about being a scientist is even the little things are big things to us. (Roderick MacKinnon)

你會聽到許多科學家說同樣的話。它不一定是大事，因為身為科學家，即便是小事對我們來說也是大事。（羅德里克·麥金農）

I wanted to be free to try any silly thing I decided to do. (Paul C. Lauterbur)

我想自由地嘗試任何自己決定做的傻事。（保羅·勞特伯）

There's a saying among scientists, that you don't know you've got a really good idea until at least three Nobel laureates have told you it's wrong. (Paul C. Lauterbur)

科學家之間流傳著一個說法：在至少三位諾貝爾獎得主告訴你它是錯的之前，你還不知道這個想法是否真正的好。（保羅‧勞特伯）

You could write the entire history of science in the last 50 years in terms of papers rejected by Science or Nature. (Paul C. Lauterbur)

你可以根據被《科學》或《自然》[19]拒絕的論文撰寫過去 50 年的科學史。（保羅‧勞特伯）

Every great idea in history has the fat red stamp of rejection on its face. It's hard to see because, once ideas gain acceptance, we gloss over the hard paths they took to get there. If you scratch any innovation's surface, you'll find the scars: they've been roughed up and thrashed around by both the masses and the leading minds before they made it in to your life. (Paul C. Lauterbur)

歷史上每種非凡的想法都曾被蓋上大大的紅色拒絕印章。這很難看出來，因為想法一旦獲得接納，我們就會掩飾它們問世的艱難歷程。揭開任何創新的表面，你都會發現累累傷痕：它們在得以進入你的生活之前，曾受到大眾與權威人物的兩面夾攻。（保羅‧勞特伯）

With luck, you have other things to do than wait for lightning to strike. (Paul C. Lauterbur)

說到運氣，除了等待閃電迸發，你還有別的事情要做。（保羅‧勞特伯）

If it doesn't seem possible, nothing much gets done. (Paul C. Lauterbur)

若非看似可能，幾乎無事可成。（保羅‧勞特伯）

---

[19] 《科學》、《自然》，均為國際頂尖科技期刊。

2001-2010 跨界融合與人文關懷

None of the work in MRI could have been achieved without the enthusiasm and dedicated support of a highly motivated team of technical and academic staff, research students and post-docs sustained over the period from 1972 —— to the present day. (Peter Mansfield)

技術和學術人員、研究學者及博士後研究員，組成了一個高度進取的團隊。如果沒有他們的積極熱忱和全力支持，自1972年持續至今，在磁共振成像技術中，沒有任何工作能夠完成。（彼得‧曼斯菲爾德）

Truth is not spoken in anger. Truth is spoken, if it ever comes to be spoken, in love. The gaze of love is not deluded. It sees what is best in the beloved even when what is best in the beloved finds it hard to emerge into the light. (John M. Coetzee)

真理不是在憤怒中說出的。真理若要被說出，就必須用愛來表達。愛的凝視並不會被矇蔽。它看到了所愛之人最好的東西，即便這種東西很難展現出來。（約翰‧馬克斯維爾‧庫切）

To bring change to the world we have to bring change to ourselves. (Shirin Ebadi)

為了改變世界，我們得改變自己。（希林‧伊巴迪）

What is important is that one utilizes one's intellect and not to be 100 percent sure about one's convictions. One should always leave room for doubt. (Shirin Ebadi)

重要的是運用自己的才智，而非百分之百地堅持自己的信念。人應當總是為懷疑留出餘地。（希林‧伊巴迪）

I find myself reflecting with great affection on smaller, perhaps less dramatic, moments. These are moments of insight; moments that started a new research topic or recognized a connection between things previously thought to be distinct. (Robert F. Engle III)

我發現自己懷著極大的熱情深入思考那些不太重要的、也許不是很起眼的瞬間。這些是洞察的時刻，它們開啟了新的研究課題，或者理解到先前以為截然不同的事物之間的連繫。（羅伯特·F·恩格爾）

Looking back now, one might think that new ideas are easy to publish. At least for me, they are not. It took quite a bit of rewriting and persuading to finally get it accepted in Econometrica. In fact, I don't think that any of my papers have had an easy time of it! (Robert F. Engle III)

如今回顧起來，人們可能以為新的想法容易發表。至少就我而言，它們不是。需要反覆的重寫和說服，才使之最終得以被《計量經濟學》所採用。事實上，我認為自己的任何論文發表都毫不輕鬆！（羅伯特·F·恩格爾）

When I am skating, economics is far away. I always return refreshed and ready to carry on. (Robert F. Engle III)

當我溜冰的時候，經濟學就遠離了我。我總是精神煥發地返回，準備好接著工作。（羅伯特·F·恩格爾）

I went to a local primary school, did well in mathematics but not much else. A teacher told my mother that "I would never become successful," which illustrates the difficulties of long-run forecasting on inadequate data. (Clive W.J. Granger)

我在當地一所小學上學，數學成績還不錯，其他就乏善可陳了。一名老師告訴我母親，我「永遠不會學有所成」。這展現了資料不充分的情況下進行長期預測之困難。（克萊夫·格蘭傑）

I think it is true to say that I am not the first Nobel Prize winner in economics to have little formal training in economics. (Clive W. J. Granger)

我想我不是第一個沒有接受過多少正規經濟學訓練的諾貝爾經濟學獎得主。（克萊夫·格蘭傑）

A recipe for success. Do not start too high on the ladder, move to a good but not top university, work hard, have a few good ideas, chose good collaborators (I had over eighty in my career), attract some excellent students, wait twenty years or so, and then retire. (Clive W.J. Granger)

成功的祕訣：起點不要太高，進入一所很好但非頂尖的大學，努力工作，有些好想法，選擇好的合作者（我在職業生涯中有 80 多位），吸引一些優秀的學生，等上 20 年左右，然後退休。（克萊夫·格蘭傑）

2004 年

Fortunately, nature is as generous with its problems as Nobel with his fortune. The more we know, the more aware we are of what we know not. (David J. Gross)

幸運的是，大自然對其問題，跟諾貝爾對其財富同樣地慷慨。我們知道得越多，就越意識到自己所不知道的東西。（大衛·葛羅斯）

From the age of 13, I was attracted to physics and mathematics. My interest in these subjects derived mostly from popular science books that I read avidly. Early on I was fascinated by theoretical physics and determined to become a theoretical physicist. I had no real idea what that meant, but it seemed incredibly exciting to spend one's life attempting to find the secrets of the universe by using one's mind. (David J. Gross)

從13歲起,我就被物理和數學吸引。我對這兩科的興趣主要來自科普圖書,我如飢似渴地閱讀它們。我很早就被理論物理學迷住了,決心當個理論物理學家。我並不真正清楚這意味著什麼,但一輩子動腦筋尋求宇宙的奧祕,這似乎令人興奮異常。(大衛・葛羅斯)

The progress of science is much more muddled than is depicted in most history books. This is especially true of theoretical physics, partly because history is written by the victorious. Consequently, historians of science often ignore the many alternate paths that people wandered down, the many false clues they followed, the many misconceptions they had. These alternate points of view are less clearly developed than the final theories, harder to understand and easier to forget, especially as these are viewed years later, when it all really does make sense. Thus reading history one rarely gets the feeling of the true nature of scientific development, in which the element of farce is as great as the element of triumph. (David J. Gross)

科學的進步比大多數史書所描述的混亂得多。理論物理學尤其如此,部分原因是因為歷史是由勝利者書寫的。所以,科學史學家經常忽略人們徘徊過的許多其他路徑、追隨過的許多不實線索、持有過的許多錯誤觀念。與最終的理論相比,這些不同的觀點發展得不是那麼清晰,比較難以理解,比較易於被淡忘,尤其是在多年後回顧,這一切真正變得有意義之時。於是,閱讀歷史,人們極少感受到科學發展的本質,其中鬧劇的成分與勝利的成分同樣多。(大衛・葛羅斯)

The neat, linear progress, as outlined by the sequence of gleaming gems recognized by Nobel Prizes, is a useful fiction. But a fiction it is. The truth is often far more complicated. Of course, there are the oft-told priority disputes, bickering over who is responsible for some particular idea. But those questions are not only often unresolvable, they are often rather meaningless. Genuinely independent discovery is not only possible, it occurs all the time. Sometimes a yet harder problem in the prize selection process is to identify what is the essential or most important idea in some particular, broader context. So it's not just a question of who did it, i.e., who is responsible for the work, but what "it" is. I.e., what is the significant "it" that should stand as a symbol for a particularly important advance. (H. David Politzer)

就像諾貝爾獎所認可的，彷彿由成串閃光寶石所勾勒出的一連串簡潔的、線性的進步，是一種實用的說法。但它只是一種說法。真相往往複雜得多。當然，也經常存在優先權之爭，為某個特定想法歸功於誰而爭執。但這些問題往往不僅無從解決，而且並無意義。真正獨立的發現不僅是可能的，而且一直都在產生。有時候，在諾貝爾獎遴選過程中，一個更加困難的問題是，認定在某些特定的、更廣闊的背景下，最本質或最重要的想法是什麼。所以問題不只是誰完成的，即成就歸功於誰，而是「它」是什麼。即，意義重大的、應當作為一大進步之象徵的「它」是什麼。（休‧波利策）

Newton said, "I know not how I appear to the world, but to myself I appear like a boy on a beach who came upon some particularly beautiful pebbles, while the great ocean of the unknown lay before me." So he realized that he understood some things very well, and he understood what it meant to really understand something, but part of that is realizing that you don't understand a lot of things. And there's a profound humility that comes from really understanding something, because then you understand what it means to really understand something. And you realize how much is missing that is different. (Frank Wilczek)

牛頓說:「我不知道在世人看來我是怎樣的,不過在我自己看來,我就像海灘上的一個孩子,偶然遇見一些特別美麗的鵝卵石,而浩瀚的未知之海在前方展開。」所以他意識到自己非常了解某些事,也了解真正理解某件事的意義,但部分原因是他意識到自己不了解很多事。真正理解某件事會令人產生深刻的謙卑感,因為這時你明白真正了解一件事意味著什麼。然後你理解到錯過了多少不同的事。(弗朗克・韋爾切克)

We humans have the fate —— which is a gift —— that we can get beyond the limitations that nature imposed, that evolution imposed on us. We really can get beyond that by thought. We have the gift of being able to understand things and go deeper and get beyond common perceptions. We can use instruments. We can use logic. We can learn from each other and traditions, and there are many surprises that get revealed. And it just enormously deepens life to participate in that. (Frank Wilczek)

我們人類有這種命運 —— 這是天分 —— 能夠超越自然及演化所強加於我們的局限。我們的確能夠經由思考超越這一點。我們有天分得以了解事物,逐漸深入,超越普遍的認知。我們能夠運用儀器。我們能夠運用邏輯。我們能夠從彼此及傳統中學習,還會發現許多驚喜。參與其中實在是極大地增加了生命的深度。(弗朗克・韋爾切克)

In theoretical physics, paradoxes are good. That's paradoxical, since a paradox appears to be a contradiction, and contradictions imply serious error. But Nature cannot realize contradictions. When our physical theories lead to paradox we must find a way out. Paradoxes focus our attention, and we think harder. (Frank Wilczek)

在理論物理中,悖論是好的。這是互相牴觸的,因為悖論看起來屬於矛盾,而矛盾意味著嚴重錯誤。但大自然無法實現矛盾。當物理理論導致悖論時,我們必須找到出路。悖論使我們集中注意力,令我們更深入地思考。(弗朗克・韋爾切克)

I've always loved all kinds of puzzles, games, and mysteries. (Frank Wilczek)

我一直鍾愛各式各樣的謎題、遊戲和難解現象。(弗朗克・韋爾切克)

I try to avoid hard work. When things look complicated, that is often a sign that there is a better way to do it. (Frank Wilczek)

我盡量避免辛苦工作。當事情看起來很複雜時,通常表示存在更好的解決辦法。(弗朗克・韋爾切克)

My immediate plan I think is to… after I talk to you… is to hang up the phone, ignore other phone calls and take a walk, take a long walk, and try to clear my head. And then I'll have a plan. (Frank Wilczek)

我想我目前的計畫是……與你談完話之後……掛斷電話,不理會其他電話,出去走走,走很長一段路,盡量清醒頭腦。然後就會有一個計畫。[20](弗朗克・韋爾切克)

---

[20] 維爾切克獲獎後接受電話採訪時說的話。

> 2004 年

I arrived at the University of Chicago with great but amorphous ambitions. I flirted with brain science, but soon decided that the central questions were not ready for mathematical treatment (and that I lacked the patience for laboratory work). I read voraciously in many subjects, but wound up majoring in mathematics, largely because doing that gave me the most freedom. (Frank Wilczek)

我懷著遠大而並不甚明確的抱負進入芝加哥大學。我曾經對腦科學有些興趣，但很快便發現其核心問題仍不適合用數學方法處理（我對實驗室工作也缺乏耐心）。我如飢似渴地廣泛閱讀，不過最終選定了數學專業，主要是因為研究數學給予我最大的自由。（弗朗克·韋爾切克）

I know enough about Nobel Prize-winning physicists to know that they come in all shapes and sizes. They don't have all that much in common, not even intelligence. But, yeah, but all of them have in common a certain kind of honesty and a certain kind of community, and they've all contributed in some significant way to human knowledge and culture and understanding. (Frank Wilczek)

我熟知獲得諾貝爾獎的物理學家，知道他們長相不同、身形各異。他們根本沒有多少共同之處，甚至智力上也沒有。然而，是的，他們全體共同具有一種真誠，一種社會性，他們都以某一種重大的方式，對人類的知識、文化和理解做出了貢獻。（弗朗克·韋爾切克）

Don't call it a failure, call it a lesson. (Aaron Ciechanover)

不要稱之為失敗，而是稱之為教訓。（阿龍·切哈諾沃）

You are not going to be successful if you don't like what you do. (Aaron Ciechanover)

你如果不喜歡所做的事，就不會成功。（阿龍·切哈諾沃）

During my medical studies I studied biochemistry. That was one of the subjects that every medical student studies, so I liked it very much. I liked, you know, the whole concept of biochemistry, of looking for chemical processes in cells, so we had, we could take off one year from the studies to spend in research in the lab. I also found a very good teacher, Jacob Mager, and I wanted to spend it with him, so I did. That's how I got involved in biochemistry. Afterwards, I finished my medical studies but already, I, after that one year, I knew that I will go to biochemistry and not to practical medicine. That's how I started. So, it's, it's, like all things in life, it starts by some kind of accident or so, that was the accident, I met a subject during my studies that I liked. (Aaron Ciechanover)

學習醫學期間，我學習了生物化學。這是醫學必修課之一，而我非常喜歡它。我喜歡，你們知道，生物化學的整體概念，即在細胞中尋找化學過程。我們可以抽出一年的時間，在實驗室中做研究。我還找到了一位非常好的老師，雅各布·馬傑，我想跟著他學習，於是就這麼做了。這就是我涉足生物化學領域的開端。後來，我完成了醫學學業，不過在那一年之後，我很清楚自己將從事生物化學而非實用醫學。我就是這樣開始的。所以，就像人生中所有的事情一樣，以某種偶然事件開始，這就是意外，我在學習中遇到了一個自己喜歡的學科。（阿龍·切哈諾沃）

I never think of winning a Nobel Prize nor assume I would be. I love taking risks. From selecting my tutors and universities to doing researches around the world, I improved little by little. I work in a team, and we will discuss together and learn from the lessons we had. At the end of the day, we are rewarded the Nobel Prize. (Aaron Ciechanover)

我從沒打算獲得諾貝爾獎,也未曾設想過。我喜歡冒險。從選擇導師和大學,到在世界各地做研究,我一點一滴地進步。我在團隊中工作,我們會一起討論,從經驗中學習。結果,我們獲得了諾貝爾獎。(阿龍‧切哈諾沃)

Success is not defined by winning a Nobel Prize, but having an impact on the world. You can be a teacher, engineer, dancer, painter, conductor of orchestra, writer and so on. (Aaron Ciechanover)

成功的定義不是獲得諾貝爾獎,而是對世界產生影響。你可以成為教師、工程師、舞蹈家、畫家、樂隊指揮、作家等等。(阿龍‧切哈諾沃)

The important thing is to do what you most love in the best way. If you love literature, you could be a great writer and perhaps one day become a Nobel Prize Laureate for Literature. (Aaron Ciechanover)

重要的是以最好的方式做最喜歡的事情。如果熱愛文學,你可以當個了不起的作家,說不定有一天會成為諾貝爾文學獎得主。(阿龍‧切哈諾沃)

Biochemistry is the science of life. All our life processes —— walking, talking, moving, feeding —— are essentially chemical reactions. So biochemistry is actually the chemistry of life, and it's supremely interesting. (Aaron Ciechanover)

生物化學是生命的科學。我們所有的生命過程 —— 行走、說話、活動、進食 —— 本質上都是化學反應。所以生物化學實際就是生命的化學,它極其有趣。(阿龍‧切哈諾沃)

We are a country that lacks riches. The Jewish brain, that's what we have. Everything that we've had and will have in this country is the direct and clear product of higher education. If we harm this system, we will drastically decline and cease to exist. (Aaron Ciechanover)

我們是個缺乏財富的國家。猶太人頭腦，這就是我們的所有。我們在這個國家已有和將有的一切，都是高等教育直接且明確的產物。我們如果破壞這個系統，就會大幅度衰退乃至消亡。（阿龍·切哈諾沃）

Science and technology are now the driving forces behind Israel's economic growth, but there can be no effective education in these fields without a corresponding investment of effort and resources in the study of the tradition, history, and archaeology of the Jewish people in Israel and the diaspora. Science and technology are universal subjects, independent of nationality, and one can study them and excel at them anywhere in the world. Israel is certainly not the best place to learn or build a career in these professions. Thus, anyone wanting to learn and apply them in Israel must do so out of a sense of national responsibility and a desire to contribute to the advancement of his country. Therefore, he needs to grow up in an atmosphere in which it is clear to him why he must study and work here and not somewhere else. (Aaron Ciechanover)

科學技術如今是以色列經濟成長背後的驅動力。然而，若沒有相應的努力和資源，以研究以色列及海外猶太人的傳統、歷史和考古學，就不可能形成這些領域的有效教育。科學技術是世界性學科，不受國家限制，在世界任何地方都可以鑽研並出眾。以色列當然不是學習或從事這些專業的最佳處所。因此，任何想要在以色列學習和應用它們的人，都必須出於國家責任感和為國家進步做出貢獻的願望。所以，他需要在這樣的氛圍中成長：他很清楚，自己為什麼必須在這裡學習和工作，而不是在其他地方。（阿龍・切哈諾沃）

I try hope that in the end, we will live in a cancer-free world. We want to live disease-free lives. (Aaron Ciechanover)

我衷心期望總有一天，我們會生活在沒有癌症的世界。我們想過沒有疾病的生活。（阿龍・切哈諾沃）

We each have a very different background, as well as very different personalities and talents. Perhaps, I may best describe myself as being intuitive and persistent, Ernie Rose as analytical and sharply critical and Aaron Ciechanover as a person of immense energies. It took the complementing talents and cumulative efforts of the three of us, together with huge efforts by dedicated research groups in Haifa and Philadelphia, building upon an important background of prior research, to reach the critical mass that resulted in the breakthrough in the research and the discovery of the ubiquitin system 25 years ago. (Avram Hershko)

我們每個人都有非常不同的背景，也有非常不同的個性和天賦。也許，我可以最好地形容自己為直覺敏銳和執著的人，歐文・羅斯善於分析且具批判力，阿龍・切哈諾沃則是個能量極大的人。由於我們三人互補的才能和累積的努力，加上海法和費城專門研究團隊的巨大付出，在前人研究的重要基礎之上，方才諸事齊備，造就研究上的突破和25年前泛素系統的發現。（阿夫拉姆・赫什科）

The discovery of this biochemical pathway has been recognized by awarding of the Nobel Prize in Chemistry, even though its implications are primarily in the biomedical sciences and hopefully, in the treatment or prevention of human diseases in the future. However, the boundaries between chemistry, biology, physics and medicine are rapidly disappearing. Only a comprehensive understanding of the chemical and physical processes in our cells and organ systems, will yield the insights needed to develop rational approaches to the prevention and treatment of disease. (Avram Hershko)

這一項生物化學途徑的發現已由諾貝爾化學獎的授予所認可，儘管它主要影響生物醫學科學，也大有希望影響未來人類疾病的治療或預防。然而，化學、生物學、物理學和醫學之間的界限正在迅速消失。為了獲得預防與治療疾病的合理方法，唯有對我們細胞和器官系統中化學和物理過程的全面了解，才會產生所需的洞察力。（阿夫拉姆·赫什科）

Initially, I thought problems on how the brain works to be the most interesting. But it was necessary to be practical and concentrate on less obscure matters when I entered Washington State College. Besides, there were no courses given in neurobiology. (Irwin Rose)

起初，我認為關於人腦如何工作的問題最有趣。但進入華盛頓州立大學時，有必要講究實際，而專注於不那麼深奧的問題。此外，學校也沒有神經生物學的課程。（歐文·羅斯）

I never wanted to work with a mentor, because I always wanted to have my own reputation and be free to do what I wanted to do. (Irwin Rose)

我從來不想跟導師一起工作，因為我一直想要擁有自己的聲譽，自由地做自己想做的事。（歐文·羅斯）

I think we all work all day and all night long. I do. I don't have any hobbies, you know, I'm very embarrassed when people ask me what are my hobbies, I don't have any hobbies. I mean, it's just enough to keep up with the things I'm trying to solve. (Irwin Rose)

我想我們全都是沒日沒夜地工作。我是這樣的。我什麼嗜好都沒有，你知道，當人們問起我的嗜好時，我會非常尷尬，我沒有任何嗜好。我的意思是，時間只夠應付正在努力解決的問題。（歐文‧羅斯）

This evening Linda Buck and I received a medal which is inscribed with three words, Creavit et promovit. He created and he promoted. The words do not honor us. They honor the vision of Alfred Nobel, the Nobel Prize that importantly encourages the freedom to acquire knowledge. This freedom cannot be taken lightly. (Richard Axel)

今天晚上，琳達‧巴克和我獲得了獎章，上面有三個詞：Creavit et promovit（他創造並促進）。這句話不是推崇我們的。推崇的是阿佛烈‧諾貝爾的願景，諾貝爾獎極力推動獲取知識的自由。這種自由不可等閒視之。（理察‧阿克塞爾）

Émile Zola asked in an address to students, "Did science promise happiness? No, I don't think so," he replied. "It promised truth and the question is whether truth will ever make us happy." Last month, science afforded me enormous happiness. (Richard Axel)

在對學生們的一次演說中，埃米爾‧左拉自問自答：「科學帶來了快樂嗎？不，我不這麼認為。它帶來了真理，而問題在於真理究竟會不會使我們快樂。」上個月，科學為我帶來了無比的快樂。（理察‧阿克塞爾）

My clinical competence was immediately recognized by the faculty and deans. I could rarely, if ever, hear a heart murmur, never saw the retina, my glasses fell into an abdominal incision and finally, I sewed a surgeon's finger to a patient upon suturing an incision… I was allowed to graduate medical school early with an M.D. if I promised never to practice medicine on live patients. I returned to Columbia as an intern in Pathology where I kept this promise by performing autopsies. After a year in Pathology, I was asked by Don King, the Chairman of Pathology, never to practice on dead patients. (Richard Axel)

教師和系主任們馬上見識了我的臨床能力。我幾乎聽不到心臟雜音，從來沒找到視網膜，我的眼鏡掉進一個腹部切口，最後，我在縫合切口時把一位醫生的手指縫到了病人身上……我獲准以醫學博士學位從醫學院提前畢業，只要承諾永遠不在活體病人身上行醫。我回到哥倫比亞大學擔任病理學實習生，在那裡我以只做屍檢，履行了承諾。學了一年病理學之後，唐‧金，病理學系主任，要求我永遠不要在死去的病人身上練習。（理察‧阿克塞爾）

If I were to talk with students, is that the joy of science is in the process, and not in the end. That science is not a move to an end, rather it is a process of discovery, which unto itself should be a meaningful pleasure. (Richard Axel)

我如果跟學生們交談，那就是科學的樂趣在於過程，而非結果。科學並不是抵達終點的一步，而是一個發現的過程，本身就應該是一種有意義的樂趣。（理察‧阿克塞爾）

Both myth and history reveal the conflict between intellect and power. With the tasting of the fruit of the Tree of Knowledge of Good and Evil and the expulsion of Adam and Eve from the garden, with Prometheus' deliverance of fire to mankind and the opening of Pandora's Box, we observe man's intellectual curiosity punished by suffering. Ironically, it is this intellectual creativity that allows man to overcome his punishment, his suffering, to allow man to prevail. Indeed, the advancement of knowledge is too often perceived as transgression. (Richard Axel)

神話和歷史都揭示了智力和權力之間的衝突。亞當和夏娃嘗到善惡知識樹的果實並被從伊甸園逐出、普羅米修斯將火傳給人類，還有打開的潘朵拉盒子，都讓我們觀察到人備受苦難懲罰的求知欲。諷刺的是，就是這種智力創造性使人克服懲罰、苦難，讓人獲得勝利。的確，知識的進步總是被視為違抗天條。（理察‧阿克塞爾）

Pick a problem that you're extremely interested in. That sounds kind of simplistic maybe, but it's not, because you don't want to just do a problem because it's easy to solve, you want to do something that you're obsessed with, that you just have to understand, because that's where the joy comes from, and that also, I think, is where the great discoveries come from, for people are really trying to try to figure out things that they don't understand. And they don't necessarily know how to do it, but they try very hard and then they succeed. (Linda B. Buck)

選擇一個你極其感興趣的問題。這聽起來也許太簡單了，其實不然。因為你想要研究一個問題，並非只是想著它容易解決，而是想探究一件自己著迷的事，你就是必須了解它，因為那是快樂的來源；那也是，我認為，偉大發現的來源，因為人們真的是無止無休，力圖釐清自己所不了解的事情。他們不一定知道如何去做，但是非常努力，然後他們成功了。（琳達‧巴克）

Looking back over my life, I am struck by the good fortune I have had to be a scientist. Very few in this world have the opportunity to do everyday what they love to do, as I have. (Linda B. Buck)

回顧此生，我為自己有幸成為科學家而驚訝。在這個世界上，極少有人得到機會天天做自己愛做的事，像我一樣。（琳達·巴克）

Every day, a piece of music, a short story, or a poem dies because its existence is no longer justified in our time. And things that were once considered immortal have become mortal again, no one knows them anymore. Even though they deserve to survive. (Elfriede Jelinek)

每天有一首樂曲、一個短篇小說或一首詩失去生命，因為不復見容於我們的時代。一度認作永恆之物重歸速朽，再也無人知曉，儘管它們值得繼續存在。（艾爾弗雷德·耶利內克）

I think what the Nobel committee is doing is going beyond war and looking at what humanity can do to prevent war. Sustainable management of our natural resources will promote peace. (Wangari Muta Maathai)

我認為，諾貝爾委員會在做的是超越戰爭，探究人類能做些什麼來防止戰爭。永續地管理我們的自然資源將促進和平。（汪蓋瑞·馬塔伊）

The key to long-run growth is usually entrepreneurial activity. (Finn E. Kydland)

長期成長的關鍵通常是創業活動。（芬恩·基德蘭德）

Mandatory retirement at 65? Forget it! (Finn E. Kydland)

65歲強制退休？忘掉它！（芬恩·基德蘭德）

One of the great joys of research —— whether it be in economics, physics, chemistry or any academic discipline —— is the act of discovery, those moments when we are surprised by what we have found... when our original ideas are turned upside down and we suddenly have to rearrange how we view the world. (Edward C. Prescott)

研究的最大樂趣之一——在經濟學、物理學、化學或任何學科都一樣——是發現的行動，我們驚奇於所發現事物的那些時刻……當我們原來的想法被徹底顛覆時，我們突然不得不調整自己看待世界的方式。（愛德華．普雷史考特）

2005 年

It's like being swept up into the vortex of a bit of a tornado. It's not quite that chaotic, but it's every bit as vigorous. (Roy J. Glauber)

獲得諾貝爾獎就像被捲入龍捲風的漩渦。昏天黑地尚不至於，但同樣充滿活力。（羅伊．格勞伯）

I have very little taste for retirement, I have to tell you. I have just taught a class and worn out my voice, doing it, as you can perhaps hear. (Roy J. Glauber)

我得告訴你，我對退休沒什麼興趣。我剛教完一堂課，嗓子都喊啞了，諸位大概聽得出來。（羅伊．格勞伯）

I am truly fortunate to have somehow always been in the right place at the right time, to capitalize on technical advances that made increasingly precise laser measurements and applications possible. I have worked with amazing colleagues and students, whose enthusiasm and vision made for excellent physics, great fun and the building of important programs. It was a great 45 years and I have really loved it. (John L. Hall)

我真是幸運，總是在適當的時間和適當的地點，利用技術進步使日益精確的雷射測量和應用成為可能。我曾與優秀的同事和學生一起工作，他們的熱情和遠見使我們獲得了出色的物理學成就、帶來無窮的樂趣並打造出重要的項目。這是非凡的 45 年，我始終真心熱愛它。（約翰·霍爾）

Well, for me, the field of light, of lasers, of atoms, molecules, has been an unending series of surprises, and I can't think of a better field. But I think we will, hopefully, find new things, in the future. (Theodor W. Hänsch)

嗯，對我來說，光、雷射、原子、分子領域一直充滿著無盡的驚喜，我想不出更好的領域了。不過我認為將來有希望找到新的東西。（特奧多爾·亨施）

My motto is more, "If you want to find something new, look for something new!" There is a certain amount of risk in this attitude, as even the slightest failure tends to be resounding, but you are so happy when you succeed that it is worth taking the risk. (Yves Chauvin)

我的座右銘是：「如果想找到新的東西，那就去尋找新的東西吧！」這種態度存在一定的風險，因為即便些微失敗也會帶來巨大的影響；然而成功之際你是如此快樂，所以值得冒險。（伊夫·肖萬）

I have always been an avid reader of chemical literature, eager for what is new. (Yves Chauvin)

我一直是化學文獻的熱心讀者，渴望新事物。（伊夫·肖萬）

> 2005 年

Like all sciences, chemistry is marked by magic moments. For someone fortunate enough to live such a moment, it is an instant of intense emotion: an immense field of investigation suddenly opens up before you. (Yves Chauvin)

跟所有的科學一樣，化學也充滿著神奇的時刻。對於有幸親歷這種時刻的人，它是瞬間的強烈情感體驗：一個巨大的探索領域突然在你面前展開。（伊夫・肖萬）

I had no training in research as such, and as a consequence, I am, in a sense, self-taught. (Yves Chauvin)

我沒有接受過任何研究方面的訓練，因此，在某種意義上，我是自學的。（伊夫・肖萬）

There is no difference between fundamental research and applied research. Although this is my view, based on personal taste and the areas I have worked in, it is not necessarily true for others. (Yves Chauvin)

基礎研究和應用研究並無區別。雖然這是我基於一己之見和個人專業領域的看法，在他人看來未必準確。（伊夫・肖萬）

We are proud to represent that group of chemists who have developed catalysts that enable new ways of coordinating the dance-like interchange of atoms in one class of molecules called olefins. Catalysts are the conductors who choreograph the chemical dance that results in the formation of new structures. Just as the influence of catalysts occurs, in a sense, behind the scenes of a chemical reactioncatalysis has been behind three of the last 6 chemistry prizes. (Robert H. Grubbs)

我們很榮幸地代表一群化學家，他們開發了催化劑，使原子得以在一類名為烯烴的分子中，採取新的方式協調舞蹈般的交換。催化劑是設計化學之舞的編導，從而產生新的結構。在某種意義上，催化劑的影響發生於化學反應的幕後，過去 6 屆的化學獎之中，有 3 屆與催化作用有關。（羅伯特・格拉布）

The science that is being honored took place over a 30 year period and hundreds of coworkers were involved in our groups. We thank them for their dedication, hard work and creative contributions. This was not a prize based on a single Eureka event. It is the accumulation of smaller triumphs and moments of excitement that have assembled to form the still-evolving whole. (Robert H. Grubbs)

獲此殊榮的科學研究歷時逾 30 年，數百名合作者參與了我們的團隊。我們感謝他們的盡心盡力、辛勤工作和創造性貢獻。這不是基於一次「我發現了！」[21]式事件而頒發的獎項。正是由一些小勝利和激動時刻的累積，組合成了這個仍處於進展中的整體成果。（羅伯特・格拉布）

I hope future generations of scientists have the freedom to pursue a topic for over 30 years and to watch it bloom from an intellectual curiosity into commercial applications. (Robert H. Grubbs)

我希望未來的科學家能夠自由地專注於一個主題 30 餘年，目睹它從對知識的好奇發展成為商業應用。（羅伯特・格拉布）

I've been enjoying doing what I'm doing for a very long time, so I see no reason to change. (Robert H. Grubbs)

我長期以來一直很享受我現在所做的事情，所以看不出有什麼理由改變。（羅伯特・格拉布）

---

[21]「我發現了！」相傳為阿基米德（Archimedes）靈機一動，根據比重原理推算出金子純度時的喊叫。

2005 年

We ultimately came to realise, step by step, that our basic research was leading to something really useful. And that is very, very pleasing to me; and I think that's what the Nobel Prize is all about: to do work that turns out to be useful to society in some way and certainly other fields in science. So I hope that I can be a spokesman for the future and what chemistry of the future will be. (Richard R. Schrock)

我們最終一步步意識到,我們的基礎研究正在引向真正實用的成果。而這對於我是非常、非常愉快的,我認為這就是諾貝爾獎的全部真諦:做對社會有一定用處的工作,當然也對科學其他領域有用。所以,我希望自己能成為未來以及未來的化學的代言人。(理察・施羅克)

Everything that's supposedly caused by stress, I tell people there's a Nobel Prize there if you find out the real cause. (Barry J. Marshall)

我告訴人們,所有一般認為由壓力導致的問題,如果你能找出真正的原因,就能獲得諾貝爾獎。(巴里・馬歇爾)

There is no other prize in any country that carries the prestige that a Nobel bestows. (Barry J. Marshall)

在任何國家,沒有其他獎項能像諾貝爾獎一樣享有如此高的聲望。(巴里・馬歇爾)

This is the story of my discovery of Helicobacter. At various times I have been asked: did I steal the discovery; did I find it by accident; did it follow some brilliant research work; or was it serendipity. My answer to most of these is a definite "No." Obviously, as with any new discovery, there is an element of luck, but I think my main luck was in finding something so important. I think the best term is serendipity; I was in the right place at the right time and I had the right interests and skills to do more than just pass it by. (J. Robin Warren)

這就是我發現幽門螺旋桿菌的故事。我屢次被問到：我是否竊取了這項發現？它是不是我偶然發現的？它是不是遵循了一些出色的研究工作？它是不是不期而至的好運？對於這些問題，我的回答大多數是明確的「不是」。顯然，跟任何新發現一樣，其中存在運氣成分，但我認為，我的主要運氣在於發現了如此重要的東西。我認為最恰當的說法是機緣。我在適當的時間、處於適當的地點，我有適當的興趣和技能並做得更多，而不僅是坐失良機。（羅賓·華倫）

One way of looking at speech is to say that it is a constant stratagem to cover nakedness. (Harold Pinter)

有一種看待言語的說法為，它是掩蓋赤裸的持續策略。（哈羅德·品特）

Once in a while, I have to pinch myself to remind myself I am Nobel laureate, but that is not part of my work plan every day. (Mohamed ElBaradei)

時不時地，我得掐自己一下，好提醒自己我是諾貝爾獎得主，不過這並非我每天工作計畫的一部分。（穆罕默德·巴拉迪）

Today, with globalisation bringing us ever closer together, if we choose to ignore the insecurities of some, they will soon become the insecurities of all. (Mohamed ElBaradei)

今天，全球化使我們的關係更加緊密，如果我們選擇漠視某些人的不安全感，他們將很快成為所有人的不安全感。（穆罕默德·巴拉迪）

Science is exploration —— exploration for the sake of exploration, and for nothing else. We must go where our curiosity leads us, we must go where we want to go. And eventually, it is sure to lead us to the beautiful, the important, and the useful. (Robert J. Aumann)

科學是探索 —— 為了探索而探索，不為任何其他目的。我們必須跟隨好奇心的指引，去自己想去的地方。而最終，它必定引領我們走向美麗、重要，和實用的事物。（羅伯特·約翰·歐曼）

What I would say to any young person is, do what you like to do, what it is that catches your attention and that you get involved in, and that you get interested in, that's what you should do. If you like to do it, go ahead and do it, that's it. (Robert J. Aumann)

我想對任何年輕人說的是，做你喜歡做的事，做那些吸引你注意、令你參與其中、使你感興趣的事，這就是你應當做的事。你要是喜歡做，就去做吧，就是這樣。（羅伯特·約翰·歐曼）

Assumptions don't have to be correct; conclusions have to be correct. (Robert J. Aumann)

假設不一定要正確，結論一定要正確。（羅伯特·約翰·歐曼）

For me, life has been —— and still is —— one tremendous joyride, one magnificent tapestry. There have been bad —— very bad —— times, like when my son Shlomo was killed and when my wife Esther died. But even these somehow integrate into the magnificent tapestry. (Robert J. Aumann)

對於我而言，生活曾經是 —— 現在依然是 —— 一次非凡的出遊，一張華麗的壁毯。曾經有糟糕的 —— 非常糟糕的時候，例如我的兒子施洛莫喪生，我的妻子埃絲特去世。然而，即便這些也以某種方式融入了華麗的壁毯之中。（羅伯特·約翰·歐曼）

There have been a lot of very good times. The excitement of research, of groping in the dark and then hitting the light. The satisfaction of teaching, of meeting someone at a party who tells you that the course in complex variables that he heard from you twenty-five years ago was the most beautiful that he ever heard. The exhilaration of climbing —— seeking and finding foot —— and handholds —— on an almost vertical rock face. The beauty of a walk in the woods with a four-year-old grandchild, who spots and correctly identifies a tiny wild orchid about which you told him last week. Dancing with your wife at your child's wedding. Unraveling an intricate passage in the Talmud with your eighteen-year-old granddaughter, or with a study partner with whom you have studied for thirty years. Slipping on a "black" (expert) ski slope, tumbling two hundred meters down, and then going back and doing the same slope again —— this time without a slip. Cooking a meal and hearing from a guest that the soup was the best she ever tasted. Raising a beautiful family. Seeing the flag of Israel fluttering in the wind, right next to that of Sweden, from the roof of the Grand Hotel in Stockholm. (Robert J. Aumann)

我的人生有過許多非常美好的時光。研究的激動，在黑暗中摸索後得見光明。教學的滿足，聚會上有人說 25 年前你講授的複變數是他聽過最美妙的課。攀岩的愉快 —— 在近乎垂直的岩石上尋覓並找到腳以及手的支撐點。攜四歲孫兒漫步林中的愜意，他指認出你上週告訴他的細小的野蘭花。在孩子的婚禮上與妻子翩翩起舞。跟 18 歲的孫女，或者一位 30 年的研習夥伴一起解開《塔木德》中一段複雜文字。在一片「黑色」（專業）滑雪坡上滑倒，滾落 200 公尺，又回到坡上再度滑下 —— 這一次全無跌倒。做一頓飯，聽一位客人說湯品是她嘗過的至美之味。養育一個

美滿的家庭。在斯德哥爾摩大飯店樓頂上,看到瑞典國旗一旁的以色列國旗迎風飄揚。(羅伯特・約翰・歐曼)

I define game theory as the study of how rational individuals make choices when the better choice among two possibilities, or the best choice among several possibilities, depends on the choices that others will make or are making. (Thomas C. Schelling)

我將賽局理論定義為對如下問題的研究:當兩種可能性之中較好的選擇,或幾種可能性之中最好的選擇,取決於他人將做出或正做出的選擇時,理性的個人如何做出選擇。(湯瑪斯・克倫比・謝林)

There is a tendency in our planning to confuse the unfamiliar with the improbable. (Thomas C. Schelling)

我們在制定計畫時傾向於將不熟悉的與不可能的混為一談。(湯瑪斯・克倫比・謝林)

And there is escaping things the knowledge of which makes one unhappy. If "truth" is what we know and are aware of, in the most engrossing fiction we escape truth. Whatever else it is, drama is forgetfulness. We can forget and forget that we are forgetting. It is temporary mind control. If memories are pain, fiction is anesthesia. (Thomas C. Schelling)

還有逃避那些令自己不開心的事。如果「真相」是我們所知道和意識到的,在最引人入勝的小說中我們便逃避了真相。戲劇是遺忘,不管在它之外是什麼。我們能夠遺忘,也能遺忘我們正在遺忘。這是暫時的精神控制。如果記憶是痛苦,小說就是麻醉。(湯瑪斯・克倫比・謝林)

Just as it may be easier to ban nuclear weapons from the battlefield in toto than through carefully graduated specifications on their use, zero is a more enforceable limit on cigarettes or chewing gum than some flexible quantitative ration. (Thomas C. Schelling)

正如完全禁止核武器上戰場，可能比透過仔細分等的使用說明規範更容易些一樣，對香菸或口香糖的零容忍，是比一些靈活的數量配額更可行的限制。（湯瑪斯‧克倫比‧謝林）

2006 年

There's no such thing as saying that we'll ever find the ultimate cause of stuff. We can only work to push our understanding one step further. (John C. Mather)

所謂我們終將找到事物的終極原因，這樣的說法不成立。我們只能努力促使自己的理解更進一步。（約翰‧馬瑟）

Every time we get a story that says there was a Big Bang, then people want to know what was before that. And if we find out, what was before that? (John C. Mather)

每當我們得到一個說法，認為有一次大爆炸，人們就想知道在那之前是什麼。而如果我們查清了，在那之前又是什麼？（約翰‧馬瑟）

There is no limit to what astrophysicists can do. We can be very curious. (John C. Mather)

天體物理學家能做的事是沒有限度的。我們可以非常好奇。（約翰‧馬瑟）

2006 年

My interest in science started quite early. My earliest school recollection, from age 6, is actually of mathematics, realizing that one could fill an entire page with digits and never come to the largest possible number, so I saw what was meant by infinity. (John C. Mather)

我對科學的興趣發生得很早。我最早的學校記憶,始於 6 歲,實際上是關於數學的,我了解到可以用數字填滿整頁紙,但永遠無法得到最大的數字,於是我領會了無窮大的意義。(約翰·馬瑟)

There is strength in numbers, but organizing those numbers is one of the great challenges. (John C. Mather)

人多力量大,然而組織這些人是最大的挑戰之一。(約翰·馬瑟)

My experience from working with people is that you can have a conversation with someone or have a meeting with a group of people, and from that meeting will derive an answer to a question that no individual could have ever thought of by him or herself. (John C. Mather)

與他人一起工作帶給我的體會是,你可以和某個人交談,或者跟一群人開會,從這種交流中,你可以得到任何一個人無法獨自想到的問題的答案。(約翰·馬瑟)

Do not make grand plans. Be flexible. (John C. Mather)

不要制定宏大的計畫。要靈活。(約翰·馬瑟)

When you have a deadline, or when you know that your equipment is about to go up in a rocket and you won't have another chance to fix it, your mind works in a way that it otherwise never would. (John C. Mather)

當你有個最後期限,或者知道自己的裝置即將搭乘火箭升空,不

會再有機會調整，你的頭腦就會以一種前所未有的方式運轉。（約翰‧馬瑟）

I think we all want to know where we came from and how we fit into the world, but some of us need to know how it all works in great detail. (George F. Smoot)

我認為我們都想了解我們是從哪裡來的，如何適應的這個世界，但我們有些人需要詳盡地了解整個宇宙是如何運作的。（喬治‧斯穆特）

The more we know of the history of the universe, the more we know about ourselves. (George F. Smoot)

我們越了解宇宙的歷史，就越了解我們自己。（喬治‧斯穆特）

When people really understand the Big Bang and the whole sweep of the evolution of the universe, it will be clear that humans are fairly insignificant. (George F. Smoot)

當人們真正了解大爆炸和宇宙演化的整個過程時，就會明白人類是相當渺小的。（喬治‧斯穆特）

I always think of space-time as being the real substance of space, and the galaxies and the stars just like the foam on the ocean. (George F. Smoot)

我總是認為時空是宇宙的本質，星系和恆星不過像是海洋上的泡沫。（喬治‧斯穆特）

When I came to Berkeley, I met all these Nobel laureates and I got to know that they were regular people. They were very smart and very motivated and worked very hard, but they were still humans, whereas before they were kind of mythical creatures to me. (George F. Smoot)

2006 年

進入柏克萊，我接觸到所有這些諾貝爾獎得主，了解到他們就是一般人。他們非常聰明，非常積極，工作非常努力，但他們仍然是人，而之前他們對我來說就像神話中的生物。（喬治・斯穆特）

I want to encourage the next generation and hand over a science enterprise to my successors, which is as good or better than the excellent one I came into as a young scientist. (George Smoot)

我想鼓勵下一代，並且把一份科學事業傳承給我的繼任者，這個事業應該和我年輕時從事的優秀事業一樣好，甚至更好。（喬治・斯穆特）

I think almost all scientists do it for the reason I do which is the challenge of solving problems, and naturally we grapple with specific problems, if one can't… and the key to solving them is actually to keep narrowing the focus until finally one has redefined the problem in a way that it can be solved, so the answer to your question is very much what motivates us and our source of satisfaction is in grappling with specific issues, and then as I say having the pleasure of finally discovering the way to either overcome a technical limitation or find an answer to a paradox about the material or whatever it may be. (Roger D. Kornberg)

我認為，幾乎所有科學家做研究的原因都跟我一樣，就是要知難而上，解決問題。我們自然會努力克服問題，如果做不到……那麼，解決它們的關鍵，實際上就是逐步收縮焦點，最終將問題重新定位於能夠解決的程度。所以，你所提問題的答案泰半在於是什麼激勵我們，而我們的滿足感來自於克服特定問題，然後如我所說，最終獲得發現解決之道的快樂，無論是克服技術上的限制，或者是找出關於材料或任何可能事項之悖論的解答。（羅傑・科恩伯格）

Even as we celebrate, and savor this moment, the work goes on. I am reminded of some lines from the American poet, Robert Frost. During the long, arduous effort of the past 20 years, I often repeated these lines to myself. I view them as a kind of metaphor for science and our ongoing commitment to it.

The woods are lovely, dark and deep,

But I have promises to keep,

And miles to go before I sleep,

And miles to go before I sleep. (Roger D. Kornberg)

在我們慶祝、並享受這個時刻之際，工作仍在繼續。我於是想起美國詩人羅伯特·佛洛斯特的幾句詩。在過去 20 年漫長而艱苦的努力中，我經常對自己複述這些詩句。我把它們看作對科學的一種隱喻，以及我們對科學的持續承諾：

樹林美好、黑暗而深幽，

可我有承諾得遵守，

睡前還有幾英哩要走，

睡前還有幾英哩要走。（羅傑·科恩伯格）

We have enjoyed the privilege of devoting our lives to the pursuit of basic knowledge. This is an extraordinary privilege. We owe it to public support of science. (Roger D. Kornberg)

我們有幸將自己的一生奉獻給對基礎知識的追求。這是一種非凡的榮幸。我們應該感謝大眾對科學的支持。（羅傑·科恩伯格）

2006 年

What we do, indeed most of the science that goes on is understandable by and could be pursued I think by an ordinary, by any ordinary person, there's nothing so profound that it requires any very rare aptitude to grasp and to do. (Roger D. Kornberg)

我認為，我們所做的事，乃至現有科學的大部分，都是任何普通人能夠理解並可以從事的，都沒有什麼事情深奧到需要任何罕見的能力才能掌握和進行。（羅傑・科恩伯格）

My wife Yahli has been my closest collaborator. She has borne a double burden. She is the wife of a scientist, and herself a scientist without a wife. Beyond her participation she has also been a source of inspiration in our work. (Roger D. Kornberg)

我的妻子亞里一直是我最親密的合作者。她承受了雙重的負擔。她是一個科學家的妻子，自己又是個沒有妻子的科學家。除了參與之外，她還是我們工作的靈感泉源。（羅傑・科恩伯格）

My own serious interest in chemistry dates from high school, and I think that's not uncommon, that young people's interests become defined at that age as they grow to maturity and they think seriously or can begin to comprehend what lies within them concerning the logical or natural directions they'll pursue. (Roger D. Kornberg)

我自己對化學認真的興趣始於高中。我認為這並非罕見，年輕人的興趣在那個年齡逐漸成熟，他們開始認真思考或開始理解他們所追求的邏輯或自然方向。（羅傑・科恩伯格）

In my personal view chemistry is really the queen of the sciences, chemistry is the common ground for all scientific investigation. So our best hope of applying physical principles for the world around us is at the level of chemistry, our best hope of understanding the biological organism and ultimately the form and function of the human body is at the level of chemistry. I have said before and I would repeat that if there is any one subject that an educated person should know in the world that is chemistry. (Roger D. Kornberg)

我個人認為，化學實在是科學中的女王，化學是所有科學研究的共同基礎。所以，我們把物理原理應用於周圍世界的最大希望是在化學層面，我們理解生物有機體並最終理解人體的形態和功能的最大希望是在化學層面。我以前說過但仍要重申，世界上如果有哪一個學科，是受過教育的人應當懂得的，那就是化學。（羅傑·科恩伯格）

One's elated, but science is a big thing. So, you immediately think of all the people that have helped make it happen and think about the fact that you're still a pretty small cog in a pretty big wheel. (Andrew Z. Fire)

獲獎者興高采烈，但科學是件大事情。所以，你馬上想到所有為獲獎出了力的人，想起自己仍然是一個龐大齒輪上的小齒輪。（德魯·法厄）

I think the successes are going to be there but it's also going to take a lot of stamina from the people doing the work. There may be things that don't work quite so well, there may be setbacks, as for any new therapeutic. (Andrew Z. Fire)

我認為成功總會出現，但它也會消耗從事者大量耐力。可能有些事情不太順利，可能挫折接二連三，跟任何新療法一樣。（德魯·法厄）

Top Ten Reasons for The Return of 2006 Nobel Laureates to Stockholm during the First Week of December 2036.

10. (And certainly least likely.) To receive an unprecedented 31st consecutive Nobel Prize in one's field of expertise...

9. To observe as one's great-great-great grandchild, having with a remarkable set of equations solved the problems of aging, time travel, and responsible investment, is awarded simultaneous Nobel Prizes in Physics, Chemistry, Physiology or Medicine, and Economics.

8. To observe (on a quick side-trip to Oslo) as one's former Nobel Attaché is awarded the Nobel Peace Prize for their outstanding career with the Swedish Foreign Ministry.

7. To observe one (or several) of one's former students from the currently-underdeveloped world receiving a prize for their efforts in the newly formed (and generously funded) international consortium on research.

6. To observe the awarding of the newly-announced "Culinary Achievement Prize in Honor of Alfred Nobel" to the room service chef from the Grand Hotel.

5. To finally observe the beauty of Stockholm covered with snow.

4. To bask and swim in the 30° C warmth of Stockholm's recently developed winter beach resorts.

3. To pursue the many productive scientific collaborations begun during one's original 2006 visit to Swedish Universities.

2. Because Sweden really knows how to throw a party.

1. Because we and our families have so much enjoyed the wonderful people, land, and traditions of Sweden we learned about on our first trip to your country. (Andrew Z. Fire)

2006 年諾貝爾獎得主們 2036 年 12 月第一週重返斯德哥爾摩的十大理由：

10. （當然最不可能。）一個人破天荒地在其專業領域連續獲得第 31 個諾貝爾獎……

9. 慶祝某個人的五世孫以一套非凡的方程式解決了衰老、時間旅行和可靠投資等諸多難題，被同時授予諾貝爾物理學、化學、生理學或醫學以及經濟學獎。

8. 慶祝（在一次短暫的順訪奧斯陸之旅中）一位前諾貝爾獎得主的隨員，由於在瑞典外交部出色的職業生涯而被授予諾貝爾和平獎。

7. 慶祝某個人的一名（或幾名）來自尚未開發國家的昔日學生，由於在新成立（並財力雄厚）的國際研究後援會中的業績而獲獎。

6. 慶祝新宣布的「諾貝爾烹飪成就獎」授予斯德哥爾摩大飯店的客房服務廚師。

5. 有幸一睹雪後斯德哥爾摩之美。

4. 在斯德哥爾摩新開發的冬季海灘度假地 30 攝氏度氣溫中作日光浴和游泳。

3. 延續自 2006 年訪問瑞典大學時展開的許多卓有成效的科學合作。

2. 因為瑞典深諳舉辦派對之道。

1. 因為我們以及家人非常喜愛初訪瑞典時見識的貴國美好的人民、土地和傳統。（德魯・法厄）

2006 年

Although there are many applications for RNAi, to me there's still a lot we don't understand about the mechanism. And it's then just really, really exciting how many different fields, seemingly unrelated, have just merged together with the understanding of the mechanism. As the understanding grows we just seem to be bringing together these very distant looking —— sort of unrelated looking stories just keep coming together and unfolding in beautiful ways. (Craig C. Mello)

雖然對核糖核酸干擾有很多應用,我認為,其機制仍有大量我們所不了解之處。令人興奮的是,許多看似毫不相關的領域,經由對機制的理解而互相融合。隨著理解的加深,我們的確看來正在把這些顯得相距遙遠 —— 看似無關的故事聚集起來,不斷地結合,再以美妙的方式展開。(克雷格・梅洛)

I want to make a difference in the world because I believe that's what science is for. (Craig C. Mello)

我想讓這個世界有所改觀,因為我相信這就是科學的目的所在。(克雷格・梅洛)

We're losing time now because we're not spending enough money to do research. As a consequence of not acting, we are sentencing people to death when we could help them be treated with new drugs. (Craig C. Mello)

我們此刻是在浪費時間,因為沒有花足夠的錢進行研究。不作為的後果是,當有可能幫助人們得到新藥治療時,我們卻在判處他們死刑。(克雷格・梅洛)

I love to do things like sail and hike, but they don't give me the satisfaction of knowing the potential of something you've learned in the lab. (Craig C. Mello)

我喜歡航海和健行等活動,但它們滿足不了我對事物潛在可能性的探求,那是在實驗室中獲得的。(克雷格‧梅洛)

I read a book one day and my whole life was changed. (Orhan Pamuk)

有一天我讀了一本書,我的整個人生由此改變。(奧罕‧帕慕克)

Unprecedented technological capabilities combined with unlimited human creativity have given us tremendous power to take on intractable problems like poverty, unemployment, disease, and environmental degradation. Our challenge is to translate this extraordinary potential into meaningful change. (Muhammad Yunus)

前所未有的技術能力加上無限的人類創造性,賦予了我們巨大的力量,解決諸如貧困、失業、疾病和環境退化等棘手問題。挑戰在於將這種非同尋常的潛力轉化為富有意義的改變。(穆罕默德‧尤努斯)

Poor people are the world's greatest entrepreneurs. Every day, they must innovate in order to survive. They remain poor because they do not have the opportunities to turn their creativity into sustainable income. (Muhammad Yunus)

窮人是天下最了不起的企業家。每一天,他們都必須創新以求存活。他們始終貧窮,因為沒有機會把創造力轉化為可持續的收入。(穆罕默德‧尤努斯)

All human beings are born entrepreneurs. Some get a chance to unleash that capacity. Some never got the chance, never knew that he or she has that capacity. (Muhammad Yunus)

所有人都是天生的企業家。一些人得到機會施展這種能力,而另一些人從未獲得機會,從來不知道自己擁有這種能力。(穆罕默德・尤努斯)

The developing world is full of entrepreneurs and visionaries, who with access to education, equity and credit would play a key role in developing the economic situations in their countries. (Muhammad Yunus)

開發中國家充滿了企業家和有遠見的人,只要他們獲得教育、公平和貸款,就能在發展本國經濟狀況中發揮關鍵作用。(穆罕默德・尤努斯)

I became involved in the poverty issue not as a policymaker or a researcher. I became involved because poverty was all around me, and I could not turn away from it. (Muhammad Yunus)

我參與貧困問題,並非作為政策制定者或研究者;參與是由於貧困無處不在,我無法置之不理。(穆罕默德・尤努斯)

I started to think about what drives innovation and what its social significance might be. The next step was to think innovators are taking a leap into the unknown. That led me to the thought that it is also a source of fun and employee engagement. (Edmund S. Phelps)

我開始思考創新的動力是什麼,創新的社會意義何在。接著想到創新者們正在跨入未知領域。這令我聯想到創新也是樂趣和員工參與的來源。(埃德蒙・費爾普斯)

Well into the 20th century, scholars viewed economic advances as resulting from commercial innovations enabled by the discoveries of scientists —— discoveries that come from outside the economy and out of the blue. (Edmund S. Phelps)

進入20世紀,學者觀察出,經濟進步是科學家們的發現引發商業創新的結果——這些發現來自經濟外部,而且出乎意料。(埃德蒙・費爾普斯)

The level of dynamism is a matter of how fertile the country is in coming up with innovative ideas having prospects of profitability, how adept it is at identifying and nourishing the ideas with the best prospects, and how prepared it is in evaluating and trying out the new products and methods that are launched onto the market. (Edmund S. Phelps)

國家的活力程度,在於它如何大量提出具有盈利預期的創意,如何擅長鑑別並培養最具前景的理念,以及如何嫻熟評估和嘗試推廣投放市場的新產品與新方法。(埃德蒙・費爾普斯)

What brought mass innovation to a nation was not scientific advances —— its own or others' —— but "economic dynamism": the desire and the space to innovate. (Edmund S. Phelps)

為國家帶來大規模創新的不是科學進步——無論是本國或他國的——而是「經濟活力」:創新的欲望和空間。(埃德蒙・費爾普斯)

Entrepreneurs' willingness to innovate or just to invest —— and thus create new jobs —— is driven by their "animal spirits," as they decide whether to leap into the void. (Edmund S. Phelps)

2006 年

　　企業家願意創新或僅僅投資——從而創造新的就業機會——是受他們的「動物精神」所驅使，在他們決定是否躍入這一片空白之際。（埃德蒙·費爾普斯）

I didn't do my work for money or prizes —— only for the excitement of discovery. (Edmund S. Phelps)

　　我不是為了賺錢或獲獎而工作——只是為了發現的激動。（埃德蒙·費爾普斯）

Without being aware, I think I was being indoctrinated into what was called Vitalism, the idea that what makes life worth living, the good life, consists of accepting challenges, solving problems, discovery, personal growth, personal change. (Edmund S. Phelps)

　　無意之中，我似乎一直被灌輸所謂生機論，讓生命變得有價值、變得美好的理念，包括接受挑戰、解決問題、探索、個人成長和個人改變。（埃德蒙·費爾普斯）

The need to encourage entrepreneurship and ensure that young people have the opportunity to start new businesses is acute. (Edmund S. Phelps)

　　鼓勵創業精神並確保年輕人有機會開創新事業，這種必要性十分迫切。（埃德蒙·費爾普斯）

If every effect of any new products or methods were required to be known before they could be produced and marketed, they would not be true innovations —— and thus not represent new knowledge of what people would like, if offered. (Edmund S. Phelps)

2001-2010 跨界融合與人文關懷

如果任何新產品或方法，在能夠生產和銷售之前都必須了解其各種效果，它們就不會是真正的創新——即便提供，也不代表是人們想要的新知識。（埃德蒙·費爾普斯）

2007 年

When I was at the university, I liked physics, but I liked the arts too, I was a good photographer, I liked cinema, I wrote and I shot a film. My main inspiration was Ingmar Bergman, my god was Bergman. I remember trying to express the feelings I wanted to express by black and white close-up and slow panning shots, inspired by the first films of Bergman, Sommarlek, Sommaren med Monika, Smultronstället. But, when I saw my film, it was not at all expressing what I wanted to express, and I realized that, unfortunately, I was at light years from what I had seen in Bergman's films. But I could remember that I had some skills in physics, I began a PhD and I found that the research can be a very creative work too. The discovery of new and beautiful landscapes in the field of knowledge was also fascinating, and this led me to be here today, partly thanks to the inaccessibility of the genius of Ingmar Bergman. (Albert Fert)

上大學的時候，我喜歡物理學，但也喜歡藝術。我是個很好的攝影師，喜歡電影，撰寫劇本並拍攝過一部電影。我的主要靈感來自英格瑪·伯格曼，伯格曼是我心目中的神。記得自己受到伯格曼《夏日戀曲》、《莫妮卡》、《野草莓》等電影啟發，試圖用黑白特寫和慢鏡頭表達心中感受。可是，看到自己的電影時，它根本沒有表達出我內心的東西。我意識到，很不幸，我跟伯格曼電影中所見比起來，相差十萬八千里。不過我還記得自己有些物理技能，就開始攻讀博士學位，並發現這種研究也可以是富於創造性的工作。在知識領域發現新的、美麗的風光，同樣令人著迷。而這使得我今天來到這裡，部分要感謝英格瑪·伯格曼的天才令人望塵莫及。（阿爾貝·費爾）

I have discovered the beauty of sciences. It is amazing for a researcher to see the product of his ideas, of purely abstract constructions with electrons and spins, becoming a concrete reality of the everyday life. (Albert Fert)

我發現了科學之美。對於一個研究人員，見到自己的思想成果，帶電子和自旋的純粹抽象結構，化為日常生活的具體現實，簡直不可思議。（阿爾貝·費爾）

My research topics gradually changed all the time but I tried always to build upon knowledge that I had gained before. So for me it was very important to have continuity. (Peter Grünberg)

我的研究課題一直在逐漸變動，不過我總是盡量以自己已有知識為基礎。所以對我來說，保持連貫性是非常重要的。（彼得·格林貝格）

I have had other ideas that could have turned out to be of importance or even a breakthrough. Whenever I have such an idea I make a corresponding note on the last pages of my notebook. But my nature is to concentrate only on one thing at a time. Of course, when you start to have doubts that your project will be successful you play with other ideas also, and then I consult my notebook. Before giving up one should carefully test out all possibilities, but also not fall into stubbornness. (Peter Grünberg)

我還有過其他的想法，它們可能會證明意義重大，甚至是個突破。每當產生這樣的想法時，我都在筆記本最後幾頁上做相應的筆記。不過我的天性是每次只專注於一件事。當然了，在懷疑起自己的項目可否成功時，人也不免嘗試一下其他的想法，這時我就查閱筆記本。放棄之前，應當仔細考量所有的可能性，但也不可陷於固執。（彼得·格林貝格）

The famous physicist Werner Heisenberg begins his autobiography with the sentence: "Science is made by men." Since in my own case you honour not a singular discovery, but the lifelong attempt to understand how chemical reactions at solid surfaces take place, this work involved in fact many people. When I was young, I was sometimes dreaming of becoming a musician. That is why I considered my co-workers often as an orchestra with me being the conductor. We know that even the best conductor cannot perform first class music with a mediocre orchestra. But I had the great luck of always being surrounded by an excellent group of co-workers whom I may compare —— not with the Royal Stockholm Philharmonic Orchestra —— but perhaps with the Berlin Philharmonic Orchestra. But in contrast to the situation with a real orchestra where the artists play notes prescribed by the composer, in our case the players themselves are the composers. By continuously crossing the border between the known and the unknown, they build on the never ending multidimensional symphony of science. (Gerhard Ertl)

著名物理學家維爾納·海森堡的自傳以這句話開頭：「科學是由人們創造的。」我本人的情況並非僅尋求單一的發現，而是畢生試圖了解固體表面的化學反應如何發生，這一些工作實際上牽涉了許多人。年輕的時候，我有時夢想著成為音樂家。這就是為什麼我經常把同事視為一支管弦樂團,由我擔任指揮。我們知道,即便是最好的指揮,也無法跟平庸的樂團合作,奏出一流的音樂。然而我具有極大的幸運,總是由一群優秀的同事簇擁,我可以將他們比作──不是皇家斯德哥爾摩愛樂樂團──而或許是柏林愛樂樂團。不過,與真正的管弦樂團情形不同,藝術家演奏出由作曲家指定的音符;我們則不然,演奏者本身即為作曲家。透過不斷跨越已知與未知的邊界,他們譜出永不停息且多元的科學交響樂。(格哈德・埃特爾)

The resulting feelings had once expressed by the greatest poet of my country, J. W. Goethe, when he was already over 80 years old: "Es geht nichts über die Freude, die uns des Studium der Natur gewährt" – "There is no greater joy than studying nature." Goethe died one year before Alfred Nobel was born, and hence he could not know that there might be an even greater joy, namely when ones own joy from studying nature is honoured in such a magnificent manner by the Nobel Prize. (Gerhard Ertl)

於是,在已經年逾八旬之時,德國最偉大的詩人約翰・沃夫岡・馮・歌德曾經有感而發:"Es geht nichts über die Freude, die uns des Studium der Natur gewährt."──「沒有比研究自然再大的快樂了。」歌德在阿佛烈・諾貝爾出生前一年去世,所以無從得知,人生還會有更大的快樂,這就是當人們自己從研究自然中獲得的快樂,又由諾貝爾獎以如此華美的方式賦予榮耀之際。(格哈德・埃特爾)

The one thing that I think is extremely important, is that anyone can do it, if given a chance, if given the opportunity. (Mario R. Capecchi)

我認為極其重要的一點是,任何人都做得到,只要有機遇,只要有機會。(馬里奧・卡佩奇)

2001–2010 跨界融合與人文關懷

As a scientist I have been fortunate to have visited many, many laboratories all over the world and to have talked with other scientists about their work and aspirations. It is through these conversations that one's vision broadens and an appreciation of the complexity and beauty of the biological world is reinforced. (Mario R. Capecchi)

作為科學家，我有幸拜訪了世界各地許許多多實驗室，與同行談論他們的工作和志向。正是透過這些對話，人的視野得以更開闊，也因而強化對生物世界之複雜和美麗的欣賞。（馬里奧·卡佩奇）

The Nobel Prize has greatly rewarded a major segment of my life and, as a kind of demarcation invites some reflection. I hope that our contributions, among other developments, will be used by many to reduce suffering, improve our health and extend the productivity and fulfillment of our lives. (Mario R. Capecchi)

諾貝爾獎極大地回報了我人生中的主要部分，並且作為一種分水嶺而引發一些反思。我希望我們的貢獻以及其他進展會被許多人用於減少痛苦、改善健康，增加人生的產出和滿足。（馬里奧·卡佩奇）

I think in my deepest recesses I've always been a scientist. (Martin J. Evans)

我認為，在內心深處，自己一直是個科學家。（馬丁·埃文斯）

In my career I've known a lot of Nobel Prize winners and, you know, they've always been the tops of the tops, amazingly. And, as I say it's a boyhood dream. And someone said "Is that like scoring the goal in the FA cup?" and I said, "No, it's like scoring a goal in the world cup!" You know, it is that sort of one-off, sort of amazing. (Martin J. Evans)

> 2007年

職業生涯中，我認識了很多諾貝爾獎得主，你們知道，他們始終是菁英中之菁英，令人驚奇。如我所說，獲得諾貝爾獎是少年時的夢想。有人問：「這像是在英格蘭足總盃比賽中進球嗎？」我說：「不，這就像在世界盃比賽上踢進一球！」你們知道，就是那種絕無僅有的，那種令人驚奇的體驗。（馬丁·埃文斯）

You probably choose the one that has the best cost-to-benefit ratio in your mind, as it were. That's to say you know there will always be a certain amount of work and uncertainty about work that you begin to think about, so then you have to ask yourself, "So what am I going to get out of this if I succeed". You pick the one where the cost is least for the greatest benefit. Amongst the benefits, of course, is whether you will enjoy it… if it's something you really enjoy and no-one else cares about it then you do it! (Oliver Smithies)

你很可能選擇心目中成本效益比最好的一個方案，這樣看來。也就是說，你明白，總會存在一定程度的工作和工作的不確定性需要考慮，於是，你就得問自己：「這件事要是成功了，我從中會得到什麼？」你選擇效益最大、成本最低的一個方案。當然，效益中包括你會喜歡它……如果它是你真心喜歡，而其他人並不關心的，那就做吧！（奧利弗·史密西斯）

I don't go to work every day; I go to play every day. And that's my advice to students here today： find something you love so much that you can say —— as I can say —— I never did a day's work in my life. (Oliver Smithies)

我不是天天上班，我是天天去玩。這就是我給今天在座的學生們的建議：找到某件事，你鍾愛得可以說 —— 就像我可以說 —— 自己這輩子從來沒做過一天工作。（奧利弗·史密西斯）

When I was a child I read a comic strip about an inventor and I decided that I wanted to become an inventor, and from then on my field evolved along the course of the natural progression of one's science. (Oliver Smithies)

小時候,我看了描寫一位發明家的漫畫,就決心要當發明家。從那時起,我所從事的領域就隨著科學的自然進步而逐漸發展。(奧利弗·史密西斯)

We also acknowledge an older debt —— to our teachers —— which I want to illustrate with three of mine.

The first, Dr. G. E. Brown, taught mathematics at Heath Grammar School in Halifax, England. "Oddy" Brown, as we called him, was a poor disciplinarian, and not much liked. But he loved mathematics, and the calculus, and he conveyed this to at least one student —— me!

The second, Field Morey, is a distinguished flight instructor. He taught me to fly 30 years ago, a difficult task because I was over 50 years of age! But he taught me something more important than flying – namely, that it is possible to overcome fear with knowledge!

This same lesson applies to scientists —— the fear of failing —— which many scientists have when trying something new —— can be overcome —— in the same way —— with knowledge.

The third of my teachers is Dr. A. G. ("Sandy") Ogston. He was my tutor as an undergraduate at Balliol College, Oxford University, and later oversaw my change from medical school to graduate school in order to take up research. Sandy was an extraordinary scientist, and a dedicated teacher. And he conveyed to his students a view of science, which I quote in closing: "For science is more than the search for truth, more than a challenging game, more than a profession. It is a life that a diversity of people lead together, in the closest proximity, a school for social living. We are members one of another." (Oliver Smithies)

我們還要感念早年所受的恩惠——來自我們的老師——我想以自己的三位恩師為例說明。

第一位，G·E·布朗博士，在英國哈利法克斯的希思文法學校教數學。我們稱他「奧迪」·布朗。他執教嚴格，不太討人喜歡。然而他熱愛數學，還有微積分，並把這傳給了至少一個學生——我！

第二位，菲爾德·莫里，是一位出色的飛行教練。30年前他教我駕駛飛機，是一項艱鉅的任務，因為我已經50多歲了！而他教會了我一些比飛行更重要的東西——那就是，以知識克服恐懼是可能的！

這同樣適用於科學家——對失敗的恐懼，許多科學家在嘗試新事物時都會感受到——可以採取同樣的方法：以知識克服。

第三位老師是A·G·(「桑迪」)·奧格斯頓博士。他是我在牛津大學貝里歐學院念大學時的導師，後來又協助我從醫學院轉入研究所以從事研究。桑迪是非凡的科學家，也是敬業的教師。他向學生傳達了一種科學觀，我在此引用作為結語：「須知科學不僅是對真理的探索，不僅是富於挑戰性的競賽，不僅是一門專業。它是一種生活，各式各樣的人聚在一起，彼此緊密地相連的社會生活群體。我們彼此皆為成員。」(奧利弗·史密西斯)

I don't know much about creative writing programs. But they're not telling the truth if they don't teach, one, that writing is hard work, and, two, that you have to give up a great deal of life, your personal life, to be a writer. (Doris Lessing)

我對創意寫作計畫所知有限。不過，他們要是不教這兩樣，他們就不是在傳授真知：其一，寫作是一種艱苦的工作；其二，要當作家，你必須放棄大量的個人生活。（多麗絲・萊辛）

They can't give a Nobel to someone who's dead so I think they were probably thinking they had better give it to me now before I popped off. (Doris Lessing)

他們不能把諾貝爾獎頒發給已經去世的人，所以我想他們很可能認為，最好在我突然離去之前就把獎頒給我。（多麗絲・萊辛）

As soon as I got the Nobel Prize my back collapsed and I was in hospital. (Doris Lessing)

一拿到諾貝爾獎我的背部就患病了，於是我進了醫院。[22]（多麗絲・萊辛）

All I do is give interviews and spend time being photographed. (Doris Lessing)

天天都在接受採訪和花時間拍照。（多麗絲・萊辛）

It's lovely to have money to give away —— that's the bonus of winning the Nobel. (Doris Lessing)

有錢能夠捐出來真是太好了 —— 這是獲得諾貝爾獎的額外福利。（多麗絲・萊辛）

Some people obtain fame, others deserve it. (Doris Lessing)

有人沽名釣譽，有人實至名歸。（多麗絲・萊辛）

---

[22] 萊辛獲獎時年屆 88 歲，為諾貝爾獎得主中最年長者。

I've worked hard all my life. You have to if you want to get things done. (Doris Lessing)

我努力工作了一生。想盡責就得這麼做。（多麗絲・萊辛）

Any human anywhere will blossom in a hundred unexpected talents and capacities simply by being given the opportunity to do so. (Doris Lessing)

任何地方的任何人都能一展各種才華與能力，猶如百花綻放，出乎他人意料，只須給予機會。（多麗絲・萊辛）

Whatever you are meant to do, do it now. The conditions are always impossible. (Doris Lessing)

無論你打算做什麼，現在就做。條件總是不具備的。（多麗絲・萊辛）

Good ideas don't get lost, though they may be submerged for a time. (Doris Lessing)

好的想法不會消失，儘管可能被埋沒一段時間。（多麗絲・萊辛）

What has happened to us is an amazing invention —— computers and the internet and TV. It is a revolution. This is not the first revolution the human race has dealt with. The printing revolution, which did not take place in a matter of a few decades, but took much longer, transformed our minds and ways of thinking. A foolhardy lot, we accepted it all, as we always do, never asked: What is going to happen to us now, with this invention of print? In the same way, we never thought to ask: How will our lives, our way of thinking, be changed by this internet, which has seduced a whole generation with its inanities so that even quite reasonable people will confess that once they are hooked, it is hard to cut free, and they may find a whole day has passed in blogging etc. (Doris Lessing)

　　我們面對驚人的發明創造——電腦、網際網路和電視。這不是人類面對的第一場革命。印刷革命，並非發生於幾十年之間，而是花了更長遠的時間，改變了我們的思想和思考方式。顢頇魯莽的我們一如既往地全盤接受，完全不問：隨著印刷術的發明，我們此時將迎來怎樣的變局？如今我們依舊完全不想問：我們的生活和思考方式會怎樣被網路改變？它以其空洞虛妄誘惑了整整一代人，影響之大，就連相當理智的人都會承認，一旦上鉤，便很難擺脫。他們可能發現，整整一天都在寫部落格等活動中消磨掉了。（多麗絲・萊辛）

When you're young you think that you're going to sail into a lovely lake of quietude and peace. This is profoundly untrue. (Doris Lessing)

　　年輕時，你以為自己將會駛入一個風平浪靜的幽美的湖。這根本不真實。（多麗絲・萊辛）

For the last third of life there remains only work. It alone is always stimulating, rejuvenating, exciting and satisfying. (Doris Lessing)

　　生命的最後三分之一時間裡剩下的只有工作。僅僅這樣就總是令人激動、煥發活力、令人興奮乃至滿意的了。（多麗絲・萊辛）

The great secret that all old people share is that you really haven't changed in seventy or eighty years. Your body changes, but you don't change at all. And that, of course, causes great confusion. (Doris Lessing)

　　所有老年人共有的一大祕密就是，七、八十年過去了，你真的一點都沒變。你的身體在改變，但你根本沒變。這當然會引發很大的困惑。（多麗絲・萊辛）

I do have a sense, and I've never not had it, of how easily things can vanish. (Doris Lessing)

我確實有種感覺,這種感覺始終存在,就是事物能夠何等輕易地消失啊。(多麗絲·萊辛)

I have always been fascinated with those who try to look over the horizon and see things that are coming at us. (Albert Arnold Gore Jr.)

我總是被一種人深深吸引,他們力圖讓視線越過地平線,看見向著我們襲來的事物。(艾爾·高爾)

Science has a culture that is inherently cautious and that is normally not a bad thing. You could even say conservative, because of the peer review process and because the scientific method prizes uncertainty and penalises anyone who goes out on any sort of a limb that is not held in place by abundant and well-documented evidence. (Albert Arnold Gore Jr.)

科學具有謹慎的天性,而這通常不是壞事。你甚至可以說是保守的,因為同儕審查的過程,也因為科學方法重視不確定性,並且懲罰任何沒有大量和充分證據支持的人。(艾爾·高爾)

If we don't succeed, we run the risk of failure. (Albert Arnold Gore Jr.)

我們如果不成功,就有失敗的危險。(艾爾·高爾)

I'm very pleased and I hope that others who deserve it also got it. (Leonid Hurwicz)

我非常高興,我希望其他有資格獲獎的人也得獎。(里奧尼德·赫維克茲)

Legal behavior is not incompatible with rational, self-interested behavior. (Leonid Hurwicz)

合法行為與合理的、利己的行為並非互不相容。（里奧尼德·赫維克茲）

The Nobel Prize is not very important for the winners —— they are usually pretty successful people already. But it is valuable as a way of drawing the public's attention to important work in economics. (Eric S. Maskin)

諾貝爾獎對獲獎者來說不太重要 —— 他們通常已經功成名就。然而作為吸引大眾關注經濟學重要工作的一種方式，它就很可貴了。（艾瑞克·馬斯金）

My parents and teachers and my friends encouraged and inspired me to work hard throughout my life. Reading Isaac Asimov's book "Foundation" inspired me to think about a career in mathematical social science. (Roger B. Myerson)

我的父母、老師和朋友支持和鼓勵我畢生努力工作。閱讀艾薩克·艾西莫夫的「基地」系列作品激發我考慮從事數學的社會科學專業。（羅傑·梅爾森）

2008 年

When you are young, you tend to be more idealistic, ambitious, and impatient, just as I was myself. You would be satisfied with nothing short of solving the great problems of physics. But at the same time, you have nagging self-doubt, constantly gauging yourself against others. I experienced this acutely when I spent two years at the Institute for Advanced Study. I could not accomplish what I had wanted to. Everybody looked smarter than I, and I had a nervous breakdown. I thought I was the only poor guy who had the problem. Much later I found out from my old rivals that they had all gone through the same experience. (Yoichiro Nambu)

年輕的時候，你往往更富有理想，雄心勃勃，急於求成，就像我一樣。非關解決物理學大哉問之事就無法令你滿足。然而同時，你又免不了自我懷疑，總是以別人衡量自己。在普林斯頓高等研究院的兩年中，我痛切地感受到這一點。我心有餘而力不足。人人都顯得比我聰明，我精神都崩潰了。我以為自己是唯一有此問題的可憐蟲。很久以後，我由老對手們那裡得知，他們都體驗過相同的感受。（南部陽一郎）

Let me also tell you another aspect of the pursuit of physics, or any discipline for that matter. It is that you enjoy it just for the fun of it. You should not be dead serious all the time. All work and no play is no good. When you are stuck, you relax and try other things that you can handle without specific purpose or ambition. Learn to be flexible in your pursuits on short term scale, and patient on long term. It happens sometimes that a paper you wrote in a casual moment gets more attention than the paper you think is the more serious and important. (Yoichiro Nambu)

我也跟你談談物理學，或任何類似學科的科學研究的另一面吧。你只是為了好玩而享受它。你無須始終認真得要死。只工作不玩耍可不好。思路卡住時，就放鬆一下，做點別的游刃有餘而並無特定目的或抱負的事情。從事研究要學會短期靈活變通，而長期保持耐心。有時偏偏

是，你不經意之間寫下的論文，比自以為更嚴謹、重要的論文得到更多的關注。（南部陽一郎）

Talent does not equal accomplishment. The latter is a more dynamical thing. You need self-confidence, but usually self-confidence and accomplishment bootstrap themselves. (Yoichiro Nambu)

才能不等於成就。後者是更動態的東西。你需要自信，不過自信和成就通常會自我實現。（南部陽一郎）

You need luck, but luck does not happen in a vacuum. It has to be cultivated. (Yoichiro Nambu)

你需要運氣，但運氣並非無端發生。它需要培養。（南部陽一郎）

Now we are waiting for some kind of new physics. In the sense theoreticians predict, propose many theories, and we just wait experimental proof of those models. (Makoto Kobayashi)

現在我們在等待某種新的物理學。在這個意義上，理論家預言、提出了許多理論，我們只是等待這些模型的實驗證明。（小林誠）

For a theorist, the most exciting period is after waking early one morning to discover a truth that you could not have imagined. (Toshihide Maskawa)

對於理論工作者，最令人激動的時候，是一天早晨醒來後，發現一個超乎你想像的真理。（益川敏英）

The point is that I don't study, I don't do my research for application or any benefit. I just do my research to understand why jellyfish luminesce, and why that protein fluoresce? (Osamu Shimomura)

> 2008 年

我並不是為了實際應用或任何益處而苦心孤詣,而從事研究。我從事研究只是想了解水母為什麼發冷光,蛋白質又為什麼發螢光。(下村脩)

Young people, study whatever if they are interested in that subject. But don't give up on the way until they finish the subject. Also, good subjects have a lot of difficulty. If one gives up, on the way; that's it, that's finished. To get success, everybody has to overcome any difficulty on the way. (Osamu Shimomura)

年輕人,他們要是對一個題目感興趣就研究它,不管是什麼。但不可半途而廢。而且,好的題目也都困難重重。人要是半途而廢,那麼就這樣結束了。為了獲得成功,人人都得克服過程中的任何困難。(下村脩)

I realised that they must have given the Prize in Chemistry, so I simply said, "Okay, who's the schnook that got the prize this time?" And so I opened up my laptop, and I got to the Nobel Prize site and I found out I was the schnook! (Martin Chalfie)

我想他們一定公布了化學獎,所以只說了句:「好吧,這次得獎的笨蛋是誰?」然後我打開筆記型電腦,找到諾貝爾獎網站,發現我就是這個笨蛋!(馬丁‧查爾菲)

I went and looked online to see who had won. I can tell you it's very, very strange to see your name listed at the Nobel Prize website. Actually, I went back several times over the following months just to make sure they haven't erased the name from the site. It was quite a surprise. (Martin Chalfie)

我上網看是誰得獎了。我可以告訴你,看到自己的名字出現在諾貝爾獎網站上,是非常、非常奇怪的。事實上,在接下來的幾個月裡,我

回去看了好幾次,只是確認他們沒有把這個名字從網站上刪除。這實在令人驚奇。(馬丁·查爾菲)

Scientific inquiry starts with observation. The more one can see, the more one can investigate. (Martin Chalfie)

科學探究始於觀察。人能看到的越多,就越能調查研究。(馬丁·查爾菲)

If you do an experiment and it gives you what you did not expect, it is a discovery. (Martin Chalfie)

如果你做了一個實驗,它也給了你出乎意料的東西,這就是一項發現。(馬丁·查爾菲)

My interest in imaging with multiple glowing colors… reflects visual interests from early childhood, which I have been lucky enough to align with a professional career. (Roger Y. Tsien)

我對多種發光顏色成像的興趣……反映了我幼時對視覺的興趣。我足夠幸運,把它跟職業生涯連繫在一起。(錢永健)

I was always obsessed by pretty colours and by technologies that seem useful. One of my earliest memories is of a beach that had a zone of coarse pebbles surrounded by two zones of sand. I tried to lay down a bridge of sand across the pebbles to make crossing more comfortable for my tiny bare feet. Of course, the bridge would have been washed away by the next big wave or high tide. Perhaps that's a metaphor for much of my career. (Roger Y. Tsien)

我總是痴迷於美麗的顏色和看來有用的技術。我最早的記憶之一是關於一處海灘,那裡有個地方遍布粗糙的鵝卵石,旁邊是兩片沙子。我賣力地在鵝卵石上鋪一座沙橋，好讓光腳走過時舒服些。不用說，它早就被下一個大浪或潮水沖走了。那也許是我大半生事業的一種象徵。（錢永健）

I've always liked pretty colors. I tell students it's valuable to get some degree of gut pleasure out of what you're doing, to keep you going. Because, yes, when experiments work, there's nothing like that thrill, but that happens once in a while, and you can go for long, long periods where nothing works. (Roger Y. Tsien)

我一向喜歡美麗的顏色。我告訴學生們，從手邊的工作中得到一定程度的內心愉悅，使你持續做下去，這是可貴的。因為，是的，實驗一旦成功，什麼都比不上那種激動；可是那難得一遇，你可能必須毫無成效地工作很長、很長的時間。（錢永健）

I have to say, that's one thing that getting some prizes for the GFP work was good for. I'd rather not just use the prizes to congratulate myself. It feels more like they've given me a license to go and try something else, like, "You've been there, you've done that, now do something better." (Roger Y. Tsien)

我必須說，這是由於綠色螢光蛋白工作而獲得一些獎項的好處之一。我寧願不以得獎向自己祝賀。我更想得到類似一種去嘗試其他事情的許可，像是「你有經驗，你做過了，現在把事情做得更好吧」。（錢永健）

I'm a muddled mix. When I was applying for my first faculty position, several biology departments rejected me on the grounds that I was a chemist, and at least one chemistry department turned me down as too much of a biologist. Almost all my work has been involved with tool building, but I have never had a formal engineering course or appointment. Fortunately, most forward looking departments have now adopted a more flexible and interdisciplinary viewpoint. Personally, I don't care much for labels. (Roger Y. Tsien)

我這個人很難歸類。最初申請教職時，幾個生物系以我是化學家為由拒絕了我，至少一個化學系認為我過多地屬於生物學家而不予考慮。我幾乎所有的工作都關係到工具製作，可是我從未獲得正式的工程學分或職位。幸運的是，大多數目光前瞻的科系，現在都採取了更靈活的、跨學科的觀點。我個人不太喜歡標籤。（錢永健）

You should take all elderly scientists with a grain of salt —— including me. (Roger Y. Tsien)

你們應當對所有的老年科學家持保留態度 —— 包括我。（錢永健）

As a child I remember my own intensive interest in biology, birds, other animals and flowers and was determined at an early age to become a scientist. (Harald zur Hausen)

我記得自己童年對生物學、鳥類、其他動物和花朵的濃厚興趣，很小的時候就決心要當個科學家。（哈拉爾德・楚爾・豪森）

What you can do today is define some interesting research topics, but I'm not willing to predict which of these research topics in 10 years from now to which extent they will be applied. Almost all of these types of predictions —— at least many of those which I have read —— turned out to be wrong in the end. (Harald zur Hausen)

你可以在今天確定一些有趣的研究主題，只是我不願預測，10 年後它們哪些會應用到何等程度。幾乎所有這一類預測 —— 至少我讀過的許多預測 —— 最終都證明是錯的。（哈拉爾德・楚爾・豪森）

2008 年

This success in the discovery of the AIDS virus is really a success of a world team with different expertise. And I think, for the future, it's also important, especially when working on infectious disease, to have a world network of clinicians, virologists and microbiologists, working in the hospitals and basic sciences. This was really essential for me in the discovery of the AIDS virus. And I think it's essential also for tomorrow for discovering new, emerging, or re-emerging agents responsible for infectious disease. (Françoise Barré-Sinoussi)

成功發現愛滋病病毒，實在是一個各具專長的世界團隊的成功。我認為，對於未來，這也有重要意義。尤其是在研究傳染病時，要有一個臨床醫生、病毒學家和微生物學家的世界網路，在醫院和基礎科學領域工作。這對於我發現愛滋病病毒實在不可或缺。並且我認為，對於未來發現新的、正在出現的或再度出現的傳染病病原，它也是不可或缺的。（法蘭索娃絲‧巴爾－西諾西）

There are many questions, which can be resolved only by hard work and innovative thinking. I hope to be able to continue both. (Luc Montagnier)

有很多問題只能藉由努力工作和創新思考解決。我希望兩者都能夠堅持下去。（呂克‧蒙塔尼耶）

Our goal is not to completely eradicate the infection —— that would be very difficult —— but to produce a vaccine that will prevent not infection but disease. I think this is more possible. (Luc Montagnier)

我們的目標不是徹底消除感染——這會非常困難——而是生產出一種並非預防感染而是預防疾病的疫苗。我認為這是更有可能的。（呂克‧蒙塔尼耶）

Literature is a good way of practicing an exchange. We have to listen to all the people of the world and there is no better voice than the voice of literature for this knowledge of the world. Because literature is done by individuals, they are not necessary specialists, they are people who feel, who experiment, sometimes suffer themselves, and they express in their books, most of the time, their hopes and their wish and their will of a better world. (Jean-Marie Gustave Le Clézio)

文學是實行交流的好方式。我們得傾聽世界上所有的人的心聲，而要了解天下人，沒有比文學之聲更好的聲音了。因為作品是由個人創作的，這些人不是必要的專家，這些人是芸芸眾生，他們感受，他們體驗，有時親身受苦。在自己的書中，大多數時候，他們表達希望和祝願，企盼更好的世界。（尚－馬利・古斯塔夫・勒克萊喬）

Peace is a question of will. All conflicts can be settled, and there are no excuses for allowing them to become eternal. (Martti Ahtisaari)

和平是意願問題。所有的衝突均可解決，也沒有任何藉口允許它們永遠存在。（馬爾蒂・阿提沙利）

The task of the mediator is to help the parties to open difficult issues and nudge them forward in the peace process. The mediator's role combines those of a ship's pilot, consulting medical doctor, midwife and teacher. (Martti Ahtisaari)

調停者的任務是幫助各方解決棘手問題，推動他們在和平進程中前行。調停者的角色結合了船舶駕駛員、諮詢醫生、助產士和教師的身分。（馬爾蒂・阿提沙利）

The point here isn't that top executives are overpaid, though they surely are; it's that the way they are paid rewards them for creating the illusion of success, never mind the reality. (Paul Krugman)

重點並非高階主管薪酬過高，儘管他們肯定如此；而是對他們的報酬方式獎勵他們製造成功假象，罔顧現實。（保羅‧克魯曼）

2009 年

The research was enthralling work and in 1966 I published the now famous ground-breaking paper, "Dielectric-fibre Surface Waveguides for Optical Frequencies". This research was to spawn a whole new industry over the next twenty years. (Charles Kuen Kao)

研究令人著迷，我在 1966 年發表了如今知名的具有開創性意義的論文，《光頻率介質纖維表面波導》，當時的研究在隨後的 20 年內催生了一個全新的產業。（高錕）

People asked me if the idea came as a sudden flash, eureka! I had been working since graduation on microwave transmissions. The theories and limitations were ground into my brain. I knew we needed much more bandwidth and thoughts of how it could be done were constantly in my mind. (Charles Kuen Kao)

人們問我，這個想法是不是靈光一閃：我想到了！我畢業後一直從事微波通訊工作，相關理論以及限制都深深地印在了我的腦海中。我知道我們需要更多的頻寬，因此我經常不斷思考如何才能做到這一點。（高錕）

Ideas do not always come in a flash but by diligent trial-and-error experiments that take time and thought. (Charles Kuen Kao)

好的想法並不是總會突然閃現。你需要花費時間，經常思考，並辛勤地不斷將想法付諸「實驗與錯誤並存」的實踐。（高錕）

One day my father brought home a big round yellow disc of food that he told us was called "cheese" that foreigners ate. Food was in short supply so we ate it, but it tasted very funny. When we went outside for some walks we sometimes passed a big tall building with Japanese soldiers standing at the door. My parents told us to walk past quickly as people inside were killed there, and to bow to the soldiers. (Charles Kuen Kao)

有一天，我父親帶回家了一些圓盤狀的黃色食物，他告訴我們，這是外國人吃的「起司」。當時食物供應短缺，所以我們吃了這些起司，但這種食物的味道確實很好笑。當我們出外散步時，有時會經過一座高大的建築物，有日本士兵站在門口把守。父母告訴我們，經過時要向士兵鞠躬並快速走過，因為有人在裡面遭到殺害。（高錕）

Food was still scarce after World War II and the slices of meat served for dinner were so thin, they were transparent when held up to the light! (Charles Kuen Kao)

由於當時戰後食物供給不足，晚餐吃的肉片很薄，以至於它們在光照下居然是透明的！（高錕）

I graduated in 1957 with a B.Sc. in Electrical Engineering. In those days the degrees were awarded as a First, Second, Pass or Fail. As I spent more time on the tennis court than with my books, my degree was a Second. (Charles Kuen Kao)

我於 1957 年獲得電氣工程的理學學士學位。當時英國大學的學位有一等、二等、及格和不及格四種類別，我由於當時在網球場上花的時間比在讀書上花的時間多，所以獲得的是二等學位。（高錕）

In 1982 I was appointed Executive Scientist at ITT in charge of all research and development activities and I moved to the Advanced Technology Center in Connecticut, U.S.A. This post was specially created and allowed me the freedom to do anything I considered important for ITT. In order to chart the waters on the ultimate limits of optical communication technology, I pioneered the Terabit Optoelectronics Technology Project to explore the technologies that could reach terabits per second of transmission capacity. (Charles Kuen Kao)

1982 年，我被任命為國際電話與電報公司的執行科學家，負責掌管公司所有的研究和開發項目。我隨後便搬到了美國康乃狄克州的高級技術中心。這個職位是特別設立的，我可以自由地做任何我認為對國際電話與電報公司重要的事。為了探索光學通訊技術的極限，我開創了太位元光電子技術項目，研究傳輸容量可達到每秒兆位元的技術。（高錕）

At the University, my role was to create space for people to grow. What I had done essentially was create situations where people would like to take on responsibilities. This had enabled the University to grow as a whole: everybody would be contributing what they should because they feel it is their responsibility and the environment allows them to do so. I created the space at the right time for talent within the University to perform as it should, thus taking it to a new level of development. (Charles Kuen Kao)

我在大學的職責是為人們的成長創造空間。我所做的基本上就是營造一種人們想要主動承擔責任的氛圍。這使得大學能夠整體發展:大家都會為學校貢獻他們應該做的事情,因為他們覺得這是他們的責任,而大學內的環境也允許他們這樣做。我在適當的時機為大學的人才營造了發展空間,讓人們能因此進一步地開發自己的能力。(高錕)

The rapid expansion of the tertiary education sector and the increased government funding that came with it have allowed us to do a lot of things to become a top university. The most satisfying change was a scholarly atmosphere on campus —— people are pursuing important things because they believe such things are important. (Charles Kuen Kao)

高等教育部門的迅速擴張以及隨之而來的政府資金增加,使我們能做很多事情來讓香港中文大學達到世界頂尖水準。其中,最令人滿意的變化是校園裡的學術氛圍 —— 人們會因相信某些事很重要的信念而鍥而不捨地進行研究。(高錕)

In the 1960s, our children were small. Charles often came home later than normal —— dinner was waiting as were the children. I got very annoyed when this happened day after day. His words, maybe not exactly remembered, were ——

"Please don't be so mad. It is very exciting what we are doing; it will shake the world one day!"

I was sarcastic, "Really, so you will get the Nobel Prize, won't you!"

He was right —— it has revolutionized telecommunications. (Gwen MW Kao)

1960年代,我們的孩子還很小。高錕常常很晚回家,以至子女經常都要在餐桌前等著吃晚飯。我對他每天晚歸感到很生氣。我依稀記得他是這麼對我說的：

「別生氣。我們現在做的是非常振奮人心的事情，有一天它會震驚全世界的！」

我略帶諷刺地說：「是嗎，那你會因此而得諾貝爾獎的，是嗎？」

他是對的——他的成果為通訊界帶來了一場驚天動地的革命。（黃美芸[23]）

I found that my career at Bell Telephone Labs thrived because of the environment, which encouraged cooperative research, offered opportunities for access to sophisticated equipment, and fellowship. (Willard S. Boyle)

我發覺，自己在貝爾電話實驗室的事業之所以興旺，是得益於環境。那裡鼓勵合作研究，提供了使用精密設備，以及爭取研究基金的機會。（威拉德·博伊爾）

I started off in the research area, where there was essentially not much direction in that you were allowed to do yourself and stand or fall on your own. And that was nice. Most of all, there were just a lot of exciting, intelligent people around that you could interact with. (George E. Smith)

我在研究領域起步，這裡基本上沒有什麼方向容許你自行其是，成敗由己。這很好。尤其是，周圍有許許多多出色的、聰明的人，你可以與之互動。（喬治·埃爾伍德·史密斯）

There is no magical formula for winning a Nobel Prize. (Venkatraman Ramakrishnan)

獲得諾貝爾獎並無神奇公式。（文卡·拉馬克里希南）

---

[23] 2009 年在斯德哥爾摩大學，高錕因病而不能親自發表諾貝爾獎演講，於是由夫人黃美芸代勞。

Science today is a highly collaborative exercise, and to convert it into a contest, as the Nobel does, is a bad way to look at science. (Venkatraman Ramakrishnan)

今日的科學是高度合作的活動，把它變成競賽，如諾貝爾獎所為，是看待科學的糟糕方式。（文卡・拉馬克里希南）

I found the most exciting thing about the ribosome was seeing a structure, seeing a large macromolecular assembly that I had no idea what it would look like. And I have to say it was the most exciting time in science that I've had, by a lot. Just, you know, it's like getting to the top of Mt. Everest and seeing the view, it's terrific. (Thomas A. Steitz)

我發現，關於核糖體，最令人激動之處是看到一個結構，看到一個很大的大分子組合，它會是什麼樣子超乎我的想像。不得不說，在科學上，這是我所經歷的最令人激動的時刻，無與倫比。你知道，簡直就像登上聖母峰頂一覽天下，美妙至極。（湯馬斯・史泰茲）

Looking back over the development and progress of my career in science, I am reminded how vitally important good mentorship is in the early stages of one's career development and constant face-to-face conversations, debate and discussions with colleagues at all stages of research. Outstanding discoveries, insights and developments do not happen in a vacuum. (Thomas A. Steitz)

回顧自己科學事業的發展和進步，使我想到，人在其事業發展早期得遇良師，以及在研究所有階段與同事經常的面對面交談、爭辯和討論，是何其重要。非凡的發現、見解和發展並非出自真空。（湯馬斯・史泰茲）

> 2009 年

I seriously considered becoming a musician, but then concluded I could do music as a hobby if I went into science, but could not do science as a hobby if I went into music. (Thomas A. Steitz)

我曾經認真地考慮成為一名音樂家，不過最終想到，我如果進入科學界，可以把音樂作為業餘愛好；但若進入音樂界，就不能把從事科學作為業餘愛好了。（湯馬斯・史泰茲）

I wanted to reveal how genetic code is translated into protein. I knew a great application could be for antibiotics, since half of the useful ones target the ribosomes, but I didn't believe I could contribute to it. It was like the next Mount Everest to conquer. It was my dream to contribute something to humanity. (Ada E. Yonath)

我想揭示遺傳密碼是如何轉譯成蛋白質的。我知道抗生素的用途非凡，因為發揮作用的那些半數指向核糖體，可是我無法置信自己能夠有所作為。這就像有待征服的下一座世界最高峰。為人類做出貢獻是我的夢想。（艾妲・尤納特）

I was described as a dreamer, a fantasist, even as the village idiot. I didn't care. What I cared about was convincing people to allow me to go on with my work. (Ada E. Yonath)

我被說成做夢的人、幻想者，甚至傻子。我不在意。我在意的是說服人們允許我繼續我的工作。（艾妲・尤納特）

The world was not supportive. They look at me as a joke for 13 to 14 years until I could prove feasibility; then I had competitors. Those that laughed at me became my competitors. (Ada E. Yonath)

人們並不支持。他們把我當笑話看了十三、四年，直到我能夠證明

可行性；然後我有了競爭者。那些嘲笑我的人成了我的競爭對手。（艾妲·尤納特）

If one has curiosity, then one stands the chance of attain a high level of scientific inquiry. (Ada E. Yonath)

人如果有好奇心，就有機會完成高水準的科學探索。（艾妲·尤納特）

I am, and always have been, passionately curious. (Ada E. Yonath)

我一向都有強烈的好奇心。（艾妲·尤納特）

People always talk about the implication and applications of a process, but for me, the goal is purely about knowledge. Knowledge can become practical today, in 20 years, or in 500 years. Ask Newton. He didn't know there would be space research based on his accident with the apple. (Ada E. Yonath)

人們總是談論一個過程的意義和用途，然而就我而言，目的純粹關乎知識。知識可以在今天、20年，或500年內變得實用。問問牛頓。他並不知道會出現基於其蘋果事件的空間研究。（艾妲·尤納特）

I was born in Jerusalem with a religious background and a rabbi as a father... it was rather poor, but what we did have, we did have books. (Ada E. Yonath)

我出生在耶路撒冷，家人信教，父親是一位拉比……家裡很窮，不過我們的確還有些東西，我們有書。（艾妲·尤納特）

Once, when I tried to calculate the height of the balcony, I broke my arm. Another time, I wanted to see if water moves faster than kerosene. When my father came out to smoke, a fire broke out. (Ada E. Yonath)

> 2009 年

　　有一次，在嘗試計算陽臺高度時，我摔斷了手臂。還有一次，我想看看水是不是比煤油流動得快。父親走出來抽菸時，一下子著了火。（艾妲・尤納特）

From the age of 11, I was cleaning floors, washing dishes, making sandwiches and being a cashier. Survival was the name of the game. Life was so hard that I had to struggle to keep up my standards. Under these conditions, I didn't think about science too much. (Ada E. Yonath)

　　從 11 歲起，我就掃地、洗盤子、做三明治，還當收銀員。一切都是為了生存。生活如此艱難，我不得不盡力維持自己的生活水準。在這樣的情況下，我並未想到科學。（艾妲・尤納特）

I don't distinguish between men and women. This is irrelevant to me, and I don't think in these terms. (Ada E. Yonath)

　　我不區分男人和女人。這與我無關，我不以這些說法思考。（艾妲・尤納特）

I don't walk into the lab in the morning thinking, "I am a woman, and I will carry out an experiment that will conquer the world." I am a scientist, not male or female. A scientist. (Ada E. Yonath)

　　早上走進實驗室，我不會想著「我是個女人，我要完成一項將征服世界的實驗」。我是個科學家，不是男性或女性。一個科學家。（艾妲・尤納特）

People are obsessed with my haircut; everyone wants to do something with my hair before the ceremony. Very senior figures tell me their hairstylist wants to do my hair for free. It's surprising. People from television are interested almost exclusively in aspects of my hair and my hairdresser. (Ada E. Yonath)

人們對我的髮型著迷；誰都想在頒獎儀式前拿我的頭髮做文章。非常顯赫的大人物對我說，他們的髮型師想免費幫我做頭髮。這令人驚訝。電視圈的人幾乎只對我的頭髮和理髮師感興趣。（艾妲・尤納特）

Challenges in medicine are moving from "Treat the symptoms after the house is on fire" to "Can we preserve the house intact?" (Elizabeth H. Blackburn)

醫學上的挑戰正在從「治療房子著火後的症狀」轉向「我們能防止房子受損嗎？」（伊莉莎白・布雷克本）

Tracing the beginnings of the interwoven stories of science can be arbitrary, as beginnings are so often lost in the mists of time. (Elizabeth H. Blackburn)

在科學上，追查相互交織的故事的開端未免任性，因為開端實在是經常消失於時間的迷霧中。（伊莉莎白・布雷克本）

Biology seemed the most interesting of sciences to me as a child. I was captivated by both the visual impact of science through science books written for young people, and an idea of the romance and nobility of the scientific quest. This latter was especially engendered by the biography of Marie Curie, written by her daughter, which I read and reread as a child. By the time I was in my late teens it was clear to me that I wanted to do science. (Elizabeth Blackburn)

小時候，生物學對於我似乎是最有趣的科學。無論寫給年輕人看的科學圖書中的科學插圖，還是科學探索浪漫而崇高的想法，都讓我入迷。其中後者尤其被居禮夫人女兒所著《居禮夫人傳》激發，我小時候一再閱讀此書。十七、八歲時，我很清楚自己想從事科學。（伊莉莎白・布雷克本）

One characteristic aspect of ageing is the increased susceptibility to disease, particularly age-related diseases such as cardiovascular diseases and cancer. (Elizabeth H. Blackburn)

衰老特有的一個方面,是對疾病敏感度的增加,尤其是與年齡相關的疾病,如心血管病和癌症。(伊莉莎白·布雷克本)

What intrigues basic scientists like me is that anytime we do a series of experiments, there are going to be three or four new questions that come up when you think you've answered one. (Carol W. Greider)

使我這樣的基礎科學家感興趣的是,每當我們做一系列實驗,當你認為已經回答了一個問題時,就會有三、四個新的問題出現。(卡蘿·格萊德)

One of the lessons I have learned in the different stages of my career is that science is not done alone. It is through talking with others and sharing that progress is made. (Carol W. Greider)

在職業生涯的不同階段,我學到的經驗之一為,科學成就並非僅憑一己之力。進步是透過交談和分享而獲得的。(卡蘿·格萊德)

It takes years to realize the multiple benefits of science; without adequate, sustained funding for research, the careers of many bright, young scientists may come to a screeching halt. (Carol W. Greider)

要實現科學的多方面效益需要若干年的時間。沒有足夠的、持續的研究資金,許多聰明的年輕科學家的事業可能戛然而止。(卡蘿·格萊德)

2001-2010 跨界融合與人文關懷

I think actively promoting women in science is very important because the data has certainly shown that there has been an underrepresentation. (Carol W. Greider)

我認為，在科學領域積極促進女性參與非常重要，因為資料的確呈現群體代表性不足。（卡蘿・格萊德）

The thing about the Nobel ceremony is that for a whole week, you get treated like a superstar. You get driven everywhere. You have minders who always make sure you get where you're going. And you always get into the back seat of the limo. (Jack W. Szostak)

諾貝爾獎頒獎儀式的情況是，整整一星期，你被當作超級明星對待。無處不是專車接送。並且總是有人照顧，確保你抵達要去的地方。你總是坐進豪華轎車後座。（傑克・索斯塔克）

You can't build a future if you don't have a past. (Herta Müller)

如果你沒有過去，就無法建立未來。（赫塔・米勒）

One is either destroyed by adapting or for refusing to. (Herta Müller)

人或是毀於適應，或是毀於拒絕適應。（赫塔・米勒）

Happiness may perhaps be shared. But not luck, sadly. (Herta Müller)

幸福也許可以被分享。然而可惜的是幸運不能。（赫塔・米勒）

Literature speaks with everyone individually —— it is personal property that stays inside our heads. And nothing speaks to us as forcefully as a book, which expects nothing in return, other than that we think and feel. (Herta Müller)

文學與每一個人個別談話 —— 它是留在我們頭腦中的個人資產。沒

2009 年

有什麼像書一樣動人地與我們談話。除了我們的思考和感受，它不指望任何回報。（赫塔·米勒）

What can't be said can be written. Because writing is a silent act, a labor from the head to the hand. (Herta Müller)

不能說的可以寫出來。因為寫作是無聲的行動，是從頭到手的勞動。（赫塔·米勒）

I have packed myself into silence so deeply and for so long that I can never unpack myself using words. When I speak, I only pack myself a little differently. (Herta Müller)

我把自己埋藏在沉默中，如此之深，如此之久，以至於完全無法用語言說明自己。我說話的時候，只是把自己包裝得略有不同。（赫塔·米勒）

Anything in literature, including memory, is second-hand. (Herta Müller)

文學作品中的一切，包括記憶，都是二手的。（赫塔·米勒）

If you're walking down the right path and you're willing to keep walking, eventually you'll make progress. (Barack H. Obama)

你如果走在正確的道路上，又願意繼續走下去，最終就會獲得進步。（巴拉克·歐巴馬）

Issues are never simple. One thing I'm proud of is that very rarely will you hear me simplify the issues. (Barack H. Obama)

問題從來都不是簡單的。我自認為得意的一件事是，你們幾乎聽不到我簡化問題。（巴拉克·歐巴馬）

The power of a theory is exactly proportional to the diversity of situations it can explain. (Elinor Ostrom)

理論的力量與其所能解釋的情況之多樣性恰成正比。（伊莉諾‧歐斯壯）

Humans are neither all angels nor all devils. (Elinor Ostrom)

人類既不是全都是天使，也並非全都是惡魔。（伊莉諾‧歐斯壯）

I've attended economic sessions where I've been the only woman in the room, but that is slowly changing and I think there's a greater respect now that women can make a major contribution. And I would hope that the recognition here is helping that along. (Elinor Ostrom)

我參加過一些經濟學會議，在那裡我是與會的唯一女性。不過情況在慢慢改變，由於女性能夠做出重大的貢獻，我認為有了更大的尊重。但願諾貝爾獎的認可有助於這一項變化。（伊莉諾‧歐斯壯）

For those who, like myself, are inclined to be eclectic, no comprehensive commitment to one approach rather than another needs to be made. What is involved, rather, is the selection of the approach best suited to deal with the problems at hand. (Oliver E. Williamson)

對於我這一類傾向於折衷的人而言，無須完全採取一種方法而非另一種方法。不如說，要做的是選擇最適合處理當前問題的方法。（奧立佛‧威廉森）

Teaching can be learning, especially if student curiosity with the question "What's going on here?" can be elicited. (Oliver E. Williamson)

教學也可以是學習，尤其是當提問「發生了什麼事」，學生的好奇心可以被引發的時候。（奧立佛‧威廉森）

2010 年

When one dares to try, rewards are not guaranteed but at least it is an adventure. (Andre Geim)

當一個人勇於嘗試時，回報是沒有保證的，但至少這是一次冒險。（安德烈‧蓋姆）

The great esteem in which the Nobel prizes are universally held is due to the fact that for several generations they have been given purely on scientific merit and not through lobbying and politicking. I do hope that it will stay this way, and the prizes will never be given according to the number of votes in live TV contests! (Andre Geim)

諾貝爾獎享有廣泛的高度尊敬，是由於幾代人以來，它們的頒發一直基於純粹的科學價值，而非透過遊說和政治活動。我衷心希望它會保持如此，且永遠不會依據電視直播比賽的投票數量而頒發！（安德烈‧蓋姆）

Ernest Rutherford's 1908 Nobel Prize in Chemistry wasn't given for the nuclear power station —— he wouldn't have survived that long —— it was given for showing how interesting atomic physics could be. (Andre Geim)

歐尼斯特‧拉塞福 1908 年的諾貝爾化學獎不是為了核電廠而授予的 —— 他不可能活這麼久 —— 它的頒發是為了表明原子物理學可以多麼有趣。（安德烈‧蓋姆）

It is impossible to learn the spirit of science from a textbook or article. They may be able to teach us physics and chemistry and many other disciplines at university, but it is up to us to develop a gut feeling for how best to "do science". I am extremely lucky to have worked with and learned from Andre Geim, who is highly innovative and broad in his perspective but, at the same time, very truthful and critical of himself, with manic attention to details. It is so easy to lose sight of the bigger picture underpinning the details or get carried away with your "beautiful theory" and stop paying attention to the facts; Andre is a master of finding the narrow path between these extremes, and, if there is one thing I am proud of in my life, it is that I have learned a little of this style. (Konstantin Novoselov)

從教科書或文章中是學不到科學精神的。大學也許能教導我們物理、化學和其他科目；但要養成直覺，知道如何最好地「做科學研究」，這取決於我們。我極為幸運，有機會與安德烈‧蓋姆共事並向他學習。他具有高度的創新精神，視野寬闊；然而，同時又對自己非常誠實和挑剔，瘋狂地關注細節。人非常容易忽視細節之下的更大圖景，或者被自己「美麗的理論」沖昏頭腦而停止關注事實；安德烈則是在這兩個極端之間找出窄路的大師。我如果此生有一件事感到自豪，那就是我學到了少許這種作風。（康斯坦丁‧諾沃肖洛夫）

When you think that we're doing physics, we're not, we're actually doing science and this means that our interests are much, much broader than any particular field of physics or just physics by itself, so we just try to be curious in everything and most important is to have fun. (Konstantin Novoselov)

當你以為我們在做物理學研究時，我們不是，我們實際上是在做科學研究，這就意味著，我們的興趣，比任何特定的物理學領域乃至物理學本身都要廣泛得很多很多。所以，我們就努力保持事事好奇，最重要

的是樂在其中。（康斯坦丁·諾沃肖洛夫）

I think there's still a lot of chemistry to be developed. (Richard F. Heck)

我認為還有大量的化學物質有待開發。（赫克）

This search for truth, one finding will lead to another so there's this tremendous scope expanding, you know, in front of you. And, then we continue. (Ei-ichi Negishi)

這種對真理的探索，一個發現會引向另一個，所以有如此巨大的、不斷擴展的範圍，你知道，擺在你面前。於是，我們持續不停。（根岸英一）

Our work in palladium-catalyzed cross-couplings in organic synthesis has been ongoing for many years and it will continue. But the full impact of it is not yet realized. Others will use what we have learned, build on what we have discovered and use this to help people and technology in ways that we can only imagine today. (Ei-ichi Negishi)

關於有機合成領域中的鈀催化偶聯工作，我們已經從事多年，而且仍將持續下去。但它的全部影響尚未實現。其他人將採取我們所學到的知識，在我們所發現的基礎上，以我們今天僅能想像的方式，用它來幫助人們，開發技術，（根岸英一）

Our pursuit in research must not be for rewards. Our pursuit in whatever we do must always be for excellence, and if we accomplish excellence, it is its own reward and recognition will follow. (Ei-ichi Negishi)

我們從事研究的追求絕不能是獲獎。無論做什麼，我們的追求永遠都必須是卓越。如果成就卓越，那就是研究的自我回報，外界的認同也會隨之而來。（根岸英一）

Receiving a Nobel Prize is the ultimate recognition for a lifetime spent questioning, exploring, experimenting; passing through the valleys of anguish to climb the mountains of success. (Ei-ichi Negishi)

獲得諾貝爾獎是對質疑、探索、實驗之一生的最終認同，穿過痛苦的谷底以攀登成功的高山。（根岸英一）

The concept of serendipity often crops up in research. Serendipity is the faculty or phenomenon of finding valuable or agreeable things that were not being sought. I believe that all researchers can be serendipitous. (Akira Suzuki)

在研究中，意外發現的創新經常冒出來。意外發現，就是發現未被尋求的可貴或可取之物的能力或現象。我相信所有的研究人員都有此可能。（鈴木章）

I learned many things from Professor Brown, including his philosophy toward research, but there is one thing he said that I recall with particular clarity: "Do research that will be in the textbooks." It is not easy to do such work, but this has remained my motto. (Akira Suzuki)

我向布朗教授學到了很多東西，包括他的研究哲學，不過他說的一句話我記得特別清楚：「要做會被載入教科書的研究。」做這樣的工作並不容易，但這句話成了我的座右銘。（鈴木章）

Memories of tough, trying experiences tend to fade with time. I think now mainly about the fun things. (Akira Suzuki)

對艱難困苦經歷的記憶往往隨著時間減退。我現在主要想些有趣的事情。（鈴木章）

A resource-poor country like Japan can only rely on people's endeavor and knowledge. I would like to continue my effort to provide help to younger people. (Akira Suzuki)

日本這種資源貧乏的國家只能依靠人民的努力和知識。我願意繼續努力向年輕人提供幫助。（鈴木章）

It struck me what we should be trying to do was pluck the egg from the ovary and fertilise it in the laboratory. We could do this in animals increasingly… this was the way to go in the human species. (Robert G. Edwards)

我突然想到，我們應當嘗試從卵巢內取出卵子，並在實驗室裡使之受精。我們可以在動物身上越來越多地做到這一點……這是探究人類的方法。（羅伯特·愛德華茲）

I wanted to find out exactly who was in charge, whether it was God Himself or whether it was scientists in the laboratory. It was us. (Robert G. Edwards)

我想查明是誰做主，是上帝本人還是實驗室裡的科學家。是我們。（羅伯特·愛德華茲）

The Nobel prize is a fairytale for a week and a nightmare for a year. You can't imagine the pressure to give interviews, to go to book fairs. (Mario Vargas Llosa)

諾貝爾獎是一個星期的童話和一年的噩夢。你無法想像接受採訪、參加書展的壓力。（馬利歐·巴爾加斯·尤薩）

Reading allows you to travel, to make other people's experiences your own. (Mario Vargas Llosa)

閱讀讓你遠行，使別人的經歷化為自身的。（馬利歐・巴爾加斯・尤薩）

Sleep is, I think, the prime celebration I'll be having! At some point the brain will shut down and the body will collapse and tomorrow we'll think of actually having enough energy to celebrate. (Peter A. Diamond)

睡覺，我想，是我心目中最好的慶祝！在某一時刻，頭腦會關閉，身體會崩潰，而明天我們會想到還有足夠精力慶祝。[24]（彼得・戴蒙德）

Family and economics have been the two poles around which I function, one a source of great joy and the other of great pleasure. (Peter A. Diamond)

家庭和經濟學一直是我圍著轉的兩極，一個是非凡歡樂之源，另一個是非凡愉快之源。（彼得・戴蒙德）

I have worked in a large number of different areas. The kind of theoretical work I most enjoy is sorting out how to approach a problem to get insights, more so than refining models to shed further light on it. Thus, it was natural for me to explore new areas once I felt I had hit diminishing returns in one area. However, revisiting a topic after years away from it has been fruitful as well. (Peter A. Diamond)

我在大量不同的領域工作過。我最喜歡的一種理論工作，是找出處理問題的思路以獲得深入見解，而不只是改進模型來進一步揭示問題。因此，一旦覺得自己在一個領域的收穫漸少，我就自然地轉而探索新的領域。然而，若干年後重拾課題也是富於成效的。（彼得・戴蒙德）

Science is a collaborative endeavour. Every great achievement is but a small peak in the mountain range of contributions. (Dale T. Mortensen)

---

[24] 在被問及「你想好今天晚些時候怎麼慶祝嗎」時戴蒙德的答話。

科學是合作的事業。每項非凡的成就只是貢獻之群山中一座小小的高峰。（戴爾·莫滕森）

Economics is a strange science. Our subject deals with some of the most important as well as mundane issues that impinge on the human condition. (Dale T. Mortensen)

經濟學是一門奇特的科學。我們的主題涉及影響人類處境的一些既平常又極其重要的問題。（戴爾·莫滕森）

Why worry about job destruction. You should have as many job destructions as the last 40 years. Because new jobs will be created. They are being created now, more efficient jobs. (Christopher A. Pissarides)

為什麼擔心就業破壞？就業破壞應當跟過去40年的一樣多。因為新的職業會被創造出來。現在正在創造更有效率的工作。（克里斯多福·皮薩里德斯）

2001–2010 跨界融合與人文關懷

2011–2020
科技反思與人性的回望

2011 年

Nobody really expects a Nobel Prize call. (Saul Perlmutter)

沒有人真的預期接到諾貝爾獎獲獎電話。（索羅‧珀爾穆特）

Probably the single most important thing about the Nobel Prize for most people is whether they get the coveted parking space on campus. (Saul Perlmutter)

對於大多數人，諾貝爾獎唯一最重要的很可能是，他們是否在校園裡獲得夢寐以求的停車位。（索羅‧珀爾穆特）

Science is not, despite how it is often portrayed, about absolute truths. It is about developing an understanding of the world, making predictions, and then testing these predictions. (Brian P. Schmidt)

科學與絕對真理無關，無論它多麼經常被說成如此。它是關於拓展對世界的理解，做出預測，然後檢驗這些預測。（布萊恩‧施密特）

There can be theory but, you know, the problem is you've got to be able to test it. So theories are one thing, testing is another. (Brian P. Schmidt)

可以有理論,但是,你知道,問題是你必須能夠檢驗它。所以理論是一回事,檢驗是另一回事。(布萊恩‧施密特)

Even if I stumble on to the absolute truth of any aspect of the universe, I will not realise my luck and instead will spend my life trying to find flaws in this understanding —— such is the role of a scientist. (Brian P. Schmidt)

即使偶然發現宇宙任一方面的絕對真理,我也不會兌現自己的運氣,反而,我會畢生努力找尋這一種詮釋的缺陷 —— 這就是科學家的角色。(布萊恩‧施密特)

Ninety-five percent of the universe is unknown, filled with dark matter and dark energy. And our job is to understand the weird stuff of that 95 percent. (Adam G. Riess)

百分之九十五的宇宙是未知的,充滿了暗物質和暗能量。我們的任務就是了解這神祕的百分之九十五。(亞當‧黎斯)

I think one of the most amazing facts about the universe is that it is expanding. I never would have guessed it. Even as an undergraduate, once I'd learned a little physics, I would have thought that the universe was eternal, static, and always in equilibrium. So in graduate school when I found out that the universe was expanding, I was awestruck. Then I learned if we could measure the expanding universe, the way we record the growth of a child with marks on a doorframe, we could determine the age of the universe and predict its ultimate fate. This was staggering! I knew this is what I wanted to do. Since that time, charting the expanding universe to determine its nature has been my passion. (Adam G. Riess)

2011 年

　　我認為，宇宙最驚人的事實之一是，它在擴張。我原來根本不會想到這個。即便作為大學生，一旦學了些物理，我就會認為宇宙是永恆的，靜止的，並且總是處於平衡狀態。所以在研究所，發現宇宙在膨脹時，我大吃一驚。隨後我了解到，如果能夠測量膨脹的宇宙，就像在門框上畫線記錄孩子的生長那樣，我們就可以確定宇宙的年齡並預測它的最終命運。這令人震驚！我意識到這就是我想做的事。從那以後，繪製不斷膨脹的宇宙以確定它的本質，就成了我熱愛的事業。（亞當·黎斯）

We've known for a long time that the universe is expanding. But about 15 years ago, my colleagues and I discovered that it is expanding faster and faster. That is, the universe is accelerating, and that was not expected, but it is now attributed to this mysterious stuff called dark energy which seems to make up about 70 percent of the universe. (Adam G. Riess)

　　我們早就知道宇宙在擴張。但大約 15 年前，我的同事們和我發現，它在越來越快地膨脹。這就是說，宇宙在加速，這是出乎意料的。而它現在被歸因於一種神祕的東西，稱作暗能量，它似乎大約構成宇宙的百分之七十。（亞當·黎斯）

Until the 1990s, there were few reliable observations about movement at the scale of the entire universe, which is the only scale dark energy effects. So dark energy could not be seen until we could measure things very, very far away. (Adam G. Riess)

　　在 1990 年代之前，對於整個宇宙規模的變動，幾乎沒有可靠的觀測，而宇宙規模是暗能量影響所及的唯一衡量標準。所以，在我們能夠測量到非常、非常遠的東西之前，暗能量是無法檢視的。（亞當·黎斯）

I think the mystery of what's out there in the universe is just very compelling. (Adam G. Riess)

我想，宇宙中遙遠事物的奧祕實在是令人著迷。（亞當‧黎斯）

We're really just the frosting on a cake and we don't know what's inside the cake. (Adam G. Riess)

我們真的只是蛋糕上的糖霜，我們不知道蛋糕裡有什麼。（亞當‧黎斯）

I was a subject of ridicule and lectures about the basics of crystallography. The leader of the opposition to my findings was the two-time Nobel Laureate Linus Carl Pauling, the idol of the American Chemical Society and one of the most famous scientists in the world. (Dan Shechtman)

關於晶體學的基本知識，我是嘲笑和指責的對象。帶頭反對我的發現的，是兩次諾貝爾獎得主萊納斯‧鮑林，美國化學學會的偶像，世界最著名的科學家之一。（丹‧謝赫特曼）

I felt I ought not to be wasting time, and I hurried to graduate from high school to enroll at UCSD. I also hurried to finish college, to go on to higher studies. By the time I was in my teens, I had a strong sense of mission, wanting to discover something important or solve a major problem in biology or medicine. (Bruce A. Beutler)

我覺得自己不該浪費時間，於是匆匆忙忙從高中畢業，去加州大學聖地牙哥分校上學。我同樣匆匆完成大學學業，以便繼續深造。十幾歲的時候，我有一種強烈的使命感，想發現某種重要的東西或者解決生物學或醫學上的一個主要問題。（布魯斯‧比尤特勒）

2011 年

There weren't the tools for understanding how the innate immune system detects infection, and I think that's where we contributed. (Bruce A. Beutler)

過去並沒有了解先天免疫系統是如何偵測感染的工具，而我認為這就是我們的貢獻所在。（布魯斯・比尤特勒）

If we think of the immune system as a machine, then we are far from even knowing all of its parts. (Bruce A. Beutler)

如果把免疫系統設想成一臺機器，那麼我們還遠遠不了解它的所有部件。（布魯斯・比尤特勒）

I was in bed. I happened to wake up in the middle of the night. I looked over at my cell phone and I noticed that I had a new email message. And, I squinted at it and I saw that the title line was "Nobel Prize", so I thought I should give close attention to that. And, I opened it and it was from Göran Hansson, and it said that I had won the Nobel Prize, and so I was thrilled. And, I was a little disbelieving and I went downstairs and looked at my laptop, and I couldn't get into the Nobel site for quite a while because it was all packed. So, I went to google news and in a few minutes I saw my name there and so I knew it was real. (Bruce A. Beutler)

我當時在睡覺。碰巧半夜醒來。看了看手機，注意到有一封新的電子郵件。瞥了一眼，見到標題是「諾貝爾獎」，想到應當予以關注。於是，我打開它，它來自戈蘭・漢松，說我得了諾貝爾獎，我因而非常激動。只是，我有一點不相信，就下樓檢視筆記型電腦，但有一段時間進不去諾貝爾獎網站，因為網站被塞爆了。所以，我前往 Google 新聞，幾分鐘後在上面見到了我的名字，由此知道這是真的。（布魯斯・比尤特勒）

251

The nicest part of the prize, perhaps, is the effect on my friends and family. Each of them feels proud and happy to have the relationship with me that they do. In a way, it's as though they received an award too, and I like that very much. (Bruce A. Beutler)

諾貝爾獎最美妙的部分，也許，是對我的朋友和家人的影響。他們每個人都為跟我有密切關係而自豪和高興。在某種程度上，就好像他們也得了獎似的，而我非常喜歡這樣。（布魯斯・比尤特勒）

My father was my most constant teacher. (Bruce Beutler)

父親是我最始終如一的老師。（布魯斯・比尤特勒）

In the sphere of antimicrobial host defenses, we unfortunately live in an environment where infectious agents can rapidly evolve and pose a constant threat to the well-being of humankind. This situation requires that we remain ever vigilant and collectively continue our efforts toward a better understanding of: how our bodies sense invading microorganisms, how we activate the appropriate counter-measures and how we can ourselves adapt to strategies by which the invaders try to elude our defenses. We hope that the studies highlighted today, will contribute to the development of new ways to protect humans against infection, now and in the future. (Jules A. Hoffmann)

在抗菌劑受體防禦方面，我們不幸生活在這樣的環境中，傳染性病原體能夠迅速演化，並對人類的福祉構成經常性的威脅。這種情況需要我們永遠保持警惕，共同持續努力深入了解：我們的身體如何感知入侵的微生物，我們如何啟動適當的應對措施，以及我們自身能夠如何適應入侵者力圖避開我們防禦的策略。我們希望，今日所強調的研究，如今以及未來會有助於開發保護人類免受感染的新方法。（朱爾斯・霍夫曼）

2011 年

That's one of the positive aspects of the Nobel Prize because it, people start wondering. (Jules A. Hoffmann)

這是諾貝爾獎積極的一面,由於它,人們開始好奇。(朱爾斯·霍夫曼)

Think about the miraculous vaccines that prevent smallpox, polio, and measles. But why do we still lack vaccines to resist AIDS, malaria, and tuberculosis? Real answers, I feel, will be to discover the principles in humans that allow dendritic cells to bring about vaccine immunity. (Ralph M. Steinman)

想想那些預防天花、脊髓灰質炎和麻疹的神奇疫苗。但是,為什麼我們仍然缺乏抗愛滋病、瘧疾和結核病的疫苗呢?我認為,真正的答案是發現人類樹突細胞產生疫苗免疫的原理。(瑞夫·史坦曼)

Consider the progress in cancer to identify the genetic and subsequent changes that drive malignancy. Again, dendritic cells and the immune system provide a distinct and potentially powerful route to therapies that recognize and attack the changes in cancer cells. (Ralph M. Steinman)

關注癌症的進展,以確定導致惡性腫瘤的基因和後續變化。此外,樹突狀細胞和免疫系統為識別和攻擊癌細胞變化的治療方法提供了一種獨特且可能有效的途徑。(瑞夫·史坦曼)

It is exhilarating to be recognized for a Lasker Award and to listen to Joe Goldstein's exceptional summary. I am so excited that I am actually feeling dendritic, wanting to embrace the members of the jury and all my friends and family who are here today. (Ralph M. Steinman)

榮獲拉斯克獎並聆聽約瑟夫·里歐納德·戈爾茨坦的精采總結令人振奮。我是這麼激動,簡直覺得自己好像樹突,只想擁抱評審委員會的成

員,以及今天在場的所有朋友和家人。[25]（瑞夫・史坦曼）

In the middle of life, death comes to take your measurements. The visit is forgotten and life goes on. But the suit is being sewn on the sly. (Tomas Tranströmer)

在生命的途中,死神來測量你的尺寸。這次來訪被忘掉了,生活繼續著。然而殮衣在暗中繼續縫製。（湯瑪斯・特朗斯特羅默）

If your dreams do not scare you, they are not big enough. (Ellen Johnson Sirleaf)

如果你的夢想沒有嚇到你,它們就不夠大。（艾倫・強森・瑟利夫）

I work hard, I work late, I have nothing on my conscience. When I go to bed, I sleep. (Ellen Johnson Sirleaf)

我努力工作,工作到很晚,我的良心全無負擔。就寢的時候,我沉沉睡去。（艾倫・強森・瑟利夫）

I'm a serious optimist. I come from a country where you have little to be hopeful for, and so you have to always be an optimist. (Leymah Gbowee)

我是個認真的樂觀主義者。我屬於一個幾乎沒有希望的國家,所以你必須永遠是個樂觀主義者。（雷嫚・葛波薇）

Peace does not mean just to stop wars, but also to stop oppression and injustice. (Tawakkol Karman)

---

[25] 史坦曼由於樹突狀細胞的發現而獲得拉斯克獎。他在頒獎典禮上發言時這麼說。
2007 年拉斯克獎頒獎典禮在皮埃爾酒店舉行,施萊辛格在場。他回憶道,史坦曼全家都出席了,包括瑞夫・史坦曼 91 歲的母親。「瑞夫事先被告知,他只有三分鐘的時間發言,不要說致謝的話。大概是主辦者不希望聽到奧斯卡獎式的演講。瑞夫針對臨床研究的重要性發表了極其精采的演講。然後他說:『恕我不聽指點,我要感謝一位在我的一生中都支持我的工作的人,就是我的母親,她今天在這裡。』」所有與會者的眼睛都溼潤了,施萊辛格講述道。

> 2011 年

和平不僅意味著停止戰爭，還意味著停止壓迫和不公平．(塔瓦庫·卡曼)

I discovered that wearing the veil is not suitable for a woman who wants to work in activism and the public domain. People need to see you, to associate and relate to you. It is not stated in my religion to wear the veil; it is a traditional practice, so I took it off. (Tawakkol Karman)

我發現，戴面紗不適合想從事行動主義和公共領域工作的女性。人們需要看到妳，與妳交流和聯繫。在我信奉的宗教中沒有規定要戴面紗；這是一種傳統習慣，所以我把它摘掉了。（塔瓦庫·卡曼）

As scientists, scientists in many fields need to speak with statistical data. In fact, we are playing the role of God at this time. What do you mean? There are many applied sciences, such as engineering, physics, and economics, which are applied sciences. We will build some models to simulate world operations. Our theory, too, is composed of a series of equations, with some random components. Our goal is to explain what we see in the world, and our key tool is to use models and then put them into computers to simulate. Take the simulated data, use mathematical methods to fine-tune its parameters, hoping to be as close to reality as possible. In this process, we play the role of God. So writing parameters and simulating is pretending that we are pretending that God generated these data. We try to get close to this accuracy. We want to approach or imitate Gods practice. It's easy to say and hard to do. People thought it was a good idea 200 or 300 years ago, but people didn't know how to do it. Why? For example, if you write a model of a particle, there is no way to calculate it. But by the twentieth century, especially after the end of World

War II, we had some great technicians, including Norman, an immigrant from Austria. My father-in-law, Tyler, studied nuclear bombs. They invented the Monte Carlo model, which was invented in their 50s. But three or four years later, statisticians came and made sure that they could do statistical analysis. So here comes a revolution that affects the work of scientists from all walks of life, and that is the benefits of technological innovation. In fact, we are playing the role of God in this process. How did I come here? Artificial intelligence is, first of all, some gorgeous rhetoric. Artificial intelligence is actually statistics, but with a very gorgeous phrase, in fact, is statistics. Many of the formulas are very old, but we say that all artificial intelligence uses statistics to solve problems. There are some new developments. In the past two or three decades, we have achieved higher quality statistics. (Thomas J. Sargent)

　　作為科學家，許多領域的科學家需要用統計資料說話。實際上，我們這時候是在扮演上帝的角色。怎麼說？有許多應用科學，如工程學、物理學，以及經濟學，都是應用科學。我們要建立一些模型來模擬世界的運行。我們的理論也是由一系列方程式組成，帶有一些隨機的成分。我們的目的是解釋我們在世界中看到了什麼，關鍵的工具是使用模型，然後把它們輸入電腦模擬。獲得模擬資料，使用數學方法微調其參數，希望盡可能接近現實。在這個過程中，我們扮演了上帝的角色。寫參數並模擬情境，我們在假裝上帝生成了這些資料。我們力圖接近準確。我們想接近或模仿諸神的行為。說來容易做來難。二、三百年前人們認為這是個好主意，但他們不知道如何去做。為什麼？例如，你寫了一個粒子模型，但沒有辦法計算它。然而到了 20 世紀，尤其是第二次世界大戰結束後，我們有了一些了不起的技術人員，包括諾曼，一位來自奧地利

> 2011 年

的移民。我的岳父，泰勒，研究過核彈。他們發明了蒙特卡洛模型，在他們 50 多歲時。然而三、四年後，統計學家來了，確保他們能夠進行統計分析。於是，一場影響各行各業科學家工作的革命到來，這就是技術創新的效益。實際上，我們在這個過程中扮演著上帝的角色。我是怎麼來到這裡的？人工智慧，首先，是些華麗的辭藻。人工智慧事實上是統計學，不過用了一個非常華麗的詞彙，實際上，就是統計學。其公式許多都很古老，但所有的人工智慧都運用統計資料來解決問題。有一些新的發展。在過去二、三十年裡，我們獲得了更高品質的統計資料。（湯瑪斯‧薩金特）

I wasn't the brightest kid, not by a long shot. I was interested in football, in girls, in getting my work done with the least amount of effort. (Thomas J. Sargent)

我不是最聰明的孩子，絕對不是。我喜歡足球，喜歡女孩子，喜歡以最少的努力完成工作。（湯瑪斯‧薩金特）

What I really don't like is oversimplification. (Thomas J. Sargent)

我真正不喜歡的是過度簡化。（湯瑪斯‧薩金特）

I think anyone who gets the Nobel Prize has to be a little bit embarrassed to be picked out when there have been so many people who have contributed. (Christopher A. Sims)

我認為，任何獲得諾貝爾獎的人被選出來都有幾分尷尬，因為有那麼多人做出了貢獻。（克里斯多福‧西姆斯）

2012 年

Creativity in science is connected to open-mindedness. (Serge Haroche)

科學上的創造力與思想的開放有關。（塞爾日・阿羅什）

You cannot get innovation without good science, and you cannot have good science without good education. (Serge Haroche)

沒有好的科學就得不到創新，沒有好的教育也無法有好的科學。（塞爾日・阿羅什）

As science progresses it discloses things that are different to nature. Much of our science education is a way to overcome what you can see directly── you have to really think about it. (Serge Haroche)

隨著自身進展，科學揭示了一些不同於自然的東西。我們的科學教育，許多是一種超越直觀可見之物的方法──你得真正地思考它。（塞爾日・阿羅什）

Science is a constant fight against common reasoning. (Serge Haroche)

科學是與普遍推理的持續抗爭。（塞爾日・阿羅什）

It is important to fund young researchers who want to do curiosity-driven research. Curiosity-driven research is a part of life. Some people are curious. They want to learn more about nature and society should help that. It's like art: you can learn more and bring more beauty. (Serge Haroche)

資助想從事出於好奇而研究的年輕研究者，這是很重要的。出於好奇的研究是生活的一部分。有些人富有好奇心。他們想更了解自然，而

社會應當幫助此事。這就像是藝術：你可以了解更多，帶來更多的美。（塞爾日·阿羅什）

It's a long way before we have a useful quantum computer. But I think most of us feel that even though that is a long, you know, long way off before we can realise such a computer, many of us feel it will eventually happen. (David J. Wineland)

在我們擁有實用的量子電腦之前，還有很長的過程。然而我想，我們大多數人都覺得，即使在能夠製成這樣的電腦之前，還有漫長的，你知道，漫長的過程，我們很多人都覺得它最終會出現。（戴維·瓦恩蘭）

Certainly my role in this work is very small when compared to that of my colleagues both at NIST and around the world, who have made so many important contributions. Having been recognized by the Nobel Foundation is really more recognition of our field rather than individual accomplishment; many others are at least as deserving. (David J. Wineland)

當然，在這項工作中，國家標準與技術研究院以及世界各地的同行做出了大量重要貢獻，與他們相比，我的作用非常之小。諾貝爾基金會的認可，實在更多地針對我們領域而非個人成就；至少還有許多人是有貢獻的。（戴維·瓦恩蘭）

As an only child lacking siblings and playmates, I was alone a great deal of the time. Much of this was spent reading virtually anything I could get my hands on. (Robert J. Lefkowitz)

作為沒有兄弟姐妹和玩伴的獨生子，我的大量時間都是孤獨的。這些時間，許多都花在了閱讀幾乎任何所能到手的讀物上。（羅伯特·萊夫科維茨）

The Nobel Prizes are often seen as, of course, awards to individuals. But beyond that they are recognition often of a field. So everybody in the field feels good about it. Especially, if they feel good about the particular people from the field who are getting the award. (Robert J. Lefkowitz)

諾貝爾獎時常被認為，當然，是對個人的獎勵。但除此之外，它們通常又是對於一個領域的認同。所以該領域中的每一個人都感到滿意。尤其是，如果他們對出自本領域的特定得獎者感到滿意的話。（羅伯特‧萊夫科維茨）

Scientists are sometimes as competitive as professional athletes, maybe. (Brian K. Kobilka)

科學家們也許有時候跟職業運動員一樣充滿競爭。（布萊恩‧克比爾卡）

If you really want something bad enough, if you're really interested in something enough, you know, you just keep working on it. (Brian K. Kobilka)

如果你真的對一件事極其想望，如果你真的對一件事足夠感興趣，不用說，你只會鍥而不捨。（布萊恩‧克比爾卡）

Of course, one is always looking for therapeutic benefits. I would say when that when the work was done there was virtually no expectation of any immediate therapeutic benefit, so the recognition as it were of the early result, one can understand has to wait. And indeed there was quite a period after the early work when people did not believe the results. So it took nearly 10 years for the major result to be accepted. (John B. Gurdon)

當然了，人們總是在尋求治療上的效益。我要說，這項工作完成的時候，幾乎沒有對任何直接療效的預期；所以，對於早期結果在某種程度上的認可,可以理解是必須等待的。的確,在早期的研究之後,有相當一段時間,人們不相信其結果。所以,花了幾乎十年時間才讓主要結果獲得承認。(約翰·格登)

Should basic science be supported if there isn't an immediate benefit to health? And, of course, I am biased but I would hope that basic science would be supported. Because so often it happens that the practical or therapeutic benefit comes along quite a long time after the initial discovery. (John B. Gurdon)

如果沒有對健康的直接效益,基礎科學應當得到支持嗎?當然了,我有所偏頗,但我希望基礎科學能夠得到支持。因為實用的或治療上的效益在最初發現的很久之後才出現,這種情況實在是經常發生。(約翰·格登)

The work I was involved in had no obvious therapeutic benefit. It was purely of scientific interest. I hope the country will continue to support basic research even though it may have no obvious practical value. (John B. Gurdon)

我所參與的工作沒有明顯的治療上的效益。它純粹出於科學興趣。我希望國家會繼續支持基礎研究,儘管它可能沒有明顯的實用價值。(約翰·格登)

It is particularly pleasing to see how purely basic research, originally aimed at testing the genetic identity of different cell types in the body, has turned out to have clear human health prospects. (John B. Gurdon)

特別令人高興的是,純粹的基礎研究,起初旨在測試人體中不同細胞類型的遺傳一致性,結果轉而釐清了人類健康的前景。(約翰·格登)

My own personal belief is that we will, in the end, understand everything about how cells actually work. (John B. Gurdon)

我的個人信念為，關於細胞如何實際工作，最終，我們會了解一切。（約翰‧格登）

I think that in the 21st century, medical biology will advance at a more rapid pace than before. (Shinya Yamanaka)

我認為在 21 世紀，醫學生物學將以比先前還要快的速度發展。（山中伸彌）

I started my career as a surgeon 25 years ago. But it turned out that I am not talented as a surgeon. So I decided to change my career, from clinics to laboratories. But I still feel that I am a doctor, I am a physician, so I really want to help patients. So my goal, all my life, is to bring this technology, stem cell technology to the bedside, to patients, to clinics. (Shinya Yamanaka)

25 年前，我作為外科醫生開始了職業生涯。然而事實表明，作為外科醫生我並無才能。所以我決定改變職業，從診所轉到實驗室。不過我仍然覺得自己是個醫生，自己是個內科醫生，所以我非常想幫助病人。所以我的目標，一生如此，就是把這項技術，幹細胞技術帶給臨床，帶給病人，帶給診所。（山中伸彌）

I can see any failure as a chance. (Shinya Yamanaka)

我可以把任何失敗都視為機會。（山中伸彌）

What's motivates me to keep writing? I can't explain it in just a few sentences. First of all, I just feel that I have something to say. I want to write down my thoughts and relate them to my readers through a polished piece of work. Secondly, there are many things in society that I feel a duty to write about. Another reason is my explorations to innovate literature as an art, which also drives me to write. Since the fictional form first emerged, at least

2012 年

a thousand years have passed. Within the art of literature and fiction there have always emerged new forms. Writers kept making changes to the form of fiction, whether in language or format. So, is there room for creativity for our generation of writers? I think there is. I see fiction as an art, and its development as infinite. Its format also has infinite possibilities. This near obsessive pursuit of fiction as an art, encourages me to keep writing. (Mo Yan)

是什麼使我繼續寫作？這個三言兩語說不清楚。首先，我只是覺得有話要說。我想把自己的想法寫下來，並經由用心經營的作品傳達給讀者。其次，社會上有許多事我覺得有責任寫。另一個原因是我對文學藝術創新的探索，這也促使我寫作。自從小說形式初現，至少過去了上千年。在文學和小說藝術中，總有新的形式湧現。作家們不斷地對小說的形式加以改變，無論語言上還是樣式上。那麼，就我們這一代作家而言，創造還有空間嗎？我想是有的。我認為小說是一門藝術，它的發展是無限的。它的樣式也有無限的可能性。對於小說藝術這種近乎偏執的追求，激勵我繼續寫作。（莫言）

In the course of creating my literary domain, Northeast Gaomi Township, I was greatly inspired by the American novelist William Faulkner and the Columbian Gabriel García Márquez. I had not read either of them extensively, but was encouraged by the bold, unrestrained way they created new territory in writing, and learned from them that a writer must have a place that belongs to him alone. Humility and compromise are ideal in one's daily life, but in literary creation, supreme self-confidence and the need to follow one's own instincts are essential. For two years I followed in the footsteps of these two masters before realizing that I had to escape their influence; this is how I characterized that decision in an essay: They were a pair of blazing furnaces, I was a block of ice. If I got too close to them, I would dissolve into a cloud of steam. (Mo Yan)

在建立我的文學領地「高密東北鄉」的過程中，美國的威廉・福克納和哥倫比亞的加布列・賈西亞・馬奎斯給了我重要啟發。我對他們的閱讀並不認真，但他們開天闢地的豪邁精神激勵了我，使我明白了一個作家必須要有一塊屬於自己的地方。一個人在日常生活中應該謙卑退讓，但在文學創作中，必須頤指氣使，獨斷專行。我追隨在這兩位大師身後兩年，即意識到，必須盡快地逃離他們，我在一篇文章中寫道：他們是兩座灼熱的火爐，而我是冰塊，如果離他們太近，會被他們蒸發掉。（莫言）

I am also well aware that literature only has a minimal influence on political disputes or economic crises in the world, but its significance to human beings is ancient. When literature exists, perhaps we do not notice how important it is, but when it does not exist, our lives become coarsened and brutal. For this reason, I am proud of my profession, but also aware of its importance. (Mo Yan)

我深知，文學對世界上的政治紛爭、經濟危機影響甚微，但文學對人的影響卻是源遠流長。當文學存在時也許我們無法意識到它的重要，但如果沒有文學，人的生活便會粗鄙野蠻。因此，我為自己的職業感到光榮也感到沉重。（莫言）

I also thank the fertile soil that gave birth to me and nurtured me. It is often said that a person is shaped by the place where he grows up. I am a storyteller, who has found nourishment in your humid soil. Everything that I have done, I have done to thank you! (Mo Yan)

　　我還要特別地感謝那片生我、養我的富饒大地，俗話說，「一方水土養一方人」，我便是這片水土養育出來的一個說書人，我的一切工作，都是為了報答你的恩情。（莫言）

For a writer, the best way to speak is by writing. You will find everything I need to say in my works. Speech is carried off by the wind; the written word can never be obliterated. (Mo Yan)

　　對一個作家來說，最好的說話方式是寫作。我該說的話都寫進了我的作品裡。用嘴說出的話隨風而散，用筆寫出的話永不磨滅。（莫言）

Our Taoist master Laozi said it best: "Fortune depends on misfortune. Misfortune is hidden in fortune." I left school as a child, often went hungry, was constantly lonely, and had no books to read. But for those reasons, like the writer of a previous generation, Shen Congwen, I had an early start on reading the great book of life. (Mo Yan)

　　就像道家先賢老子所說的那樣：「禍兮福之所倚，福兮禍之所伏。」我童年輟學，飽受飢餓、孤獨、無書可讀之苦，但我因此也像我們的前輩作家沈從文那樣，及早地開始閱讀社會人生這本大書。（莫言）

I was a modern-day storyteller who hid in the background of his early work; but with the novel Sandalwood Death I jumped out of the shadows. My early work can be characterized as a series of soliloquies, with no reader in mind; starting with this novel, however, I visualized myself standing in a public square spiritedly telling my story to a crowd of listeners. This tradition is a worldwide phenomenon in fiction, but is especially so in China. At one time, I was a diligent student of Western modernist fiction, and I experimented with all sorts of narrative styles. But in the end I came back to my traditions. To be sure, this return was not without its modifications. Sandalwood Death and the novels that followed are inheritors of the Chinese classical novel tradition but enhanced by Western literary techniques. What is known as innovative fiction is, for the most part, a result of this mixture, which is not limited to domestic traditions with foreign techniques, but can include mixing fiction with art from other realms. Sandalwood Death, for instance, mixes fiction with local opera, while some of my early work was partly nurtured by fine art, music, even acrobatics. (Mo Yan)

在我的早期作品中，我作為一個現代的說書人，是隱藏在文字背後的，但從《檀香刑》這部小說開始，我終於從後臺跳到了前臺。如果說我早期的作品是自言自語，目無讀者，從這本書開始，我感覺到自己是站在一個廣場上，面對著許多聽眾，繪聲繪色地講述。這是世界小說的傳統，更是中國小說的傳統。我也曾積極地向西方的現代派小說學習，也曾經玩弄過形形色色的敘事花樣，但我最終回歸了傳統。當然，這種回歸，不是一成不變的回歸，《檀香刑》和之後的小說，是繼承了中國古典小說傳統又借鑑了西方小說技術的混合文字。小說領域的所謂創新，基本上都是這種混合的產物。不僅僅是中國文學傳統與西方小說技巧的混合，也是小說與其他的藝術門類的混合，就像《檀香刑》是與民間戲曲的混合，就像我早期的一些小說從美術、音樂、甚至雜技中汲取了營養一樣。（莫言）

Possibly because I've lived so much of my life in difficult circumstances, I think I have a more profound understanding of life. I know what real courage is, and I understand true compassion. I know that nebulous terrain exists in the hearts and minds of every person, terrain that cannot be adequately characterized in simple terms of right and wrong or good and bad, and this vast territory is where a writer gives free rein to his talent. So long as the work correctly and vividly describes this nebulous, massively contradictory terrain, it will inevitably transcend politics and be endowed with literary excellence. (Mo Yan)

可能是因為我經歷過長期的艱難生活,使我對人性有較為深刻的了解。我知道真正的勇敢是什麼,也明白真正的悲憫是什麼。我知道,每個人心中都有一片難以用是非善惡準確定義的朦朧地帶,而這片地帶,正是文學家施展才華的廣闊天地。只要是準確地、生動地描寫了這個充滿矛盾的朦朧地帶的作品,也就必然地超越了政治並具備了優秀文學的特質。(莫言)

Disease is more expensive than health. (Alvin E. Roth)

疾病比健康還要昂貴。(阿爾文・羅思)

It turns out that a Nobel is also followed by other recognitions, and perhaps the most unexpected of these is that the Japan Karate Association in Tokyo has now made me an honorary 7th-degree black belt, something that, given my athletic abilities, is even more unimaginable than being an Economic Sciences Laureate. (Alvin E. Roth)

原來諾貝爾獎也有其他美譽跟隨。也許其中最意想不到的是,東京的日本空手道協會現已授予我名譽黑帶七段。而鑒於我的運動技能,這一項稱譽比成為經濟學獎得主還要不可思議。(阿爾文・羅思)

We would play mathematical games sometimes around the house, play with cards and multiply them, do things like that. So I had this kind of boost from trying to out-excel my brothers. I had a family reputation of being the math whiz. (Lloyd Shapley)

在家中我們有時會玩數學遊戲，玩紙牌並用牌演算乘法之類的事。於是我從超越兄弟們的努力中得到了鼓勵。在家人中我有作為數學奇才的名聲。（勞埃德・沙普利）

Now, I'm ahead of my father. He got other prizes… But he did not get a Nobel Prize. (Lloyd Shapley)

現在，我領先於我父親。他得了另一些獎。……但他沒得諾貝爾獎。（勞埃德・沙普利）

2013 年

Fundamental research is needed to make progress, which you cannot do solely by copying others. If you only do applied research, you quickly lose creativity. (François Englert)

獲得進步需要基礎研究，無法僅僅經由複製他人而達到。如果只做應用研究，你很快就會失去創造力。（法蘭索瓦・恩格勒）

It's not necessary to have read everything about a particular subject in order to get interested in it. The main thing is to sort out what's important and what is peripheral in order to be able to dive in. (François Englert)

要對特定題目產生興趣，沒有必要遍讀關於它的一切。主要是必須釐清什麼是重要的，什麼不是，從而得以深入研究。（法蘭索瓦・恩格勒）

2013 年

When the basic status of a theory is clear, and all that needs to be cleared are details, you can collaborate. But if the main structure of a hypothesis isn't established, and you want to change the paradigm —— like it was the case in the 1960s —— it's better to work alone. (Peter W. Higgs)

當一種理論的基本形態是清晰的,需要釐清的均屬細節,你就可以採取合作。但是如果一個假設的主要結構沒有建立,而你想要改變典範 —— 就像 1960 年代的情況一樣 —— 則以單獨進行較好。(彼得・希格斯)

Nobody else took what I was doing seriously, so nobody would want to work with me. I was thought to be a bit eccentric and maybe cranky. (Peter W. Higgs)

沒有人認真看待我在做的事情,所以沒人願意和我一起工作。我被認為有點反常,甚至怪異。(彼得・希格斯)

When my wife and I got married, she thought of me being an easygoing person, and I warned her I wasn't. (Peter W. Higgs)

結婚時妻子以為我是個隨和的人,我警告她我不是。(彼得・希格斯)

In 2002, a Scottish journalist, during a dinner meant to be private, absolutely wanted me to react to Stephen Hawking's comments. I said one shouldn't pay too much attention to what Hawking was saying because he was a celebrity but not a specialist of elementary particle theory. (Peter W. Higgs)

2002 年,一個蘇格蘭記者在一次本屬私人性質的晚餐中,非要我對史蒂芬・霍金的評論做出反應。我就說,無須過多關注霍金在說什麼,因為他是名人但非基本粒子理論專家。(彼得・希格斯)

I was an embarrassment to the department when they did research assessment exercises. A message would go round the department: "Please give a list of your recent publications." And I would send back a statement: "None." (Peter W. Higgs)

每當系裡做研究評鑑時我都讓他們難堪。全系都會收到一個通知：「請列出你最近發表的文章。」我則會回覆：「沒有。」（彼得・希格斯）

My inbox and doormat are full with emails and letters from people who want me to endorse their Higgs board game or to inaugurate the walkway of their new office atrium. There's even a microbrewery in Barcelona which wants to know what my favourite beer is so they can brew a similar one in my honour. It is quite mad. (Peter W. Higgs)

我的收件匣裡和門墊上滿是電子郵件和信件，來信者想請我支持希格斯棋盤遊戲，或者為新辦公室中庭走道揭幕。甚至有一家巴塞隆納小啤酒廠，想知道我愛喝什麼啤酒，以便能夠釀造類似啤酒以示敬意。這相當瘋狂。（彼得・希格斯）

I don't regard television as the outside world. I regard it as an artefact. (Peter W. Higgs)

我不認為電視是外部世界。我認為它是人工製品。（彼得・希格斯）

When you appear to have discovered something new and exciting, you should be doubly careful to make certain that there is no mistake in what you have done. (Martin Karplus)

在似乎發現了某種新的、令人興奮的東西時，你應當加倍小心，以確定做過的無誤。（馬丁・卡普拉斯）

2013 年

My philosophy in graduate and postgraduate education has been to provide an environment where young scientists, once they have proved their ability, can develop their own ideas, as refined in discussions with me and aided by other members of the group. (Martin Karplus)

我的研究生教育理念是，為年輕科學家提供環境，在其中他們一旦證明了自己的能力，就可以在跟我的討論中改善，並經由群體其他成員幫助，從而發展自己的想法。（馬丁·卡普拉斯）

I very much want to mention one other person, my wife Marci, who was willing to live with me, someone "who spent all his time working," in her words. Even more than just living with me, she was brave enough to be my laboratory administrator. (Martin Karplus)

我非常想提到另一個人，我的妻子馬西，她一心一意地和我（一個她說是「把所有時間都用於工作」的人）一起生活。不僅和我一起生活，她還有足夠的勇氣擔任我的實驗室管理員。（馬丁·卡普拉斯）

Don't do something that you think is going to be important, because the important things are always surprising. (Michael Levitt)

不要做你以為將變得重要的事情，因為重要的事情總是出乎意料的。（邁可·列維特）

I had most of the research work for my Nobel work done before the age of 25. (Michael Levitt)

我獲得諾貝爾獎的大部分研究工作，都是在 25 歲之前完成的。（邁可·列維特）

Science is a bit strange because the old people are sitting in a chair, giving advice. The job of the old people is to make life easier for young people, to give them opportunities and resources. (Michael Levitt)

科學有一點奇怪,因為老年人坐在椅子上,指指點點。老年人的任務是讓年輕人的日子過得容易些,給他們機會和資源。(邁可・列維特)

It's sort of nice in more general terms to see that computational science, computational biology is being recognized. It's become a very large field, and it's always in some ways been the poor sister, or the ugly sister, to experimental biology. (Michael Levitt)

從更普遍的方面而言,目睹計算科學、計算生物學不斷得到認可,相當令人欣慰。它成為一個非常大的領域。而對於實驗生物學,它在某種程度上一直是可憐的姊妹,或醜陋的姊妹。(邁可・列維特)

I love the Swedish people for their detective novels, their archipelago, their sense of humor, their carbonated vodka, and most especially, for their wonderful hospitality. (Michael Levitt)

我喜歡瑞典人,由於他們的偵探小說,他們的群島,他們的幽默感,他們的碳酸伏特加,尤其是他們無與倫比的熱情好客。(邁可・列維特)

Advice to the young: Be passionate. Be persistent. Be original. Be kind and good. Adults tend give too much advice, so this is given in the expectation that it will be ignored. These four points are rather obvious but they certainly worked for me. Passion is needed for any endeavor. Being persistent means you believe in yourself and if you do not, why should anyone else? By being original, competition is less of a concern. By being kind and good, you make friends and not enemies.（Michael Levitt）

對年輕人的建議：要熱情。要執著。要獨創。要善良。長者時常給出過多的建議，所以這是以姑妄言之、姑妄聽之為前提的建議。這四點有些平淡無奇，不過對於我無疑是有效的。熱情是任何努力都需要的。執著意味著你相信自己，你若不相信，別人憑什麼要信？由於獨創，競爭就無須多慮。由於善良，你結交朋友而非樹敵。（邁可‧列維特）

Take risks. It is difficult to predict the outcome of most actions. Taking some risks can lead you to wonderful places that would have been missed otherwise. This is true in science as it is in life.（Michael Levitt）

要勇於冒險。大多數行動的結果難於預測。冒險可以使你到達一些若非如此就會錯過的奇境。在科學中確實如此，跟生活中一樣。（邁可‧列維特）

Multiscale modeling provides a very powerful tool in modeling non-biological systems. Promising directions here include the design of catalysts for a wide range of applications, the design of advanced materials, and the optimization of nanotechnological devices. Overall, the use of computer modeling is likely to increase enormously in any branch of molecule science, as well as in modeling very large systems that can be considered as macroscopic systems. (Arieh Warshel)

多重規模模型為非生物系統模型的建構提供了非常強大的工具。富於前景的方向包括大範圍應用催化劑的設計、先進材料的設計，以及奈米技術設備的優化。整體而言，在分子科學的任何分支中，電腦建模的運用很可能大幅增加，同樣情況也適用於建構被視為宏觀系統的大型系統模型。（阿里耶‧瓦舍爾）

The enormous increase in computer power makes it virtually certain that computer simulations will increasingly become the key tool in modeling complex systems. (Arieh Warshel)

電腦能力的大幅成長,使得這一點實為定論:電腦模擬將逐漸成為建構複雜系統模型的關鍵工具。(阿里耶・瓦舍爾)

The truth is that anyone, almost anyone, who receives the Nobel Prize has some indirect knowledge of one sort or another that they may be a candidate. (James E. Rothman)

實際上,任何一個,幾乎任何一個諾貝爾獎得主,事先都這樣或那樣地間接知道,自己可能是一名候選人。(詹姆斯・羅思曼)

As physics students, we are taught that physicists are smart, that chemists are moderately acceptable, and that biologists are certainly not very intelligent. So I wasn't inclined to take a biology course. But my father insisted, and maybe what he had in mind was that, if there were no jobs in physics, I would end up being a doctor. (James E. Rothman)

作為物理系學生,我們被教導說,物理學家是睿智的,化學家尚可接受,而生物學家肯定不太聰明。所以我並不打算上生物課。但是父親執意要我上,也許他心裡想的是,如果在物理學領域無法就業,到頭來我會當個醫生。(詹姆斯・羅思曼)

I started taking a basic biology course, and I really loved it. I started asking research questions incessantly. I was drawn very quickly to biology. (James E. Rothman)

我開始上基礎生物課,而我真的喜歡它。我開始不停地詢問研究問題。我很快就被生物學吸引了。(詹姆斯・羅思曼)

2013 年

I had five years of failure, really, before I had the first initial sign of success. (James E. Rothman)

我經歷了 5 年的失敗，真的，在首次見到成功的初步跡象之前。（詹姆斯·羅思曼）

I was driven completely by a desire to understand how cells worked. (Randy W. Schekman)

我完全被理解細胞如何工作的欲望所驅使。（蘭迪·謝克曼）

When I was a postdoc, I jotted every fresh thought on a three-by-five card and kept them in a card catalogue. (Randy W. Schekman)

成為博士後研究員時，我把每一個新想法都寫在 3×5 英寸的卡片上，並將它們保存在卡片目錄中。（蘭迪·謝克曼）

Everything I did in high school was focused on microbiology, looking at things like algae under a microscope for hours on end. When I was 13, I saved up $100 to buy a good used microscope. I was obsessed with microorganisms. (Randy W. Schekman)

高中時，我全神貫注於微生物學，在顯微鏡下觀察水藻之類，一連好幾個小時。13 歲的時候，我存了 100 美元，買了一架用得很舊的顯微鏡。我對微生物著了迷。（蘭迪·謝克曼）

I got into science because I thought that, with inspiration and hard work, I could figure out how life works. (Randy W. Schekman)

我一頭栽進了科學領域，因為我認為，憑藉靈感和勤勉，我能夠查明生命如何運作。（蘭迪·謝克曼）

I am a scientist. Mine is a professional world that achieves great things for humanity. (Randy W. Schekman)

我是一名科學家。我致力於一個專業領域，它為人類獲得非凡的成就。（蘭迪・謝克曼）

Basic science is underfunded. And yet it is basic science that will lead to cures. (Randy W. Schekman)

基礎科學經費不足。然而將帶來治癒的是基礎科學。（蘭迪・謝克曼）

Much remains to be done, and I hope to see at least some of these intriguing questions addressed in my lifetime! (Thomas C. Südhof)

還有很多工作要做。這些有趣的問題，我希望在有生之年見到至少有一些得到解決！（托馬斯・聚德霍夫）

I cannot tell you how much I enjoy what I do, so I will always consider it an enormous privilege to be a scientist, and... of course, this honour is very... incredibly beautiful. (Thomas C. Südhof)

我無法說明我多麼鍾愛所做的事情，所以我會永遠認為當科學家是極大的榮幸，而且……當然，這項榮譽非常……不可思議地美麗。（托馬斯・聚德霍夫）

I want the reader to feel something is astonishing —— not the "what happens " but the way everything happens. (Alice Munro)

我想讓讀者感到情節之驚人——不是「發生了什麼事」，而是每件事發生的方式。（艾莉絲・孟若）

I threw out more stuff than I ever sent away or finished, and that went on all through my twenties something. But I was still learning to write the way I wanted to write. (Alice Munro)

我扔掉的作品比曾經尋求發表的或完成的還多，在我 20 幾歲的時候一直如此。但我仍在學習以我想採用的方式寫作。（艾莉絲·孟若）

When I was into my 30s, I became increasingly depressed by rejection letters. I had had the feeling that by the time I was 30, I would be established. But I was not at all. By the time of Lives of Girls and Women, I was into my 40s and I had become more thin-skinned. (Alice Munro)

30 多歲時，退稿信使得我越來越沮喪。我曾有 30 歲會功成名就的預感。可是根本沒有實現。寫《女孩和女人們的生活》時，我已經年屆四十，變得更加敏感。（艾莉絲·孟若）

I can't remember when I wasn't writing stories. (Alice Munro)

我想不起來自己有什麼時候沒在寫作。（艾莉絲·孟若）

I want my stories to move people, I don't care if they are men or women or children. I want my stories to be something about life that causes people to not say "isn't that the truth" but to feel some kind of reward from the writing and that doesn't mean that it has to have a happy ending or anything. But everything that the story tells moves the reader in such a way that you feel you are a different person when you finish. (Alice Munro)

我希望我的故事感動人，無論他們是男人、女人還是孩子。我希望我的故事是關於生活的，並非使人們說「這不是事實嗎」，而是從作品中感受到某種回報，這並不意味著它得有個幸福的結局或任何東西。然而故事所講的一切都以這樣的方式打動了讀者：讀完的時候，你覺得自己是個不同的人。（艾莉絲·孟若）

I feel that I've done what I wanted to do, and that makes me feel fairly content. (Alice Munro)

我覺得自己做到了想做的事，這讓我感到相當滿足。（艾莉絲·孟若）

The constant happiness is curiosity. (Alice Munro)

好奇是無盡的快樂。（艾莉絲·孟若）

Research in finance has been and continues to be a great ride. It has been incredibly satisfying to participate in the growth of finance and to know and learn from all the old giants who created the field and the new giants (like Lars and Bob) who continue to push its boundaries. (Eugene F. Fama)

金融研究一直是也繼續是非凡的歷程。親身體驗金融學的成長，並從所有開創這一領域的老巨人和拓展其疆土的新巨人（如拉爾斯和鮑勃[26]）那裡獲得知識，這始終令人無比滿足。（尤金·法馬）

I think all points of view should get a full airing, and that's why I'm thrilled to get the prize with Shiller. (Eugene F. Fama)

我認為所有的觀點都應當得到充分傳播，這就是為什麼我非常高興跟席勒一起獲獎。（尤金·法馬）

You make enough mistakes by mistake, don't make one on purpose. (Eugene F. Fama)

你無意間犯了夠多無意的錯，不要有意地犯錯。（尤金·法馬）

I work on the boundary between economics and statistics in this field called econometrics. Part of my interest is understanding how you use statistics in productive ways to analyze dynamic economic models. (Lars Peter Hansen)

---

[26] 拉爾斯和鮑勃，即拉爾斯·彼得·漢森和羅伯特·席勒。法馬和他們共同獲得了 2013 年諾貝爾經濟學獎。

2013 年

我的研究著力於經濟學和統計學的交會之處,稱為計量經濟學的這個領域。我的一部分興趣,是了解如何有效運用統計學來分析動態經濟模型。(拉爾斯·彼得·漢森)

I view the work I've done related to statistics and economics as roughly speaking, how to do something without having to do everything. So economic models —— how any model by definition isn't right. When someone just says, "Oh, your model is wrong. " That's not much of an insight. What you want to know is, is wrong in important ways or wrong in ways that are less relevant? And you want to know what does the data really say about the model? (Lars Peter Hansen)

在我看來,我所做的與統計學和經濟學相關的工作,大致說來,就是設法靜觀其變。也就是研究經濟模型 —— 各種模型是如何地顯然不正確。當有人只是說「哦,你的模型錯了」,這算不上多深刻。你想知道,是錯得嚴重還是關係不大。你想知道,關於模型,資料究竟說明了什麼。(拉爾斯·彼得·漢森)

We don't know the probabilities of future events. Still, you have to take action, and so you do it on gut feeling. That's the world we live in. (Robert J. Shiller)

我們不知道未來事件的機率。儘管如此,你還是得採取行動,所以你憑直覺行事。這就是我們生活的世界。(羅伯特·席勒)

I often tend to think that things are not what they seem. (Robert J. Shiller)

我常常傾向於認為事物並不是它們看起來的樣子。(羅伯特·席勒)

As a child, I was fascinated by any branch of physical or biological science. Even today, I find great excitement in discovering the complexity and variability of the world we live in, getting a glimpse into the deeper reality that we mostly ignore in our everyday human activities. (Robert J. Shiller)

兒時，物理或生物科學的任何分支都使我心馳神往。即使在今天，發現我們所生活的世界之複雜和可變，得以一窺我們在日常人類活動中大多忽略的更深層次的現實，也讓我十分激動。（羅伯特‧席勒）

I want to know diverse facts about such things as galaxies or molecules or proteins or insect species. I have an impulse to want to know the little details, which are usually of no significance to non-specialists. I own a dissection microscope, and if there is an insect in the house, I sometimes catch it and look at it under the microscope. (Robert J. Shiller)

我想知道五花八門的事實，關於星系、分子、蛋白質或昆蟲物種，諸如此類事物。我急於了解微小的細節，它們對於非專業人士通常並不重要。我有一架解剖顯微鏡，如果室內有一隻昆蟲，我有時會抓住它，在顯微鏡下觀察。（羅伯特‧席勒）

I think that a lot of people in all walks of life have the impression, of course, that, "I specialize in something. I can't —— I don't have the time to read other things. I'll just go to pure entertainment when I'm relaxing, and then I'll come back to my pure specialty. " That produces —— that attitude produces idiot savants, unfortunately. (Robert J. Shiller)

我認為，各行各業的許多人都有一種想法，那就是：「我專注於一件事。我沒有辦法 —— 沒有時間閱讀別的東西。空閒時我會參加純粹的娛樂，然後回到我純粹的專業。」不幸的是，這產生了 —— 這種態度產生了白痴專家。（羅伯特‧席勒）

2014 年

I was overwhelmed by so many interviewers and then messages of congratulations. So many congratulation messages. I feel this shows the authority and the greatness of the Nobel Prize. (Isamu Akasaki)

我被這麼多的採訪者淹沒了,然後是祝賀訊息。這麼多的祝賀訊息。我覺得這顯示了諾貝爾獎的權威性和非凡之處。(赤崎勇)

No pain, no gain. And as Thomas Edison said, "Genius is one percent inspiration and 99 perspiration." I say this to younger people, experience is the best teacher. That is, sometimes there is no royal road to learning. (Isamu Akasaki)

不勞則無獲。如湯瑪斯・愛迪生所說:「天才是百分之一的靈感加上百分之九十九的汗水。」我對年輕人說,經驗是最好的老師。也就是說,有時學無坦途。(赤崎勇)

I was very lucky to have carried out research under the excellent supervision of Prof. Akasaki and many distinguished colleagues. These days, facilities and funding are much better than in the 80s. So, I would like to see the younger generation attempting to tackle subjects which will greatly contribute to improving the quality of human lives. By doing so, the younger generation can develop a much better world for themselves. (Hiroshi Amano)

我非常幸運,在赤崎教授和許多傑出同事的出色指導下展開了研究。如今,設備和資金比 1980 年代時好得多。所以,我樂於看到年輕世代有志於解決難題,攻克它們將大大有助於提高人們的生活品質。年輕的世代可以由此為自己造就一個更美好的世界。(天野浩)

When I started on my research, I never expected I could invent the LED and laser diode. (Shuji Nakamura)

剛開始研究的時候，我從沒想到自己能發明LED和雷射二極體。（中村修二）

For people who currently have to burn fossil fuels to produce meager, polluting light, LED lighting is a game changer. (Shuji Nakamura)

對於目前不得不燃燒化石燃料來產生微弱的、汙染的光的人們，LED照明是徹底的變革。（中村修二）

It is very satisfying to see that my dream of LED lighting has become a reality. (Shuji Nakamura)

目睹我的LED照明夢想成為現實，我覺得心滿意足。（中村修二）

Basically I like research because research is like to solve the quiz, you know. Always there is a problem and I have to solve the problem. (Shuji Nakamura)

從根本上來說，我喜歡研究，是由於研究就像解謎，你們知道。總是有個難題而我必須解決它。（中村修二）

Breakthroughs are born out of unusual circumstances. (Shuji Nakamura)

突破源自於不尋常的情況。（中村修二）

It's good to have high-quality competition. It helps drive research forward at a faster pace. (Shuji Nakamura)

存在高品質的競爭是好事。它有助於推動研究以更快的速度前進。（中村修二）

Basically physics, it means that usually people was awarded for the invention of the basic theory. But in my case, not a basic theory, in my case just making the device, you know. So I'm not sure whether I could win a Nobel Prize or not, but the Nobel Committee called me and "You got the Nobel Prize". So, I was so, so happy, and I was so surprised. (Shuji Nakamura)

基本上,物理學科意味著,人們通常由於基本理論的發明而獲得獎勵。但在我的例子中,不是由於基本理論,在我的例子中只是製造設備,你們知道。所以我不確定自己是否能夠獲得諾貝爾獎。然而諾貝爾委員會致電給我:「你獲得了諾貝爾獎。」所以,我是這麼,這麼高興,我又是這麼驚訝。(中村修二)

Honestly, I feel you are poisoned if you read too much of the scientific literature because it makes you start thinking like other people. You're better off having a vague sense of what's going on and making your own way. (Eric Betzig)

老實說,我覺得,如果你讀了過多的科學文獻就會中毒,因為這會讓你開始跟別人一樣地思考。明智的是,對現狀具有模糊的概念,並找出自己的思路。(艾力克·貝齊格)

It always irritated me that people think they have to be locked into a career path. (Eric Betzig)

人們認為自己就得被鎖定於職業道路上,這總是使我惱怒。(艾力克·貝齊格)

You get so tied up with the minutiae of the day-to-day, there's never a chance to sit back and let your subconscious run wild. (Eric Betzig)

日常瑣事纏身,你永遠都沒機會放鬆下來,聽任潛意識馳騁。(艾力克·貝齊格)

I'm spoiled. All of my adult jobs have left me with complete freedom to come up with what I wanted. (Eric Betzig)

我是被寵壞了。我成年後所有的工作都給予我完全的自由，可以任意發揮。（艾力克‧貝齊格）

Frankly, I guess, I don't really understand why people, why so many people, are so risk averse. You know, there's always ways to wiggle your way out of any situation if you're motivated enough. (Eric Betzig)

坦率地說，我想，我不太明白為什麼人們，為什麼這麼多的人，對風險這麼避之唯恐不及。要知道，只要有足夠的衝勁，任何困境都有辦法擺脫。（艾力克‧貝齊格）

In my opinion, the only real asset one has is one's reputation, right? I mean, any company and institution can go belly up at any time. But if you have a good reputation, you know, you can usually find somebody who can —— who thinks they can use what you have to offer. (Eric Betzig)

在我看來，唯一真正的資產是一個人的名聲，對吧？我是說，任何公司和機構都可能在任何時候倒閉。然而如果你有好名聲，你知道，你通常就能發現，有人可以 —— 有人認為可以採用你所能提供的東西。（艾力克‧貝齊格）

I love to be a scientist. I've always enjoyed being curious. (Stefan W. Hell)

我喜歡當科學家。我總是樂於好奇。（斯特凡‧赫爾）

I've always enjoyed doing challenging things and also challenging common wisdom. (Stefan W. Hell)

我一向樂於做具有挑戰性的事，也樂於挑戰共識。（斯特凡‧赫爾）

I think that's something a scientist can do because a scientist works at a border, at the edge of science, at the edge of knowledge, and so there's a lot of fun of reaching out and thinking about things that other people didn't think about. And so it has a kind of exploratory notion, kind of adventurous part in it. (Stefan W. Hell)

我認為這是科學家能做的事，因為科學家在邊界工作，在科學的邊緣，在知識的邊緣，興味盎然地接觸和思考別人未曾思考的事情。因此它有一種探索的概念，其中有一些冒險的成分。（斯特凡‧赫爾）

When morning comes, you would better find yourself saying: "I have so many choices of what to do or what to leave —— every morning, every day. I better judge for myself, and —— go ahead and do it." (Stefan W. Hell)

早晨到來之際，你最好發現自己在說：「關於做什麼或不做什麼，我有這麼多的選擇，每一個早晨，每一天。我理當自行判斷，然後 —— 著手實行吧。」（斯特凡‧赫爾）

I imagined there would be a way to crack the diffraction barrier. But of course I didn't know exactly how it would work, but I had a gut feeling that there must be something, and so I tried to think about it, to be creative. (Stefan W. Hell)

我設想會有什麼方法打破繞射屏障。當然我並不確切知道它會如何作用，不過我有種直覺，必定有什麼東西，我就努力地思索它，努力尋求創意。（斯特凡‧赫爾）

I got bored with the topic; I felt this was 19th century physics. I was wondering if there was still something profound that could be made with light microscopy. So I saw that the diffraction barrier was the only important problem that had been left over. (Stefan W. Hell)

我對這個主題感到厭煩，我覺得這是 19 世紀的物理學。我一心在想，是否還有什麼艱深的難題，可以運用光學顯微鏡探索。於是我發現，繞射屏障是剩下的唯一重大問題。（斯特凡·赫爾）

Today, super-resolution microscopy is a powerful application of single molecules that has broad impact across many fields of science, and new and amazing discoveries continue, such as the observation of actin bands in axons. All of this has occurred due not only to my efforts, but also due in major part to the clever and insightful research performed by many researchers around the world too numerous to mention here. (William E. Moerner)

今天，超解析度顯微技術是單分子的一種強而有力應用，它在許多科學領域都有廣泛的影響，驚人的新發現持續不斷，例如對軸突中肌動蛋白帶的觀察。這一切不僅源自我的努力，大部分還要歸功於全世界許多研究人員機智而深入的研究，在此無法歷數。（威廉·莫爾納爾）

My wife, Sharon, has been an indispensable source of love, companionship, patience, and encouragement to me throughout our marriage, and I cannot thank her enough. (William E. Moerner)

我的妻子，莎倫，在我們的婚姻中一直是愛、陪伴、耐心和鼓勵不可或缺的來源，我對她感激不盡。（威廉·莫爾納爾）

I think it's fair to say that the Nobel Prize is the highest honor any scientist or artist can achieve. (John O'Keefe)

我認為，說諾貝爾獎是任何科學家或藝術家所能獲得的最高榮譽，這種說法是公允的。（約翰·奧基夫）

Science is the quintessential international endeavour, and the sterling reputation of the Nobel awards is partly due to the widely-perceived lack of national and other biases in the selection of the laureates. (John O'Keefe)

科學是最典型的國際努力,而諾貝爾獎崇高的聲譽,部分來自於廣泛的共識:獲獎者的遴選不帶國家和其他偏見。(約翰·奧基夫)

Our search for knowledge is a search that sometimes feels like wandering in a fog landscape where we see things close to us but fail to obtain a global view. Research is a bit like that but sometimes we make breakthroughs and see far. During the past few decades there have been many breakthroughs in systems and circuit neuroscience. The prize to the three of us is recognition of this exciting development. (May-Britt Moser)

我們對知識的尋求有時感覺像是在霧氣中摸索,我們看到眼前的東西,但無法獲得全面性的視野。研究也有點類似,但有時我們做出突破,就能看得遠了。過去幾十年裡,在系統和迴路神經科學中有了許多突破。我們三人的獲獎[27]是對這種令人激動的發展的認同。(邁-布里特·莫澤)

All children are born with stars in their eyes, and they are curious. It is important for teachers to be careful not to kill this curiosity. A lot can go wrong. Children can be teased, even by teachers. (May-Britt Moser)

所有的孩子生來眼中有星星,他們很好奇。重要的是,老師們要小心不要扼殺這種好奇心。很多事可能出錯。孩子們可能受到嘲弄,甚至出自於老師。(邁-布里特·莫澤)

Children need teachers who have stars in their eyes themselves and who treat them with respect. (May-Britt Moser)

孩子們需要自己眼中有星星的老師,這樣的老師尊重孩子。(邁-布里特·莫澤)

---

[27] 奧基夫、邁-布里特·莫澤和愛德華·莫澤共同獲得 2014 年諾貝爾生理學或醫學獎。

It is so important to allow children to bloom and to be driven by their curiosity. (May-Britt Moser)

聽任孩子們如花綻放，受自己的好奇心驅使，這極其重要。（邁─布里特・莫澤）

I learned at an early age that work makes you happy. (May-Britt Moser)

我早年就懂得了工作使人快樂。（邁─布里特・莫澤）

I was not always the best student with the highest grades, but my teachers saw something in me and tried to encourage me. (May-Britt Moser)

我並非總是分數最高的傑出學生，然而老師們看出我的潛能，熱情鼓勵我。（愛德華・莫澤）

Perhaps my personality also helped a little bit. I have a strong will and can be extremely focused on a particular goal, even if it is decades away. My slight enthusiasm for mathematics has been useful, as well as my passion for putting together disparate pieces of information. With the help of May-Britt I felt I could sometimes see the whole picture and the path forward. (Edvard I. Moser)

也許我的個性也有所幫助。我有堅強的意志，能夠極度專注於特定的目標，即便它處於數十年後。我對數學的小小熱情一直很有用，對整合不同資訊的熱衷也是這樣的。在邁─布里特・莫澤的幫助下，我覺得自己有時看得見整體全貌和前方坦途。（愛德華・莫澤）

Science is team work so you need a team of people who like to work together. (Edvard I. Moser)

科學是團隊工作，所以你需要一群樂於合作的人。（愛德華・莫澤）

2014 年

You were right to tell me that in life it is not the future which counts, but the past. (Patrick Modiano)

你們跟我這麼說是對的：在生活中，重要的不是未來，而是過去。（派屈克·莫迪亞諾）

Childhood means simplicity. Look at the world with the child's eye —— it is very beautiful. (Kailash Satyarthi)

童年意味著單純。用孩子的眼睛看世界 —— 它非常美麗。（凱拉西·沙提雅提）

There is no greater violence than to deny the dreams of our children. (Kailash Satyarthi)

沒有比否定我們孩子的夢想更大的暴力了。（凱拉西·沙提雅提）

The power of youth is the common wealth for the entire world. The faces of young people are the faces of our past, our present and our future. No segment in the society can match with the power, idealism, enthusiasm and courage of the young people. (Kailash Satyarthi)

年輕人的力量是整個世界的共同財富。年輕人的面孔是我們過去、現在和將來的面孔。社會中沒有任何部分能與年輕人的力量、理想、熱情和勇氣相匹配。（凱拉西·沙提雅提）

From my own experience, I want to say that you should follow your heart, and the mind will follow you. Believe in yourself, and you will create miracles. (Kailash Satyarthi)

根據我自己的經驗，我想說，你應當跟隨你的內心，思想就會跟隨你。相信自己，你就會創造奇蹟。（凱拉西·沙提雅提）

India may be a land of over a 100 problems, but it is also a place for a billion solutions. (Kailash Satyarthi)

印度可能是個問題數以百計的國家,但它也是個對策成千上萬的地方。(凱拉西・沙提雅提)

Let us remember: One book, one pen, one child, and one teacher can change the world. (Malala Yousafzai)

讓我們記住:一本書,一支筆,一個孩子,一位老師可以改變世界。(馬拉拉・尤沙夫賽)

There are many problems, but I think there is a solution to all these problems; it's just one, and it's education. (Malala Yousafzai)

問題有很多,但我認為有一個解決所有這些問題的辦法;只有一個,就是教育。(馬拉拉・尤沙夫賽)

There is so much we still have to learn, and the world changes faster than our understanding can keep up. (Jean Tirole)

有這麼多的東西我們還得學習,世界變化得比我們的理解力所能跟上的更快。(讓・梯若爾)

Research is largely a question of motivation and passion. (Jean Tirole)

研究相當程度上是個動力和熱情問題。(讓・梯若爾)

I'm very proud, this is true, I mean. But, you know, it's also being with the right people, in the right place, at the right moment. And, you know, it's a team work too. (Jean Tirole)

我非常自豪,我是說,真的。但是,你們知道,它也需要合適的人,在合適的地方,於合適的時刻。而且,你們知道,它又是一項團隊

工作。（讓·梯若爾）

Our failure to foresee or prevent the financial crisis is a sore reminder of the dangers of hubris. True enough, we had worked on most of its ingredients. But like a virus that keeps mutating, new dangers emerged when we thought we had understood and avoided the existing ones. (Jean Tirole)

我們未能預見或預防金融危機，這是對傲慢之危險的痛切提醒。確實，我們研究過危機的大部分成因。但就像不斷變異的病毒一樣，當我們認為自己已經了解並避開現存的病毒時，新的危險出現了。（讓·梯若爾）

Humility is not easy to preserve when receiving such a prestigious award. Albert Camus in his acceptance speech wondered how he, rich only in his doubts and his work still in progress, could cope with being at the center of a glaring light. His answer was that he could not live without his art. The great French scientist Henri Poincaré described the unmatched pleasure of discovery："Thought is only a flash in the middle of a long night. But this flash means everything." Wisdom therefore encourages me to return as soon as possible to my lab, to the colleagues to whom I am indebted for the Prize, in short to the wonderful life of a researcher. (Jean Tirole)

接受這樣一個聲望卓著的獎項時，保持謙遜並不容易。阿爾貝·卡繆在獲獎演說中自問，僅僅在自己的懷疑和工作持續時才感到充實的他，如何應對身在奪目光輝中心的處境？他的回答是，沒有他的藝術，他就無法生存。偉大的法國科學家亨利·龐加萊描述了發現的無與倫比的快樂：「思想不過是漫漫長夜中的一道閃光。然而這閃光意味著一切。」因此，智慧催促我，盡快回到自己的實驗室裡，回到幫助我得獎的同事之間，總之回到一個研究人員的美妙人生中。（讓·梯若爾）

2015 年

When I entered Saitama University, I had not even considered becoming a researcher. However, I did know that I primarily wanted to focus on physics. As with so many other things in life, you never know what will happen next until you first try it out. (Takaaki Kajita)

當我進入埼玉大學時,我甚至從沒想過成為研究人員。不過,我確實知道自己最想專攻物理。跟生活中眾多其他事情一樣,你永遠不知道接下來會發生什麼,直到初次嘗試過。(梶田隆章)

For a few years, before I received the Nobel Prize, journalists always discussed our work especially around September, just before the announcements. But I had always treated it with detachment because it had nothing to do with me. I felt that I would probably never actually win a Nobel Prize. So that was the extent of my thoughts on becoming a Nobel Laureate. (Takaaki Kajita)

有幾年了,在我獲得諾貝爾獎之前,記者們總是議論我們的工作,尤其是 9 月左右,快到宣布名單的時候。但我總是以超然的態度對待這件事,因為它跟我無關。我覺得我很可能永遠不會真的獲得諾貝爾獎。這就是我對成為諾貝爾獎得主的想法。(梶田隆章)

I think, nowadays, young researchers and people in positions hired for a limited term are unable to work on one large theme over a long period of time with their research the way I did. I think we are now living in a time where we are told, "You must publish a paper each year," or we are pushed to publish just about anything as often as we can for the sake of evaluations. Back in the day, nobody demanded that out of young researchers. Despite this, we were writing a paper every two years or so. That is to say, in my days, nobody felt rushed just because research was making slow progress. I think the fact that we were allowed to study and research subjects that we cared about contributed greatly in continuing such long-term research projects. (Takaaki Kajita)

我認為,如今,年輕的研究人員和所處職位聘期有限者,無法像我一樣,長期從事一個大的研究課題。我認為我們現在生活在這樣的時期,我們被告知,「你必須每年發表一篇論文」;或者為了評鑑,被迫盡可能頻繁地發表不拘議題的文章。回到過去,沒有人要求年輕研究人員這麼做。儘管如此,我們保持每兩年左右寫一篇論文。這也就是說,在我那時候,沒有人只是由於研究進展緩慢而感到倉促。我認為,我們獲准學習和研究自己喜歡的科目這一個事實,對於持續如此長期的研究項目有很大的貢獻。(梶田隆章)

Occasionally, I feel that in Japan, government-led policies on science and technology focus entirely on "innovation." Everything is viewed from the same lens. In recent years, it has been all about "innovation." I think this is concerning because this has initiated a sort of trend that deals with pursuing science for the sake of innovation. I do not know how this trend will impact basic science in the long run. For example, during some of my recent talks at high schools and junior high schools about neutrino research, I am shocked to find that there is always at least one student who asks, "What good is that research for?" What I expect from them is pure curiosity and interest in these topics of research. Today, however, the mindset among the youth is such that before everything else, they question the value of an academic subject from the perspective of whether or not it would be useful for them in the future. This worries me a lot. I truly hope that my talks would make young students realize that there are amazing natural phenomena and mysteries in the universe, and that there is a body of research dedicated to unraveling those mysteries. (Takaaki Kajita)

　　我偶爾覺得，在日本，政府主導的科技政策完全聚焦於「創新」。事事都以同樣的眼光看待。近年來，一直只關心「創新」。我認為這令人擔心，因為這引發了一種傾向，事關為了創新而投身科學。我不知道這種傾向終將如何影響基礎科學。例如，我最近在高中和國中做了一些關於中微子研究的演講，其間驚訝地發現，總有至少一個學生問道：「這一項研究有什麼用？」我所期待於他們的，原本是對這些研究課題純粹的好奇心和興趣。如今，然而，年輕人的心態是這樣的：別的均屬次要，先從將來對他們有用與否的角度質疑一個學術科目的價值。這使我非常擔憂。我真心希望，所做的演講會讓年輕學生們意識到，宇宙中存在驚人的自然現象和神祕之處，並且有大量的研究致力於解開這些神祕的謎團。（梶田隆章）

It has been said that behind every success there is effort, behind the effort there is passion and behind the passion there are people with the courage to try. (Arthur B. McDonald)

　　有人說過，所有成功背後都有努力，努力的背後是熱情，熱情的背後是勇於嘗試的人們。（阿瑟・麥克唐納）

Work on something most of your colleagues think is boring or off track. You might be lucky and find an area where there isn't much competition. (Tomas Lindahl)

　　從事大多數同事認為乏味或偏離軌道的課題。你可能很幸運，找到了一個沒有太多競爭的領域。（托馬斯・林達爾）

Don't do what everybody else is doing. (Tomas Lindahl)

不要做別人都在做的事。（托馬斯·林達爾）

I got my initial training in Sweden, and I also had the difficult decision to do there, in that I was studying medicine, and research started looking very interesting and intriguing, so should I put aside my clinical studies for some time and concentrate on the research instead. And that's a risky decision to make for a young fellow, but I took the chance and I think it has worked out. (Tomas Lindahl)

我在瑞典接受了最初的培訓，在那裡我也有個艱難的決定要做，就是在我學習醫學時，研究開始顯得非常有趣和吸引人，那麼我應當暫且擱置臨床學業，代之以專心從事研究嗎？對一個年輕人來說，下這個決心是有風險的，但我把握住了機會，我認為結果還不錯。（托馬斯·林達爾）

At school I had a teacher that didn't like me and I didn't like him. At the end of the year he decided to fail me. The ironic thing is that the topic was chemistry. I have the distinction of being the only Chemistry Laureate who failed the topic in high school! (Tomas Lindahl)

學校裡有一個老師不喜歡我，我也不喜歡他。學年結束時，他決定讓我不及格。諷刺的是那一門科目是化學。作為唯一在高中這科不及格的化學獎得主[28]，我就出了名！（托馬斯·林達爾）

It's always nice at the end of your career to have recognition that what you have done is actually important. (Tomas Lindahl)

在職業生涯結束時，認定自己所做的事情的確重要，這總是美好的。（托馬斯·林達爾）

---

[28] 林達爾是 2015 年諾貝爾化學獎得主。

A research laboratory in many ways is like an extended family, and the longterm personal connections have always been a source of pleasure to me. (Paul Modrich)

在很多方面，研究實驗室就像個大家庭，長期的人際關係一直是我的快樂之源。（保羅‧莫德里奇）

Science is not done in a vacuum. We have greatly benefited from work done on these topics by our predecessors as well as our contemporaries who carried out similar work on these topics. Their ideas, findings, and shared reagents have been critical to the success of my laboratory. (Aziz Sancar)

科學成果不是在真空中獲得的。前人對這些課題做過探討，同時代的人也就這些課題展開了類似研究，對此我們實在受益匪淺。他們的想法、發現，以及共同的反應物，對我的實驗室得以成功十分重要。（阿齊茲‧桑賈爾）

In late afternoon I often climb a nearby hill —— not a mountain, just a grassy half-mile hill called "Half-mile Hill." From the top I see a marvelous vista of woodland and lake, and a sky often tinted with color as evening falls. It is a moment of uplifting tranquility; and with it comes the realization that many do not live amidst natural beauty and peace. To redress the terrible imbalance, many people around the world are making heroic efforts, and one of their objectives is the improvement of global public health. (William C. Campbell)

下午晚些時候，我經常爬上附近的一處山岡 —— 不是大山，只是一座長滿草的半英哩小丘，就叫「半哩岡」。從山頂上，看得見一片神奇的遠景，有林地和湖水；還有天空，薄暮時分往往盡染霞光。這種寧靜時刻令人心情為之一振,它又讓人意識到,許多人沒有生活在天然美景和安寧靜謐之中。為了糾正這種嚴重的不平衡,世界各地很多人都在做出崇高的努力,目標之一就是改善全球公共衛生。(威廉·塞西爾·坎貝爾)

I firmly believe that Nature's microbes produce metabolites offering unmatched promise toward meeting our needs, although the introduction of novel screening methods will be key to achieving optimal results. Thus, success will only be restricted by our vision and our innovation —— or lack of it. Fortunately, we have access to some of the innovation we need through genetic engineering and the number of non-natural compounds obtained is increasing rapidly to supplement the never-ending stream of novel compounds that Nature can supply. (Satoshi Ōmura)

我堅信,大自然的微生物產生代謝物,它們為滿足我們的需求提供了無與倫比的前景,儘管全新篩選方法的引入將是實現最佳結果的關鍵。所以,成功只會受限於我們的眼界和創新 —— 或者創新不足。幸運的是,我們可以憑藉基因工程獲取一些所需創新,而得到的非天然化合物的數量正在迅速增加,以補充大自然所能供應的源源不斷的全新化合物。(大村智)

My work has always been guided by five fundamental creeds: the almost unlimited abilities of microorganisms to produce novel compounds; the crucial need to establish "gold-standard" screening systems; recognition that screening is not just a routine exercise; the major contribution of basic research; and the need to assign the highest value to maintaining human relationships and partnerships. (Satoshi Ōmura)

我的工作一直受到五大基本信條的指導：微生物產生全新化合物的近乎無限的能力、建立「黃金標準」篩選系統的重大需要、了解篩選工作並非僅屬於常規流程、基礎研究的主要貢獻，以及賦予維護人際關係和夥伴關係最高價值的需要。（大村智）

For 50 years, I have worked alongside specialised researchers in fields such as Biochemistry, Microbiology, and Clinical medicine. My approach has always been influenced by the tenet "One encounter, one chance." This encompasses the deep reverence that is an essential part of the Tea Ceremony (or Chanoyu), which is held in the highest esteem in Japanese culture. As well as the certain fact that exact circumstances at any point in time will never happen again, I believe it is important to seize opportunities as and when they arise. And to maintain profound respect and consideration for all my colleagues —— as well as for Nature and the microorganisms I work with. Such sentiments form the fundamental basis for all good scientific research and discovery. (Satoshi Ōmura)

50年來，我曾與生物化學、微生物學和臨床醫學等領域的專業研究人員並肩工作。我的研究方法始終受到「一期一會」的信條影響。這一項信條包含屬於茶道精神的深切敬意，而茶道在日本文化中受到無上尊崇。任何時刻的確切情況都不會再度發生；與這一項當然的事實相應，我相信當機遇一旦出現就把握住它們是重要的。重要的還有對所有的同事 —— 以及對共處的大自然和微生物 —— 保持深厚的尊敬和周到的考慮。這樣的情感構成一切優秀科學研究與發現的根本基礎。（大村智）

It was not a simple and easy journey in the discovery of the artemisinin from Qinghao, a Chinese herbal medicine with over two thousand years of clinical application. (Tu Youyou)

自中國已有兩千多年沿用歷史的中藥青蒿之中發掘出青蒿素的歷程相當艱辛。（屠呦呦）

"Fortune favors the prepared mind" and "What's past is prologue." My prologue of integrated training in both modern and Chinese medicine prepared me for the challenges when the opportunities to search for antimalarial Chinese medicines became available. (Tu Youyou)

「機會垂青有準備的人。」、「凡是過去，皆為序曲。」然而，序曲就是一種準備。當抗瘧項目給我機會的時候，融合現代醫學和中醫的訓練為我從事青蒿素研究提供了良好的準備。（屠呦呦）

After accepting the tasks, I collected over two thousand herbal, animal and mineral prescriptions for either internal or external use by reviewing ancient traditional Chinese medical literature and folk recipes, interviewing well-known and experienced Chinese medical doctors who provided me prescriptions and herbal recipes. I summarized six hundred forty prescriptions in a brochure. It was this information collection and deciphering that laid a sound foundation for the discovery of artemisinin. (Tu Youyou)

接受任務後，我收集整理歷代中醫藥典籍，走訪名老中醫並收集他們用於防治瘧疾的方劑和中藥、同時調閱大量民間方藥。在彙集了包括植物、動物、礦物等兩千餘內服、外用方藥的基礎上，編寫了以640種中藥為主的《瘧疾單驗方集》。正是這些資訊的收集和解析造就了青蒿素發現的基礎。（屠呦呦）

Joseph Goldstein has written in this journal that creation (through invention) and revelation (through discovery) are two different routes to advancement in the biomedical sciences. In my work as a phytochemist, particularly during the period from the late 1960s to the 1980s, I have been fortunate enough to travel both routes… In keeping with Goldstein's view, the discovery of artemisinin was the first step in our advancement —— the revelation. We then went on to experience the second step —— creation —— by turning the natural molecule into a drug. (Tu Youyou)

約瑟夫・里歐納德・戈爾茨坦曾在《自然醫學》上寫道，發明創造和發現揭示是生物醫學研究進步的兩條道路。作為植物化學家，在1960年代末到1980年代期間，我非常幸運地走在這兩條路上。……依戈爾茨坦的看法，青蒿素的發現是研究進展的第一步，即揭示。我們隨即轉向第二步，即創造，將這個天然的分子變為藥物。（屠呦呦）

Artemisinin is a true gift from old Chinese medicine. The route to the discovery of artemisinin was short compared with those of many other phytochemical discoveries in drug development. But this is not the only instance in which the wisdom of Chinese medicine has borne fruit. (Tu Youyou)

青蒿素是中國醫學給予人類的一份珍貴禮物。和其他植物化學的發現在藥物開發中的應用相比，青蒿素的歷程相對短暫。但這絕不是中醫智慧的唯一果實。（屠呦呦）

We have a substantial amount of natural resources from which our fellow medical researchers can develop novel medicines. Since "Tasting a hundred herbs by Shen Nong," we have accumulated substantial experience in clinical practice, integrated and summarized the medical application of most nature resources over the past several thousand years through Chinese medicine. Adopting, exploring, developing and advancing these practices would allow us to discover more novel medicines beneficial to global healthcare. (Tu Youyou)

大自然為我們提供了大量的植物資源，醫藥學研究者可以從中開發新藥。中醫藥從神農嘗百草開始，在幾千年的發展中累積了大量臨床經驗，對於自然資源的藥用價值已經有所整理歸納。透過繼承、發揚、發掘、進步，一定會有所發現，有所創新，從而造福人類。（屠呦呦）

From our research experience in discovering artemisinin, we learned the strengths of both Chinese and Western medicine. There is great potential for future advances if these strengths can be fully integrated. (Tu Youyou)

透過抗瘧藥青蒿素的研究經歷，深感中、西醫藥各有所長，二者有機結合，優勢互補，當具有更大的開發潛力和良好的發展前景。（屠呦呦）

My name, Youyou, was given by my father, who adapted it from the sentence "呦呦鹿鳴，食野之蒿" translated as "Deer bleat 'youyou' while they are eating the wild qinghao" in the Chinese Book of Odes. How this links my whole life with qinghao will probably remain an interesting coincidence forever. (Tu Youyou)

我的名字，呦呦，是父親取的，摘自《詩經》中的句子「呦呦鹿鳴，食野之蒿」，意思是「鹿呦呦地鳴叫，吃著野生青蒿」。這如何把我的一生都與青蒿連繫起來，大概永遠都是個有趣的巧合。（屠呦呦）

I would like to share with you a well-known poem, On the stork tower, written during the Tang Dynasty by Wang Zhihuan (688–742 AD)：

The sun along the mountain bows;

The Yellow River seawards flows;

You will enjoy a grander sight;

By climbing to a greater height.

Let us reach to a greater height to appreciate Chinese culture and find the beauty and treasure in the territory of traditional Chinese medicine. (Tu Youyou)

我想與各位分享一首唐代有名的詩，王之渙（688～742）所寫的〈登鸛雀樓〉：

白日依山盡，

黃河入海流，

欲窮千里目，

更上一層樓。

請各位有機會時更上一層樓，去領略中華文化的魅力，發現蘊含於傳統中醫藥中的寶藏。（屠呦呦）

The discovery of artemisinin was an example of successful collective efforts. (Tu Youyou)

青蒿素的發現是集體發掘中藥的成功範例。（屠呦呦）

This is not only an honor for myself, but also a recognition and motivation for all scientists in China. (Tu Youyou)

諾貝爾獎不僅是授予我個人的榮譽，也是對全體中國科學家團隊的認同和鼓勵。（屠呦呦）

It is my dream that Chinese medicine will help us conquer life threatening diseases worldwide, and that people across the globe will enjoy its benefits for health promotion. (Tu Youyou)

我的夢想是中國醫藥幫助我們征服全世界危害人們生命的疾病，提升全球人民的健康和福祉。（屠呦呦）

Death is the fairest thing in the world. No one's ever gotten out of it. The earth takes everyone —— the kind, the cruel, the sinners. Aside from that, there's no fairness on earth. (Svetlana Alexievich)

死亡是世界上最公平的東西。從無一人躲得過它。大地吞噬每一個人——善良的，凶殘的，有罪之人。除此之外，世上再無公平。（斯維拉娜·亞歷塞維奇）

I'm one of these people who are fortunate enough to have my recent project be the one I'm most excited by; it always seems to be the best. Some people would call that fickle, in that I'm always giving up on one thing and moving onto something else. It sort of keeps you young, I think. I'm always very excited about what I'm doing. (Angus Deaton)

我屬於這樣的幸運者，最新的項目就是最讓自己興奮的一個，它看起來總是最棒的。有人會稱此為善變，因為我總是放棄一件事而轉向另外的事。這在一定程度上使人年輕，我認為。我總是為手邊的事興高采烈。（安格斯·迪頓）

Boredom and loneliness have been familiar visitors throughout my life, though I have come to (reluctantly) accept that the turning inwards that they bring is linked to creativity, at least for me. (Angus Deaton)

無聊和孤獨是我一生的熟客，雖然我已經（無奈地）承認，它們所導致的令人轉為內向與創造力有關，至少就我而言如此。（安格斯·迪頓）

If you're my age and you've been working for a long time you know this is a possibility. But you also know there are a huge number of people out there who deserve this. That lightning would strike me seemed like a very small probability event. It was sort of like, "Oh my goodness, it's really happening." (Angus Deaton)

如果你到了我的年紀,而且已經工作了很長時間,你知道這是可能的。但你也知道,此外還有大量的人值得獲得這個獎。閃電會擊中我的機率看來似乎非常小。這有一點像是,「哦,我的天,這真的發生了。」(安格斯・迪頓)

The Nobel thing is like dying and going to heaven for a while. It's like being transported to a fairyland. (Angus Deaton)

得諾貝爾獎就像死後進入天堂一陣子。就像被送到了仙境一般。(安格斯・迪頓)

It's been a whirlwind, but a very pleasant one. You know, I live a reasonably quiet life, and now all of a sudden my life is not a quiet one anymore. Some of it is sort of irritating —— there are lots of people who want to talk to you who you have no particular interest in talking with. But there are a lot of people who you really do want to talk to, which is giving me a chance for my ideas to reach audiences that they wouldn't otherwise reach. I've also received emails from people I haven't heard from in 40 to 50 years, perhaps even longer than that, and that's a real treat. It does have a reach that other things, other prizes that are academic recognitions, don't seem to have. (Angus Deaton)

獲得諾貝爾獎是陣旋風,不過是非常愉快的一陣。要知道,我過著相當平靜的生活,現在一下子不再平靜了。多少有點讓人煩惱 —— 許多人想跟你說話,而你沒有特別的興趣與之交談。不過有許多人你是真的想跟他們說話,這給了我機會,把自己的想法傳遞給本來傳遞不到的聽眾。我還收到了四、五十年,乃至也許更久沒有聯絡的人發來的電子郵件,這是真正的愉悅。這個獎項的確有種影響力,是其他獎勵,其他作為學術認可的獎項,看來所不具備的。(安格斯‧迪頓)

I really haven't recovered from last Monday. I don't know what the rest of my life is going to be like. I have a couple of fairly substantial projects going on right now, so as soon as I recover from this train that's hit me, I would like to get back to those; there's a lot of work to be done on those. (Angus Deaton)

我實在還沒從上週一[29]恢復過來。我不知道自己的下半輩子會是什麼樣子。現在我有幾個相當重大的項目正在進行,所以一旦從這次火車撞擊恢復過來,我願意馬上回到那些項目上,還有許多工作得做。(安格斯‧迪頓)

One of the things I was delighted to hear was them saying they'd found a thread through my work about looking at well-being and behavior, which integrates almost everything I've done; they managed to make it into a discovery, but also to make it a sort of lifetime achievement award, and for that I'm enormously grateful. (Angus Deaton)

我很高興聽到的一件事是,他們說,找到了一條貫串我所做工作的線索,即觀察幸福和行為,這整合了我所做的幾乎所有事情。他們設法使這成為一項發現,而且使之成為一種終身成就獎,對此我極為感激。(安格斯‧迪頓)

I think the sense of people having the will and drive to prosper and to find their own meaning in life —— that's just something that's very deeply engrained in human beings. That's the wellspring of scientific progress, and

---

[29] 指 2015 年 10 月 12 日被授予諾貝爾經濟學獎。

that scientific progress, that curiosity, that will to be happy and prosperous, is something that's never going to leave us. I'm not an optimist in the sense that I think nothing bad is ever going to happen again; terrible things do happen, and bad politics can do awful things. But there's this will, which is never going to go away, to make the world better. (Angus Deaton)

人們有意願和動力過好日子，求得自己生活的意義，我認為這種意識完全是深入人心的。這是科學進步的泉源。這種科學進步，這種好奇心，這種追求幸福美滿的意願，是永遠不會離開我們的。我不是那種樂天派，以為糟糕的事情永不再來；可怕的事情確實發生，糟糕的政治也能鑄成大錯。然而這種意願永遠不會消失，它使世界更加美好。（安格斯·迪頓）

We forget that ageing is a really good thing and a great achievement. Ageing is a great mark of success! (Angus Deaton)

我們忘了，年老是一件好事，是偉大的成就。年老是成功的一大標記！（安格斯·迪頓）

I can think of three of them: computers, computers, and computers. (Angus Deaton)

我能想到其中三種：電腦、電腦、電腦。[30]（安格斯·迪頓）

---

[30] 在被問及「你能想到職業生涯中有什麼特別的工具讓你把工作做得更好嗎」時，迪頓如此回答。

2016 年

We worked well together, since I had the broad ideas and tried to understand the big picture, whereas Mike would find the holes in my arguments and ways to solve the problems I had ignored. (David J. Thouless)

我們合作得很好，因為我有了大致想法，力圖理解整體局面，而邁克[31]會發現我的論證的漏洞，找出解決我所忽視問題的方法。（大衛·杜列斯）

Getting to know Kac and to learn from him was one of the unexpected benefits of going to Cornell. I treasured his explanation of the difference between a physicist and a mathematician: that a physicist was interested in the simple properties of complicated systems, but a mathematician was interested in the complicated properties of simple systems. (David J. Thouless)

得以結識卡茨[32]並跟從他學習，是進入康乃爾大學的意外得益之一。我非常喜歡他對物理學家和數學家二者差異的解釋：物理學家對複雜系統的簡單性感興趣，而數學家對簡單系統的複雜性感興趣。（大衛·杜列斯）

We should never say things like "What's it used for?" Because all the big discoveries of really useful things don't really come about because someone sits down and thinks "I want to discover something useful". They occur because someone discovers something interesting and it turns out to be tremendously useful. I mean that's the history of everything, in the transistors. (F. Duncan M. Haldane)

---

[31] 邁克，即約翰·科斯特利茲（J. Michael Kosterlitz），與杜列斯共同創造了相變理論。
[32] 卡茨，即馬克·卡茨（Mark Kac），一位數學家。

我們絕不該問「它是用來做什麼的」這種話。因為所有真正有用的東西的重大發現，都不是由於有人坐下來想「我要發現某種有用的東西」而真的出現的。它們之所以產生，是由於有人發現了某種有趣的東西，結果它極其有用。我認為，這就是各種東西的發展史，在電晶體方面。（鄧肯・哈爾丹）

The surprise in everything is that quantum mechanics is so much richer than we dreamed. Quantum mechanics is so bizarre! The things it can do, we didn't discover them earlier because it was just difficult to actually even imagine that quantum mechanics might do these kinds of things. And now we've found a whole lot of new topological physics and quantum mechanics and it's starting to become a big field. (F. Duncan M. Haldane)

令人百般驚訝的是，量子力學比我們所能設想的遠為豐富得多。量子力學真是匪夷所思！它能夠做的事情，我們先前沒有發現，因為我們實在是難以想像，量子力學可以做這些事情。而現在我們發現了眾多新的拓撲物理學和量子力學，它已經開始成為一大領域。（鄧肯・哈爾丹）

J. Michael Kosterlitz: Hello?

Adam Smith: Oh Hello, my name is Adam Smith. I'm calling from Nobel Media, which is the media organisation of the Nobel Foundation in Stockholm. We run the official website for the Nobel Prize. Have you already heard the news of the announcement of the Physics?

MK: No, I haven't heard anything. I'm talking from an underground car park in Helsinki, Finland, right now so I can barely hear you.

AS: It has just been announced in Stockholm that you are one of the recipients of the 2016 Nobel Prize in Physics.

MK: Jesus. That's incredible.

AS: (Laughs)

MK: That's amazing.

AS: So the Prize is given to yourself, Duncan Haldane and David Thouless for theoretical discoveries of topological phase transitions and topological phases of matter.

MK: Oh that's, yes, thank you, that's, this is quite amazing. Thank you very much indeed.

AS: I must say you sound very calm.

MK: Er, yes. It just feels a little bit odd getting this news in an underground car park outside Helsinki.

AS: (Laughs) Actually, maybe remaining in the underground car park is a good option because you'll be safe from the onslaught of press that will now descend.

MK: True, yes, but I guess I'll have to face it eventually.

AS: I actually was given your number by your son at home, and I have to say he was absolutely elated.

MK: I'm sure that he is elated, but not half as elated as I am.

AS: (Laughs) That's lovely. Oh, well, many congratulations from Nobelprize.org, and if you go to Nobelprize.org you will of course see the announcement of the news there.

MK: Thank you very much.

約翰・科斯特利茲：你好。

史密斯：你好。我叫亞當・史密斯。這個電話我是從諾貝爾媒體打的，它是位於斯德哥爾摩的諾貝爾基金會的媒體組織。諾貝爾獎官方網站由我們營運。你聽說了物理學獎宣布的消息嗎？

科：沒有，我什麼都沒聽說。我現在是在芬蘭赫爾辛基的一個地下停車場接電話，所以幾乎聽不清楚你說的話。

史：在斯德哥爾摩剛剛宣布，你是2016年諾貝爾物理學獎的得主之一。

科：天哪。這難以置信。

史：（笑）

科：這令人吃驚。

史：就是說，這個獎項授予你本人、鄧肯・哈爾丹和大衛・杜列斯，以表彰物質的拓撲相變和拓撲相的理論發現。

科：哦，是這樣啊，是啊，謝謝，是這樣啊，這很令人吃驚。真的非常感謝。

史：我得說你聽起來非常平靜啊。

科：嗯，是啊。只是在赫爾辛基郊外的地下停車場得知這個消息有點奇怪。

史：（笑）實際上，也許待在地下停車場是個很好的選擇，因為可以躲避即將降臨的猛烈轟炸。

科：沒錯，是啊，但是我想我最終不得不面對它。

史：你的號碼其實是你在家裡的兒子告訴我的，我得說他極為高興。

科：我肯定他很高興，但比不上我一半高興。

史：（笑）這太好了。哦，對了，Nobelprize.org 衷心祝賀你。如果上 Nobelprize.org 網站，你當然會在那裡看到這個消息的宣布。

科：非常感謝。

In fact, when I was in my twenties, I was one of the best climbers in Britain and even considered giving up physics in favor of a professional climbing career. My teaching duties prevented me from going on any of the Himalayan expeditions I could have joined. However, on thinking about the possible consequences of this choice, sanity and my wife finally prevailed. I realized that, although I was technically good enough, a career in academia and physics would allow me enough vacation time to indulge in my climbing obsession. (J. Michael Kosterlitz)

事實上，20 幾歲的時候，我是英國最好的攀岩者之一，甚至考慮過為從事專業攀岩而放棄物理學。教學職責使我無緣於任何一次喜馬拉雅山遠征，我本來可以參加的。不管怎樣，考慮到這一項選擇的可能後果，理智和我妻子最終占了上風。我理解到，儘管自己在運動技術上足夠優秀，從事學術和物理學工作也會有足夠的假期，任我沉湎於對攀岩的痴迷。（約翰・科斯特利茲）

I am happy that I have managed to work since that dreadful day in September 1978 when I was diagnosed with MS. The twenty-five years have gone and, as predicted by the neurologist then, I now know the outcome.

I was not a bad case. I had attacks every 18 months from age 35 to 55, some quite bad, some small relapses. When I was 55 my neurologist put me into a trial for a new MS drug. This was very successful and opened up a whole new field of pharmacological drugs for the easing of MS.

Since then, I have been lucky in that I have never had another attack. I only battle the deadly fatigue that comes with the disease. I want to take this space to tell any budding scientist that, however bleak the future may seem due to illness or other problems, one cannot say you will not be successful. (J. Michael Kosterlitz)

1978 年 9 月，我確診罹患 MS（多發性硬化症）。欣慰的是，從那可怕的日子後，我一直盡力工作。25 年過去，一如神經科醫生當時預告，我現在得知了結果。

我的病情不算糟糕。35 到 55 歲，每 18 個月發作，有時很嚴重，有時稍微復發。55 歲時，神經科醫生讓我試用一種 MS 新藥。這非常有效，開闢了藥理學上藥物緩解 MS 的全新領域。

從那以後，我一直很幸運，再也沒有發作。我只與疾病帶來的致命疲勞抗爭。我想藉此機會，告訴所有起步階段的科學家，無論疾病或其他難題導致的未來多麼黯淡，都不能說自己不會成功。（約翰‧科斯特利茲）

Physics still fascinates me because there are so many problems waiting for a solution that, despite my increasing incompetence, I would like to see understood before I retire. Perhaps in this respect, I am like my father who refused to give up working until he was over 90! (Michael Kosterlitz)

物理學仍然深深吸引我，因為有太多的問題猶待解決。儘管日漸不夠勝任，我還是希望在退休前見到人們對我的理解。也許在這方面，我跟父親一樣，過了 90 歲還不肯放棄工作！（約翰‧科斯特利茲）

I started to be very interested in chemistry when I was 15 or 16 years old and, in particular, I liked to play with natural molecules such as chlorophylls which I extracted from plants. I had a small and very primitive chemistry lab in the cellar where I was separating chlorophylls on paper or distilling various mixtures. (Jean-Pierre Sauvage)

十五、六歲時，我對化學產生了很大的興趣，尤其是，喜歡把玩天然的分子，比如從植物中提取葉綠素。在地窖裡，我有個小小的、非常原始的化學實驗室。我置身其中，在紙上分離葉綠素，或者蒸餾各種混合物。（尚－皮耶・索法吉）

In spite of all the possibilities offered by molecular machines in terms of potential applications for the future, it should be stressed that basic research is still of utmost importance and is or has been at the origin of the many technologies which are nowadays part of our daily life. (Jean-Pierre Sauvage)

儘管分子機器為未來潛在的應用提供了各式各樣的可能性，應當強調的是，基礎研究仍然具有極為重要的意義，並且居於日常生活當中許多技術的源頭。（尚－皮耶・索法吉）

You've got to break the rules. (J. Fraser Stoddart)

你不得不打破規則。（佛瑞塞・史多達爾）

I was in bed. It was 4:05 a.m. when I got a call. So, of course, I thought something bad had happened, either in Japan or in the UK, where my daughters live. When I answered the phone and got told about the Prize, I also thought it could be a hoax. Fortunately, I am good at detecting English being spoken by people of different nationalities. I soon understood that: "Yes, this person is speaking Swedish-English". Then I knew it was for real. (J. Fraser Stoddart)

我當時在睡覺。凌晨 4 點零 5 分，我接到一通電話。所以，當然，我以為發生了不好的事，在日本或者英國，我的女兒住在那裡。接聽電話並被告知獲得諾貝爾獎的消息時，我還是以為這可能是惡作劇。好在，我擅長辨別不同國家的人所說的英語。我很快明白了：「對，這個人說的是瑞典英語。」於是我知道這通電話是認真的。（佛瑞塞・史多達爾）

I am 75 going on 76 years old. One of the projects that I am most excited about is giving the 30 to 35 very bright young people in my lab, from all over the world, pretty much free rein to do what they like. If only one or two of them come up with something out of this world, it would be a rewarding experience. The Prize has done a lot to open up these opportunities as well as funding for the project. (J. Fraser Stoddart)

我 75 歲，即將 76 歲了。我的實驗室有 30 至 35 個年輕人，非常聰明，來自世界各地。最讓我心動的項目之一，是給予他們極大的自由去做自己喜歡的事。只要有一、兩個人由現實世界得出某種想法，這種經歷就是值得的。諾貝爾獎為提供這些機會發揮了很大作用，也為這個項目提供了資金。（佛瑞塞・史多達爾）

I find it difficult when people ask: "How do you win a Nobel Prize?" First of all, statistically it is absolutely reigned against you. And secondly, you should not pursue your profession as a scientist with this mission as your goal. You should do your research and enjoy doing it. Maybe a Nobel Prize will happen for you, but the likelihood is very small. (J. Fraser Stoddart)

人們問起「你是怎麼獲得諾貝爾獎的」時，我覺得難以作答。首先，從統計角度而言，這絕對由不得你。其次，作為科學家，也不應將獲獎使命視為目標而從事專業。應當專心於研究，並樂於做此事。也許諾貝爾獎會落到頭上，但可能性非常之小。（佛瑞塞・史多達爾）

I am totally taken over by Twitter. I feel that I must reach out to the young people who are coming into science at the moment. Twitter breaks down a lot of barriers and I become one of them. I was persuaded by my ex-graduate student Stuart Cantrill to start tweeting when I went to Stockholm. I took his advice and I am now labelled as a twitter monster! My mission is to try and get my co-Laureates and people from my generation involved. (J. Fraser Stoddart)

我被推特徹底地征服了。我覺得必須接觸到此刻進入科學界的年輕人。推特克服了許多障礙，我也算其中之一。去斯德哥爾摩的時候，我被我之前的研究生斯圖爾特・坎特里爾說服，開始使用推特。我接受了他的建議，現在被貼上了推特怪物的標籤！我的使命是，爭取讓我的共同獲獎者和我們這一代的人加入。（佛瑞塞・史多達爾）

For me being a scientist engaged in designing new molecules and chemical systems is a life-long "adventure into the unknown," entering an uncharted territory of astonishing beauty, surprises and amazing perspectives. (Bernard L. Feringa)

對我來說，做一名從事新分子和化學系統設計的科學家，是畢生「探索未知的冒險」，進入一片具有攝魂美麗、眾多奇觀和驚人遠景的神祕地域。（伯納德・佛林加）

So we use molecules as a kind of Lego kit. And so we have access to this unlimited number of molecules and we use them to build the new materials, the drugs of the future, and in this case also the nanomachinery and the smart materials of the future. And yes, I feel often, and me and my students and the team, and I'm sure that it's the same for the other teams of Stoddart and Sauvage, we feel sometimes like kids playing with these molecules and seeing what are the possibilities to build, like with Lego. (Bernard L. Feringa)

於是我們把分子當成一種樂高積木來用。我們用上了如此無限數量的分子，以之建造新的材料、未來的藥物，同樣也運用奈米機器和未來的智慧材料。是的，我經常感到，我和我的學生與團隊，我確定，史多達爾和索法吉[33]他們的團隊也一樣，我們有時覺得像是孩子似的把玩這些分子，看看有可能建造些什麼，就像玩樂高積木。（伯納德‧佛林加）

It is a great privilege to be able to stand on the shoulders of the giants of chemistry and in doing so experience the marvels of the molecular world and provide challenges for our youth, dreams for the people, and opportunities for industry. For me being a scientist engaged in designing new molecules and chemical systems is a life-long adventure into the unknown, entering an uncharted territory of astonishing beauty, surprises and amazing perspectives. Over the past decades on many occasions we have lost track on our intended journeys, reaching places in chemical space we could never have imagined. (Bernard L. Feringa)

能夠站在化學巨人的肩膀上，從而體驗分子世界的奇蹟，並為年輕人提供挑戰、為人們提供夢想、為產業提供機遇，這是莫大的榮幸。對於我，作為從事新分子和化學系統設計的科學家，是進入未知世界的畢生冒險，涉足陌生而神祕的領域，領略炫目的美麗、奇異的現象和驚人的景緻。過去幾十年中我們一次次迷失於預期的旅途上，在化學的天地裡到達完全無法想像的境界。（伯納德‧佛林加）

---

[33] 佛林加與史多達爾和索法吉三人，由於分子機器的設計和合成而共同獲得 2016 年諾貝爾化學獎。

> 2016年

When I draw a molecule in China or in Argentina, it is the same molecule. People understand immediately without knowing Spanish or Chinese. That is beautiful. Our common goal is not about power or borders of the country, it is about bringing forward human knowledge. (Bernard L. Feringa)

當我在中國或阿根廷畫分子時,它是同樣的分子。不懂西班牙文或中文,人們也馬上理解。這很美妙。我們的共同目標不是權力或國界,而是推動人類知識的進步。(伯納德·佛林加)

Autophagy was a very good topic to work. Still we have so many questions. Even now we have more questions than when I started. (Yoshinori Ohsumi)

自噬是個非常好的研究課題。我們還有非常多的問題。即便現在,我們的問題比我剛開始時的還多。(大隅良典)

My autophagy research has always been driven by nothing more than intellectual curiosity and a thirst to get a better understanding of life through protein dynamics within the cell. When I started my work, I never thought it would become relevant in diseases as diverse as neuro-degeneration, infectious disease, cancer and others in such a short time. But now autophagy research has become a major field in biology. (Yoshinori Ohsumi)

我從事自噬研究,動機一直不過是求知欲,以及透過細胞內的蛋白質動力學深入理解生命的渴望。開始研究時,我絕對沒想到,在這麼短的時間內,它會與神經變性、傳染病、癌症等如此多樣的疾病連繫起來。然而現在,自噬研究已經成為生物學的一個主要領域了。(大隅良典)

Science is a system of knowledge that is gradually accumulated over many years by society, but it is also an inherently human activity. I believe that every scientist is a product of the era in which they live. (Yoshinori Ohsumi)

科學是一個知識體系,由社會長年逐漸累積,但它也是根本上屬於人的活動。我相信,每一個科學家都是所處時代的產物。(大隅良典)

If someone had ever told me that I had the slightest chance of winning the Nobel Prize, I would have to think that I'd have about the same odds as standing on the moon. (Bob Dylan)

假如有人對我說,我有獲得諾貝爾獎的一丁點機會,我都會認為,機率跟我登上月球幾乎相同。(巴布‧狄倫)

There is nothing so stable as change. (Bob Dylan)

天下沒有比變化更穩定的事情了。[34](巴布‧狄倫)

Yesterday's just a memory, tomorrow is never what it's supposed to be. (Bob Dylan)

昨天只是記憶,明天絕不會一如設想。(巴布‧狄倫)

The only thing people really have in common is that they are all going to die. (Bob Dylan)

人們真正具有的唯一共同之處是全都會死。(巴布‧狄倫)

He not busy being born is busy dying. (Bob Dylan)

人不是忙著出生就是忙著死去。(巴布‧狄倫)

You're going to die. You're going to be dead. It could be 20 years, it could be tomorrow, anytime. So am I. I mean, we're just going to be gone. The world's going to go on without us. All right now. You do your job in the

---

[34] 對照:萬物變化兮,固無休息。(賈誼)

face of that, and how seriously you take yourself you decide for yourself. (Bob Dylan)

你會死。你會死的。也許 20 年，也許明天，隨時。我也一樣。我是說，我們早晚都會離去。世界會沒有我們而繼續。有的只是當下。你面對這一個現實做事，如何認真對待自己，你自己決定。（巴布・狄倫）

Some people seem to fade away but then when they are truly gone, it's like they didn't fade away at all. (Bob Dylan)

有些人看似逐漸消逝，不過當他們真的離去時，又彷彿完全沒有消逝。（巴布・狄倫）

A man is a success if he gets up in the morning and goes to bed at night and in between does what he wants to do. (Bob Dylan)

早上起床，晚上睡覺，中間做想做的事，即為成功。（巴布・狄倫）

The only thing I knew how to do was to keep on keeping on. (Bob Dylan)

我知道的唯一辦法是繼續堅持。（巴布・狄倫）

Some people feel the rain. Others just get wet. (Bob Dylan)

有些人感受雨。另一些人只是被淋溼。（巴布・狄倫）

That has been the concept to my life —— setting very high objectives and trying to fulfil them. (Juan Manuel Santos)

這就是我的人生觀 —— 設立很高的目標，並努力實現它們。（胡安・曼努埃爾・桑托斯）

It is far more difficult to make peace than it is to wage war, I know it because I have done both. (Juan Manuel Santos)

實現和平比進行戰爭困難得多，我明白，因為兩樣我都做過。[35]（胡安・曼努埃爾・桑托斯）

Some of the mathematics that had seemed very dry seemed much less so when I saw how it could tie in with the world. (Oliver Hart)

當我看到工作如何能夠與世界連繫起來的時候，一些看起來非常單調的數學運算似乎就不那麼枯燥了。（奧立佛・哈特[36]）

Well I think you have to have a goal, but yes research that takes its own path, an unexpected path, that's a very essential part of doing research. So research that exactly goes where you expected it to go is uninteresting on the whole. You need to start travelling somewhere, you know you have to decide you want to get to Stockholm, but if on the way, you know, you see Paris you may want to stop there, to give you a sort of metaphorical answer. Research is a trip, and you have to be attentive to all the things you see and be able also to move away from the planned path. (Bengt Holmström)

沒錯，我想你是得有個目標；不過研究是走自己的路，一條出乎意料的路徑，這是做研究非常基本的部分。所以，完全如你所期望而展開的研究，整體而言是索然寡味的。你需要從某地起程，你知道自己得決定想到斯德哥爾摩去，但是如果半路上，你知道，看到巴黎，你可能想停留在那裡，這是給你一個比喻式的回答。研究是一次旅行，你得留意所看到的一切，並能離開規劃好的路線。（本特・霍姆斯壯）

To my wife Anneli and my son Sam: Thank you for your love and support. You have shared the pain and you deserve to share the gain from the

---

[35] 2016 年，桑托斯作為哥倫比亞總統與反政府武裝簽訂協議結束內戰，同年獲諾貝爾和平獎。他年輕時曾經入伍。
[36] 哈特為 2016 年諾貝爾經濟學獎得主。

award. (Bengt Holmström)

致妻子安妮莉和兒子薩姆：謝謝你們的愛和支持。你們分擔了我的困苦，也理應分享這個獎項的收穫。（本特・霍姆斯壯）

2017 年

Let me tell you how you really do science. You have an idea that you want to do something, and then you make a plan —— you need to build this, you have to make this, you have to design that. And if the process of doing that doesn't give you pleasure and fun you're not going to do it. (Rainer Weiss)

我來說說怎樣真的從事科學。你有個想法，想做一件事，你就制定計畫 —— 需要建立這個、得製造這個、得設計那個。而如果做這些事的過程無法帶來愉快和樂趣，你就不會做它了。（萊納・魏斯）

Most of us fully expect that we're going to learn things we didn't know about. (Rainer Weiss)

我們大都滿懷期待，一心要學到些未知的東西。（萊納・魏斯）

What was done is measure directly, with exquisitely sensitive instruments, gravitational waves predicted about 100 years ago by Albert Einstein. These waves are a new way to study the universe and are expected to have significant impact on astronomy and astrophysics in the years ahead. (Rainer Weiss)

我們所從事的，是運用精密靈敏的儀器，直接測量阿爾伯特・愛因斯坦一百年前所預言的引力波。這些波是研究宇宙的新途徑，可望在今後的歲月裡，對天文學和天體物理學產生重大影響。（萊納・魏斯）

Why do you do science? In this particular case, we don't have a very good reason to be doing this except for the knowledge that it brings. This research is especially important to young people. We all want to know what's going on in the universe. (Rainer Weiss)

問我們為什麼研究科學？就這個具體的項目來說，我們研究它沒有特別好的理由，除了它所帶來的知識。這項研究對年輕人尤其重要。我們都想知道宇宙中發生著什麼。（萊納‧魏斯）

Over and over in the history of astronomy, a new instrument finds things we never expected to see. (Rainer Weiss)

在天文學史上，新型的儀器屢屢發現我們根本不曾期待會見到的東西。（萊納‧魏斯）

We'll have all sorts of crazy signals. And you'd be a damned fool if you didn't look for things you weren't expecting, because that's probably what you're going to see first. (Rainer Weiss)

我們會收到五花八門的奇異訊號。要是不從中尋找些出乎意料的東西，你就是個頭號傻瓜，因為那很可能是你首先見到的。（萊納‧魏斯）

One of the things I sort of dreamt about awhile ago is that if Einstein were still alive, it would be absolutely wonderful to go to him and tell him about the discovery, and he would have been very pleased, I'm sure of that. (Rainer Weiss)

不久前我想到的事包括，如果愛因斯坦還活著，去告訴他這個發現將會妙不可言，他會非常高興的，我肯定。（萊納‧魏斯）

We live in an epoch where rational reasoning associated with evidence isn't universally accepted and is, in fact, in jeopardy. That worries me a lot. (Rainer Weiss)

我們生活在這樣一個時代,伴隨證據的合理推論得不到普遍接受,實際上,處於危險邊緣。這讓我非常擔心。(萊納·魏斯)

I prefer really often to talk to high school students, mostly because I think they're the future for us. (Rainer Weiss)

我的確更喜歡多跟高中生談話,主要是由於我認為,他們是我們的未來。(萊納·魏斯)

I wasn't unpopular. I didn't have any trouble getting girls. (Rainer Weiss)

我並非不受歡迎。我要找女友毫無困難。(萊納·魏斯)

The detection of gravitational waves is truly a triumph of modern large-scale experimental physics. (Barry C. Barish)

引力波的探測確實是現代大規模實驗物理學的勝利。(巴里·巴利許)

The technical challenges were technical challenges that were not unbeatable; it was just that we had to learn how to do things and how to build a sensitive enough device. That took us 20 years after we built the first version of the LIGO detector. (Barry C. Barish)

這個項目技術方面的挑戰並非不可戰勝,我們只須學習如何從事,如何建造一個足夠敏感的設備。建造第一版探測器,雷射干涉儀引力波觀測臺,花了我們 20 年時間。(巴里·巴利許)

I always wanted to be an experimental physicist and was attracted to the idea of using continuing advances in technology to carry out fundamental science experiments that could not be done otherwise. (Barry C. Barish)

我一直想成為實驗物理學家,一心想要利用技術的持續進步,從事非此即無法完成的基礎科學實驗。(巴里・巴利許)

I think the scientific goals and the technical challenges were the two things that equally motivated me. (Barry C. Barish)

我認為,科學目標和技術挑戰是兩件同樣激勵我的事情。(巴里・巴利許)

I've typically had between five and ten for most of my career, but now I can't —— I just don't have time for that. And I like graduate students; I can work well with them. They're great, too. You get a lot back from graduate students; you put a little bit in, and then they give you so much back. (Barry C. Barish)

我在職業生涯的大部分時間裡,通常都帶領5到10名研究生,但現在不行了 —— 實在沒時間再帶了。我喜歡研究生,能夠跟他們合作愉快。他們很了不起。你從研究生那裡得到大量回饋。你投入少許,而他們回報給你那麼多。(巴里・巴利許)

The problem for large scientific projects is to do something that is being done for the first time, balanced against cost, schedule, and promises to the government. That is a hard balancing act. (Barry C. Barish)

大型科學項目的問題,在於做首次做的事情之際,要權衡成本,安排進度,並對當局做出承諾。這是一種難以平衡的行為。(巴里・巴利許)

The most exciting science requires the most complex instruments. (Barry C. Barish)

最令人激動的科學需要最複雜的儀器。(巴里・巴利許)

I actually spent a lot of time reading about how professional managers work. And how people build bridges. (Barry C. Barish)

實際上，我花了大量時間閱讀，了解專業經理人如何進行管理。以及人們怎樣建造橋梁。（巴里·巴利許）

In some ways, abstractly, I wish I were in a university that had a lot of culture around. I'd rather meet somebody who's an artist or philosopher than another engineer or physicist. (Barry C. Barish)

大體而言，在理論上，我希望自己身處一所文化特別多元的大學。我更願接觸一位藝術家或哲學家，而非另一名工程師或物理學家。（巴里·巴利許）

Everything we know about the universe is studied by using telescopes or other instruments that look at visible light, infrared, ultraviolet or X-ray —— different wavelengths of electromagnetic interactions. Only 4 percent of what's in the universe gives off electromagnetic radiation, so we don't have any handle on the rest. (Barry C. Barish)

關於宇宙，我們所了解的一切，都是運用望遠鏡或其他儀器研究的，以之觀察可見光、紅外線、紫外線或 X 射線 —— 不同波長的電磁相互作用。宇宙中僅有百分之四的物質發出電磁輻射，所以我們對其餘的成分沒有任何掌握。（巴里·巴利許）

I can't imagine not being in a phase where I'm trying to understand something or create something. That's the essence of life. (Kip S. Thorne)

我總是在努力理解或創造某種東西。這是人生的本義。我設想不出自己處於相反的狀態。（基普·索恩）

The human race has a yearning to explore. That's part of our biological and psychological makeup. (Kip S. Thorne)

人類有一種探索的渴望。這是我們生理和心理的組成部分。（基普‧索恩）

We're born with a curiosity about the universe. Those people who don't have it because it's gotten beaten out of them in some way. (Kip S. Thorne)

我們生來具備對宇宙的好奇心。那些漠視宇宙的人缺乏這種好奇心，是由於它已經消磨殆盡。（基普‧索恩）

We have to have a combination of general relativity that describes the warping of space and time, and quantum physics, which describes the uncertainties in that warping and how they change. (Kip S. Thorne)

我們必須擁有廣義相對論與量子物理的組合。前者描述空間和時間的扭曲；後者則描述這種扭曲中的各種不確定，以及它們如何變動。（基普‧索恩）

We're going to need a definitive quantum theory of gravity, which is part of a grand unified theory – it's the main missing piece. (Kip S. Thorne)

我們將需要一種決定性的引力量子理論，作為大一統理論的一部分——它是主要缺失的那一塊。（基普‧索恩）

We'll have four different gravitational wave windows open within the next 20 years, and each of them will see something different. We'll be probing the birth of the universe with this. The so-called "inflationary era" of the universe. We'll be probing the birth of the fundamental forces and how they came into being. (Kip S. Thorne)

今後 20 年裡，我們將打開 4 個不同的引力波視窗，每一個都會看到不同的東西。我們要以之探測宇宙的誕生。宇宙的所謂「暴漲時期」。我們要探索宇宙基本力的誕生，以及它們是如何形成的。（基普・索恩）

When I ask myself what are the great things we got from the Renaissance, it's the great art, the great music, the science insights of Leonardo da Vinci. Two hundred years from now, when you ask what are the great things that came from this era, I think it's going to be an understanding of the universe around us. (Kip S. Thorne)

我若自問，我們從文藝復興中得到的非凡之物是什麼，它就是非凡的美術、非凡的音樂、李奧納多・達文西的科學洞察。由此兩百年後，你若問，出自我們這個時代的非凡之物是什麼，我認為它會是對我們周圍宇宙的理解。（基普・索恩）

As a true scientist, I have been proved wrong so many times that I'm very humble. (Kip S. Thorne)

作為實實在在的科學家，我再三地被證明出錯，以至於我非常謙卑。（基普・索恩）

I wanted to be a snowplow driver when I was a kid. Growing up in the Rocky Mountains, that's the most glorious job you can imagine. But then my mother took me to a lecture about the solar system when I was 8, and I got hooked. (Kip S. Thorne)

小時候，我想當個除雪車司機。在洛磯山區長大，這是想像得出的最神氣的職業。然而在我 8 歲時，母親帶我去參加一個關於太陽系的講座，我被迷住了。（基普・索恩）

Knowledge is our greatest wealth and the love of others is the most beautiful human value. (Jacques Dubochet)

知識是我們最偉大的財富，而對他人的愛是最美好的人類價值。（雅克・杜巴謝）

We three have never been very good chemists but we are gratified with a Nobel Prize in Chemistry. The Peter Principle says that everyone is promoted until they reach their level of incompetence. We are worried that we may have reached this remarkable point. (Jacques Dubochet)

我們三人從來算不上特別出色的化學家，但我們對榮獲諾貝爾化學獎心滿意足。「彼得原理」說：人人都得到升遷，直至其無能的程度。恐怕我們已經達到這種引人注目的程度了。（雅克・杜巴謝）

Rather big part of my time is to read scientific journals and to discover what others are doing. (Jacques Dubochet)

我的很大一部分時間用於閱讀科學期刊，以及發現別人在從事什麼研究。（雅克・杜巴謝）

Normally, my dog wakes me early in the morning. But today, it was the Nobel Prize! (Joachim Frank)

通常，我的狗一早把我叫醒。但今天，喚醒我的是諾貝爾獎！（姚阿幸・法蘭克）

I thought the chances of becoming a Nobel Prize laureate were minuscule because there are so many other innovations and discoveries that happen almost every day. (Joachim Frank)

我認為成為諾貝爾獎得主的機會微乎其微，因為幾乎每天都有那麼多其他的創新和發現。（姚阿幸・法蘭克）

Medicine is no longer looking at organs. It looks at the processes inside the cell. (Joachim Frank)

醫學不再著眼於器官。它著眼於細胞內部的過程。（姚阿幸・法蘭克）

I love the English language, the colors of it, the many, many nuances, the different influences. (Joachim Frank)

我喜歡英語，它的各種色彩，許許多多細微差異，各具不同的作用。（姚阿幸・法蘭克）

They told me that the Chemistry Prize was going to be awarded with Jacques Dubochet and Joachim Frank who of course I know very well, so I think that's quite delightful really. Of course there were a few other people who also contributed. But I think all of us know the Nobel Prize awards are always, usually only to three people. So there are often one to two others who've made strong contributions who didn't quite cross the threshold. (Richard Henderson)

他們告訴我，化學獎將與雅克・杜巴謝和姚阿幸・法蘭克共享。我跟他們自然非常熟，所以我覺得這真的很令人愉快。當然還有一些人也做出了貢獻。然而我想我們都知道，諾貝爾獎一向如此，通常只授予三個人。所以常常另有其他一、兩位貢獻良多卻受限於名額。（理察・韓德森）

I think the feeling is that the three of us who have been awarded the prize are sort of acting on behalf of the whole field. It's kind of a worldwide effort that's just now come to fruition. (Richard Henderson)

我想，感受就是，我們三個人，可以說是在代表整個領域領獎。這一項研究屬於全世界範圍的努力，正當此時獲得成果。（理察・韓德森）

People used to think that biological clocks were not only mysterious, they were seen almost as miracles. This is no longer the case. (Jeffrey C. Hall)

人們不僅一向認為生理時鐘不可思議,而且幾乎視之為奇蹟。現在就不是這樣了。[37]（傑佛瑞‧霍爾）

I admit that I resent running out of research money. (Jeffrey C. Hall)

我承認,我討厭研究經費耗盡。（傑佛瑞‧霍爾）

I stand on the shoulders of giants. (Michael Rosbash)

我站在巨人們的肩膀上。（麥可‧羅斯巴希）

You've got to go for what you love and not look back 30 years, 40 years later and say, "I never tried." You got to try. (Michael Rosbash)

你必須追求你所鍾愛的,而非 30 年、40 年後回顧說：「我根本沒嘗試。」你得試試。（麥可‧羅斯巴希）

Scientific careers rely on inheritance, environment, and random events, like all biological phenomena. (Michael Rosbash)

科學職業依賴遺傳、環境,以及隨機事件,跟所有的生物現象一樣。（麥可‧羅斯巴希）

I am grateful to my colleagues at Brandeis and to the unusual environment here that allows researchers to explore without boundaries while also engaging students in the process of discovery. (Michael Rosbash)

我非常感謝布蘭戴斯的同事們,感謝這裡不同尋常的環境,學校容許研究人員跨界探索,並安排學生參與發現的過程。（麥可‧羅斯巴希）

---

[37] 霍爾、羅斯巴希和楊恩發現了控制畫夜節律的分子機制,因而獲得 2017 年諾貝爾生理學或醫學獎。

I was smart enough to get out of the way of talented people and let them make progress. (Michael Rosbash)

我的自知之明足以使我避讓有才能的人,讓他們出人頭地。(麥可・羅斯巴希)

We were built to be rhythmic. (Michael W. Young)

我們生來就是有節奏的。(麥可・楊恩)

The physical malaise we feel when we travel reflects a desynchronizing of all the clocks that reside in our tissues. (Michael W. Young)

我們旅行時感到的身體不適,反映了人體組織內所有生理時鐘的不同步。(麥可・楊恩)

I wouldn't want to try to adapt something of my own. It would be like going back to school and doing all my exams again. (Kazuo Ishiguro)

我不會願意嘗試改編自己的作品。那就像重回學校,所有的考試再來一遍。(石黑一雄)

When I got to 40 or so... I had the sense when I looked back over my life I would actually see a mess of decisions, a few of which I had thought about, some of which I had sort of stumbled on, and many that I had no control over whatsoever. (Kazuo Ishiguro)

到了大約40歲時……我有種感覺,回顧自己的生活,我實際上會看到一大堆決定,其中少許是經過思考的,有些要算誤打誤撞的,還有很多就是隨隨便便的。(石黑一雄)

I'm not at all interested in the brave who fight against the odds and win. I am interested in those who accept their lot, as that is what many people in the world are doing. They do their best in ghastly conditions. (Kazuo Ishiguro)

我完全不關注迎難而上並戰而勝之的勇者。我關注那些逆來順受的人，世上許多人正在這麼做。他們在極差的條件下盡力而為。（石黑一雄）

I don't hang out with the glitteringly successful people; I hang out with people who've been friends for many years, and to some extent I feel my worldly success is a bit uncomfortable for them. (Kazuo Ishiguro)

我不跟耀眼成功的人士來往；我跟多年為友的人來往，多少感到我的世俗成功讓他們有幾分不適應。（石黑一雄）

I have been a very lucky man. The academic life can be solitary, especially when many of your colleagues think you are nuts. I have been fortunate to have had a fabulous set of collaborators, all of whom became friends. (Richard Thaler)

我一向是個非常幸運的人。學術生涯可能是孤獨的，尤其在許多同事認為你瘋了的時候。我一直走運，有一群非凡的合作者，他們都成了我的朋友。（理查‧塞勒）

The Nobel Prize is going to be "fun money"—— for an occasion, when my wife and I want a $50 bottle of wine. (Richard H. Thaler)

這筆諾貝爾獎金將用於隨心所欲的開銷，比如當我們夫妻一時興起，想喝一瓶 50 美元的葡萄酒的時候。（理查‧塞勒）

2018 年

The combination of deep engagement on the ground with intellectual rigor is producing very exciting work, both in terms of understanding the world and in helping to provide practical solutions to problems affecting some of the poorest people in the world. (Michael Kremer)

深入的實地參與和理智上的嚴謹互相結合，正在產生非常令人激動的成果，既在於了解世界，也有助於為影響世界上一些最貧困人口的難題提供實際的對策。（麥可‧克里莫）

I would say choose something that you care about and that's important. "Care about" could be this puzzle that you just can't get out of your head and you want to try to solve. (Michael Kremer)

我會說選擇某件你關心的事情，這很重要。「關心」可能是這個謎題令你始終無法忘懷，一心嘗試解決。[38]（麥可‧克里莫）

I didn't realise I'm the oldest ever! So I just about made it, huh? Because you can't be dead and win… If you're a winner of the National Inventors Hall of Fame you can be dead. I won that prize a couple of years ago and I was very proud of that. (Arthur Ashkin)

我沒想到自己是迄今最老的！這麼說我屬於險勝，哈？因為逝者不能入選。……入選國家發明家名人堂的人可以是逝者。前幾年我得了這個獎，我也因此非常自豪。[39]（阿瑟‧亞希金）

---

[38] 在被問到研究人員如何產生突破性想法時，克里莫如此回答。
[39] 亞希金獲獎後接受電話採訪時說的話。諾貝爾獎只接受對在世候選者的提名（入選後逝世者仍可獲獎）。美國國家發明家名人堂表彰對人類社會和經濟進步有重大貢獻的個人，亞希金是 2013 年入選者之一。

I'm writing a paper now and I'm not celebrating about old stuff. I've got something new and important. I'm working on solar energy and I think I've gotten some important stuff. And the world badly needs science in climate change. (Arthur Ashkin)

我眼下正在寫一篇論文[40]，沒工夫慶祝過去的事情。我有了新的重要的想法。我在研究太陽能，自認獲得了一些重要進展。面對氣候變化，世界急需科學。（阿瑟·亞希金）

I'm very old and had given up worrying about things like Nobel Prizes. (Arthur Ashkin)

我年事已高，已經不再操心得諾貝爾獎之類事情了。（阿瑟·亞希金）

That's my hobby, more or less. I was interested in science since I was a kid, so I tell my wife that's the only thing that I'm really good at. (Arthur Ashkin)

埋頭工作，這多少是我的愛好。我從小就對科學感興趣，所以我告訴妻子，這是我唯一真正擅長的事情。（阿瑟·亞希金）

It's an amazing moment. Nobody is prepared for that kind of moment. (Gérard Mourou)

得諾貝爾獎令人一時不知所措。沒人為這種時刻做好準備。（熱拉爾·穆胡）

In laser high-field science, I think the best is really yet to come. (Gérard Mourou)

---

[40] 亞希金獲獎時年屆 96 歲，仍在從事新的研究。

2018 年

在雷射高場科學領域，我認為最好的成果還在後面。（熱拉爾・穆胡）

If somebody else thinks something that you don't believe in, just think they're wrong and you're right and keep going. That's pretty much the way I always think. (Donna Strickland)

如果別人持有某種想法而你不相信，那就認為他們錯了而你是對的，然後我行我素好了。我幾乎一直都是這麼想的。（唐娜・史垂克蘭）

In high school, I was very good in math and physics. I wasn't good at much of anything else. Some people are good at a lot of things. I don't know how they choose what to do. I couldn't do athletic stuff, I wasn't artistic, I have no musical ear, and I wasn't good at writing. So I was pretty narrow in what I could do. I wasn't thinking, "Can I do science?" I was thinking, "That's the only thing I can do, so let's do it." (Donna Strickland)

高中時，我的數學和物理都很好。許多別的我就不擅長了。有些人擅長很多事情。我不知道他們如何選擇從事什麼。我無法做體育相關的事，我缺乏美術天賦，我沒有音樂鑑賞力，我也不擅長寫作。所以我能從事的行業相當有限。我沒想著「我能從事科學嗎」，我是在想「這是唯一我能做的事，那就做吧」。（唐娜・史垂克蘭）

I never applied. (Donna Strickland)

我從沒申請過。[41]（唐娜・史垂克蘭）

Is that all, really? I thought there might have been more. We need to celebrate women physicists, because we're out there. Hopefully, in time, it will

---

[41] 在接受 BBC 採訪，被問及何以身為諾貝爾獎得主而仍非正教授時，史垂克蘭做出了這樣的解釋。

start to move forward at a faster rate. I'm honoured to be one of those women. (Donna Strickland)

真的就這幾位？我本以為會有更多。我們需要讚美女物理學家，因為我們就在這裡。但願，隨著時間推移，人數將開始以更快的速度增加。我很榮幸成為這些女性的一員。[42]（唐娜‧史垂克蘭）

I remember being told over and over again: Women, you can do anything, so it never entered my mind that I couldn't. (Donna Strickland)

我記得一再受到叮囑：女人，妳們無所不能。所以我從來沒想過自己不行。（唐娜‧史垂克蘭）

What I'm going now is looking at this question of how do you evolve innovation. How does innovation happen? How do get a whole new chemical reactivity that you don't know already exists in nature? How can I evolve a whole new species in essence, a whole new species of enzyme? (Frances H. Arnold)

我現在所從事的，是探究如何展開創新這個問題。創新是怎麼發生的？怎樣才能獲得一種全新的、你不知道已經存在於自然界的化學反應？如何得以形成一個實質上全新的物種，一種全新的酶？（弗朗西絲‧阿諾德）

I am very interested in the evolution of novelty —— how do new functions appear in the biological world. I am tackling this question by evolving enzyme catalysts that catalyze chemical reactions not known in the biological world. (Frances H. Arnold)

---

[42] 在一次新聞發表會上，對自己成為諾貝爾物理學獎第三位女性得主，史垂克蘭這麼說。

> 2018 年

我對新事物的演化非常感興趣——新的功能是怎樣在生物世界中出現的。我以形成酶催化劑來探究這一項課題，這種催化劑促進生物世界中未知的化學反應。（弗朗西絲·阿諾德）

Most innovative things are not obvious to other people at the time. You have to believe in yourself. If you've got a good idea, follow it even though others tell you it's not. (Frances H. Arnold)

大多數創新性的東西對於當時其他的人並非顯而易見。你得相信自己。如果想到了一個好主意，即使別人告訴你它不是，你也要實行。（弗朗西絲·阿諾德）

I've jumped into all sorts of things during my life. Learning new things has always been fun for me. (Frances H. Arnold)

此生我嘗試過各式各樣的事情。學習新事物對於我一向都是樂趣。（弗朗西絲·阿諾德）

If you're going to change the world, you've got to be fearless. (Frances H. Arnold)

你若要改變世界，你就得無所畏懼。（弗朗西絲·阿諾德）

I said "OK, if one experiment doesn't work I'm going to do a million experiments, and I don't care if 999,999 don't work. I'm going to find the one that does." (Frances H. Arnold)

我說：「好吧，如果一次實驗失敗，我就要做一百萬次實驗，我不在乎九十九萬九千九百九十九次是否失敗。我要找到成功的那次。」[43]（弗朗西絲·阿諾德）

---

[43] 對照：我沒失敗。我只是發現了行不通的一萬種方法。（湯瑪斯·愛迪生 Thomas Edison）

I did not choose to become a researcher until I was almost 30. I tried other careers, but science spoke to me more and more, especially after I started studying the biological world and all the amazing molecular machines made by nature. As a little girl, I thought I might be a heart surgeon, CEO of a multinational company or even a diplomat someday (until I figured out I had no diplomatic skills). When I went to college, I never really thought about being a scientist or an engineer, but of course that was always on the list of possibilities. I had tried lots of odd jobs —— from taxi driver to waitress to assembling electronic devices —— and later a few science and technology jobs in nuclear power and solar energy. But I loved languages, I enjoyed economics, I spent every break traveling and seeing different cultures. I loved learning and did not think too much about the future until one day it happened! (Frances H. Arnold)

我直到快30歲時才選擇做研究人員。我嘗試過另一些職業，但科學越來越吸引我，尤其在開始研究生物世界，以及大自然製造的所有神奇的分子機器之後。小時候，我以為自己會成為心臟外科醫生、跨國公司執行長，甚至有朝一日成為外交官（直到明白自己沒有外交技能）。上大學的時候，我從沒真正想過成為科學家或工程師，不過當然了，那總是處於可能性的清單上。我試過很多零工——從計程車司機到服務生，到組裝電子設備——後來還有核能和太陽能方面的幾種科技工作。然而我鍾愛語言，我喜歡經濟學，我一有空就到處旅行，遍覽不同的文化。我熱愛學習，對未來沒想太多，直到有一天它出現了！（弗朗西絲·阿諾德）

I meet so many young people who want to plan out their lives and want a recipe. They want me to tell them how to succeed. I didn't follow a recipe. I followed my instincts. I was lucky to be passionate about a field that was full of opportunity. (Frances H. Arnold)

我接觸過許許多多年輕人,他們想規劃自己的生活,想要有個祕方。他們希望我告訴他們怎樣成功。我不曾依照祕方。我依照直覺。我很幸運,對一個充滿機遇的領域懷有熱情。(弗朗西絲・阿諾德)

It differs from natural evolution in that it is directed by the researcher. Mutations are directed (by me) to a specific gene, and since the researcher has a goal in mind, it is also directed in that sense. (Frances H. Arnold)

它(定向演化)與自然演化的不同之處在於,它是由研究者引導的。突變(由我)導向一個特定的基因,而且由於研究者心中有一個目標,它也在這個意義上受到引導。(弗朗西絲・阿諾德)

It's a technology that allows us to reliably create improved proteins for a wide range of applications. Just as farmers and breeders have used artificial selection processes over thousands of years to create higher-yielding crops or pets that please us, we can direct the evolution of proteins to perform better in applications, from laundry detergents to green chemistry. Modern methods of DNA manipulation allow us to make iterations of mutations and artificial selection on a gene rather than in an organism, and to shorten the generation time to a few days. That way we can accumulate beneficial mutations in the gene that encodes the protein, making it better and better until it meets our needs. (Frances H. Arnold)

它(定向演化)是一種技術,容許我們可靠地為廣泛的應用創造改良的蛋白質。幾千年來,農民和飼養者都在運用人工選擇流程,造就高產的作物或我們喜歡的寵物。與此相同,我們也能夠引導蛋白質的演化,使之在各種應用中表現得更好，從衣物洗滌劑到綠色化學。現代的 DNA 操作方法，容許我們在基因上而非有機體中進行反覆的突變和人工選擇，並將每一代用時縮短至幾天。從而，我們得以在對蛋白質編碼的基因中累積有益的突變，使它越來越好，直到滿足我們的需要。（弗朗西絲‧阿諾德）

The wonderful thing about directed evolution is that it is both simple and general. Because the technology is accessible, it can be implemented in any laboratory. It opened up a new way for people to look at the inventions of the biological world and fit them into their own creations. So many clever people all over the world have taken this technology and done all manner of brilliant things with it, things I would never have thought of. This will continue in the future. (Frances H. Arnold)

定向演化的絕妙之處，在於它既簡單又廣泛。由於這項技術門檻不高，它可以在任何實驗室實施。它為人們開闢了新途徑來看待生物世界的發明，並將它們融入自己的創造。全世界有那麼多聰明的人接受了這項技術，並運用它獲得了各式各樣輝煌的成就，我絕對想不到的成就。這將會持續下去。（弗朗西絲‧阿諾德）

Pesticides get into our food, streams and rivers and cause all manner of harm. Imagine spraying a little bit of "perfume" in a field to confuse the insect pests so that they can't mate. If they can't mate they are not going to damage your crops. Wouldn't it be wonderful to do that instead of dumping highly toxic pesticides? Our hope is to make these complicated insect perfumes quite cheaply using enzymes. (Frances H. Arnold)

2018 年

殺蟲劑進入我們的食物，溪水與河流，造成各式各樣的傷害。想像一下，在田野裡噴灑一點「香水」來迷惑害蟲，使牠們無法交配。牠們要是無法交配，就不會傷害你的莊稼。以此來取代傾倒劇毒殺蟲劑，不是很奇妙嗎？我們的希望是，用酶來製造這些複雜的昆蟲香水，而成本相當低。（弗朗西絲・阿諾德）

I hope that my getting this prize will highlight the fact that, yes, women can do this, they can do it well and that they can make a contribution to the world and be recognized for it. I hope that women will see that one can have a rewarding career in science and technology. (Frances H. Arnold)

我希望，我獲得這個獎項[44]會突顯一個事實：是的，女性能夠做到，她們能夠做得很好，她們能夠為世界做出貢獻並為此獲得認同。我希望女性會看到，一個女人能夠在科學技術領域擁有有意義的事業。（弗朗西絲・阿諾德）

Talented women choose to do other things. But if they knew how important technology is for supporting our well-being and that of the planet, and how fun it can be, more would choose STEM fields. (Frances H. Arnold)

有才華的女性選擇做其他工作。不過，她們如果得知，技術對於提供我們的福祉、維護地球的平安是多麼重要，以及它可以多麼有趣，更多的人就會選擇 STEM[45] 領域。（弗朗西絲・阿諾德）

I believe that some women still face external barriers, but other barriers are more self-imposed： lack of confidence or desire to compete and a misun-

---

[44] 指阿諾德於 2016 年獲得的千禧年科技獎（Millennium Technology Prize）。她是此獎的首位女性得主。該獎由芬蘭技術學院評選，自 2004 年始兩年頒發一次，有高額獎金。與諾貝爾獎主要表彰對於科學的貢獻不同，它側重表彰技術方面的成就。

[45] STEM, Science, Technology, Engineering and Mathematics 的縮寫，即科學、技術、工程學與數學。

derstanding of what science and technology can contribute to society. Science is not for everyone; it takes a lot of time and devotion to become really good, and the same is true for engineering. You have to love it. What I see is that the most talented women have many opportunities. Whether they choose to pursue science or engineering depends on how they feel about their whole life experience, perhaps more so than men. Opportunities today are excellent, but there are challenges to having a family and competing at the highest levels that women often feel more acutely. (Frances H. Arnold)

我相信有些女性仍然面臨外部障礙，然而其他障礙更多地是強加於自我的：缺乏自信或競爭欲望，以及對科學技術能夠為社會所做貢獻的誤解。科學事業並不適合所有人；成為真正優秀的一員需要大量的時間和熱忱，工程學也完全如此。你必須鍾愛它。我看到最有才華的女性有很多機會。她們選擇從事科學或工程學與否，取決於對自己整個人生經歷的感受如何，或許比男性更甚。當今的機會非常好，但是要兼顧家庭和最高層次的競爭，其中挑戰重重，對此女性通常感受更強烈。（弗朗西絲·阿諾德）

I think all Nobel laureates understand they are in the middle of a huge web of science, of influence and ideas, of research and results that impinge on them and that emanate from them. (George P. Smith)

我想所有的諾貝爾獎得主都明白，他們處於一個巨大的科學網路中，有關他們所激發和創造出的影響和創意、研究和成果的網路。（喬治·P·史密斯）

Very few research breakthroughs are novel. Virtually all of them build on what went on before. It's happenstance. That was certainly the case with my work. Mine was an idea in a line of research that built very naturally on the lines of research that went before. (George P. Smith)

研究上的突破極少是新穎的。它們幾乎全都建立在先前的進展上。它是偶發事件。我的工作當然如此。我的成果就是一系列研究中的一種想法，非常自然地建立在先前展開的各種研究之上。（喬治‧P‧史密斯）

I happened to be in the right place at the right time to put those things together. I am getting an honor that has been earned by a whole bunch of people. (George P. Smith)

我碰巧在合適的地方、合適的時間把這些東西組合起來。我是在接受一項由整整一群人贏得的榮譽。（喬治‧P‧史密斯）

There are times when a teacher does something that can light a fire when the teacher isn't even aware of it. (George P. Smith)

有時候教師做了某一件事，而那能夠在教師甚至沒有意識到之際點燃一團火焰。（喬治‧P‧史密斯）

At Mizzou, I had a tremendous amount of freedom to explore what I think is interesting. Not all universities give you the freedom to do that, and I think science really depends on that. (George P. Smith)

在密蘇里大學，我有極大的自由去探索我認為有趣的東西。並不是所有的大學都給你這麼做的自由，而我認為科學真的有賴於此。（喬治‧P‧史密斯）

For a scientist, a Nobel Prize is the highest accolade you can get, and I'm so lucky because there are so many brilliant scientists and not enough Nobel Prizes to go around. (Gregory P. Winter)

對於科學家，諾貝爾獎是所能得到的最高榮譽。我真是幸運，因為有這麼多傑出的科學家，卻沒有足夠的諾貝爾獎分發。（葛瑞格‧溫特）

It's terribly important that scientists don't ignore the opportunities that may come from their work. (Gregory P. Winter)

極其重要的是，科學家們從不忽視可能從他們工作中產生的機會。（葛瑞格‧溫特）

My personal strategy has been to do the basic research, but to be mindful of opportunities that may arise. In other words not to say "that's applied, I'm not going to do it". (Gregory P. Winter)

我的個人策略是做基礎研究，但要留意可能出現的機會。換句話說，不要說「這是應用研究，我不會染指」。（葛瑞格‧溫特）

I'm one of those people who has always wanted to solve puzzles. As a kid, I wanted to be the first to know something that no one else did. I think that's true of a lot of scientists. (James P. Allison)

我屬於那種總是想解決難題的人。小時候，我一心要當這樣的人：別人不知道的事情我先知道。我認為許多科學家都是如此。（詹姆士‧艾立遜）

Meeting the people who have benefitted from our research is the real prize for me. (James P. Alliso)

見到得益於我們研究的人，是給予我的真正獎勵。（詹姆士‧艾立遜）

I always consider myself a basic scientist, but not any more I suppose! (James P. Allison)

> 2018 年

> 我一向認為自己是一名基礎科學家，不過現在看來不再是了！[46]（詹姆士・艾立遜）

Many people tried very hard to cure the cancer but fortunately we, Jim Allison and myself, studied this checkpoint inhibitor therapy. I mean, we discovered the principle, and this is really working. So for me it's more than happy to see many patients – often I can see them telling me, "You saved my life". This is my most enjoyable and, I would say, I'm very pleased to hear what I have done is really meaningful. (Tasuku Honjo)

許多人都竭盡全力地治療癌症，只是我們，詹姆士・艾立遜和我本人，幸運地研究了檢查點抑制劑療法。我是說，我們發現了這個原理，而這一項原理確實有效。所以對於我，遇到很多病人 —— 我經常能遇到他們 —— 對我說，「你救了我一命」，是格外快樂的。這是我最享受的，並且我要說，我非常高興聽到人們講，我的成果的確富於意義。（本庶佑）

Biology is such a complex system. It's totally different from the engineering. We cannot design. Many people tried to find the therapy for cancer, but all failed. And myself, I never expected my research, working on the immune system, would lead to the cancer therapy. But, in a sense, I'm very fortunate that I also thought about it. You know, you have to try many things and if you're lucky you can hit, but you have to pursue. (Tasuku Honjo)

生物學是個如此複雜的系統。它與工程學完全不同。我們無法設計。許多人試圖找到治療癌症的方法，然而都失敗了。而我本人，我從未料想，自己致力於免疫系統的研究，會引向癌症治療。不過，在某種

---

[46] 艾立遜和本庶佑發現了以抑制免疫負調節來治療癌症的方法，因而獲得 2018 年諾貝爾生理學或醫學獎。

意義上，非常幸運的是，我也思考過這個問題。你知道，你得嘗試許多事情，運氣好的話也能成功，不過你得執著。（本庶佑）

I think that diversity is important for successful research, especially in the life sciences. We don't know exactly where to target. We must try many things. For that purpose, everybody has to think different ideas and to discuss. (Tasuku Honjo)

我認為多樣性對於成功的研究很重要，尤其在生命科學領域。我們不確切知道目標何在。我們必須嘗試許多事情。為此，每個人都得思考不同的想法並討論。（本庶佑）

We need the power of many, many people to push this therapy in a really satisfactory level. This is just the beginning of the whole story. (Tasuku Honjo)

我們需要許多、許多人的力量，來將這種療法推向真正令人滿意的程度。這只是整個故事的開端。（本庶佑）

I generally accept that necessity is the mother of discovery. But in biology, we cannot design any strategy to reach the end goal. Most of the findings in biology are serendipitous or accidental, because there are so many unknown factors. (Tasuku Honjo)

我大致接受需要是發現之母的說法。不過在生物學中，我們無法設計任何策略來達到最終目標。生物學上的大多數發現都是偶然或意外的，因為有太多的未知因素。（本庶佑）

Science cannot make progress without studies ambitious enough to overturn established theories. (Tasuku Honjo)

沒有雄心十足的研究以推翻既定理論，科學就無法獲得進步。（本庶佑）

2018 年

The more difficult a goal is to achieve, the more attractive the task is for accomplishing the challenge. Pick up a stone that everyone else has disregarded and polish it up until you find that it is a diamond. I've found a lot of fun in pursuit of making a discovery in the face of a chaos of things the future of which you never know. (Tasuku Honjo)

目標越難達成，完成挑戰的任務就越吸引人。撿起一塊人人不屑一顧的石頭，擦淨，直到查明它是一顆鑽石。我發現，面對亂成一團的事物，其未來你無從得知，這時尋求發現非常有趣。（本庶佑）

Follow your curiosity. Sometimes, a direct attack may be difficult. You can take a round route or a side tour but never forget what you really want to do. (Tasuku Honjo)

跟隨你的好奇心。有時，正面進攻是困難的。你可以取道周遭或側翼，但切勿忘記真正想做之事。（本庶佑）

What is important is to always hold a feeling of wanting to know something and to hold a sense of wonder. (Tasuku Honjo)

重要的是始終保持想要有所了解的感覺，保持新奇感。（本庶佑）

I never tried to keep my curiosity, it comes from inside. When I learn something new I always： Oh, this is quite interesting but why? Curiosity is just endless; it just comes from inside. (Tasuku Honjo)

我從不努力保持好奇，它發自於內心。學到新東西時，我總是想：哦，這很有趣，但為什麼？好奇原無止境，它只發自於內心。（本庶佑）

To make yourself a good scientist I would say first, you have to have curiosity. If you don't have any curiosity you better choose something else. To be good scientists we have to solve something new. Something new usually is not easy because it is difficult, that is why it remains unknown. You need enough courage to tackle the difficult problems and you need courage and that is a challenge. Challenge with courage. I call this three primary C's. And then once you decide to tackle, you have to concentrate and continue and eventually you build up confidence. So this is another three C's. That is what I tell my students. (Tasuku Honjo)

要使自己成為優秀的科學家，我會說，首先得有好奇心（curiosity）。如果全無好奇心，就以另選行業為好。要成為優秀的科學家，必須解決新問題。新問題通常不易解決，就因為它難，這就是它為什麼始終處於未知。你需要足夠的勇氣（courage）應對這些難題，你需要勇氣，這是個挑戰（challenge）。伴隨勇氣的挑戰。我稱之為首要的三個C。而一旦決定應對，你就得專注（concentrate）而持續（continue），最終建立信心（confidence）。這就是另外的三個C。這是我對學生們說的。（本庶佑）

I think it is important to continue until one can confirm the results with one's own eyes. (Tasuku Honjo)

我認為重要的是堅持下去，直到能夠親眼確認結果。（本庶佑）

Exactly when you think that what's written in a schoolbook is entirely correct, you will be bound to cease to be a promising scientist. (Tasuku Honjo)

一旦以為寫在教科書上的便完全正確，你就注定不再是個有前途的科學家了。（本庶佑）

Do not trust what is written in textbooks. You should have a feeling of wanting to find out what is really going on. Do not give up. (Tasuku Honjo)

2018 年

不要盡信寫在教科書上的東西。你應當保持想釐清實情的感覺。不要放棄。（本庶佑）

My parents were very supportive, psychologically and financially they supported and my family, wife and children —— I was kind of workaholic. I don't spend much time with my family, I feel sorry for them, but they just allowed me to concentrate on my research, so I am very fortunate. (Tasuku Honjo)

我的父母非常支持，在心理上和經濟上支持；還有我的家人，妻子和孩子——我多少屬於工作狂。我和家人共處的時間不多，對他們感到歉疚，但他們只是讓我專注於研究，所以我非常幸運。（本庶佑）

In every raped woman, I see my wife. In every raped mother, I see my mother and in every raped child, my own children. (Denis Mukwege)

在每一個被強姦的女人身上，我都看到了我的妻子。在每一個被強姦的母親身上，我都看到了我的母親，在每一個被強姦的孩子身上，我都看到了我自己的孩子。[47]（德尼·穆克維格）

The goal is to transform their pain into power. We can change hate by love. (Denis Mukwege)

我們的目標是將她們的痛苦轉化為力量。我們能夠以愛改變仇恨。（德尼·穆克維格）

I want to be the last girl in the world with a story like mine. (Nadia Murad)

但願我成為世界上最後一個有像我這樣經歷的女孩。（娜迪雅·穆拉德）

---

[47] 穆克維格和穆拉德致力於反對戰時性暴力，因而獲得 2018 年諾貝爾和平獎。

It never gets easier to tell your story. Each time you speak it, you relive it. But my story, told honestly and matter-of-factly, is the best weapon I have against terrorism, and I plan on using it until those terrorists are put on trial. (Nadia Murad)

講述親身經歷從來都不容易。每次訴說都是重新感受。但是我的經歷，實在地說，的確就是我所擁有能對抗恐怖主義的最好武器，而我打算運用它，直到那些恐怖分子受到審判。（娜迪雅・穆拉德）

An economist is a scoundrel who tells you the way things are rather than the way you want them to be. (William D. Nordhaus)

經濟學家是個惡棍，他告訴你事物原本的樣子，而非你所期望的樣子。（威廉・諾德豪斯[48]）

The most important job I do is teaching. (William D. Nordhaus)

我所做的最重要的工作是教學。（威廉・諾德豪斯）

Putting a low price on valuable environmental resources is a phenomenon that pervades modern society. Agricultural water is not scarce in California; it is underpriced. Flights are stacked up on runways because takeoffs and landings are underpriced. People wait for hours in traffic jams because road use is unpriced. People die premature deaths from small sulfur particles in the air because air pollution is underpriced. And the most perilous of all environmental problems, climate change, is taking place because virtually every country puts a price of zero on carbon dioxide emissions. (William D. Nordhaus)

對於昂貴的環境資源估價過低，是現代社會普遍存在的現象。農業用水在加州並不缺乏，而是價值被低估了。飛機擠在跑道上，因為起飛

---

[48] 諾德豪斯，2018年諾貝爾經濟學獎得主。

和降落的費用被低估。人們在交通堵塞中等待數小時,因為道路的使用沒有標價。空氣中細微的硫顆粒導致人們提早死亡,因為空氣汙染受到低估。而所有環境問題中最危險的一種,氣候變化,正在發生,因為對於二氧化碳排放,實際上每一個國家都採取了零定價。(威廉‧諾德豪斯)

One feature of knowledge can be summarized by Isaac Newton's statement that he could see far because he could stand on the shoulders of giants. In other words, his notion was that knowledge builds on itself, which means that as we learn more, we get better and better at discovering new things. It also means that there's no limit to the amount of things we can discover. (Paul M. Romer)

知識的一個特點可以由艾薩克‧牛頓的說法概括:他能夠看得遠,是由於能夠站在巨人的肩膀上。換言之,他認為知識建立在自身之上,意即,我們學習得越多,就越來越擅長發現新事物。這也意味著,我們能夠發現的事物是無限的。(保羅‧羅莫)

Every generation has underestimated the potential for finding new ideas.... Possibilities do not add up. They multiply. (Paul M. Romer)

每一代人都低估了發現新想法的潛力。……可能性並非相加。它們相乘。(保羅‧羅莫)

Now it could have been —— I suppose —— that with each new discovery, it got harder and harder to make additional discoveries. In that case, we would —— at some point —— simply give up. Progress would be slowing down and eventually would come to a halt. Of course, this is not what we see when we look at history. From one century to the next, the rate of technological change and the rate of growth of income per capita has been speeding up. (Paul M. Romer)

如今，我推測，隨著每一次新發現，做出更多的發現也許會變得越來越艱難。既然如此——在某個時候——我們會索性放棄。進展會逐漸放慢並最終止步不前。當然了，這並不是我們觀察歷史時所見到的。從一個世紀到下一個世紀，技術變革的速度和個人所得的成長速度一直都在加快。（保羅・羅莫）

If you look at the very long sweep of history what you see is that the rate of growth has been speeding up, the rate of progress, and that's because there's more and more people who are all engaged in this process of discovery. (Paul M. Romer)

縱觀漫長的歷史，你看到的是成長的速度一直在加快，進步的速度，這是由於有越來越多的人都投身於發現的過程。（保羅・羅莫）

We've maintained accelerating growth over time in part because of changes in our institutions. We have things like universities… patent laws, and research grants which have created incentives for those individuals who develop innovations to engage in more discovery… The rules of the game create incentives. (Paul M. Romer)

隨著時間的推移，我們一直保持加速成長，部分由於機制的變化。我們有像大學這樣的東西⋯⋯專利法，還有研究資助，激勵開發創新的個人從事更多的發現。⋯⋯遊戲規則產生激勵。（保羅・羅莫）

Once we admit that there is room for newness —— that there are vastly more conceivable possibilities than realized outcomes —— we must confront the fact that there is no special logic behind the world we inhabit, no particular justification for why things are the way they are. Any number of arbitrarily small perturbations along the way could have made the world as we know it turn out very differently. Human material existence is limited by ideas, not stuff, people don't need copper wires they need ways to communicate, oil was a contaminant, then it became a fuel. (Paul M. Romer)

一旦承認新事物有存在的空間——與已經實現的結果相比，存在極其眾多不難設想的可能性——我們就必須面對這樣的事實：在我們居住的世界背後，沒有特別的邏輯，沒有特殊的理由，來解釋各種事物的現狀。在形成過程中，任何數量的無論何其微小的擾動，都可能使我們所知的世界變得大為不同。人類的物質存在受限於理念，而非材料。人們不需要銅線，他們需要溝通的路徑；石油曾經是汙染物，後來成了燃料。（保羅・羅莫）

We have taken the fixed quantity of matter available to us and rearranged it. We have changed things from a form that is less valuable into a form that is more valuable. Value creation and wealth creation in their most basic senses have to do with taking physical objects and rearranging them. Now, where do ideas come in? Quite simply, ideas are the recipes we use to rearrange things to create more value and wealth. For example, we have ideas about ways to make steel by combining iron with carbon and a few other elements. We have ideas about how to take silicon —— an abundant element that was almost worthless to us until recently —— and make it into semiconductor chips. So we have physical materials to work with —— raw ingredients —— which are finite and scarce, and we have ideas or knowledge, which tell us how to use those raw materials. When I say there are always more things to discover, what I mean is that there are always more recipes that we can find to combine raw materials in ways that make them more valuable to us. (Paul M. Romer)

我們已經取得現存的定量物質並將其重新安排。我們已經把事物從價值較低的形式變為價值更高的形式。價值創造和財富創造，在它們最基本的意義上，都關係到取得並重新安排物理對象。那麼，創意何來？很簡單，創意就是用於重新安排事物以創造更多價值和財富的祕方。例如，我們有了創意，設法將鐵和碳以及另一些元素結合來製造鋼鐵。我們有了創意，研究如何取得矽——一種直到不久以前都對我們幾無價值的豐富元素——並把它做成半導體晶片。所以，我們有備用的物理材料——原料——它們是有限的和稀缺的；我們又有創意或知識，它們告訴我們如何使用這些原料。我說總是有更多的東西等待發現，我的意思是，總是有更多的祕方，我們可以找到它們，以各種方式結合原料，從而使它們對我們更有價值。（保羅・羅莫）

Economic growth springs from better recipes, not just from more cooking. New recipes produce fewer unpleasant side effects and generate more economic value per unit of raw material. (Paul M. Romer)

經濟成長來自更好的食譜，而非更多的烹飪。新食譜造成的令人不快的副作用較少，而每一個原料單位產生的經濟價值更高。（保羅・羅莫）

Why was progress... speeding up over time? It arises because of this special characteristic of an idea, which is if a million people try to discover something, if any one person finds it, everybody can use the idea. (Paul M. Romer)

進步為什麼⋯⋯隨著時間的推移而加速？它來自創意的這種特別的

性質，就是，如果有一百萬人試圖從事某項發現，如果任何一個人成功了，每個人都可以使用這個創意。（保羅·羅莫）

My number-one recommendation is to invest in people. Humans that are well trained are the inputs into this discovery process. And there's big opportunities still, I think, to do a better job of investing in people. (Paul M. Romer)

我的首要建議是投資於人。獲得良好訓練的人是對於發現過程的投入。我認為，還有很大的機會更好地投資於人。（保羅·羅莫）

A crisis is a terrible thing to waste. (Paul M. Romer)

危機的浪費是一件可怕的事情。（保羅·羅莫）

Many people think that dealing with protecting the environment will be so costly and so hard that they just want to ignore the problem. I hope the prize today could help everyone see that humans are capable of amazing accomplishments when we set about trying to do something. (Paul M. Romer)

許多人認為，著手保護環境將是如此昂貴，如此困難，於是他們只想忽略這個問題。我希望，今天的獎項能有助於每個人看到，當我們努力從事時，人類是能夠獲得驚人成就的。（保羅·羅莫）

Science may have actually been more important for the West in developing a culture where a reputation for integrity and telling the truth became something that was valued. Science may have actually been more important than we realize for that. (Paul M. Romer)

對於西方，實際上，科學可能在發展一種文化方面更重要，在這種文化中，正直和說真話的名聲成為受重視的東西。就此而言，實際上，科學可能比我們所意識到的更重要。（保羅·羅莫）

A fact beats a theory every time, and theories have to be logically coherent. If we stay committed to those principles, then we'll make progress. (Paul M. Romer)

事實總是勝過理論，而理論須得邏輯連貫。如果堅持這些原則，我們就會獲得進展。（保羅・羅莫）

2019 年

The universe is capable of surprising us. I don't think there's a final theory of everything. It's theories all the way down. We can be very sure that my theory isn't the final answer. And we can be very sure that as we discover new aspects of the expanding and evolving universe we will be amazed once again. I hope you guys hurry up and make those discoveries. (James Peebles)

宇宙能夠使我們驚奇。我不認為存在萬事通用的終極理論。只有不斷發展的各種理論。我們可以非常確定，我的理論並非最終答案。我們可以非常確定，一旦發現宇宙膨脹和演化的新現象，我們將再度吃驚。期望諸位加快研究，獲得這些發現。（吉姆・皮博斯）

I think I'd be depressed if everything were nearly all known, but I don't feel any danger of that happening. (James Peebles)

我想，如果一切都幾乎已經知曉，我會感到沮喪，但我絲毫不覺得此事有發生的危險。（吉姆・皮博斯）

What might we learn from lines of research that are off the beaten track? They check accepted ideas, always a good thing, and there is the chance nature has prepared yet another surprise for us. (James Peebles)

我們可能從脫離常規的研究中學到什麼？它們查驗公認的觀念，這總是好事，大自然也有可能為我們準備了另一個驚喜。（吉姆·皮博斯）

Don't judge your career by the number of prizes and awards. I have so many. It's wonderful and the Nobel Prize is absolutely spectacularly wonderful, but to get such a prize requires not only dedication and creativity, it requires eventualities. (James Peebles)

不要以獲獎數量評價自己的職業生涯。我擁有了這麼多。這十分美妙，諾貝爾獎絕對是驚人地美好，但獲得這樣的獎項不僅需要奉獻和創造力，它更需要不期而然。（吉姆·皮博斯）

My advice is not to aim for prizes or awards. We're in this for the joy of research, the fascination, the love of science⋯⋯. I remember being amazed that I could get paid for this. (James Peebles)

我的建議是不以獲獎為目標。我們投身於此是為了研究的快樂，醉心於對科學的熱愛。⋯⋯我還記得自己曾驚訝於能夠為此得到報酬。（吉姆·皮博斯）

My advice, my central advice to a young person considering entering science of any sort, say in natural science： look around, discover what really interests you. It may not be the first thing that you notice, you may find something mildly interesting, but if you look a little harder, you'll find something even better. Don't jump into a particular line of research until you have looked around quite carefully and discover that which really fascinates you. If you are fascinated, you'll do well. (James Peebles)

我的建議，給有意進入自然科學任何學科的年輕人的主要建議是：

四處觀察，找出真正使你感興趣的事情。它可能不是你注意到的第一件事，你可能發現某一件事有幾分趣味，然而再仔細看看，你會發現還要更好的。在仔細地四處觀察並找出真正使你著迷的事情之前，不要一頭栽進特定的研究領域。一旦你著迷了，你就會做得好。（吉姆・皮博斯）

Research in the natural sciences operates in successive approximations. We are glad to be able to offer many good problems for research by generations to come. (James Peebles)

自然科學研究的運作是連續的近似值。我們很高興能夠為後代的研究提供許多出色的問題。（吉姆・皮博斯）

I advise young researchers to be ambitious, to do what they are interested in and to carefully choose the right place to do their thesis. (Michel Mayor)

我建議年輕的研究人員立下志向，做自己感興趣的事情，審慎選擇合適的議題撰寫論文。（米歇爾・梅爾）

This has been humanity's dream for more than 2,000 years. Today, we are in a privileged position: the technology we have allows us to transform this ancient dream into what is an immensely vibrant chapter of scientific history. We can't see these planets, but we can tell they are there using stringent scientific methods. (Michel Mayor)

這是人類兩千多年來的夢想。今天，我們處於特別的位置：我們所擁有的技術，得以將這個古老的夢想化為科學史上活力四射的一章。我們看不見這些行星，但能夠運用嚴謹的科學方法說出它們在那裡。（米歇爾・梅爾）

What would the German physicist Wilhelm Conrad Röntgen have said if someone had asked him what the point was of investigating cathode rays?

> 2019 年

(Michel Mayor)

　　如果有人問德國物理學家威廉・康拉德・倫琴研究陰極射線的意義何在，他會說什麼？[49]（米歇爾・梅爾）

　　It's an amazingly powerful process, that of curiosity, it's an extraordinary gift. We should stimulate this curiosity on every different level. As children we are more curious than ever. (Didier Queloz)

　　這是個驚人地充滿力量的過程，好奇是一項非凡的天賦。我們應當在每一個不同層面激發這種好奇心。作為孩子，我們比任何時期都更好奇。（迪迪埃・奎洛茲）

　　All myths and religions ask the same questions: where do we come from? What is our place in the universe? (Didier Queloz)

　　所有的神話和宗教都在問同樣的問題：我們從哪裡來？我們在宇宙中的位置何在？（迪迪埃・奎洛茲）

　　To make a revolutionary discovery, you have to do research without thinking about any sort of application. You can go on improving steam locomotives for as long as you like, they will never take you to the moon. (Didier Queloz)

　　要獲得革命性的發現，你就得做研究而不考慮任何程度的應用。只要願意，你可以繼續改良蒸汽火車，可是它們永遠不會把你帶到月球去。（迪迪埃・奎洛茲）

　　Yes, I'm in the lab every day. I'm still working. What would I do, just retire and wait to die? No, I don't think so. (John B. Goodenough)

---

[49]　有疑問曰：研究一顆 5,000 萬光年之外，人類完全力所不及的行星值得嗎？梅爾和奎洛茲不約而同地做出了回答。

是，我天天都在實驗室，我還在工作。不然要做什麼，就是退休等死？不，我沒有這種想法。[50]（約翰・B・古迪納夫）

First, don't copy. Think about the problem and to remember that we compete against problems, not against people. Well as I say, don't believe everything that you read and don't be afraid to think and it is alright to understand what has gone before but don't just rely on copying but develop your internal voice and your own internal means of interpreting. That is a very individual thing and there are many different ways to be successful. Some people are very good at building equipment, you got to be able to measure and you got to be able to know what you are measuring and to interpret and so on. There are other people who do theory and develop theoretical understanding. And then there are people who develop intuition. You have to have some scientific intuition as well. And every scientist is an individual and brings a different talent to the problem. But you have to be willing to dialogue so that we can all benefit from one another's intuition. (John B. Goodenough)

首先，不要模仿。要思考問題，記住我們的對手是問題，而不是人。就像我說的，不要讀到什麼都相信，不要害怕思考，了解過往沒錯，但是不要一味依賴模仿，而要發展你內心的聲音和自己的解讀方法。這是非常個人的事情，成功有很多不同的途徑。有些人非常擅長製作設備，你必須能夠測量，必須知道在測量什麼，必須能夠解釋等等。另一些人研究理論並發展出對理論的詮釋。還有些人發展直覺。你也必須具備某種科學直覺。每位科學家都是個體，為解決問題提供不同的才能。但你得願意對話，從而我們都能從彼此的直覺中獲益。（約翰・B・古迪納夫）

---

[50] 古迪納夫獲獎時年屆97歲，刷新了2018年獲獎者阿瑟・亞希金（Arthur Ashkin）的紀錄。

> 2019 年

I have learned to be open to surprises, not have preconceived ideas or close your mind from listening to what might work. (John B. Goodenough)

我學會對意想不到的事物保持開放態度，不抱持先入之見，或者封閉自己的心智而不傾聽可能有用的東西。（約翰·B·古迪納夫）

I think dialogue is very important for thinking. And sometimes when you have to write something up, you are dialoguing with yourself as you are writing something up and you think about things. You have to try to be clear when you write. And you have to try to be brief. Get away with the clutter and just get to the point. (John B. Goodenough)

我認為，對話對於思考非常重要。有時候，在需要訴諸文字時，你就是在一邊寫作、一邊跟自己對話的同時動腦思索。寫作的時候，你應該力求表達清晰。力求簡短、擺脫雜亂、直奔主題。（約翰·B·古迪納夫）

Is science fun? It's hard work, but it's satisfying. (John B. Goodenough)

科學有趣嗎？它是艱苦的工作，然而令人心滿意足。（約翰·B·古迪納夫）

Being able to satisfy your curiosity is fun. (John B. Goodenough)

好奇心獲得滿足是快樂的。（約翰·B·古迪納夫）

There's some goal in mind; it's not just research for its own sake. I like to feel it makes a difference. (M. Stanley Whittingham)

心存目標。這不僅是專注於研究本身。我喜歡感受這其中的差異。（史丹利·惠廷安）

The biggest perk is I'm allowed to park my car inside the college. (M. Stanley Whittingham)

（獲諾貝爾獎）最大的優待，是允許我把車子停在學校裡。（史丹利・惠廷安）

Innovation all around will enable a sustainable society to be achieved very soon. (Akira Yoshino)

全方位的創新將快速實現永續發展的社會。（吉野彰）

Many unknown aspects still remain in science, including chemistry. The natural world is deep. Environmental problems provide the greatest challenges, a chance to become world heroes. Young researchers should see them as a great opportunity. (Akira Yoshino)

科學中仍然存在許多未知的方面，包括化學。自然界是深奧的。環境問題提供了最大的挑戰，一個成為世界英雄的機會。年輕的研究人員應當將其視為巨大的機會。（吉野彰）

While the IT Revolution occurred in the field of information, I believe the next revolution will be in the field of energy. Preparations for the upcoming revolution are already advancing. One thing that never changes is that scientists who clearly grasp society's emerging needs and boldly take on new research challenges will be the leaders who open the path to the future. (Akira Yoshino)

雖然資訊科技革命發生在資訊領域，我認為下一次革命將是在能源領域。對即將到來的革命的準備已經開始了。永遠不變的是，清楚把握社會的新興需求，並大膽接受新研究挑戰的科學家，將成為開關未來道路的領導者。（吉野彰）

2019 年

You need to be able to set goals as if it's a marathon. Although it's difficult to do, what is important is to be able to anticipate what will be needed 10 or 15 years from now. Then you calculate what experience and expertise, and what research, is necessary to get there. What is of utmost importance is to have confidence in yourself. Then, you can overcome the hurdles you will undoubtedly encounter. (Akira Yoshino)

你需要像參加馬拉松一樣設定目標。儘管難以做到，重要的是能夠預見 10 或 15 年後的需求。然後你推測要達到它需要什麼經驗和專長，以及什麼研究。最重要的是具備自信。然後，你便能克服即將遭遇的阻礙。（吉野彰）

If you hit the wall, you should thank God for placing it in front of you —— that's when something new is born. (Akira Yoshino)

如果碰壁，你應當感謝上帝把它放到你面前 —— 這是新事物誕生的時候。（吉野彰）

I try to consider what people need, what the world really needs, based on my own experience in daily life. Then I think about how technology can be a means to accomplish it. I've found that it's more likely for a good technology idea to pop into my head when I'm relaxing, with a clear mind, rather than when I'm concentrating hard trying to think of something. (Akira Yoshino)

我努力依據本身的日常生活經驗考慮人們需要什麼，世界真正需要什麼。然後思考技術如何得以成為滿足這種需要的手段。我發現，好的技術概念更可能在自己放鬆、頭腦清晰之際湧現，而非集中精力苦苦思索的時候。（吉野彰）

Since we live in a society flooded with so much information, it may be hard for young scientists to appreciate that there are many fields where unknown things are waiting to be discovered. There are many opportunities for groundbreaking R&D. With a clear objective and persistent effort, the possibilities are endless. As for me, I intend to remain on the front line of research, taking on challenges in new fields. (Akira Yoshino)

我們生活在資訊氾濫的社會，年輕的科學家可能難以意識到，有許多領域的未知事物等待發現。有許多突破性研發的機會。具備明確的目標和執著的努力，可能性是無窮的。就我而言，我打算留在研究的前線，在新的領域接受挑戰。（吉野彰）

Curiosity was the main driving force for me. (Akira Yoshino)

好奇心是我的主要動力。（吉野彰）

I just sort of sniffed out the direction that trends were moving. You could say I had a good sense of smell. (Akira Yoshino)

我只是多少嗅出了趨勢發展的方向。你不妨說我的嗅覺很靈敏。（吉野彰）

I think it is important to thinking every day. (Akira Yoshino)

我認為每天都思考是很重要的。（吉野彰）

Flexible thinking, and its direct opposite: tenacity of purpose. You've got to be persistent and never give up until the end. (Akira Yoshino)

靈活的思考，和它的直接相反面：目標之執著。你必須堅持到底，永不放棄。[51]（吉野彰）

---

[51] 被問及傑出研究者必備的特質時，吉野彰不假思索地如此回答。吉野彰本人即為堅韌不拔的典型：他 2005 年獲得博士學位時 57 歲。2019 年獲得諾貝爾獎時 71 歲。接受採訪時還說，要

Today's students have goals, but they have yet to discover the path to get there. There are too few people around them who have experienced success. They don't know how to pursue their goals, and end up confused about what direction to take. I'd like to tell them to look ahead to the time when they are in their mid-30s, and study and gain the experience they need to pursue their goals when the time comes. (Akira Yoshino)

今天的學生具有目標，但還有待找出達到目標的途徑。他們身邊經歷過成功的人太少了。他們不知道如何追求目標，結果迷失了方向。我想告訴他們，35歲左右時要向前看，學習並獲得所需的經驗，當時機到來時追求目標。（吉野彰）

I think parents should encourage their children to have an interest in something. However, they must not push them... When a child becomes interested in something after being given the right stimulus, they will naturally find their own way of pursuing it. (Akira Yoshino)

我認為，父母應當鼓勵孩子對某件事具有興趣。然而，千萬別逼他們。……受到適當的刺激後，孩子對某件事產生了興趣，自然會找到自己的追求方式。（吉野彰）

Live for those moments when you have the privilege of seeing or understanding something that's never been seen or understood before. (William G. Kaelin Jr)

為這樣一些時刻而活：你有幸見識或理解以前從未見識或理解的事物。（威廉·凱林）

向97歲仍在工作的共同獲獎者古迪納夫學習，「只要活著就要繼續研究」。

I'm a big believer of curiosity-driven, hypothesis-driven research… I think in the end what drew me to science and what draws a lot of scientists to science is that we like interesting puzzles. (William G. Kaelin Jr)

我是好奇心驅動、假說驅動研究的忠實信徒。……我認為最終吸引我和許多科學家投身科學的，是我們喜歡有趣的謎題。（威廉·凱林）

I think scientists in general, and in particular physician scientists, are under tremendous pressure these days, to try to justify the importance of their work in terms of potential clinical applicability. And yet I like to point out that our story is one of trying to generate knowledge and to understand how things work. And if you go deep enough and you understand things well enough, occasionally opportunities for translation or therapeutic application will arise. So I'm so happy to be involved with this story because I think that's how real translation happens. People like to take short cuts, or they are sometimes told to try to take short cuts, but there are no short cuts as far as I'm concerned. (William G. Kaelin Jr)

我認為，一般來說，科學家，尤其是醫學家，現在都承受著巨大的壓力，力圖證明所做工作在潛在臨床適用上的重要性。然而我想指出，我們的故事，是試圖產生知識、理解事物運作的故事。如果探究足夠深入，理解足夠透澈，就偶爾出現轉化或治療應用的機會。所以我非常高興置身於這個故事，因為我認為真正的轉化就是如此發生。人們樂於走捷徑，或者有時被告知盡量走捷徑，但是就我而言，並無捷徑可行。（威廉·凱林）

Yes, I think the courage, and I think this is an important issue, that we make knowledge, that's what I do as a publicly-funded scientist. That knowledge has only one quality that's definable really: it's good knowledge, it's true, it's correct. The idea at the outset that some knowledge might be more valuable than some other knowledge, well probably that's true also, but it's extremely difficult to assess in prospect, and this is an example where we set out on a journey without the clear understanding of the value of that knowledge, and I guess it has gained in value. Quite what the future holds of course is yet another question, but it is important that scientists have the courage and are allowed to derive knowledge for its own sake, i.e. independent of the perceived value at the point of creation. And history of science tells us over and over again that the value of that knowledge can increase with the impact on other people's research, other circumstances, all sorts of random and unpredictable issues brought to bear. (Peter J. Ratcliffe)

是的,我認為勇氣,我認為這是個重要問題,我們創造知識,這就是我作為受公共資助的科學家所做的事。知識唯有一種真正可以確定的品質:它是優良的知識,它是真實的,它是正確的。起初的想法,認為有的知識也許比另一些更有價值,這也很可能是真的,然而極其難以預先評估。此為一例,即我們在出發點對於此知識的價值並無明確的理解,我想它的價值提升了。未來究竟如何當然是另一個問題,然而重要的是,科學家有勇氣並被允許為了知識本身而研究,也就是說,與創造時所感知的價值無關。科學史一再告訴我們,隨著對於其他人的研究、其他的情況、各種隨機和莫測的問題所帶來的影響,知識的價值能夠提升。(彼得・雷克里夫)

If a journal ever says they are having difficulty in finding reviewers —— this is good! It means you're in a small pool of people and working on something nobody else is. (Peter J. Ratcliffe)

如果一家期刊說他們難以找到審稿人──這很好！這意味著你處於一小群人中，在做沒有其他人做的事情。（彼得‧雷克里夫）

Our eureka moment didn't come out of the blue. (Peter J. Ratcliffe)

我們的靈光一現並非憑空而來。（彼得‧雷克里夫）

These splendid celebrations have blown us away. New experiences. We have had a lot of interview questions. What is my favourite Beatles song, what is my favourite time of day, what is my favourite food? We have learned so much about ourselves; the answers to all those questions. (Peter J. Ratcliffe)

這些慶祝的大場面可把我們鎮住了。新體驗。採訪問及的問題眾多。我最喜歡的披頭四歌曲是什麼？我最喜歡一天中的什麼時間？我最喜歡的食物是什麼？我們已經對自己有了這麼多了解，對所有這些問題的回答。（彼得‧雷克里夫）

This is my religion: I am filled with Wonder at the outcome of 4 billion years of evolution here on our speck in the universe and Hope regarding our opportunity to improve the lives of those around us through basic science discoveries and their translation to clinical practice. (Gregg L. Semenza)

這就是我的信仰：對於這顆宇宙塵埃上 40 億年演化的結果，我充滿了驚奇；對於我們的機會，透過基礎科學的發現及其向臨床實務的轉化來改善周遭人們的生活，也滿懷希望。（格雷格‧塞門薩）

I think it's really important to have people who are kind of there at the boundary between research and medicine to facilitate the discovery of knowledge that will translate ultimately to improvements in clinical practice. (Gregg L. Semenza)

我認為，真正重要的，是讓處於研究和醫學交界地帶的人們促進知識的發現，這將最終轉化為臨床實務的進步。（格雷格·塞門薩）

Yes, and unexpected turns. That's what makes science so exciting, you never quite know where your studies are going to lead you. (Gregg L. Semenza)

是的，還有意想不到的轉折。這就是科學如此令人激動的原因，你永遠不太清楚，你的研究將把你引向何方。（格雷格·塞門薩）

I would like to dedicate this lecture to Rose Nelson. She was my high school biology teacher and my inspiration in science. I am here because of her. (Gregg Semenza)

我願把這個演講獻給羅絲·納爾遜。她是我的高中生物老師，在科學上激勵我的人。我站在這裡是由於她。（格雷格·塞門薩）

Many of us who conduct biomedical research do so with what could be described as a religious fervor. This would not have come as a surprise to Mary Lasker. She once told a reporter, "I am opposed to heart attacks and cancer the way one is opposed to sin." Amen. (Gregg L. Semenza)

我們許多從事生物醫學研究的人，工作時都懷著不妨稱為宗教狂熱的情緒。對於瑪麗·拉斯克[52]，這不會令人感到意外。她有一次告訴記者：「我反對心臟病和癌症，就像人們反對罪惡。」阿門。（格雷格·塞門薩）

Creating stories means constantly bringing things to life, giving an existence to all the tiny pieces of the world that are represented by human experiences, the situations people have endured and their memories. (Olga Tokarczuk)

---

[52] 瑪麗·拉斯克，美國健康活動家和慈善家。

創作意味著不斷賦予事物生命,使人類的經歷所展現的塵世所有細節、人們的境遇和他們的記憶得以存在。(奧爾嘉・朵卡萩)

Standing there on the embankment, staring into the current, I realized that —— in spite of all the risks involved —— a thing in motion will always be better than a thing at rest; that change will always be a nobler thing than permanence; that which is static will degenerate and decay, turn to ash, while that which is in motion is able to last for all eternity. (Olga Tokarczuk)

站在堤岸上,凝視著激流,我意識到:儘管包含所有風險,變動的事物永遠比靜止的好;變化永遠優於持久的事物;靜態的事物會退化、衰減,化為灰燼,而變動的事物能夠永恆延續。(奧爾嘉・朵卡萩)

Every single human being is the source of a novel, it's a source of many stories. So, we are living in a world that like, more or less, five billion of stories, novels, in potential state existing still around us. (Olga Tokarczuk)

每個人都是一部小說的來源,是許多故事的來源。所以,我們生活在如此這般的世界裡,大約有 50 億個潛在的故事、小說,靜靜地處於我們周圍。(奧爾嘉・朵卡萩)

I write fiction, but it is never pure fabrication. (Olga Tokarczuk)

我寫小說,但它從來不是純粹的虛構。(奧爾嘉・朵卡萩)

Today it is exactly one hundred-ten years since the first woman won the Nobel Prize in Literature —— Selma Lagerlöf. I bow low to her across time, and to all the other women, all the female creators who boldly exceeded the limiting roles society imposed on them, and had the courage to tell their story to the world loud and clear. I can feel them standing behind me. (Olga Tokarczuk)

2019年

　　今日恰逢第一位女性獲得諾貝爾文學獎110週年——塞爾瑪·拉格洛夫。跨越時間，我向她，向所有其他女性，所有大膽超越社會強加的角色限制、勇於向世人大聲且明確地講述自己故事的女性創作者深深鞠躬。我感受得到站在身後的她們。（奧爾嘉·朵卡萩）

I also owe a great deal to my translators. They will continue to be the most attentive readers of everything I write, they'll catch every little inconsistency, and they'll kick up a fuss about every mistake I make. (Olga Tokarczuk)

　　我也非常感謝我的譯者。他們將繼續作為我每篇作品最專心的讀者，他們將抓住每一個細小的扞格之處，他們將對我所犯的每一項錯誤大加撻伐。（奧爾嘉·朵卡萩）

Make no decisions you don't feel excited about. Let yourself fail. Above all, give yourself time and take the long way round. (Peter Handke)

　　不要做你不感到心動的決定。允許自己失敗。尤其是，給自己時間，不走捷徑。（彼得·漢德克）

Most older people don't talk about the past so they won't have to admit that their life ran on the wrong rail. (Peter Handke)

　　大多數老年人不談論過去，這樣他們就無須承認自己的生活行駛在錯誤的軌道上。（彼得·漢德克）

We live as Ethiopians and die as Ethiopia. (Abiy Ahmed Ali)

　　我們作為衣索比亞人而生，也作為衣索比亞人而死。（阿比·阿邁德）

My hope for the next 15 years is very much that I continue to do what I am doing. I enjoy very much what I am doing, I think that this might open some more doors, give us a chance to do some more useful interventions or study some more useful interventions, make the case that these things actually matter. Maybe people will listen to us a little bit more as a result of the prize. (Abhijit Banerjee)

我對今後 15 年的期待,是非常希望繼續做正在做的事情。我非常喜歡正在做的事情,我認為這可能打開更多扇門,提供我們機會去從事或研究一些更有用的干預,以證明這些事實際上很重要。也許由於諾貝爾獎,人們會多聽取我們的意見。(阿巴希‧巴納吉)

Talking about the problems of the world without talking about some accessible solutions is the way to paralysis rather than progress. (Abhijit Banerjee)

談論世界的問題卻避談一些可及的對策,乃是導致癱瘓而非進步之道。(阿巴希‧巴納吉)

What is dangerous is not making mistakes, but to be so enamored of one's point of view that one does not let facts get in the way. To make progress, we have to constantly go back to the facts, acknowledge our errors, and move. (Abhijit Banerjee)

危險不在於犯錯,而在於如此沉迷於個人觀點而排斥事實。要獲得進步,我們就得不斷地回顧事實,承認錯誤,然後行動。(阿巴希‧巴納吉)

For each successful entrepreneur in the Silicon Valley or elsewhere, many have had to fail. (Abhijit Banerjee)

就矽谷或其他地方的每一個成功企業家而言,許多人都曾難免失敗。(阿巴希‧巴納吉)

Poverty is not just a lack of money; it is not having the capability to realize one's full potential as a human being. (Abhijit Banerjee)

貧窮不只是缺錢，是無力於實現一個人作為人的充分潛能。（阿巴希・巴納吉）

Economics is too important to be left to economists. (Abhijit Banerjee)

經濟學太重要了，不能交給經濟學家。[53]（阿巴希・巴納吉）

I think it is very important to ask questions that can be answered. And that can be answered in as rigorous and scientific way as possible. The question can be broader or it can be narrow but it should be specific... I think to me it is very essential to try to ask these questions that are very well defined and on which you can train your kind of gaze as a scientist in trying to answer them rigorously and that involve usually not answering the whole problem you would like to answer at once. (Esther Duflo)

我認為，提出能夠回答的問題是非常重要的。這種問題能夠以盡量嚴謹和科學的方式回答。問題廣狹無妨，但應當是明確的。……我認為，就我而言，尤其必要的是，盡量提這樣的問題，它們定義得非常明確，你在力圖嚴謹作答時得以訓練自己那種科學家的專注，且通常你不會一次回答你想作答的整個問題。（艾絲特・杜芙洛）

People are not so different. People live in very different circumstances but at heart we have the same type of strengths and weaknesses, just happen to be in different contexts. (Esther Duflo)

人們沒那麼不同。人們生活在非常不同的情況裡，但實質上我們具

---

[53] 喬治・克里蒙梭（Georges Clemenceau）曾說：戰爭過於重大，不能交給將軍。（War is too important to be left to the generals.）巴納吉這裡是在幽默地模仿。巴納吉，2019 年諾貝爾經濟學獎得主。

有相同類型的優點和缺點，只是碰巧處於不同的環境中。（艾絲特·杜芙洛）

This prize has come at an extremely important time. I am incredibly humbled to be only the second woman awarded, and I hope to represent all women in economics... Showing that it is possible for a woman to succeed, and to be recognised for success, I hope is going to inspire many, many other women to continue working and many other men to give them the respect that they deserve. (Esther Duflo)

這個獎項頒發於極其重要的時刻。我極其榮幸，竟然成為第二位女性獲獎者。我希望代表經濟學領域的所有女性……表明女性的成功並獲得認可是可能的，我希望能激勵許許多多女性繼續工作，並使許多其他男性給予她們應得的尊重。（艾絲特·杜芙洛）

I've never felt that being a woman was a problem in my profession, but I did feel isolated in my field. So as a woman it's an honour to receive this prize. (Esther Duflo)

在我的職業中，我從未覺得身為女人是個問題，但在我的領域裡，我確實覺得孤獨。所以作為女性，獲得這個獎項是一種榮譽。（艾絲特·杜芙洛）

In a way, it has been an advantage for me to be a woman because there is always some academic committee that needs you to fill a quota! (Esther Duflo)

在某種程度上，身為女性對於我一直是有益的，因為總是有些學術委員會需要妳充數！（艾絲特·杜芙洛）

I've never had a TV in my whole life. Television passed by me. (Esther Duflo)

我整整一輩子都沒有電視機。電視跟我擦肩而過。（艾絲特・杜芙洛）

I don't go to the beach. There is no value in going to the beach. If I did go I would probably read economics books. (Esther Duflo)

我不去海灘。去海灘沒有價值。若真的要去的話，我多半會讀經濟學的書。（艾絲特・杜芙洛）

2020 年

Science and fun cannot be separated. (Roger Penrose)

科學與樂趣密不可分。（羅傑・潘洛斯）

My own way of thinking is to ponder long and I hope deeply on problems and for a long time which I keep away for years and years and I never really let them go. (Roger Penrose)

我自己的思考方式是長時間思索。我深切地、長久地寄希望於多年沒觸碰的難題，從不真正放過它們。（羅傑・潘洛斯）

I'm pretty tenacious when it comes to problems. (Roger Penrose)

就難題而言，我非常執著。（羅傑・潘洛斯）

Sometimes it's the detours which turn out to be the fruitful ideas. (Roger Penrose)

有的時候，迂迴而行才是富於成效的主意。（羅傑・潘洛斯）

I think I am intrigued by paradoxes. If something seems to be a paradox, it has something deeper, something worth exploring. (Roger Penrose)

我想我著迷於悖論。如果一件事看來是個悖論，它就具有更深入之處，值得探索之處。（羅傑‧潘洛斯）

People think of these eureka moments and my feeling is that they tend to be little things, a little realisation and then a little realisation built on that. (Roger Penrose)

人們思索這些靈光一閃的時刻，而我的感覺為，它們往往是些小事，一點領悟，接著在此基礎上又是一點領悟。（羅傑‧潘洛斯）

And these little things may not seem like much but after a while they take you off on a direction where you may be a long way off from what other people have been thinking about. (Roger Penrose)

這些小事也許看似無關緊要，然而一段時間之後，它們就把你帶到一個方向，那可能與他人所想相去甚遠。（羅傑‧潘洛斯）

It took quite a long time. I was surprised —— well there was actually wasn't a great deal of interest to begin with. It took —— I used to go to these meetings called the Texas Meetings on Relativistic Astrophysics. I was there at the first one. That was when people were just beginning to realize that you had situations which might be something like a black hole. And it took a long time, I remember going to several of these meetings, every two years or so, and each time there was a bit more interest and a bit more interest. And it took quite a while before people really swung around and the general community believed that these objects were really likely to be there. (Roger Penrose)

這花了很長時間。我感到驚訝，其實起初並沒有太大興趣。我參加了相對論天體物理學德克薩斯會議。第一次會議我就出席了。那時人們才開始了解有可能是黑洞之類的狀況。這花了很長時間，我記得數次參加此會，兩年左右一次，興趣逐步一點點加大。過了很長一段時間，人們才真的轉變，廣泛相信這些事物真的可能存在。（羅傑·潘洛斯）

I was indeed very slow as a youngster. (Roger Penrose)

我年輕時確實非常遲鈍。（羅傑·潘洛斯）

I have certainly enjoyed puzzles since an early age, and things that look like impossible things are often particularly intriguing. (Roger Penrose)

我從小就喜歡謎題，看似不可能的事通常都特別有趣。（羅傑·潘洛斯）

Might we... be doing something with our brains that cannot be described in computational terms at all? How do our feelings of conscious awareness —— of happiness, pain, love, aesthetic sensibility, will, understanding, etc. —— fit into such a computational picture? (Roger Penrose)

可能我們……我們的大腦在做完全無法以計算術語描述的事情？我們有意識的感覺 —— 快樂、痛苦、愛、美感、意志、理解等等 —— 如何融入這種計算畫面？（羅傑·潘洛斯）

If you look at the Nobel Prize for physics over the last five years, you'll see that they have been awarded for neutrinos, gravitational waves, cosmology and exoplanets. Was it to be astrophysics again? You can perhaps imagine that people in other fields of physics might start grumbling. (Reinhard Genzel)

看看過去五年的諾貝爾物理學獎，你會發現他們授予了中微子、引

力波、宇宙學和系外行星。又要授予天體物理學嗎？你也許想像得到，物理學其他領域的人會開始抱怨。（賴因哈德・根舍）

We've known for a long time that the object in the galactic centre has a very high mass, and that it is highly plausible that it is a black hole. However, there's a difference between plausibility and physical certainty. That's why we design all kinds of tests, for which the centre of our Milky Way offers wonderful opportunities. In short: our current measurement of the gravitational redshift is already providing very strong evidence of the existence of the black hole in the galactic centre —— and of the general theory of relativity. (Reinhard Genzel)

我們早就知道，銀河系中心的物體有非常高的質量，它看似極可能是個黑洞。然而，看似可能不等於物理確定。因而，我們設計出各式各樣的測試，銀河系中心為之提供了絕妙的機會。簡而言之：我們目前對重力紅移的測量，已經為銀河系中心黑洞 —— 以及廣義相對論 —— 的存在提供了非常有力的證據。（賴因哈德・根舍）

There's so much that we don't understand, and from a scientist's point of view it's really most interesting to be working in the frontier area of our knowledge. (Andrea M. Ghez)

我們所不了解的東西如此眾多。從科學家的角度來看，在我們知識的前端領域工作，真是有趣極了。（安德烈婭・蓋茲）

As I've gotten older I've had a chance to think a little bit more about the question of diversity, and one of the things that I think can be an asset is not being part of the majority gives you an opportunity to do something that's new and different. It's often hard to do things that are different, and if you're already different there's I think, in some sense, there's an opportunity as long as you have the confidence to do things that are indeed different. (Andrea M. Ghez)

隨著年齡增加,我有了更多機會去思考多樣性的問題。我認為可以認定的好處之一是,不從眾,給自己機會去做新的、不同的事情。做與眾不同的事情通常很難。如果你已經與眾不同,我認為,在某種意義上,只要你有信心去做的確不同的事情,就會有機會。(安德烈婭・蓋茲)

I think it's a passion for the universe. I think the questions of the universe just inspired me, so I⋯ for me it was really following my passions, my curiosity about the universe. (Andrea M. Ghez)

我認為這是一種對宇宙的熱情。我認為宇宙問題恰好啟發了我,所以我⋯⋯對我來說,這就是追隨我的熱情,我關於宇宙的好奇心。[54](安德烈婭・蓋茲)

Black holes, because they are so hard to understand, is what makes them so appealing. I really think of science as a big, giant puzzle. (Andrea M. Ghez)

黑洞之所以如此吸引人,是因為它們這樣地難以理解。我實在認為科學是個龐大的、巨大的謎。(安德烈婭・蓋茲)

It amazes me every time we go to the telescope to think about "here is this light that we're capturing that's been on a journey for 26,000 years." And you know, if you think about 26,000 years ago when these photons left the vicinity around the black hole it's just ⋯ it's rather amazing to think we can do this as human beings. (Andrea M. Ghez)

---

[54] 在被問及是什麼促使她成為天體物理學家時,蓋茲這樣回答。

每當我們走向天文望遠鏡，想起「這就是我們正在捕捉的光線，它經歷了 26,000 年的旅程」時，我都大為驚奇。要知道，如果你想起 26,000 年前，這些光子離開黑洞附近之時，再想到我們作為人類，能夠做到這一點，這真是……實在是太不可思議了。（安德烈婭・蓋茲）

Nothing like competition to keep you going, to propel you forwards. (Andrea M. Ghez)

沒有什麼像競爭一樣保持你前進，推動你向前。（安德烈婭・蓋茲）

I think seeing people who look like you, or people who are different, succeeding shows you that there's an opportunity there, that you can do it, that this is a field that is open to you. (Andrea M. Ghez)

我認為，目睹跟你相似的人，或者不同的人成功，代表著其中有機會，你可以做到，這是向你開放的領域。（安德烈婭・蓋茲）

I hope I can inspire other young women into the field. It's a field that has so many pleasures, and if you are passionate about the science, there's so much that can be done. (Andrea M. Ghez)

希望我能激勵其他年輕女性進入這一領域。這是個樂趣叢生的領域，你如果對科學滿懷熱情，就有眾多的事情可做。（安德烈婭・蓋茲）

For sure one always needs to have some kind of big hypothesis or direction or interest, but sometimes you just hit something, certain components that you want to put together in a way that maybe does not make sense but you just want to do it. Scientists need to have the support to be able to do some crazy experiments to see where they go. My discovery has been a lesson for me that it's important to give scientists the freedom and the time to do such work. (Emmanuelle Charpentier)

2020 年

確實，一個人總是需要某種大的假設，方向或興趣；但有時你只是碰上什麼東西，某些部分你想以某種方式組合起來。這可能不合情理，可是你就是想這麼做。科學家需要得到支持，才能做一些瘋狂的實驗，看看它們結果如何。我的發現使我領會到，給科學家自由和時間去做這樣的工作是重要的。（埃馬紐埃爾・夏彭蒂耶）

For me, it was important to be independent and not to have anyone around me, and just to start my research the way I wanted to start my research. (Emmanuelle Charpentier)

對我來說，重要的是獨立自主，周圍不要有任何人，只是以我希望的方式開始研究。（埃馬紐埃爾・夏彭蒂耶）

I miss the time where I could be in the lab and a little bit freer, quieter, being able to focus on research. (Emmanuelle Charpentier)

我懷念能夠待在實驗室的時光，更自由一點，更安靜，能夠專注於研究。（埃馬紐埃爾・夏彭蒂耶）

That's life itself, with all its various aspects. Of course, I'd like more time. But I'm betting on becoming pretty old. I know so many scientists over 90 who are very active. I think I'm still going to be doing some great things later in life than most other people. So for that, I keep myself fit. (Emmanuelle Charpentier)

這[55]就是生活本身，包括它的各個方面。當然，我想要更多的時間。但肯定會變得很老。我認識許多年逾九十的科學家，都很活躍。我認為與大多數人相比，自己在晚年仍會做些大事。為此，我保持健康。（埃馬紐埃爾・夏彭蒂耶）

---

[55] 指科學。

I think we had a sense in those very early days, in my work with Emmanuelle, that you know we were onto something big, but I think we had no idea how big. And it still amazes me every day to see the extraordinary work that's going on now globally with this technology, and yeah, thinking back about how it really started with just a curiosity driven project. (Jennifer Doudna)

我想，在很早的那些日子，和埃馬紐埃爾[56]合作時，我們就有一種感覺，就是我們在做一件大事，不過我想我們不清楚有多大。現在每天看到全世界都在運用這種技術所做的非凡工作，我仍然大為驚奇，是的，回想一下當初，它是如何真的僅以一個由好奇心驅動的項目開始。（珍妮弗·道德納）

It's a great story of how curiosity driven research, aimed in one direction, ended up uncovering something that could be employed in a completely different way. (Jennifer Doudna)

這是個非凡的故事，講述了好奇心驅動的研究，如何朝向某一個方向發展，最終揭示了能夠以完全不同的方式運用的東西。（珍妮弗·道德納）

I hope that this prize and this recognition changes that at least a little bit, and that it's encouraging to other women who are in science, or even in other fields, to realise that, you know, their work can be honoured and that their work can have a real impact. And whether or not, you know, it's a Nobel Prize or something else, that women have a really important role to play in the world, and that their contributions are, you know, can have real impact that is noticed. (Jennifer Doudna)

---

[56] 即埃馬紐埃爾·夏彭蒂耶，兩人同獲 2020 年諾貝爾化學獎。

> 2020 年

我希望這個獎項和這種認可，至少造成些許改變，鼓勵從事科學工作的其他女性，甚或其他領域的女性，使她們意識到，就是，她們的工作能夠得到尊敬，她們的工作能夠產生真正的影響。要知道，無論是諾貝爾獎還是其他獎項，女性在世界上都扮演非常重要的角色。要知道，她們的貢獻能夠產生真正的影響，引起關注。（珍妮弗·道德納）

It was 4:45 I think on the east coast here. The phone rang… and who the heck is calling? And I didn't answer it. And then about 5 minutes later it rang again and still, still didn't answer it, and the third time I got up angrily to answer it. It was Stockholm. It was a weird, weird experience. (Harvey J. Alter)

東海岸這邊的時間是 4：45。電話響了……到底是誰打來的？我沒有接。接著大約 5 分鐘後它又響了，照舊，我還是沒接。第三次我生氣地起來去接。是從斯德哥爾摩打來的。這是一次非常、非常奇怪的經歷。（哈維·阿爾特）

It's so kind of other-worldly. Its something that you don't think will ever happen, and sometimes don't think you deserve it to happen. And then it happens in this crazy COVID year, just where everything is turned upside down. This is another, nice upside down for me. (Harvey J. Alter)

它實在非同尋常。它是你認為永遠不會發生的事情，有時你認為它不應該發生。然而它發生在這個瘋狂的新冠疫情之年，事事顛倒的時候。對我來說，這是另一種不錯的顛倒。（哈維·阿爾特）

My composite of awards leaves me with pangs of guilt that I have been singled out for accomplishments that were achieved only through vital collaborations. I owe everything to these collaborations and the associated investigators. Perhaps my main strength is that I chose my collaborators well and then built lifelong friendships with most of them. (Harvey J. Alter)

獲得的各種獎項使我深感內疚，因為入選所憑藉的成就是經由十分重要的合作獲得的。我將一切歸功於這些合作和有關研究人員。也許我的主要長處是合作者選得好，並與他們大多數人建立了一生的友誼。（哈維‧阿爾特）

College was where you really grow up. I changed, I think, dramatically in my first year of college. The lessons I learned just kind of stayed with me. (Harvey J. Alter)

大學是你真正成長的地方。我想，在大學第一年，自己發生了顯著的變化。學到的東西就那麼始終不忘。（哈維‧阿爾特）

You have to work on something that excites you a little bit. Find a field you like. Find a mentor who's known in that field. Cut your teeth in that environment. Then branch out. (Harvey J. Alter)

你必須從事某種能激發你的工作。找一個喜歡的領域。找一位在此領域有名氣的導師。在這個環境中獲得初步經驗。然後擴展專業。（哈維‧阿爾特）

Try to be the person that other people either want to come to you for advice, or want you to be their collaborator… It's very hard to do anything just by yourself these days, you gotta really work with others if you want to delve into something really deeply. (Harvey J. Alter)

盡力成為別人想向你尋求建議，或者想與你合作的人。現在單靠自己做什麼都非常難，想深入探究某事，你就得真正與人合作。（哈維‧阿爾特）

The biologic sciences always seemed more interesting to me than any other discipline… except, of course, baseball. I would have dropped medicine in a millisecond to play for the Brooklyn Dodgers. There were, however, certain impediments to my becoming a professional baseball player —— I couldn't hit and I couldn't field. Thus, I sublimated my "field of dreams" to become a doctor. (Harvey J. Alter)

在我看來，生物科學總是比其他任何學科更有趣。……當然了，棒球除外。假如能為布魯克林道奇隊打球，我會在一毫秒內放棄醫學。只是，要成為職業棒球手，還是有一定困難的 —— 我不會擊球，也當不了外野手。於是，我昇華了自己的「夢想場地」，成為一名醫生。（哈維・阿爾特）

I do not ruminate about death, but I empathize with Dylan Thomas who "raged against the dying of the light." My research light is dimming and I plan to retire before someone turns the light off for me. Retirement will be a difficult step, but I am beginning to come to grips with its inevitability and its prospects. (Harvey J. Alter)

我不思索死亡，但我能同理狄蘭・湯瑪斯[57]，他「怒斥光的消逝」。我的研究之光正在變暗，我打算在有人為我熄滅研究之光以前退休。退休將是艱難的一步，但我開始理解到它的必然性和可能行。（哈維・阿爾特）

A recurrent dilemma is how to give each member enough time, especially while continuing to work. Time has been my constant enemy. I have never had enough and never given enough to my family. I think I have been a reasonably good father and husband, but all of my relationships have suffered, to varying

---

[57] 狄蘭・湯瑪斯（1914—1953），英國詩人。

degrees, by the conflicting pull of time devoted to work. I have stolen time from my family not just to achieve professional goals, but also merely to keep up with all that was required. I have already written my graveside epitaph to encompass my recurrent temporal dilemma, namely, "As in life, he ran out of time." (Harvey J. Alter)

一個反覆出現的難題,是如何留給家裡每個人足夠的時間,尤其在持續工作之際。時間是我的宿敵。我從來沒有足夠的時間,也從來沒有滿足家人。我認為自己一直是個相當不錯的父親和丈夫,然而在不同程度上,由於工作時間導致的衝突,我所有的關係都受到了影響。我從家人那裡竊取時間,不僅是為了要達到職業目標,也是為了想跟上所有的要求。我已經擬就自己的墓碑銘文,概括反覆產生的現世困境,就是「猶如在生命中,他耗盡了時間」。(哈維・阿爾特)

We must have tried 30 different approaches at least over 7 or 8 years, and eventually we got one clone, after screening probably hundreds of millions of clones. So, yes, I work with some great people, without whom I would not have had this success. And we worked very hard, and so a lot of hard work and persistence was part of our success story, for sure. (Michael Houghton)

我們肯定至少用了七、八年時間,嘗試過 30 種不同的方法,終於在篩選數億個殖株之後,得到一個殖株。所以,是的,我和一些了不起的人一起工作,沒有他們,我不會獲得這一項成就。我們的工作非常艱苦,所以,大量的艱苦工作和堅持不懈是我們成功故事的一部分,毫無疑問。(麥可・霍頓)

It is, I think, a success story for biomedical science and team science. (Charles M. Rice)

我認為，這是生物醫學科學和團隊科學的一個成功故事。（查爾斯·M·賴斯）

The activity around the world on this virus is breath taking, and it's changing the way that science is done. It shows you what can be done if people really mobilise and work together and bring different expertise to a common problem. (Charles M. Rice)

全世界對這種病毒的研究令人驚嘆，它在改變科學的行動方式。它顯示了，人們如果真正動員起來，一起工作，帶著不同的專業知識解決共同的問題，就能夠獲得怎樣的成就。（查爾斯·M·賴斯）

I am suspicious of my existing ideas, my conscious thoughts and convictions. They are what I need to get beyond, into ignorance and after that, with luck, discovery. (Louise Glück)

我懷疑自己既有的想法，自己意識到的思想和信念。我需要超越它們，進入無知，隨後，幸運的話，獲得發現。（露伊絲·葛綠珂）

You have to live your life if you're going to do original work. Your work will come out of an authentic life. (Louise Glück)

想成就原創作品，你就得認真生活。你的作品將出自真正的人生。（露伊絲·葛綠珂）

Some work is done through suffering, through impoverishment, through the involuntary relinquishing of a self. (Louise Glück)

有些工作是經由受苦、清貧、無意間忘卻自我而完成的。（露伊絲·葛綠珂）

It had occurred to me that all human beings are divided into those who wish to move forward and those who wish to go back. Or you could say, those who wish to keep moving and those who want to be stopped in their tracks as by the blazing sword. (Louise Glück)

我認為，人分成兩類，一類想前進，一類想後退。或者可以說，一些想繼續走的人，以及一些彷彿被炙熱的劍攔住而想停下來的人。（露伊絲・葛綠珂）

He was the advisor everybody recommended you should have. (Paul Milgrom)

他[58]是人人都建議你應當找的指導老師。（保羅・米爾格龍）

We're both nerds in, you know, in a certain way. (Paul Milgrom)

你知道，在某種意義上，我們[59]都是書呆子。（保羅・米爾格龍）

I've been more of a speculative thinker, and he is very precise. (Robert B. Wilson)

我更多地是個慣於思索的人，他[60]則行事一絲不苟。（羅伯特・B・威爾遜）

I take great pride in him because he was my PhD student so I take a lot of pride in having sort of at an early stage influenced him, and in this whole field of market design and auction design. This of course, by the way, is the third of my students who've won Nobel Prizes. (Robert B. Wilson)

---

[58] 指羅伯特・B・威爾遜（Robert B. Wilson），米爾格羅姆的博士指導老師。兩人共同獲得了2020年諾貝爾經濟學獎。
[59] 指他本人和威爾遜。
[60] 指米爾格龍。

2020 年

　他[61]使我大為得意，因為是我的博士生，所以我為對他有所影響而格外自豪，在早期，以及在整個市場設計和拍賣設計領域。當然了，順帶一題，這是我第三位獲得諾貝爾獎的學生。（羅伯特・B・威爾遜）

---

[61]　指米爾格龍。

2011–2020 科技反思與人性的回望

2021–2024
危機年代的希望之聲

2021 年

The medal was heavier than I thought.（Syukuro Manabe）

這個獎牌的分量比我想像的重。[62]（真鍋淑郎）

I never imagined that this thing I was beginning to study would have such huge consequences. I was doing it just because of my curiosity. I really enjoyed studying climate change. Curiosity is the thing which drives all my research activity. It is great fun to use a model to study how climate change over the last 400 million years has evolved.（Syukuro Manabe）

我從未想到我開始研究的這個東西會有如此巨大的影響。我這麼做只是出於好奇心。我真的很喜歡研究氣候變化。好奇心是我所有研究活動的動力。用一個模型來研究氣候變化在過去 4 億年裡如何演變是非常有趣的。（真鍋淑郎）

I must have been about 13 years old… I wanted to better understand the puzzling phenomenon that you could get something from nothing. I went to the town library in order to find out in books on physics for beginners how

---

[62] 頒獎儀式後真鍋淑郎告訴記者。

electricity and radios work. That was my introduction to physics. At that time, it was an exciting experience for me, completely independent of the fact that I was taught physics in school. I did not see any connection between our physics lessons in school and my personal learning from the books in the library —— I think this experience of personal learning and discovery was very important for me. (Klaus Hasselmann)

那時我應該是13歲左右。……我想更了解人們憑空可見的費解現象。我去了鎮上的圖書館，以便在物理初級讀物中了解電力和無線電的工作原理。那是我的物理學入門。當時，它是一種使我感到激動的經歷，跟學校實際上教授的物理完全無關。在學校的物理課與我由圖書館書中的個人所學之間，我看不到任何關聯 —— 我認為這種個人學習和發現的經歷，對於我非常重要。（克勞斯・哈塞爾曼）

I wanted to work in an area in which I thought I would be able to contribute something. I always had a practical bent; I wanted to work on problems which I thought I would be able to solve. I did not want to work on abstract, theoretical problems, and I did not have enough self-confidence to think I could make significant contributions to such difficult fields as general relativity or quantum field theory. (Klaus Hasselmann)

我想在一個自認能有所貢獻的領域工作。我總是趨於務實，我想從事自認能解決的問題。我不想研究抽象的、理論上的問題，也沒有足夠的自信，以為有能力在諸如廣義相對論或量子場論等高難度領域做出重大貢獻。（克勞斯・哈塞爾曼）

My mentor Nicola Cabibbo was usually saying that we should work on a problem only if working on the problem is fun. (Giorgio Parisi)

我的導師尼古拉・卡比博經常說，只有在解決問題是有趣的時候，我們才應該解決問題。（喬治・帕里西）

There are very, very simple problems that are very hard to understand. (Giorgio Parisi)

有些非常、非常簡單的問題非常難以理解。（喬治・帕里西）

Fundamental science is crucial. It's crucial for understanding everything, and will not go too much towards, only in applied science, but it's important that applied science and fundamental science go together. Because many times the application from fundamental science to applied science, applications that can be useful to humanity come in some unexpected ways from your science. (Giorgio Parisi)

基礎科學十分重要。它對於理解一切都十分重要，並且不會前進過遠，只是涉及應用科學，然而重要的是應用科學和基礎科學是分不開的。因為許多時候，從基礎科學到應用科學的應用，有利於人類的應用，會以一些意想不到的方式來自於你的學科。（喬治・帕里西）

It's difficult to explain to people who are not chemists, and specially not synthetic chemists, because we really think, and maybe it's naive or weird, but we really think our molecules have a certain beauty to them. And then, making them is like creating something beautiful… And then there's another aspect. It's not just the molecules that are beautiful but also the way to making them… Yeah, honestly it's just a joy, and I would argue most chemists do this because they love it and enjoy it. (Benjamin List)

很難對不是化學家，尤其非合成化學家的人解釋，因為我們真的認為，也許天真或怪異吧，但我們真的認為，我們的分子具有某種美感。

然後，製作它們就像創造美麗的東西。……然後還有另一個方面。美麗的不僅僅是分子，還有製作它們的方法。……是的，老實說，這只是一種樂趣，我會說大多數化學家這樣做是由於熱愛它並享受它。（本亞明・利斯特）

The beauty of catalysis is that it's a very important technology, some would say the most important technology that we have on the planet for humanity. (Benjamin List)

催化的美妙之處在於它是一項非常重要的技術，有人會說是我們在這個星球上為人類所擁有的最重要的技術。（本亞明・利斯特）

I thought it was a prank. I've had a lot of mischievous grad students and co-workers over the years. I got a text from Ben saying, "I just got off the phone with the Swedish Academy, they're trying to reach you," and I said, "Somebody is pranking us. I bet you a thousand dollars it's not real. I'm going back to bed." And I did go back to sleep! But then my phone started blowing up with calls and texts, and I realized it was really happening. So I'm a thousand dollars poorer, but happier! (David W.C. MacMillan)

我還以為是惡作劇呢。這些年來，我遇到過很多淘氣的研究生和同事。我收到本[63]的簡訊說：「我剛和瑞典學院通完電話，他們想聯絡你。」我說：「有人在捉弄我們。我跟你賭一千塊這不是真的。我要回去睡覺了。」我真的又睡著了！但後來我的電話和簡訊都被打爆了，我意識到這一切真的發生了。所以我少了一千塊錢，但多了快樂！（戴維・麥克米倫）

What we care about is trying to invent chemistry that has an impact on society and can do some good, and I am thrilled to have a part in that. Organo-

---

[63] 本，即與麥克米倫同獲 2021 年諾貝爾化學獎的本亞明・利斯特。

catalysis was a pretty simple idea that really sparked a lot of different research, and the part we're just so proud of is that you don't have to have huge amounts of equipment and huge amounts of money to do fine things in chemistry. (David W.C. MacMillan)

我們意在設法發明對社會產生影響並能帶來一些益處的化學過程，我非常高興參與其中。有機催化是個很簡單的想法，它確實引發了許多不同的研究，而我們尤其引以為傲的是，你不必擁有大量的設備和大量的資金，就可以在化學領域做各種精妙的事情。（戴維·麥克米倫）

We all know there's a real lack of drugs and approaches to treat chronic pain. I think we need some new insights and new ideas for treating pain, pharmacologically and other ways, and I think our work will contribute to that. (David Julius)

我們都知道治療慢性疼痛的藥物和方法是真正缺乏的。我認為我們需要一些藥理學和其他方式的新見解和新想法來治療疼痛，而我認為我們的工作將為此做出貢獻。（戴維·朱利葉斯）

We don't go into this thinking we're going to win prizes, we just do it for the thrill of discovering something. There's a time when you make a discovery when you're the only person on the planet —— or at least you think you're the only person on the planet —— who knows the answer to a particular question, and that's a really thrilling moment. That's what most of us live for. (David Julius)

我們不沉迷於爭取獲獎這種想法，我們只是為了有所發現的激動而行事。一時之間，當你做出發現，而這時你是地球上唯一 —— 或者至少自認是地球上唯一 —— 知道特定問題答案的人時，這才是真正令人激動的時刻。這才是我們大多數人夢寐以求的事情。（戴維·朱利葉斯）

In science many times it's things we take for granted that are of high interest. (Ardem Patapoutian)

在科學中，很多時候，人們以為理所當然的事情才是我們具有高度興趣的。（阿登・帕塔普蒂安）

One of the beautiful things about basic science is that it takes you in directions that you never anticipate. There's a long way ahead of us to figure out what indications this could be useful for as well as actual treatments that we could develop. (Ardem Patapoutian)

基礎科學的一個美妙之處，是它帶你前往從未想到的方向。要釐清這可能對哪些症狀有用，以及我們可以開發的實際療法，我們還有很長的路要走。（阿登・帕塔普蒂安）

Writing has always been a pleasure. Even as a boy at school, I looked forward to the class set aside for writing a story or whatever our teachers thought would interest us more than to any other class on a timetable. (Abdulrazak Gurnah)

寫作一直都是一種樂趣。甚至在上小學時，我就期盼專門用來寫故事的課堂，或者老師認為會比課程表上其他任何內容都使我們更感興趣的課堂。（阿卜杜勒－拉扎克・古納）

I'm not perfect. I'm unfulfilled. (Abdulrazak Gurnah)

我不完美。我不滿足。（阿卜杜勒－拉扎克・古納）

Close your eyes. Imagine the world as it should be. Now go and make it happen. (Maria Ressa)

閉上眼睛。想像理想的世界。現在就去實現它。（瑪麗亞・雷薩）

When you play football or hockey, you can win the championship, take your prize, go home and get ready for the next season. Here it's the exact opposite. It's not a prize in the sense of a celebration for the journalistic community. It feels like getting a magic wand that you don't quite know how to use. (Andreyevich Muratov)

參加足球或曲棍球賽時，你可以贏得冠軍，獲獎凱旋，為下一個賽季做好準備。這裡情況截然相反。這個獎對於新聞界來說稱不上是種慶賀。這種感覺就像得到一根你不清楚該如何使用的魔杖。（德米特里·穆拉托夫）

I don't really know. Sometimes there are questions that have been hanging out there in the world for a very long time. And I see myself as having a list of those questions at the back of my head and someone then creates a new dataset or a new theoretical model that makes me rethink them. (David Card)

我真的不確定。有時候一些問題已經在世間存在了很長的時間。我自己覺得心底有一串這一類的問題，然後有人建立了新的資料庫或新的理論模型，使我重新思考這些問題。[64]（戴維·卡德）

I always do one thing at a time. I prefer to get really into one project, have it all in my head, remember exactly what I'm doing, and then finish it and move on. I hate multitasking. (David Card)

我一向每次只做一件事。我更願意扎扎實實地專注於一個項目，把它完全放在心上，牢記自己在做什麼，然後完成它，再做別的。我討厭一併承擔多項任務。（戴維·卡德）

---

[64] 對「你的研究想法從何而來」之問的回答。

I had great teachers, and great teachers make all the difference in a student's life. Looking back on it, the important thing was I discovered economics and it's something I loved and was good at. And everything else is sort of second-order in retrospect. (Joshua D. Angrist)

當年我有出色的老師，而出色的老師使學生的人生大為改觀。如今回首，重要的是我發現了經濟學，它是我熱愛和擅長的事情。回想起來，其他一切均屬次要。（約書亞·D·安格里斯特）

Acts demolish their alternatives, that is the paradox. We can't know what lies at the end of the road not taken. (Joshua D. Angrist)

行動銷毀了他們的其他選擇，這就是悖論。我們無法知曉在不曾選取的道路的終點有些什麼。（約書亞·D·安格里斯特）

There's a lot of projects I'm working on that I'm excited about, and the only sad thing is there's not more hours in the day. (Guido W. Imbens)

我手邊在做的項目很多，它們令我興奮，而唯一難過的事情是，一天中沒有更多的時間。（吉多·因本斯）

I like working with the students, working with young, smart people. There's nothing better than that. (Guido W. Imbens)

我喜歡和學生們一起工作，和年輕、聰明的人們一起工作。沒有比這更好的事情了。（吉多·因本斯）

2022 年

Well, it's of course a surprise because we know that there are so many outstanding physicists who deserve it⋯ (Alain Aspect)

（被問及對獲獎消息的反應）嗯，這當然是個驚喜，因為我們知道有這麼多傑出的物理學家值得擁有它⋯⋯（阿蘭·阿斯佩）

The development of quantum mechanics early in the twentieth century obliged physicists to change radically the concepts they used to describe the world. (Alain Aspect)

20 世紀早期量子力學的發展，迫使物理學家從根本上改變他們用來描述世界的觀念。（阿蘭·阿斯佩）

The main ingredient of the first quantum revolution, wave-particle duality, has led to inventions such as the transistor and the laser that are at the root of the information society. (Alain Aspect)

第一次量子革命的主要成分，波粒二象性，導致了電晶體和雷射等發明，它們是資訊社會的根源。（阿蘭·阿斯佩）

If he/she is deeply attracted by the domain, he/she should go without too much thinking and hesitation, because things are totally open and we have no idea of how it will evolve in the coming years. But it is sure that all the efforts that are invested will give interesting results, many unexpected. So better be in the action rather than observing it. (Alain Aspect)

他或她（有意加入量子領域的科學家或企業家）若深為這個領域所吸引，就應當不存過多的考慮和猶豫，因為前景是完全開放的，我們不清楚未來幾年它將如何發展。但肯定的是，投入的所有努力都會產生有趣的結果，許多是意想不到的。所以最好是行動起來而非一味觀望。（阿蘭‧阿斯佩）

History of inventions (eg transistor, laser, optical fibers) show that when there is a need and a market, engineers are extraordinary good at fighting noise, this is why I am confident. (Alain Aspect)

根據發明史（例如電晶體、雷射、光纖），當需求和市場存在時，工程師們是極其擅長抵制非議的，這就是我具備信心的原因。（阿蘭‧阿斯佩）

It will remain remarkable, in whatever way our future concepts may develop, that the very study of the external world led to the scientific conclusion that the content of the consciousness is the ultimate universal reality. (Alain Aspect)

無論我們未來的觀念可能如何發展，對外部世界的研究都得出了科學結論，即意識的內容是最根本的普遍現實，這將始終值得注意。（阿蘭‧阿斯佩）

I got waked up at three in the morning. So far it took me over an hour to even get my pants on, there were so many phone calls. (John Clauser)

（獲獎消息傳開當天）我凌晨3點就被叫醒了。到現在甚至花了一個多小時才套上褲子，接到這麼多的電話。（約翰‧克勞澤）

We can see that too often scientists are conservative and sometimes even emotionally against what they perceive as speculation. The really new in science cannot be logical consequences of what we know already⋯ that would just be the next logical step. I don't want to belittle the more down-to-earth approach in the sciences but I find it more interesting to ask bold new questions. (John Clauser)

不難看到，科學家常常是保守的，有時甚至出於情感而反對他們視為推論的見解。科學中真正的新事物不可能是已知事理的邏輯推論……那只是下一個邏輯階段。我不想貶低科學中更腳踏實地的方法，但我發現提出大膽的新問題更有趣。（約翰‧克勞澤）

You have to set goals that are wildly ambitious. The point is that completely new technologies will emerge that we never predicted. Look at the laser. When it was invented (50 years ago) nobody predicted the two most common applications we see today —— the CD player and the supermarket scanner. Nobody predicted this —— that's the way it always works. (John Clauser)

你得設立雄心勃勃的目標。關鍵是會冒出我們從未料到的全新技術。看看雷射。當它發明時（50 年前），沒人預料到我們如今所見的兩種最常見的應用 —— CD 播放器和超市掃描器。沒有人預料到這個 —— 這就是它一向的做法。（約翰‧克勞澤）

Even in the most basic sciences you cannot work without bold attempts taking risks. You have to be open, you have to be challenging —— this is the interesting stuff. I wouldn't like to look at science as just one more step here or one more step there. (John Clauser)

即使在最基本的科學中，沒有大膽的冒險嘗試你也無法工作。你必須保持開放，必須富於挑戰性 —— 這是有趣的事情。我不願將科學視作淺嘗輒止、零打碎敲。（約翰‧克勞澤）

I was having fun. It was a challenging experiment. I thought it was important at the time, even though everybody told me I was crazy and was going to ruin my career by doing it. And to some extent I did —— I've never been a professor. (John Clauser)

（對貝爾定理進行首次實驗測試）我做得心情舒暢。它是個具有挑戰性的實驗。我那時就認為它意義重大，儘管人人都對我說我瘋了，這麼做將毀掉我的職業生涯。在某種程度上的確如此 —— 我始終沒當上教授。（約翰・克勞澤）

My dad was absolutely a marvelous teacher, my whole formative years. Every time I asked a question, he knew the answer and would answer it in gory detail so that I would understand it. I mean, he didn't force feed me, but he did it in such a way that I continuously hungered for more. (John Clauser)

在我的整個成長歲月中，我老爸絕對是一位了不起的老師。每次我提出問題，他都知道答案，並不厭其詳地回答，從而讓我理解。我要說，他並非硬性灌輸，而是因勢利導，以使我接著渴求更多。（約翰・克勞澤）

I think there is a need for something completely new. Something that is too different, too unexpected, to be accepted as yet. (Anton Zeilinger)

我認為需要某種全新的東西。某種大為不同，大出意料，以至尚難以接受的東西。（安東・蔡林格）

You have to have some confidence in your intuition and crazy ideas. (Anton Zeilinger)

你必須對自己的直覺和瘋狂的想法具備一定信心。（安東・蔡林格）

2022 年

I don't want to do things that are mainstream. (Anton Zeilinger)

我不想做主流的事情。（安東・蔡林格）

Real breakthroughs are not found because you want to develop some new technology, but because you are curious and want to find out how the world is. (Anton Zeilinger)

真正的突破不是由於你想開發些新技術而找到，而是由於你好奇，想釐清世界是何等樣貌。（安東・蔡林格）

Vienna was a special place. My supervisor Helmut Rauch created a climate where you could do things. That was unusual and not often the case around the world: that you could just pursue your curiosity. (Anton Zeilinger)

維也納是個特別的地方。指導我的赫爾穆特・勞赫製造了一種你可以為所欲為的氛圍。這是不尋常的，全天下都不常見：你可以只追求自己的好奇心。（安東・蔡林格）

During the first experiments, I was asked what it was supposed to be good for. I answered proudly: it's not good for anything. I am just doing this out of curiosity because I have been completely fascinated by quantum physics from the start. (Anton Zeilinger)

在最初的實驗中，有人問我它會有什麼益處。我自鳴得意地答道：什麼益處都沒有。我這樣做只是出於好奇，因為我從一開始就徹底被量子物理迷住了。（安東・蔡林格）

Someday, when we truly understand quantum physics, it will be even more revolutionary than the achievements of Copernicus and Columbus —— and for everyone, not just us physicists. (Anton Zeilinger)

有朝一日，當我們真正理解量子物理學時，它將甚至比哥白尼和哥倫布的成就更具革命性 —— 對每個人而言，不僅對我們物理學家。（安東‧蔡林格）

I believe in the future of humankind. As long as there are children, as long as there are people who look up at the night sky in sheer wonder, as long as there is music and poetry and the Mona Lisa —— and old monasteries and young artists and fledgling scientists and all the other expressions of human creativity —— I will remain optimistic. (Anton Zeilinger)

我信任人類的未來。只要有孩子，只要有人純粹驚奇地仰望夜空，只要有音樂、詩歌和〈蒙娜‧麗莎〉—— 還有古老的修道院、年輕的藝術家、初出茅廬的科學家以及人類創造力的所有其他表現 —— 我就會保持樂觀。（安東‧蔡林格）

I love organic chemistry, I'm fascinated by biology. Like all of us, you know, I've had family members and close friends who've suffered from ailments that were so untreatable. It was always my hope that as a scientist I could make some contributions that might benefit human health, either in the near term or the long term, or not even necessarily in my lifetime, but that was always my goal. (Carolyn R. Bertozzi)

我鍾愛有機化學，我深為生物學所吸引。跟大家都一樣，你知道，我有親人和好友苦於很難醫治的病痛。我總是希望，作為科學家，我能做出一些有益於人類健康的貢獻，或早或晚，甚至並非得在我有生之年，但這始終是我的目標。（卡羅琳‧貝爾托西）

Chemistry is the central science, as we call it. And it's such an exciting area of science for people who want to have an impact in biology and medicine and materials and climate and sustainability, right? Chemistry is so central to all of it. (Carolyn R. Bertozzi)

化學是核心科學,如我們所稱。而對於想在生物學、醫學、材料、氣候和永續性方面產生影響的人們,它是個非常激勵人心的科學領域。(卡羅琳・貝爾托西)

Opportunities drive by you and if you are lucky you notice a few. We probably miss a lot as we cannot pay attention to every little thing and only have so much bandwidth. But opportunities are always driving by, and if you see it, you should get on the bus and see where the path takes you. (Carolyn R. Bertozzi)

機會總是從你身旁駛過,你如果夠幸運,就會注意到一些。我們很可能錯過許多,因為只有這麼大的頻寬,無法關注每件小事。但機會總是在駛過,你要是看到,就應當上車,看看這條路線把你帶到何處。(卡羅琳・貝爾托西)

Great discoveries are not done behind the office desk, they are done in the laboratory. Having an idea, making very creative experiments, having a keen observational eye —— you'll see that there's always something odd going on because nature is very, very complex. (Morten Meldal)

了不起的發現不是在辦公桌後做出來的,它們是在實驗室裡完成的。產生一個想法,進行富於創造性的實驗,擁有敏銳觀察的眼睛——你會發現總是有奇怪的事情發生,因為大自然非常、非常之複雜。(莫滕・梅爾達爾)

The reality is much more complex than we as chemists are able to imagine, and new things come up all the time, and will forever. And I think there is no way that we will ever know everything. And the complexity of organic chemistry, also reflected in complexity of life, is very, very high. (Morten Meldal)

現實比我們身為化學家所能想像的複雜得多,新事物不斷出現,而且永無休止。我認為我們不可能事事盡知。有機化學的複雜性是非常、非常高的,這也反映在生命之複雜性上。(莫滕‧梅爾達爾)

There are two really fundamental sciences, and that is chemistry and physics. Because chemistry and physics, those describe everything that happens everywhere, whereas the other science fields —— like biology and so on —— is very, very interesting, and essential to our understanding of life, and our own lives as well. But it's not a fundamental understanding of reality as it is with chemistry. (Morten Meldal)

真正的基礎科學有兩門,那就是化學和物理學。因為化學和物理學,它們描述到處發生的一切,而其他科學領域 —— 如生物學等 —— 非常、非常有趣,對於我們理解生命,以及我們自己的生活十分重要。但它不像化學那樣,不是對現實的根本理解。(莫滕‧梅爾達爾)

One of my favourite quotes is by Einstein "If at first the idea is not absurd, then there's no hope for it". (Karl Barry Sharpless)

我最喜歡的引語之一出自愛因斯坦:「想法如果起初不荒唐,那就沒有希望。」(卡爾‧巴里‧沙普利斯)

When I started doing chemistry, I did it the way I fished —— for the excitement, the discovery, the adventure, for going after the most elusive catch imaginable in uncharted seas. (Karl Barry Sharpless)

> 2022 年

　　我開始從事化學研究時，是以自己釣魚的方式進行的——為了興奮、發現、冒險，為了追求未知海洋中所能設想出最難的捕獲。（卡爾・巴里・沙普利斯）

　　You should be drawn to uncertainty, that's the point I guess. And as a discoverer, or adventurer, or somebody who wants to be a hero, basically we're all trying to do something that most people aren't. (Karl Barry Sharpless)

　　你應當受不確定性吸引，我認為這就是重點。作為發現者，或冒險家，或想成為英雄的人，基本上我們都在力圖做大多數人不做的事情。（卡爾・巴里・沙普利斯）

　　Chemists usually write about their chemical careers in terms of the different areas and the discrete projects in those areas on which they have worked. Essentially all my chemical investigations, however, are in only one area, and I tend to view my research not with respect to projects, but with respect to where I've been driven by two passions which I acquired in graduate school: I am passionate about the Periodic Table (and selenium, titanium and osmium are absolutely thrilling), and I am passionate about catalysis. What the ocean was to the child, the Periodic Table is to the chemist; new catalytic reactivity is, of course, my personal coelacanth. (Karl Barry Sharpless)

　　化學家們書寫自己的化學生涯，通常根據不同的領域，以及工作過的諸領域中的各個項目。然而，我所有的化學研究基本都只在一個領域中，我也傾向於無視項目，而是看重自己始終被兩種熱情驅動所至之處，這兩種熱情則是我在研究所時獲得的：我熱衷於元素週期表（硒、鈦和鋨絕對令人激動），我熱衷於催化。海洋之於幼童，即為元素週期表之

於化學家；新的催化活性，當然就是我個人的腔棘魚[65]了。（卡爾‧巴里‧沙普利斯）

I think instinct is important for me, I know that. And I told you that if I come back at an idea after whatever small timescale or large one, but if the damn thing comes back to me and says "you don't know the answer to this," why is it coming back? And then I'd say, I've got to give that respect and try it again because it's subconsciously alive, right? And, yeah. (Karl Barry Sharpless)

我認為直覺對於我很重要，這個我很清楚。我跟你講過，如果我不論多久之後記起一個想法，而如果這個該死的東西回來對我說：「你不知道這個問題的答案」，它為什麼要回來？這時我會說，我必須重視它，再試一下，因為它在潛意識中是活的，對吧？而且，是的。（卡爾‧巴里‧沙普利斯）

We have a word game in English called "Twenty questions." To play Twenty Questions, one player imagines some object, and the other players must guess what it is by asking questions that can be answered with a "yes" or a "no." I imagine every language has a similar game, and, for those of us who speak the language of science, the game is called The Scientific Method. (Karl Barry Sharpless)

有一個英文文字遊戲，叫做「20 問」。要提 20 個問題，一個玩家設想某個物體，其他玩家則必須透過提出可以用「是」或「否」回答的問題，來猜測它是什麼。我想，每種語言都有類似的遊戲，而對於我們這些使用科學語言的人，這個遊戲稱為科學方法。（卡爾‧巴里‧沙普利斯）

---

[65] 腔棘魚長期被認為數千萬年前即已滅絕，20 世紀中葉卻在非洲捕到個別現生種類。

2022 年

There were errors and setbacks along the way, but today the information extracted from ancient genomes contributes to our understanding of the evolution and history of humans and many other organisms. (Svante Pääbo)

一路上不乏錯誤和挫折，但今天從古代基因組中提取的資訊有助於我們理解人類和許多其他生物的演化和歷史。（斯萬特・帕博）

The development of this research field has been —— and continues to be —— a great adventure for me! (Svante Pääbo)

這個研究領域的發展對於我一直是 —— 並繼續是 —— 非凡的冒險！（斯萬特・帕博）

I accept this honor as a recognition not only of the work of our research group, but of everybody who has contributed to this field as well. (Svante Pääbo)

我接受這一項榮譽，不僅作為對我們研究團隊工作的認同，同樣作為對在這個領域做出貢獻的每個人的認同。（斯萬特・帕博）

The biggest influence in my life was for sure my mother, with whom I grew up. And in some sense it makes me a bit sad that she can't experience this day. She sort of was very much into science, and very much stimulated and encouraged me through the years. (Svante Pääbo)

對我生命影響最大的無疑是我的母親，我的成長離不開她。她無法親身經歷這一天多少使我有些難過。她真的非常喜歡科學，多年來一直大力激勵和支持我。（斯萬特・帕博）

I live for writing. I write most of the time here in my house. Sometimes I wonder if I've missed out on something because I've subordinated everything to writing. But when I read the many letters in which people tell me how important my books are to them and how they have changed their lives, then I think to myself: it was worth it. Maybe that's exactly what I'm here for. (Annie Ernaux)

我為寫作而活。大多數時間都在家中寫作。有時我想知道，自己是不是錯過了什麼，使一切都服從了寫作。然而當我讀到許多來信，人們從中告知，我的書對他們有多麼重要，以及它們如何改變了其生活時，我自忖：這是值得的。也許這正是我在此處的目的。（安妮・艾諾）

It's the work of a novelist to tell the truth. Sometimes I don't know what truth I'm looking for, but it's always a truth that I'm seeking. (Annie Ernaux)

說實話是小說家的工作。有時我不知道自己在尋找什麼真相，但它始終是我在尋覓的一種真相。（安妮・艾諾）

When I think of my life, I see my story since childhood until today, but I cannot separate it from the world in which I lived; my story is mixed with that of my generation and the events that happened to us. In the autobiographical tradition we speak about ourselves and the events are the background. I have reversed this. This is the story of events and progress and everything that has changed in 60 years of an individual existence but transmitted through the "we" and "them". The events in my book belong to everyone, to history, to sociology. (Annie Ernaux)

想到自己的生活時，我看見自己從小至今的故事，但無法將它與我生活的世界分開；我的故事與我這代人的故事以及發生在我們身上的事件混合在一起。在自傳傳統中，我們談論自己，事件是背景。我已經扭轉了這一點。這是關於事件和發展在個人存在的 60 年中變化的故事，但

2022 年

經由「我們」和「他們」訴說。書 [66] 中的事件屬於每個人，屬於歷史，屬於社會學。（安妮・艾諾）

The book has been well received in Germany and Italy and has been translated into Chinese, so it must have an appeal that is greater than just (as) a history of France. Even if I don't say it directly, it's clearly history through an individual life, my life, and through my memory. I am recounting this collective history via my feelings and recollections. The main character is time and its passing, which takes everything with it including our lives. (Annie Ernaux)

這本書 [67] 在德國和義大利都大受好評，並被譯成中文，所以它必定比一本法國史更具有吸引力。雖然我不直說，它顯然是經由個人生活，我的生活，經由我的記憶的歷史。我在透過我的感受和回憶來敘述這段集體歷史。主角是時間及其流逝，它帶走一切，包括我們的生活。（安妮・艾諾）

In research, that you have a program, you have a plan, but on any given day, you have a set of specific problems you have to solve. And keeping your mind focused on those problems helps you keep things in balance. (Ben Shalom Bernanke)

在研究中，你有個規畫，有個計畫，但在每個具體的日子，你都有一系列特定的問題需要解決。而把注意力集中在這些問題上有助於保持平衡。（班・柏南奇）

A perennial question is whether economics is really a science. It's true, for example, that we economists can't do large-scale controlled experiments,

---

[66]　指《悠悠歲月》（Les Années）。
[67]　即《悠悠歲月》。

although neither can evolutionary biologists or seismologists. However, one thing we surely have in common with physics, chemistry, and the rest, is that ignorance or misapplication of basic principles can result in enormous damage. In economics, that damage can take the form of financial crises and economic depressions. (Ben Shalom Bernanke)

一個長期的問題是，經濟學是否真的是一門科學。例如，我們經濟學家確實不能做大規模的控制實驗，儘管演化生物學家或地震學家也不能。然而，我們肯定與物理學、化學和其他學科有一個共同點，即對基本原理的無知或誤用會導致巨大的損害。在經濟學中，這種損害可以表現為金融危機和經濟蕭條。（班·柏南奇）

While financial and economic crises often have terrible human costs, at least they can give us insight into how economies and financial systems work, why they break down, and how we might avoid such outcomes. For that reason, all this year's economics laureates have been recognized for work on banking and financial crises and their effects. (Ben Shalom Bernanke)

儘管金融和經濟危機常常造成人們慘重的損失，它們至少可以讓我們深入了解經濟和金融體系如何運作，它們為什麼崩潰，以及我們如何避免這種後果。由於這個原因，今年的經濟學獎得主均因在銀行和金融危機及其影響方面的工作而得到認可。（班·柏南奇）

The famous investor Warren Buffet once said, "It's when the tide goes out that you can see who is swimming naked." Financial crises separate the prepared from the unprepared. Our work, and that of many other economists, is aimed at assuring both that the financial system is prepared, and that the tide doesn't go out very often. (Ben Shalom Bernanke)

> 2022年

著名投資人華倫・巴菲特說過：「退潮時你才能看到誰在裸泳。」金融危機將有準備的人和沒有準備的人區分開來。我們，還有許多其他經濟學者的工作，旨在確保金融體系做好準備，並且潮水不致輕易退去。（班・柏南奇）

I think this research area is still incomplete, and I hope more people keep thinking about it. But the thing I'm most excited about is that this is still an important area where we only know this much. (Douglas W. Diamond)

我認為這個研究領域仍然不完善，希望更多的人繼續思考它。但我最興奮的是，這仍然是一個重要的領域，我們只知道這麼多。（道格拉斯・戴蒙德）

We all take our each other's research very seriously, so we all go to seminars and listen and try to make sure there aren't any holes in the research. We're all sort of research-aholics here. This is part of our fun —— doing the research. (Douglas W. Diamond)

我們都非常認真地對待彼此的研究，所以都去參加研討會，傾聽並設法確保研究沒有任何漏洞。我們在這裡都多少是研究狂。這是我們樂趣的一部分 —— 做研究。（道格拉斯・戴蒙德）

We had a more complicated idea in the beginning and we kept simplifying it. And Phil is among the clearest thinkers of anyone I know in social science. So the fact that our model is quite clear and simple would not be possible without him as a co-author. (Douglas W. Diamond)

我們起初有個更複雜的想法，我們一直在簡化它。在社會科學界，菲爾[68]屬於我所知頭腦最清晰的人。所以，我們的模型非常清晰簡單這

---

[68] 即菲利普・迪布維格。

一項事實，沒有他作為共同作者是不可能的。（道格拉斯·戴蒙德）

I really wish my PhD adviser Steve Ross could be here to see this. He should have had a Nobel Prize. He would have been happy to see one of his students receive this. (Philip H. Dybvig)

我真的希望我的博士指導老師史蒂芬·羅斯能在這裡看到這個。他應當獲得諾貝爾獎的。他會很高興看到他的一個學生獲得這個。（菲利普·迪布維格）

Doug is an amazing guy and he's a great co-author. And we worked so hard to make the paper simple⋯ And I think it paid off some because the model's pretty simple. It's easy to extend, with you know, we've left some room where people can add some things and still solve the model. (Philip H. Dybvig)

道格[69]是個了不起的人，是個非凡的共同作者。我們極其努力地使論文變得簡單⋯⋯我也認為獲得了一定效果，因為模型非常簡單。它很容易擴展，你知道，我們已經留下了一些空間，人們可以新增一些東西，而仍然可以說明模型。（菲利普·迪布維格）

In recent years, I have spent a significant time visiting the Far East, mostly China⋯ Some of my leisure activities include playing jazz and blues keyboards and playing some traditional instruments such as the erhu and the hulusi. I also enjoy weightlifting, Taiji, Qigong, Tui Shou (push hands), and walking. (Philip H. Dybvig)

近年來，我花了許多時間訪問遠東，主要是中國。⋯⋯我的閒暇活動包括演奏爵士樂和藍調鍵盤，以及演奏一些傳統樂器，如二胡和葫蘆絲。我也喜歡舉重、太極拳、氣功、推手和步行。（菲利普·迪布維格）

---

[69] 即道格拉斯·戴蒙德。

2023 年

I was soon convinced that experiment is the key in Physics, and even though it was slow, required a lot of money, had all kind of pitfalls, it was the way to go. (Pierre Agostini)

我很快就確信實驗是物理學的關鍵，儘管它進展緩慢，需要很多錢，有各式各樣陷阱，然而是必經之路。（皮耶‧亞谷斯蒂尼）

Time and time again, though, new developments appeared —— either technological or theoretical —— which opened new roads. (Pierre Agostini)

然而，新的發展一次又一次地出現 —— 無論技術上的還是理論上的 —— 開闢了新的道路。（皮耶‧亞谷斯蒂尼）

First of all, clearly defining the questions we wanted to answer and the concrete research objectives that we should derive from these questions —— and firmly believing that we can achieve them in the short or long run despite all setbacks. Persistence and obsession are important qualities here, as are self-confidence and a positive attitude. It's also vital to have a healthy measure of discipline, so that you do not allow yourself to be distracted by the interesting new questions that pop up on almost a daily basis but which do not bring you closer to your goal. (Ferenc Krausz)

首先，確定我們想要回答的問題以及應當從中得出的具體研究目標 —— 並堅信儘管遇到所有挫折，也可以在短期或長期內實現它們。堅持和執著是重要的特質，自信和積極的態度亦如此。具有健全的紀律措施也十分重要，這樣你就不許自己被幾乎天天跳出來的有趣的新問題分心，它們只是妨礙你接近自己的目標。（費倫茨‧克勞斯）

It has been a tremendous privilege to stand on the shoulders of scientists, including many Nobel laureates, who made seminal contributions to our understanding of electrons and light, when walking the path to exploring sub-atomic motions. To eventually exploit them for addressing grand challenges. To the benefit of humankind. (Ferenc Krausz)

眾多科學家，包括不少諾貝爾獎得主，為我們理解電子和光做出了開創性的貢獻。在探索亞原子運動的過程中，站在他們的肩膀上是非凡的榮幸。最終利用成果應對重大挑戰，並造福人類。（費倫茨·克勞斯）

Back then, I never thought that this could lead to a Nobel Prize one day. I wanted to keep looking into this, as I saw a possibility that it could be attosecond pulses. It went against what others thought. But my intuition told me that there could be opportunities to create something that would lead me onwards. (Anne L'Huillier)

那時[70]，我完全沒想到這有朝一日能獲得諾貝爾獎。我想繼續研究這個問題，因為我看到了它可能是阿秒脈衝的可能性。這與其他人的想法相悖。但直覺告訴我，這可能有機會創造出某種引導我前進的東西。（安妮·呂利耶）

It is crucial to uphold scientific rigour. Passion and motivation are essential for a successful research career. There will inevitably be difficult moments, and you must be deeply passionate and motivated about your work to avoid giving up. (Anne L'Huillier)

堅持科學的嚴謹性十分重要。熱情和動力對於成功的研究生涯不可

---

[70] 呂利耶的這項工作始於 1987 年。

或缺。艱難時刻難免，你必須對工作充滿熱情和動力，以避免放棄。（安妮・呂利耶）

Scientists are explorers, we ask questions and resolve to find answers about the world around us. The answers sometimes change us profoundly, and sometimes they lead to technologies with big impact. In our case the exploration began with a simple question about the emergence of properties from the atomic to the macroscopic. The building up of a macroscopic crystal begins with a few atoms or molecules that are then joined with more atoms or molecules. The initial atoms or molecules look nothing like the final product. In the beginning stages of growth, the magical laws of quantum mechanics dominate, but as the crystal grows the more mundane properties of classical mechanics emerge. Wondering about how the atomic world evolves into the macroscopic one inevitably leads us through a wonderful new world, the nano-world, which we now call the realm of nanoscience and nanotechnology. Quantum dots, for which we are being honored here today were at the birth of this new realm. They shine brightly on its future and the yet un-imagined possibilities it offers. (Moungi G. Bawendi)

科學家是探險家，我們提出問題並決心尋找關於周圍世界的答案。這些答案有時深刻地改變我們，有時帶來具有重大影響的技術。在我們的例子中，探索始於一個簡單的問題，關於從原子到宏觀層面的特性的出現。宏觀晶體的建構從幾個原子或分子開始，然後與更多的原子或分子連線。初始的原子或分子看起來與最終產物截然不同。在生長的開始階段，量子力學的神奇定律主導，但隨著晶體生長，古典力學的更平凡特性出現了。想知道原子世界如何演變成宏觀世界，不可避免地引導我們穿越一個奇妙的新世界，奈米世界，我們現在稱為奈米科學和奈米技術的領域。我們今天在這裡因而受到表揚的量子點，正處於這個新領域的誕生。它們閃耀著它的未來以及它所提供的尚且無法想像的可能性。（蒙吉・巴汶帝）

  If you look at technologies that we have today, they have roots 20, 30, 40 years ago in curiosity based research questions that people were asking because they saw something that they didn't expect or because they were exploring a topic with no real idea of where to go. It's not something you can write in a grant proposal. I'm going to do this, this, and this, and in three years I'm going to get this. That's not how curiosity based research work. You start off with an idea and then you've got to switch. There's always these bifurcations and you change path depending on what you see. You have no idea really where it's going to go. You certainly don't know what the applications are going to be. (Moungi G. Bawendi)

  如果你看看我們今天擁有的技術，它們植根於20、30、40年前基於好奇心的研究問題，人們提出它們是由於看到出乎預料的東西，或者由於正在探索一個懵然不知前路的題目。這不是你可以寫在資助提案中的東西。我要做這個、這個、這個，三年後我要得出這個。基於好奇心的研究不是這麼運作的。你從一個想法開始，然後又得轉換方向。總是有這些分岔，你依據所見而改變路徑。你不了解它真正要去哪裡。你當然不知道其應用何在。（蒙吉・巴汶帝）

  So often, the research needs to be somehow motivated by some societal need or application, which is fine, but there also needs to be space for just being curious, because that's where the discoveries actually come from. (Moungi G. Bawendi)

很多時候，研究需要以某個方式、受到某種社會需求或應用的激勵，這很好，但也需要存在純粹好奇的空間，因為那是發現的真正來源。（蒙吉·巴汶帝）

Now it has to be the creative mind that has to try to make educated guesses on what's going to be interesting and important, and then try some things, see what happens, and use those results or the failures or the new understanding that comes to guide you into making it better. Combined with theory, I think theory has definitely a place to play in that exploration. (Moungi G. Bawendi)

現在需要具有創造性的頭腦，嘗試對於什麼是有趣和重要的做出基於一定知識的推測，然後嘗試某些事情，看看會發生什麼，並運用得出的這些結果，無論是失敗的或是全新的理解，指導你使之改善。結合理論，我認為理論在這種探索中肯定有一席之地。（蒙吉·巴汶帝）

I think people sometimes misunderstand the role of theory. They think that you have to have theory that exactly explains the data that matches all the numbers that come out. But really what we're looking for is a theory that explains the trends. It doesn't have to be perfect, but if it can catch the interesting parts of the trend where the trend begins to deviate from a linear line, for instance, or things like this, right? It may not be at exactly the right size, but it catches this evolution and simple theory, like if it's simple enough, then an experimentalist like me can get intuition out of that to begin to ask new questions. Guided by this understanding… It's something that you try to teach graduate students how to get intuition. If you have enough background and you see something happening that can be explained by fairly simple theory, then you can use your background to add on top of that simple theory, or you can try to apply that simple theory to other materials. Or basically you try to extrapolate from what you think you understand to outside of the gram where that simple theory may be applicable. Intuition is hard to teach and hard to explain. (Moungi G. Bawendi)

我認為人們有時誤解理論的作用。他們認為你得具備理論，準確解釋與得出的所有數字相符合的資料。但實際上，我們在尋求的是一種解釋趨勢的理論。它不一定必須完美，但應該要能抓住趨勢有趣的部分，例如，趨勢開始偏離直線，或者諸如此類，對吧？它可能規模並不恰如其分，但它抓住了這種演化和簡單的理論，比如如果它足夠簡單，那麼像我這樣的實驗者就可以從中獲得直覺，開始提出新的問題。以這種理解為引導。……這是你試圖教研究生們如何獲得直覺的方法。如果你有足夠的背景，並且看到某種現象可以由相當簡單的理論解釋，你就可以利用自己的背景疊加這一項簡單的理論，或者可以嘗試將這一項簡單的理論應用於其他素材。或者基本上，你嘗試從自認理解的部分推廣到這一項簡單理論可能適用的範圍之外。直覺很難教授也很難解釋。（蒙吉‧巴汶帝）

I'm a really strong believer of a liberal arts education, the kind that we have in small colleges here, or some universities. I think that there's a certainly a trend towards a more career oriented education that focuses too quickly on one subject, let's say, or a couple subjects. I think it's so important to be well read, to understand history. Science is a part of history to understand science's role in our community and the world. You need to understand all these other things. You need to understand social dynamics… When you're 20 years old, you may not know what you really want to do. That's really perfectly fine. You can come to figure out what it is that interests you a little later, and you've lived a life that you can bring to that field and contribute things from a different direction. I think that's really important. (Moungi G. Bawendi)

我全心全意地堅信人文教育,例如我們現有的在地小規模學院或一些大學進行的這種教育。我認為當然有一種趨勢,傾向於更加以職業為導向的教育,過於急切地專注於一門學科,或幾門學科。我認為廣泛閱讀、了解歷史非常重要。科學是歷史的一部分,用於了解科學在我們的社會和世界中的作用。你需要了解所有這些其他的事情。你需要了解社會動態。……20歲時,你可能不知道自己真正想做什麼。這真的非常好。稍後,你就能釐清使你感興趣的是什麼,你過著可以帶入那個領域、從另一方面做出貢獻的生活。我認為這真的很重要。(蒙吉·巴汶帝)

Over the past two centuries, curiosity —— driven basic research has led, eventually and inexorably, to new technologies that have hugely improved our lives. Yet, discoveries and new knowledge are often unpredictable in their application. For example, we first thought that semiconductor nanocrystals would be used in transistors. Actually, nanocrystals were first used as luminescent tags in biological imaging. Basic research is best supported by society as a whole, and its natural home is in the universities. By its very nature, basic research tends to advance an entire industry, not one specific company. (Louis E. Brus)

在過去的兩個世紀裡,好奇心驅動的基礎研究最終勢不可擋地導致新技術的出現,大幅地改善了我們的生活。然而,在其應用中,發現和新知識往往是不可預測的。例如,我們起初以為,半導體奈米晶體將用於電晶體。實際上,奈米晶體最初是在生物成像中用作發光標籤的。基礎研究最受整體社會的支持,而其發源地是在大學之中。就其本質而言,基礎研究往往推動整個產業的發展,而非一家特定的公司。(路易斯·布魯斯)

Bell Labs believed that in research, working scientists were best positioned to figure out where the real opportunities were. There was substantial leeway to define your own project. If I wanted to discuss something, I could almost always find an expert somewhere in the building. The culture strongly encouraged open discussion. There were no students, and very few postdocs. Many projects required collaboration to assemble the necessary expertise and equipment. Over time, the management tried to assess who was especially creative in defining projects and building teams to get them done. (Louis E. Brus)

貝爾實驗室認為,在研究中,在職科學家最可能找出真正的機會何在。在這裡,有充分的自由空間闡發自己的項目。如果想討論某件事,我幾乎總是不用走出大樓就能找到專家。這種文化強烈鼓勵公開討論。沒有學生,博士後研究員也極少。許多項目需要合作來整合必要的專業知識和設備。隨著時間推移,管理階層盡力評估誰在闡發項目和建立團隊以完成它們方面特別有創意。(路易斯·布魯斯)

Back then, it was a career based on curiosity, not for making money or anything else (Aleksey Yekimov)

那時,它是一種基於好奇心的事業,不是為了賺錢或其他任何事情。(阿列克謝·葉基莫夫)

It's not just a surprise happening, its based on textbook quantum chemistry, on established chemical protocols bringing together previous knowledge in new ways. (Aleksey Yekimov)

它不僅僅是個意外事件，它基於教科書上的量子化學，基於既定的化學方案，以新的方式將以往的知識整合起來。（阿列克謝・葉基莫夫）

My mother listened always to the announcement of who gets the Nobel Prize because she told me, "Oh next week they will announce, maybe you will get it." You know I was laughing, I was not even a professor, no team, and I told my mom, don't listen, and she said, "Yes but you know, you work so hard." And I told her that all scientists work very hard. She believed, and my daughter she watched me work hard, and she became two-times Olympic champion. Rowing, and she is a five times world champion, and I went to this, she was inducted in the hall of fame, she was rowing here and there, and I was always introduced like "She's Susan's mom." I was Susan's mom. And now that my daughter came several times to the awards ceremony with me, and she was introduced as "Kati's daughter." To persevere, and I believe the first 14 years of your life, your genes, your parents, your teachers, your friends, they shape you, the person who you will be. I also, as a woman and a mother, I try to tell fellow female scientists that you don't have to choose between having a family, you can have it, you don't have to over your child, your child will watch you and they will do, because that's what counts, the example that you present. (Katalin Karikó)

我母親總是在聽誰獲得了諾貝爾獎的消息，因為她告訴我，「哦，下週他們會宣布，也許妳會得到它」。你知道我笑起來，我甚至不是教授，沒有團隊，我告訴媽媽，別聽，她說，「好吧，可是妳知道，妳這麼努力工作。」我告訴她，所有科學家都非常努力地工作。她相信，我女兒看著我努力工作，她成了兩屆奧運冠軍。划船比賽，她是五次世界冠軍，我去參加了這個場合，她入選了名人堂，她在各地競賽，我總是被介紹說「她是蘇珊的媽媽」。我是蘇珊的媽媽。現在，女兒跟我一起出席了好幾次頒獎典禮，她被介紹為「凱蒂的女兒」。堅持下去，我相信你生命的前14年，你的基因、你的父母、你的老師、你的朋友，他們塑造了你，你將成為什麼樣的人。作為一名女性和母親，我也想告訴女科學家們，不必為擁有家庭的兩難而選擇，妳可以擁有它們；不必為孩子過度憂慮，孩子會觀察你，他們也會成人，因為妳們樹立的榜樣才是重要的。（卡塔琳・卡里科）

When I went from academia to a company, they don't care how many committees you are on, how many papers you have. What counts is that you have a product that has an effect. The ego is wiped out. It is so much better. (Katalin Karikó)

當我從學術界轉到公司時，他們不在乎你名列多少個委員會，你擁有多少篇論文。重要的是你有個發揮效用的產品。自我被抹去了。這實在是好多了。（卡塔琳・卡里科）

Kati and I spent 25 years working on this, with people telling us the whole time, "Give it up. It isn't going to work. Why are you bothering?" The NIH (National Institutes of Health) not giving us money, people not wanting to publish our papers. And then, to suddenly see it come out to the market and be the major vaccine that has tamed the pandemic is a fantastic experience. My dream has been to develop something that helps people and I think I've done that. I've never gotten used to getting awards. They're things that Hollywood people like to get, to march down the red carpet and to show off. I'm happy back in the lab and working. (Drew Weissman)

凱蒂[71]和我花了25年時間研究這個項目，人們一直對我們說，「算了吧。它行不通。你們為什麼要操心？」國家衛生研究院不給我們錢，人們不想發表我們的論文。然後，突然看到它進入市場並成為制伏疫情大流行的主要疫苗，是妙不可言的經歷。我的夢想是開發某種有助於人的東西，我認為自己做到了。我從不習慣得獎。它們是好萊塢的人們喜歡得到的東西，可以走上紅地毯並炫耀。我樂於回實驗室工作。（德魯·魏斯曼）

In general, people don't understand what lab work is. It, of course, varies by your age and experience. In general, I characterise it as four steps back, one step forward. It isn't a place where if you seek pleasure, you go. You have to tolerate frustration to be able to work in a lab. When you do make a finding, even if it's a little finding, because of all of the frustration and all of the difficulty getting it, it makes it that much more important. At least for me, it wasn't one big finding. It was 25 years of finding after finding, some very small, some moderately big. It was a continuous development. The vaccine, the RNA just didn't pop off the page one day. It was years and years of work and continued development and optimisation. To see something come along, to see something develop. It's kind of like a child growing up. It's 21 years of taking care of something with lots of frustration and potentially setbacks to then see them go off to college or get married or do whatever. It's really kind of an inner joy. (Drew Weissman)

---

[71] 即卡里科。

一般來說，人們不了解實驗室的工作。當然，它會因你的年齡和經驗而異。一般來說，我將其描述為後退四步，前進一步。這不是一個你若想尋求快樂就去的地方。你得忍受挫折才能在實驗室工作。當你真的獲得一個發現時，即使是小小的發現，你經歷的所有挫折和所有困難，都使它變得更加重要。至少就我而言，它不是一個大的發現。它是 25 年來一次又一次的發現，有的非常小，有的算是一般大。它是持續的發展。疫苗、核糖核酸，絕非一夕之間由紙面跳出來的。它是年復一年的工作和持續的發展和優化。看著某種東西出現，看著某種東西發展。它有點像是孩子的成長。它是 21 年來持續照顧某種東西，伴隨大量挫折，潛在的各種阻礙，直至看到他們上大學或結婚或做任何事情。這實在是一種衷心的快樂。（德魯・魏斯曼）

It's very easy to use a lot of words and then write in a complicated way. That's the easiest thing to do. But what's hard to manage? It's to write in a simple and deep way. (Jon Fosse)

使用大量的詞彙，然後以複雜的方式寫作，這非常容易。做起來最簡單不過了。而什麼是難於從事的呢？就是以簡單而深入的方式寫作。（庸・佛瑟）

There's something that cannot be said directly, and you have to turn to literature in a way to manage to say it. I think Jacques Derrida was quite right when he said that, what you cannot say, you should write. Or something close to that. I experienced that as a simple truth. You can write, manage to write very, very complex emotions or a way of experiencing life that's impossible to speak. I guess that's somehow the gift of a real author to be able to write in such a way. (Jon Fosse)

2023 年

有些東西無法直接說出來,你得以某種方式轉化為文學才能設法表達出來。我認為雅克・德希達講得非常對:說不出口的,你應當寫。諸如此類。我體驗到這個簡單的事實。你可以寫作,設法寫下非常、非常複雜的情感,或一種無以言傳的體驗人生的方式。我想,這就是真正的作家能夠以這種方式寫作的天賦。(庸・佛瑟)

You must stick to yourself, you must listen to yourself, to your inner voice and not to others. When I, my first books were published, and my first play was produced, the reviews, they were almost really, really, bad. I decided not to listen to it, but to listen to myself —— to what I knew was good writing. (Jon Fosse)

你必須堅持自己,你必須傾聽自己,聽你內心的聲音,而不是聽別人的。當我的第一本書出版,第一部劇本上演時,評論幾乎非常、非常糟糕。我決定不聽那些評論,而是聽我自己 —— 我知道什麼是好作品。(庸・佛瑟)

For his ideals and his objectives, the human being is capable of accepting all suffering and despite it arousing, experimenting, and spreading hope and passion to give meaning and brilliance to his life. (Narges Mohammadi)

為了理想和目標,人類能夠承受一切痛苦,而任其激發、驗證和傳播希望和熱情,賦予生活意義與光輝。(納爾吉斯・穆罕默迪)

It's endless curiosity, but it's also curiosity about something in particular. I find that I'm curious about an extraordinarily wide range of subjects. Most of them have to do with economics or education or the labour force. But I'm curious about many things and you can't follow all of those threads. You have to limit yourself somewhat. (Claudia Goldin)

這是無窮的好奇心，但也是對特定事物的好奇心。我發現自己對非常廣泛的議題感到好奇。它們大都涉及經濟、教育或勞動力。但我對很多事情都好奇，你不可能跟著所有這些線索走。你得在一定程度上限制自己。（克勞蒂亞・戈丁）

I think we all have doubts about what we're doing. I wouldn't call that failure. It's a sense that we question our own work. I always tell my students, be your own worst enemy or else someone else will be. (Claudia Goldin)

我認為我們都對正在做的事情抱持疑惑。我不會稱之為失敗。這是一種質疑自己工作的感覺。我總是告訴學生，做自己最大的敵人，不然那就會是別人。（克勞蒂亞・戈丁）

2024 年

How mind emerges from brain is, to me, the deepest question posed by our humanity. (John Hopfield)

對我來說，思想如何從頭腦中產生，是我們人類所提出的最深刻的問題。（約翰・霍普菲爾）

I slowly wove my way from an interest in how the brain functioned to a question of how could hardware or software, or whatever you want to call it, wetware, produce such a thing. And the centre of gravity of my knowledge and understanding moved slowly from much more physics oriented to the neurobiological one. And somewhere along the line, this connection between AI, networks, neural networks and physics developed. (John Hopfield)

2024 年

慢慢地，我把研究方向從對腦如何運作的興趣，移向硬體或軟體，或者無論你想怎麼稱呼它，溼體，如何能夠產生這樣一種東西的問題。我的知識和理解的重心，慢慢地從物理學指向移至神經生物學指向。在此過程中，人工智慧、網路、神經網路和物理學之間的這種連繫得到了發展。（約翰·霍普菲爾）[72]

I think that the prize is recognizing, in part, the fact that understanding the deep problems of things like mind is not going to come forth in some simple way like Newtonian physics. It really requires much more understanding of the relationship between structure and properties, and structure dynamics and properties. And that's a mixture of some corners of physics, some corners of chemistry, some corners of biology, coming together to understand and create an area of study. (John Hopfield)

我認為，此獎項在一定程度上認同這個事實，即理解像心靈這些事物的深層問題，不會像牛頓物理學一樣，以某種簡單的方式呈現。它確實需要對結構與屬性、結構動力學與屬性之間的關係有更多的理解。這是物理學的一隅、化學的一隅、生物學的一隅的綜合，它們結合起來理解和建立一個研究領域。（約翰·霍普菲爾）

My answer to "Now What" is "here is a research problem which is unusual, perhaps significant, novel, that I can pose and probably solve because of my background in physics". The situation would not be readily identified as a problem at all by those whose background seems much more relevant than my own. Choosing problems is the primary determinant of what one accomplishes in science. I have generally had a relatively short attention span in science

---

[72] 2024 年諾貝爾物理學獎授予霍普菲爾和辛頓的理由，為「透過人工神經網路實現機器學習的基礎發現和發明」。

problems (note the fine line between the polymath and the dilettante, where I am often offside). Thus I have always been on the lookout for more interesting questions either as my present ones get worked out, or as they get classified by me as intractable, given my particular talents. (John Hopfield)

我對「現在怎麼辦」的回答是,「這是一個不尋常的、也許很重要、新穎的研究問題,由於我的物理學背景,我可以提出並可能解決它」。那些背景看來比我更相關的人,根本不會輕易將這種情況認定為問題。選擇問題是決定一個人在科學中獲得什麼成就的主要決定因素。一般來說,在科學問題上,我的注意力持續時間相對較短(注意博學和一知半解之間的細微區別,我經常越位)。因此,我總是在尋找更有趣的問題,若不是手邊的問題解決了,就是考量到自己的能力,它們被歸為棘手的一類。(約翰・霍普菲爾)

The selection of what to work on as the most important factor in a career in research… There was a slow personal accumulation of the effects of deliberate steps and chance events that shaped the way that I viewed the world of science. This accumulation would shape my choice at the next fork in the pathway of possibilities. (John Hopfield)

在研究生涯中,對於所從事項目的選擇是最重要的因素。……深思熟慮的步伐和偶然的事件都會對個人逐漸累積影響力,它們塑造了我看待科學世界的方式。這種累積會在可能性之路的下一個岔路口塑造我的抉擇。(約翰・霍普菲爾)

Physics was not subject matter. The atom, the troposphere, the nucleus, a piece of glass, the washing machine, my bicycle, the phonograph, a magnet —— these were all incidentally the subject matter. The central idea was that the world is understandable, that you should be able to take anything apart, understand the relationships between its constituents, do experiments, and on that basis be able to develop a quantitative understanding of its behavior. Physics was a point of view that the world around us is, with effort, ingenuity, and adequate resources, understandable in a predictive and reasonably quantitative fashion. Being a physicist is a dedication to a quest for this kind of understanding. (John Hopfield)

物理學不是主要的課題。原子、對流層、原子核、一塊玻璃、洗衣機、我的腳踏車、留聲機、磁鐵——這些都是隨機的主要課題。中心思想為，世界是可以理解的，你應當能夠拆解任何東西，理解其組成部分之間的關係，做實驗，並在此基礎上能夠對其行為形成一定程度的理解。物理學是一種觀點，即我們周圍的世界，透過努力、聰明才智和足夠的資源，可以經由預測和合理定量的方式理解。作為物理學家即致力於尋求這種理解。（約翰·霍普菲爾）

I grew up taking things apart, seeing how they worked, repairing bicycles, exploring chemistry in the kitchen (or better, out of sight in the cellar), building flyable model airplanes, crystal sets and simple radios, playing with batteries and coils of wire, and learning to think with my hands and manipulate real objects. One of my earliest memories is of a small screwdriver that was kept in a drawer of the treadle —— operated sewing machine my mother used. It was for minor sewing machine adjustments, but I was allowed to use it on anything in the house —— as long as I put it back in the drawer. And if I occasionally could not reassemble the object I had attacked, my father would patiently do so in the evening. My early concept of what it would be like to be a physicist was a somewhat mystical idea of carrying on such playful explorations at a more abstract level. (John Hopfield)

我從小就拆東西，看它們是怎麼回事，修腳踏車，在廚房裡（或者更好，躲在地窖裡）探究化學，做飛得起來的模型飛機、礦石和簡單的收音機，玩電池和線圈，還學著動手思索和操作實物。我最早的記憶之一是關於一把小螺絲刀，它放在我母親踏板縫紉機的抽屜裡。它用於縫紉機的細微調整，但我可以用在家裡的任何東西上——只要把它放回抽屜。如果我拆了東西偶爾裝不回去，晚上我的父親會耐心地把它裝好。我對當物理學家的早期概念是個有點神祕的想法，即在更抽象的層面上從事這種有趣的探索。（約翰·霍普菲爾）

A long series of unpredictable events had led me from a childhood exposure to "he world as physics" from my physicist parents, to condensed matter physics, to Cornell and Bell Labs, from there to the chemical physics of proteins, and finally to be teaching a Princeton course for which I had too little background. (John Hopfield)

一連串出乎意料的事情，把我從童年的接觸引向「物理世界」，從我的物理學家父母，到凝聚體物理學，再到康乃爾大學和貝爾實驗室，再到蛋白質的化學物理學，最後在普林斯頓大學講授一門我個人缺乏背景的課程。（約翰·霍普菲爾）

What I have done in science relies entirely on experimental and theoretical studies by experts. I have a great respect for them, especially for those who are willing to attempt communication with someone who is not an expert in their field. I would only add that experts are good at answering questions. (John Hopfield)

> 2024 年

　　我在科學領域所做的工作完全依賴專家的實驗和理論研究。我非常尊重他們，尤其是那些願意嘗試與一個其他領域專家交流的人。我只想補充一點：專家們擅長回答問題。（約翰・霍普菲爾）

　　I would say I am someone who doesn't really know what field he's in but would like to understand how the brain works. And in my attempts to understand how the brain works, I've helped to create a technology that works surprisingly well. (Geoffrey Hinton)

　　我想說，我是個不太了解自己處於哪個領域的人，但我想要了解大腦如何工作。在試圖了解大腦如何工作的過程中，我協助創造出一種效果奇佳的技術。[73]（傑佛瑞・辛頓）

　　I think we should think of AI as the intellectual equivalent of a backhoe. It will be much better than us at a lot of things. (Geoffrey Hinton)

　　我認為，我們應該將人工智慧視為智力的挖土機。在很多事情上，它將比我們好得多。（傑佛瑞・辛頓）

　　I'm hoping AI will lead to tremendous benefits, to tremendous increases in productivity and to a better life for everybody. I'm convinced that it will do that in health care. My worry is that it may also lead to bad things, and in particular, when we get things more intelligent than ourselves, no one really knows whether we're going to be able to control them. We don't know how to avoid "catastrophic AI scenarios" at present. That's why we urgently need more research. So I'm advocating that our best young researchers, or many of them, should work on AI safety. (Geoffrey Hinton)

---

[73] 有學者稱：辛頓對人工神經網路這個新奇但未經證實的概念感興趣，這個領域有時候被描述為人工智慧研究「無望的死水」。

我希望人工智慧將帶來極大的益處，大幅增加生產力，讓人人都能擁有更好的生活。我相信它將在醫療保健領域奏效。我擔心的是，它也可能導致壞事，尤其是，當外物比我們自身更聰明時，沒有人真正知道我們能否控制它們。目前我們不知道如何避免「災難性的人工智慧場景」。這就是為什麼我們迫切需要更多的研究。因此我提倡，我們最優秀的年輕研究人員，或者其中許多人，應當致力於人工智慧安全。（傑佛瑞・辛頓）

Did industrial farming eliminate some forms of farming? Absolutely, but it amplified our capacity to produce agricultural goods. Not all of this was good, but it allowed us to feed more people. When you use a phone, you amplify the power of human speech. You cannot shout from New York to California and yet this rectangular device in your hand allows the human voice to be transmitted across three thousand miles. Did the phone replace the human voice? No, the phone is an augmentation device. The cognitive revolution will allow computers to amplify the capacity of the human mind in the same manner. Just as machines made human muscles a thousand times stronger, machines will make the human brain a thousand times more powerful. (Geoffrey Hinton)

工業化農業是否消除了某些形式的農業？確實如此，但它放大了我們生產農產品的能力。這並非完美無缺，但它使我們養活更多的人。使用電話時，你放大了人類言語的力量。你無法在紐約朝著加州喊叫，然而你手中這個矩形設備使得人聲傳播 3,000 英哩。電話是否取代了人聲？沒有，手機是一種增強設備。認知革命將使得電腦以同樣的方式放大人類思考的能力。就像機器使人類肌肉強壯上千倍一樣，機器會使人腦有力上千倍。（傑佛瑞・辛頓）

2024 年

In science, you can say things that seem crazy, but in the long run they can turn out to be right. We can get really good evidence, and in the end the community will come around. (Geoffrey Hinton)

在科學領域，你可以說些看似瘋狂的話，但長遠而言，它們可能被證明是正確的。我們能夠得到非常好的證據，最終人們也會接受。（傑佛瑞・辛頓）

The future depends on some graduate student who is deeply suspicious of everything I have said. (Geoffrey Hinton)

未來取決於某個研究生，他對我說過的一切都深為懷疑。（傑佛瑞・辛頓）

If you want to build an airplane, you don't start by modifying a bird; instead, you understand the first principles of aerodynamics and build flying machines from those principles. (David Baker)

如果想建造飛機，你不能從改裝鳥兒開始；相反地，你了解空氣動力學的第一原理，並根據這些原理建造飛行器。[74]（大衛・貝克）

I'm really optimistic about really a wide range of applications. So just thinking about the things that we're working on now, in health and medicine, I think smarter therapeutics that are more precise, and act only in the right time and place in the body, could get around a lot of the problems of systemic drugs. We have the first really de novo design medicine that's been approved for use in humans. That's a vaccine designed by my colleague Neil King at the Institute for Protein Design. Then outside of medicine, I think we're making

---

[74] 貝克的獲獎理由為：電腦蛋白質設計。他開發出電腦化的方法，實現了幾乎不可能的事情：創造本來不存在的蛋白質。它們具有全新的功能。

435

great strides now in developing new catalysts, and that could be for things like breaking down pollutants and plastics and things in the environment to coming up with sort of greener chemistry, you know, better routes to new molecules. I think there's a lot of sustainability applications, you know, once you start just thinking about all the different things proteins do in nature that, and they really just evolved over random chance over, you know, over millions of years of natural selection. Now with the ability to design new proteins, specifically to solve problems there's just so many possibilities. It's really exciting. (David Baker)

我對於非常廣泛的應用十分樂觀。所以，只要想想我們現在正在研究的事情，在健康和醫學方面，我認為更精確、更智慧的治療方法，並且只在正確的時間及體內位置發揮作用，可以解決系統性藥物的許多問題。我們擁有第一個被批准用於人類、真正從頭設計的藥物。那是我在蛋白質設計研究所的同事尼爾·金設計的疫苗。然後在醫學之外，我認為，我們此時在開發新催化劑方面正獲得長足的進步，這將可能用於分解環境中的汙染物、塑膠等，從而提出某種更綠色的化學方法，你知道，更好的新分子途徑。我認為有大量可持續性的應用，你知道，一旦你開始考慮蛋白質在自然界中所做的所有不同事情，它們真的只是在，你知道，數百萬年的自然選擇之中隨機演化而成。現在，有了設計新蛋白質的能力，尤其是用於解決各種問題，可能性就太多了。這實在激勵人心。（大衛·貝克）

You never know where life is going to take you. Being an entrepreneur and starting companies really grew out of the work that we were doing. (David Baker)

2024 年

你永遠不知道生活會把你帶到哪裡。成為企業家和創辦公司真的出自於我們從事著的工作。（大衛・貝克）

The key thing is there has to be a really important unsolved problem that should be solvable in the next couple of years. That's a real art, though, to find those problems. And you can't pick something that's too easy —— you have to really push the envelope. And if you choose a problem that's way too hard then you won't get anywhere either. But if you choose the right problems, where this is the time to solve them, a surprisingly large fraction will have some commercial potential —— maybe in a way that you didn't anticipate. And that certainly happened with a lot of the things we've done. (David Baker)

關鍵是得有個真正重要的未解問題，它應當在隨後數年內可以解決。不過，找出這些問題是真正的藝術。你不能選擇太容易的事情——你得真正挑戰極限。而如果選擇一個太難的問題，你也不會有任何進展。但是，如果選擇正確的問題，在解決它們的適當時機，極大一部分就將具有一定的商業潛力—— 也許以你不曾預料的方式。我們做過的很多事情都是如此。（大衛・貝克）

In fact, in every problem we work on, we only work on problems which are kind of at the cutting edge of what's possible. Because the really easy problems we figure people in other places could do with the software we're releasing. And whenever you work on a hard problem, you only understand about 30, 40% of what's going on. And so one of the things, the really key thing, is you start working on a problem like targeting a tumour or breaking down plastic. And the first few designs you make don't work or they don't work very well, and then you have to look at what's going on that's wrong. Then that gives you ideas on what you need to improve about your design strategy or the methods to really solve those problems. And so that's really largely what science is about, is having some hypothesis about how to solve a problem, trying to solve it, and then it doesn't work as well as you thought. And then trying to figure out what the basis for that is and improving your method and approach accordingly. (David Baker)

事實上，在我們所面臨的每一個問題中，我們只處理位於最前端的部分。因為我們認為，其他人可以用我們釋出的軟體解決真正簡單的問題。每當處理一個難題時，你只能理解正在發生之事的大約三、四成。所以，真正關鍵之事在於你正著手處理的是一個有如打擊腫瘤或分解塑膠的問題。你做的前幾個設計沒有效果，或者效果不夠好，你就必須檢視發生了什麼錯誤。於是這為你提供了想法，關於設計策略需要改進之處，或者真正解決這些問題的方法。所以，這在相當程度上就是科學的意義所在，對於如何解決問題提出一些假設，試圖解決它，而它並非如你所想的那麼有效。然後再盡力釐清其基礎是什麼，並相應改進方法和路徑。（大衛・貝克）

What I should tell you about is a little bit about my work environment. Because this area is so exciting now, there are many, many brilliant, super motivated, energetic people at all career stages from around the world who are coming to my group to explore new areas like breaking down plastic or fixing CO2 and it's really an amazing place. We don't have very much space, so everyone's very close together and everyone's kind of talking and brainstorming about the next frontier. And because it's a big group, there's new exciting results popping up pretty much every day. And so it's this incredibly exhilarating environment. (David Baker)

　　我應當稍微談論關於我的工作環境。由於這個領域現在如此令人激動，有很多才華洋溢、極為進取、精力充沛的人，來自世界各地所有職業，他們來到我的團隊，探索新的領域，比如分解塑膠或固定二氧化碳，這真的是個令人驚嘆的地方。我們沒有太多空間，於是人人靠得很近，人人都在縱論和暢想下一個疆界在哪。而且由於它是個很大的團體，所以幾乎每天都有令人興奮的新成果湧現。它就是如此令人難以置信且振奮人心的環境。（大衛·貝克）

I think collaboration is just absolutely central to science. I encourage my students to just email people. If they're working on a problem, I say figure out who the best three people are in the world and email them. Sometimes you won't get an answer, but other times you will, and that can start a connection which could really transform your research. (David Baker)

　　我認為合作絕對是科學的核心。我鼓勵學生發電子郵件給別人。學生如果在處理一個難題，我會建議找出世界上最優秀的三個人，發電子郵件給他們。有時你不會得到答覆，但有時會，而這能夠建立一種連結，且很可能真正改變你的研究。（大衛·貝克）

Research is never a straight line. If it is, then it's not real research. If you knew the answer before you started it, then that's not research. (Demis Hassabis)

　　研究從來都不是一條直線。如果是，它就不是真正的研究。如果你在開始之前就知道答案，那就不是研究。（德米斯·哈薩比斯）

I want to understand the big questions, the really big ones that you normally go into philosophy or physics if you're interested in. I thought building AI would be the fastest route to answer some of those questions. (Demis Hassabis)

我想了解重大的問題,那些你通常會訴諸於哲學或物理學的真正重大的問題,如果你有興趣的話。我認為建構人工智慧會是回答其中一些問題的最佳捷徑。(德米斯・哈薩比斯)

The reason I've worked on AI my whole life is that I'm passionate about science and finding out knowledge, and I've always thought if we could build AI in the right way, it could be the ultimate tool to help scientists, help us explore the universe around us. (Demis Hassabis)

我一生都在研究人工智慧的原因,是由於我對科學及獲取知識充滿熱情,而且我一直認為,如果我們能以正確的方式建構人工智慧,它可能會成為幫助科學家、幫助我們探索宇宙的終極工具。(德米斯・哈薩比斯)

At least for the next foreseeable future, I feel like this allows individual scientists to do so much more. Because, these systems, they're tools. They're very good for analyzing data and finding patterns and structure in data. But, you know, they can't, figure out what the right question is to ask, or the right hypothesis, or the right conjecture. All of that's got to come from the human scientist. I think the best scientists paired with these kinds of tools will be able to do incredible things. (Demis Hassabis)

我認為,至少在接下來可預見的未來,人工智慧能讓各個科學家們大展身手。因為,這些系統,它們是工具。它們非常適合分析資料以及

2024 年

尋找資料中的模式和結構。但是，你知道，它們無法理解要問的正確問題是什麼，或正確的假設，或正確的推論。這些全都得出自人類科學家。我認為，最好的科學家與這些工具搭配，將能夠做不可思議的事情。（德米斯・哈薩比斯）

It is in this collaboration between people and algorithms that incredible scientific progress lies over the next few decades. (Demis Hassabis)

正是在人和演算法之間的這種合作之中，存在今後幾十年裡不可思議的科學進步。（德米斯・哈薩比斯）

We've been talking a lot about science, and a lot of science can be boiled down to if you imagine all the knowledge that exists in the world as a tree of knowledge, and then maybe what we know today as a civilization is some, you know, small subset of that. And I see AI as this tool that allows us, as scientists, to explore, potentially, the entire tree one day. And we have this idea of root node problems that, like AlphaFold, the protein-folding problem, where if you could crack them, it unlocks an entire new branch of discovery or new research. And that's what we try and focus on at DeepMind and Google DeepMind to crack those. And if we get this right, then I think we could be, you know, in this incredible new era of radical abundance, curing all diseases, spreading consciousness to the stars. You know, maximum human flourishing. (Demis Hassabis)

我們一直在大量談論科學，而大量科學可以歸結為，如果你把世界上存在的所有知識設想成一棵知識之樹，那麼也許，我們今天作為一種文明，你明白，只是它的一小部分。我將人工智慧視為一種工具，它容許我們，作為科學家，可能有一天將能探索整棵樹。我們目前有了根節點問題的想法，像 AlphaFold[75]，蛋白質摺疊問題，在此你若能破解它們，那就開啟了一個全新的發現或新研究分支。這就是我們在 DeepMind 和 GoogleDeepMind 所著力關注以求破解的問題。如果我們做對了，那麼我認為我們可能，你明白，在這個極其豐富的嶄新時代，治癒所有疾病，讓意識散播到群星。你明白，最大限度的人類繁榮。（德米斯·哈薩比斯）

When we started working with artificial intelligence (AI) more than a decade ago, people were skeptical about whether this technology would develop enough in the foreseeable future to do anything useful. But we held on to our faith in AI's potential to benefit humanity. We used games like chess, Go and Atari to train and test our AI systems to become smarter and more capable. In 2016, we decided to use our smart systems to try to solve a 50-year-old fundamental problem in biology, called the protein-folding problem. This was the birth of AlphaFold, our AI system that predicts the three-dimensional structures of proteins based on their amino acid sequence. (Demis Hassabis & John Jumper)

十多年前，當我們開始使用人工智慧（AI）時，關於這項技術是否會在可預見的未來發展到足以做任何有用的事情，人們持懷疑態度。但我們堅信 AI 有可能造福人類。我們用西洋棋、圍棋和雅達利等遊戲來訓練和測試我們的 AI 系統，使其變得更智慧、更有能力。2016 年，我們決定使用我們的智慧系統，嘗試解決一個 50 年歷史的生物學基本問題，名為蛋白質摺疊問題。這就是 AlphaFold 的誕生，我們的 AI 系統根據蛋白質的氨基酸序列預測蛋白質的三維結構。（德米斯·哈薩比斯、約翰·江珀）

---

[75] 一種人工智慧系統，能夠以前所未有的準確性和速度經由計算預測蛋白質結構。

We are so honored to be recognized for delivering on the long promise of computational biology to help us understand the protein world and to inform the incredible work of experimental biologists. It is a key demonstration that AI will make science faster and ultimately help to understand disease and develop therapeutics. (John Jumper)

我們非常榮幸得到認同，由於投身計算生物學的長期發展，幫助我們了解蛋白質世界，並為實驗生物學家不可思議的工作提供資訊。這是個關鍵的證明：人工智慧將使科學發展得更快，並最終有助於了解疾病和開發療法。（約翰·江珀）

I think to be a researcher you really want to be a researcher in an area that's ready to make big breakthroughs. I've worked both in areas that aren't ready to make big breakthroughs and ones that are. It's a lot more fun to be in the latter. The other point is just to be active, to be engaging. Don't be the person who sits inside and never asks a question —— that doesn't get you very far in science. (John Jumper)

我認為，要成為研究人員，你實在需要成為準備好做出重大突破的領域中的研究人員。我在還沒有準備好做出重大突破的領域和準備好的領域中都工作過。在後者之中有趣得多。另一點就是要積極，要投入。不要成為坐在裡面而從不提出問題的人 —— 那樣無法讓你在科學上走得很遠。（約翰·江珀）

I believe in interdisciplinary, but I think what is most important is that people are interdisciplinary. I've benefited quite a bit in my career by learning from some incredible physicists, biologists, chemists and computer scientists and then being able to work as myself at the intersection. I think if you want to do intersectional science, and that's very important, you should find the very best. Go talk to the very best machine learners. Go talk to the very best experts in this field. Figure out what problems they really have. Do the interdisciplinary part yourself by going to both sides and not seeking out too much of the interdisciplinary spaces yourself. (John Jumper)

我相信跨學科，但我認為最重要的是跨學科的人。職業生涯中，我曾向一些非凡的物理學家、生物學家、化學家和電腦科學家學習，然後得以在人生十字路口上以自己的身分工作，從而受益匪淺。我認為，如果你想從事跨領域科學，這就非常重要，你應當找到最好的。去與非常優秀的機器學習者談話。去與這個領域非常優秀的專家交談。釐清他們真正存在的問題。兩邊都去探訪，而非自己尋求過多的跨學科空間——由此發掘屬於自己的跨學科領域。（約翰・江珀）

I found it a lot more fun to do science in teams and often in an industrial setting than to do it academically. It's a lot more fun to chase the constant failure and occasional success of science in a group, so the social aspect of science just can't be underestimated. (John Jumper)

我發現，在團隊中，而且常常是在實務環境中從事科學，比學術式地研究有趣得多。在一個團體中追求科學的不斷失敗和偶爾成功有趣得多，所以科學的社會面向實在不容小覷。（約翰・江珀）

I led a team of around 15 people that worked on "AlphaFold" full time, and collaboration was extremely intense. We would have a daily stand-up meeting where we would all talk about what we did yesterday and what we were going to do today. More importantly, we built on each other's ideas enormously. I remember a senior scientist at DeepMind telling me afterward that he was so impressed because he would watch one person propose an idea, a second person refine it and the third person implement it. And we give credit to everyone, right? We were building off each other's ideas day to day —— not month to month or year to year. (John Jumper)

我帶領一個大約 15 人的團隊，全力從事 AlphaFold 工作，合作極其熱烈。我們每天舉行一次站立會議，大家談論我們昨天做了什麼，和今天要做什麼。更重要的是，我們極大地信賴彼此的想法。我記得 DeepMind 的一位高級科學家事後告訴我，他印象非常深刻，因為他目睹有個人提出一個想法，第二個人完善它，然後第三個人實施它。我們讚揚每個人，對吧？我們在彼此想法的基礎上行事，每天如此 —— 而非每月或每年。（約翰・江珀）

There's an enormous qualitative difference between learning really great facts that have been discovered and really learning new facts and building new ideas. (John Jumper)

在學習已經發現的真正非凡的事實與真正學習新事實和構成新想法之間，存在巨大的性質的差異。（約翰・江珀）

We're conditioned to think we understand most of what we need to understand to function. But in science, you constantly have to work against the instincts that assume that we know everything we need to know. I think we have to learn to have faith in the idea of mysteries. (Victor Ambros)

我們通常以為，自己已經理解研究所需理解的大部分內容。然而在科學中，你始終得與假設自己知道需要知道的一切這種本能抗爭。我認為，我們必須學會對有關神祕事物的想法有信心。（維克多・安布羅斯）

Every day, in these rooms, here, in these labs on this campus and everywhere else, people are finding surprises about biological systems that they don't understand and they can't explain, and then when they investigate them and really get to the bottom of it, new principles emerge, new kinds of molecules, new kinds of machines become discovered. That's going to keep going indefinitely. (Victor Ambros)

每天，在這些房間裡，在這裡，在這個校園的這些實驗室和其他地方，人們正在發現有關生物系統的各種驚奇，那是他們所不了解並無法解釋的；然後，當他們調查它們並真正深入探究時，新的原理出現了，新種類的分子、新種類的機制於是被發現。這個過程將無限持續。（維克多・安布羅斯）

And so it has very little to do, frankly, with the particular person getting the award. What the award represents is a process that involves interactions amongst many, many people. And the end, one person ends up getting the award. It's really important to try to acknowledge that and understand the fact that really everything that happens in science, including the discoveries that people try to acknowledge by awards, are really the products of this confluence of people's histories and people's interactions. I really believe that science gets done by people with average abilities and talents, for the most part, and when something special happens, enough so that people want to acknowledge it with an award, it was really… in large part… luck! (Victor Ambros)

因此，坦率地說，這個獎與特定的得主幾乎沒什麼關係。它所代表的是一個涉及許多人互動的過程。最終，結果是一個人得了獎。嘗試承認此事並理解這個事實真的很重要，即科學中發生的實際上一切，包括

2024 年

人們試圖以獎項認可的發現，真的是人們的歷史和人們的互動兩相匯合的產物。我真的認為，在多數情況下，科學是由能力與天賦普通的人完成的；當某種特別的事情發生，以至讓人們想以一個獎項來認可它，這真的是……在相當程度上……運氣！（維克多‧安布羅斯）

It is possible that my undergraduate training in physics taught me not quantitative reasoning, but rather how a scientific revolution at its very beginning can be recognized. (Gary Ruvkun)

我在大學受到的物理學訓練，可能不是定量推理，而是如何能夠當即認出一場科學革命的發端。（加里‧魯夫昆）

The joy of doing genetics… is the surprises. The surprises are what keep you young in science. I'm constantly surprised, and my ignorance is bliss. (Gary Ruvkun)

從事遺傳學研究的樂趣……就是驚喜。驚喜是讓你在科學領域保持年輕的原因。我總是感到驚奇，我的無知是天賜之福。（加里‧魯夫昆）

The Nobel is just mythic in how it transforms the life of people who are selected. The Nobel Prize is a recognition that's sort of 100 times as much press and celebration as any other award. So, it's not part of a continuum. It's a quantum leap. (Gary Ruvkun)

在如何改變入選者生活方面，諾貝爾獎簡直是神話。諾貝爾獎是一種認同，其報導和慶祝的程度是其他任何獎項的一百倍。所以，它不是一個漸進過程的段落。它是一個巨大的突破。（加里‧魯夫昆）

I've always been fascinated by language. I enjoy contemplating the great depth, complexity and delicacy of the layers of a culture in which a single language is in-built. (Han Kang)

我始終著迷於語言。我喜歡思考單一語言所包含文化層次的非凡深度、複雜與細膩。（韓江）

When I write fiction, I put a lot of emphasis on the senses. I want to convey vivid senses like hearing and touch, including visual images. I infuse these sensations into my sentences like an electric current (Han Kang)

寫小說的時候，我非常注重感覺。我想傳達生動的感覺，如聽聞和觸碰，包括視覺意象。我將這些知覺如電流般注入語句之中。（韓江）

We can try to understand that via sort of proximate causes of economic development. Differences in education, differences in efficiency with which you use things, differences in the amount of machinery you have and some other important factors, but then you go one layer down, and that's where we think that institutional factors are the most dominant. Of course, other things influence human capital, other things influence efficiency. But institutions, especially your broad institutional trajectory over time is a major determinant. (Daron Acemoglu)

我們不妨透過經濟發展的某種直接原因來理解它。教育的差異、手段之效率的差異、所擁有機器數量的差異，以及其他一些重要因素；然而再深入一層，那就是我們認為制度因素最重要之處。當然，其他因素影響人力資本，其他因素影響效率。但制度，尤其是隨時間變動的廣泛的制度軌跡，是最主要的決定因素。（達龍·阿傑姆奧盧）

Economic institutions determine the incentives of and the constraints on economic actors, and shape economic outcomes. As such, they are social decisions, chosen for their consequences. Because different groups and individuals typically benefit from different economic institutions, there is generally a conflict over these social choices, ultimately resolved in favor of groups with greater political power. The distribution of political power in society is in turn determined by political institutions and the distribution of resources. Political institutions allocate de jure political power, while groups with greater economic might typically possess greater de facto political power. We therefore view the appropriate theoretical framework as a dynamic one with political institutions and the distribution of resources as the state variables. These variables themselves change over time because prevailing economic institutions affect the distribution of resources, and because groups with de facto political power today strive to change political institutions in order to increase their de jure political power in the future. Economic institutions encouraging economic growth emerge when political institutions allocate power to groups with interests in broad-based property rights enforcement, when they create effective constraints on power-holders, and when there are relatively few rents to be captured by power-holders. (Daron Acemoglu)

經濟制度決定經濟行為者的激勵和約束，並塑造經濟成果。因此，它們是社會決策，是為其結果而選擇的。由於不同的群體和個人一般受益於不同的經濟制度，在這些社會選擇上通常有衝突，最終決定有利於擁有更大政治權力的群體。政治權力在社會中的分布轉而取決於政治制度和資源分布。政治制度分配法律上的政治權力，而擁有更大經濟實力的群體一般擁有更大的實際上的政治權力。我們因而認為，適當的理論框架是一個以政治制度和資源分布為狀態變數的動態框架。這些變數本身隨時間變動，因為主流的經濟制度影響資源的分布，因為今天擁有實際上的政治權力的群體努力改變政治制度，以便在未來增加其法律上的政治權力。當政治制度將權力分配給在廣泛的產權執法中有利益的群體時，當它們對權力持有者產生有效約束時，當由權力持有者獲得的租金相對較少時，鼓勵經濟成長的經濟制度於是出現。（達龍‧阿傑姆奧盧）

Allowing people to make their own decisions via markets is the best way for a society to efficiently use its resources. When the state or a narrow elite controls all these resources instead, neither the right incentives will be created nor will there be an efficient allocation of the skills and talents of people. (James Robinson)

允許人們經由市場做出自己的決定，是社會有效運用其資源的最佳方式。反之，當國家或狹隘的菁英控制所有這些資源時，既不會創造正確的激勵措施，也不會有效地分配人們的技藝和才能。（詹姆斯‧羅賓遜）

You've got to create a system of rules which can harness all that latent talent. And that's this idea of inclusive institutions that create broad based incentives and opportunities. So people with ideas and talent and creativity can come to the top. And we know that's what drives innovation and productivity and prosperity. (James Robinson)

必須建立一個能夠利用所有潛在的人才的規則體系。這就是包容性制度的理念，它創造基礎的、廣泛的激勵和機會。因此，有想法、才華和創造力的人可以登上頂峰。而我們知道，這就是推進創新、生產力和繁榮的動力。（詹姆斯‧羅賓遜）

Today, the accelerated arrival of enhanced Artificial Intelligence capabilities provides the world with a choice: Will we develop technologies that enhance the productivity and improve the life chances of everyone, or will we slip into another phase of excessive automation, contributing to further job market and social polarisation? (Simon Johnson)

今天，增強的人工智慧能力的加速到來為世界提供了一個選擇：我們要開發提高生產力和改善每個人生活機會的技術，還是進入另一個過度自動化的階段，導致就業市場和社會進一步兩極化？（西蒙・詹森）

Many algorithms are being designed to try to replace humans as much as possible. We think that's entirely wrong. The way we make progress with technology is by making machines useful to people, not displacing them. (Simon Johnson)

許多演算法都設計來試圖盡可能地取代人類。我們認為這是完全錯誤的。我們利用技術獲得進步的方式是讓機器對人們有用，不是取代他們。（西蒙・詹森）

2021–2024 危機年代的希望之聲

編譯者後記

諾貝爾獎得主托妮・莫里森（Toni Morrison）說過：要是有一本書你想讀，可是還沒人寫，你就必須寫出來。（If there's a book that you want to read, but it hasn't been written yet, then you must write it.）諾貝爾獎得主堪稱人中龍鳳，我很想集中地、大量地讀到他們的言論，且所論最好聚焦於一些重要的事情，比如創新，比如人生。創新是科學技術的本質，是發展進步的動力。人生則屬於人們世代探究的永恆課題。關於它們，這些菁英肯定說過不少，必定值得一讀，只是百餘年來，漸近千人，地北天南，零金散玉，又如何得知？

於是我很早就萌生了收集素材、編譯成書的設想。然而憚於其難，遲遲未曾著手。是2015年屠呦呦先生獲獎強化了實行的信心。且不說當有不少讀者也需要這樣一本書。

苦心人，天不負。幾年下來，累積的有關英文語錄終於足以成書了，包括一些與創新和人生的話題雖無關聯，但趣味盎然的話。初具規模，欣喜之餘，便壓抑急切的心情，而細細品味，推敲譯出。筆者本人是深為這些話語所吸引的，因為它們具有獨特的魅力，更充滿真知灼見。尤其是大量的第一人稱講述，富於夫子自道的色彩，隨和親切，本色天然，時見推心置腹，多有現身說法，總之令人傾倒。

下面具體說說編譯工作。

在編選方面，細心的讀者可能注意到，所收內容不夠均衡，表現在兩方面，即收錄的每人條數和每條字數。

編譯者後記

　　先說每人條數。大部分人只錄兩、三條，也有少數人入選較多。其中緣由，大體有二。一是個人原因。編者身處地球一隅，眼界有限，雖積年搜求，仍有個別獲獎者連一句合用的都難得，甚至根本找不到的。尤其是上個世紀前葉的一些人，可謂個個深思熟讀，學富五車，不知說過多少精警剴切的話，奈何未見報刊（包括網路）記載，又囿於條件無法遍尋其著作。二是實際情況。這些獲獎者個性非常，有的話沒少講，然而只談專業不及其餘；有的乾脆惜字如金，端坐無言，令人氣惱他直似深水老蚌，就是不肯開口！好在此書雖非披沙揀金，或可比作海灘拾貝，正是一本聞見錄，原本無須也無法求全。吉光片羽，思想火花，只要對讀者有所啟迪，或已足矣。

　　至於每條字數，差別也不小。有的寥寥數語，也有的連續幾段。按理以簡短為上，只是有些話語或文字一氣呵成、十分精采，實在難於摘錄取捨，而並非編者不肯用心。體例不夠一致，還請讀者理解。精心剪裁，先得有下手的餘地。璞玉渾金，自有其特別的韻致。行於所當行，止於不可不止，其此之謂歟？

　　在翻譯方面，筆者首先慮及的，是專業內容的譯出精度。瑞典皇家科學院祕書長、諾貝爾生理學或醫學獎評審諾比（Erin Norby）說：諾貝爾獎不啻一部科學發展史。（The Nobel Prize describes a history of scientific development.）獲獎者無不處於有關領域前端，見識博大精深。數理化天地生，放談縱論，譯者如何應對得了？無奈過河卒子只能向前。每逢緊要，格外謹慎。現在的譯文猶如交出的試卷，固然談不到完美，總是盡力而為的結果，敬待讀者教正。倒是有個意外發現，令人釋然，值得一說。就是學術性極強的文字，比如術語專名，由於概念清晰，內涵明確，邏輯嚴整，表述周詳，反而未必難譯。

迻譯之際，除了注意不同人的不同語風，追求聲口畢肖，譯者心中還存了一份時代感，即想到社會變化對個體語言的影響。雖然譯今人的言語也不妨略「文」一些，畢竟盡為學者大家；轉達舊時人的話則不宜過於直白──聯想汪曾祺與魯迅的文字可知。全書內容按年度排列的方式也與此相關。跨越百年帶來了歷史意味。不僅科學的發展，細細揣摩，竟連社會的進步、思想的深入，乃至風氣的演化、語言的變遷，都不無痕跡在焉。譯者筆拙，難以準確傳達，讀者，尤其是原文讀者，閱讀時兼顧此點，當會多出一重趣味。

閱讀這些非凡人物的語錄，筆者時而會產生恍惚的感覺，就是自己彷彿身處他們的課堂上、實驗室中，或學術演講廳裡，乃至頒獎現場，親聆高論，但覺振聾發聵在在皆有，感動人心莫過於是，總之自然生動，聞所未聞，聲欬珠玉，美不勝收。他們的言論或樸實，或深邃，或睿智，或幽默，有的與前人所說暗合，更多的是自出機杼，不少說法具有強烈的個人風格。於是自己在讚嘆之餘，只想選得精些再精些，著意譯得好些再好些。甚至考慮到它們許多摘自演講或訪談，還試圖呈現幾分現場感，爭取讀者會心的共鳴。無奈天賦有限，學力不逮，交出的書稿未必合乎眾意，更唯恐存在差錯，只有寄希望於再版修訂的機會。

接近完工時，初稿中出現了 1910 年諾貝爾獎得主保羅·海澤（Paul Johann Ludwig Heyse）的一段話：

It was so refreshing to be tramping along this path, overgrown with bushes, fifty feet above the torrent, to feel the fine spray of the waterfall dash… to see the lizards slipping over the stones, and the graceful butterflies chasing the furtive sunlight.

走在這條小路上令人實在神清氣爽。灌木叢生，山溪在下方 50 英呎

編譯者後記

處流淌，感受瀑布飛落濺起的水霧……看蜥蜴在石頭上竄過，蹁躚的蝴蝶追逐閃爍的陽光。

這竟使我無端遐想，能讀到如此優美的文字，算不算對編譯工作的別樣獎勵。

個人譯出之書雖有若干，然而格外關心發行量的還要數這一本。期盼此書能夠流傳得廣泛些。如果它得以列入一些學校的課外書單，或者成為研究單位的年終獎品，或由企業管理者指定為員工讀物，或被專家學者推薦給年輕人，乃至書中的語錄出現在閱覽室或圖書館之類場所的牆壁上，總之被更多的讀者看到，從而多少有助於科技創新，有益於即將大展身手的新一代成長，編譯者就如願以償了！

用諾貝爾金句拯救你的破英文！詞窮到詞王，就是這麼簡單！

思路變清晰、語感變靈動、作文變好玩，打開腦袋讓靈感發光！

作　　　者：	詹森
發 行 人：	黃振庭
出 版 者：	財經錢線文化事業有限公司
發 行 者：	崧燁文化事業有限公司
E-mail：	sonbookservice@gmail.com
粉 絲 頁：	https://www.facebook.com/sonbookss
網　　　址：	https://sonbook.net/
地　　　址：	台北市中正區重慶南路一段 61 號 8 樓 8F., No.61, Sec. 1, Chongqing S. Rd., Zhongzheng Dist., Taipei City 100, Taiwan
電　　　話：	(02)2370-3310
傳　　　真：	(02)2388-1990
印　　　刷：	京峯數位服務有限公司
律師顧問：	廣華律師事務所 張珮琦律師

-版權聲明

本書版權為出版策劃人：孔寧所有授權財經錢線文化事業有限公司獨家發行電子書及繁體書繁體字版。若有其他相關權利及授權需求請與本公司聯繫。

未經書面許可，不得複製、發行。

定　　　價：580 元
發行日期：2025 年 06 月第一版
◎本書以 POD 印製

國家圖書館出版品預行編目資料

用諾貝爾金句拯救你的破英文！詞窮到詞王，就是這麼簡單！思路變清晰、語感變靈動、作文變好玩，打開腦袋讓靈感發光！/ 詹森 著 .-- 第一版 .-- 臺北市：財經錢線文化事業有限公司，2025.06
面；　公分
POD 版
ISBN 978-626-408-286-0(平裝)
1.CST: 英語 2.CST: 讀本 3.CST: 格言
805.18　　　　　114007122

電子書購買

爽讀 APP　　臉書